INNER
Demons

AMANDA STRONG

CLEAN TEEN PUBLSHING

For my daughter, Isabella.
You will always be my princess.
Never give up on your dreams!

INNER *Demons*

ISBN: 978-1-63422-193-1
Cover Design by: Marya Heiman
Typography by: Courtney Nuckels
Editing by: Cynthia Shepp

For more information about our content disclosure,
please utilize the QR code above with your smart phone
or visit us at

www.CleanTeenPublishing.com.

CHAPTER One

I dreamt of Sammy. Not every night, but often enough to leave dark rings under my eyes. Dreams of her haunted me, leaving me drenched in cold sweats. Were they really just random thoughts passing through my subconscious? Or could it be Sammy's distant memories coming out when my mind was stilled? The nightmares were so vivid, so draining, that most mornings I struggled to even climb out of bed. My muscles protested, my body begging for more rest. My mom kept offering me sleeping pills. Apparently, my night terrors kept her up as well. Tempting as it was for even a few hours of dreamless sleep, I hadn't tried them yet.

Of course, I never mentioned any of this to Dr. Killian, who leaned back into her leather chair, her hazel eyes appraising me through thin-rimmed glasses.

"So why don't you walk me through the past few days?" Dr. Killian coaxed, crossing her long legs. "How have you been?"

I stiffened, choosing to pick at the armrest of the faux leather couch next to the chair instead. Like usual, I'd sat in the opposite corner, sitting as far away from my new therapist as possible.

Since I knew about Sammy now, my parents had swapped out my usual therapist for a psychologist. Guess they felt I needed a 'doctor' to figure me out. If they only knew how messed up I really am, they'd be sending me to every specialist they could get their hands on. It was why my decision not to tell them about the Dragon Fae world I was a part of was easy. Blake said Tonbo didn't want the world to know about us, and that was good enough for me. I didn't care to become a science-experiment freak show anyway.

I'd never been a fan of my old therapist before. Honestly, she'd drove me bananas, always insisting my answers were in my subconscious. She could have just told me I had a split personality and that all the answers really were inside of me—inside Sammy.

However, compared to how I felt about Dr. Killian, my old therapist seemed like a warm sunset at the beach with a lounge chair and book to enjoy. The woman in the button-up blouse, gray slacks, and tight chignon had so far been nothing but pleasant. She was willing to talk about whatever topic I chose. I eyed her warily from my usual spot.

I don't care if it doesn't make sense... that woman makes my skin crawl. One thing I'd learned since becoming a damsel was to trust my instincts, and right now, they told me not to trust her.

Dr. Killian gave me a reassuring smile, waiting for my response.

I cleared my throat. "Nothing's happened. No blackouts. No waking up in weird places."

"So you don't think Sammy has been around?" she asked, tilting her head to the side.

"Nope," I said simply.

She scrawled something into her notebook. I couldn't imagine what it was. I hadn't said anything groundbreaking, had I?

"How have you been feeling lately?"

"Great," I lied. I wasn't about to tell her how conflicted I felt. Or how utterly exhausted the nightmares left me.

"How have things been with your family? Your mom, for starters?" she asked, breaking my line of thought.

I stared at her. "Good, I guess. Just the same as last week."

"Mm," she hummed, again writing something in her notebook. "You wouldn't say it's been a bit more strained over the past week?"

My eyes narrowed. What's she getting at? "No, why? Did she say something to you?"

"Oh no, I wasn't meaning to cause alarm, Samantha. Of course she hasn't said anything to me. Our sessions are completely between you and me." Dr. Killian smiled, but it didn't reach her eyes.

"My mom and I are great. Sure, we disagree at times, but it has nothing to do with Sammy."

"Wonderful. So glad to hear that. And your dad? It's much the same, I presume?"

I wanted to shout, You should presume nothing. I don't know why I'm even talking to you. But instead, I nodded.

"How about your sisters? Jocelyn and Krista?"

"Krista and I are great," I answered without thinking. It came easily because it was the truth. I felt my face flush, realizing my blunder.

She cocked an eyebrow at me. "Oh? Are things not good between you and Jocelyn?"

Darn. I berated myself for not simply lumping my sisters together. I hated to admit it... to this doctor especially, that I hardly saw Jocelyn lately, and when I did, there was tension between us. I wondered if it had always been there, and I was just more sensitive to it now. At times, I'd catch her staring at me with disdain in her expression. Like she'd tasted something sour. Was she ashamed of me? She'd always known about Sammy; why would me knowing change that?

It brought me to the conclusion that maybe something had happened. And if I have no memory of it, it means someone else does. Sammy. I hadn't lied to Dr. Killian when I'd said I hadn't blacked out in a while. I had to fudge a bit when I retold the last time I thought Sammy had taken over. I wasn't about to tell her I'd been sitting in Tonbo's theater, watching a production put on by flying dragons and damsels. I'd awoken in Jaxon's cave after that.

That lapse in memory tormented me. What had Sammy done? I hoped to ask Jaxon since he'd been the one to capture Sammy and throw her, or me, into his cave. But Blake didn't want me anywhere near his brother, which I could understand. Last time we'd been together, things had gotten pretty hairy. Blake had questioned Jaxon for me, but got little other than he'd found me not far from my own house. For some reason, that was enough for Blake. It wasn't for me. All it did was solidify my hunch that something might have happened between Sammy and Jocelyn.

There were two others who might have answers—Kory and Mack. However, no one could find Kory, not even Blake, and it wasn't for lack of trying. He'd gone off grid, moving his 'bug' operations underground. A terrifying thought in and of itself. The other option filled my heart with a sad longing.

I missed Mack, more than I cared to admit. The last time Blake had come back from the island, he said he'd discovered Mack in one of Tonbo's holding cells. There were rules about changing someone against their will, and since Tonbo could hardly hold Sammy, my other half, accountable, Kate and Mack were the ones being punished. Blake had told me that even though Mack's trial was over, and Tonbo had granted him pardon for his part, Mack still refused to leave his prison cell.

My eyes pricked at the thought that my friend could hold himself so personally accountable for what Sammy had put him up to. That's going to change, I decided. I can do something about Mack. I'm not a helpless bystander anymore.

A soft cough reminded me I wasn't alone at the moment. I turned and stared at the woman still waiting for a response.

"Jocelyn and I are even better," I said firmly, knowing we both saw straight through my fabrication. What happened between my sister and me is none of your dang business, lady, so stop smiling at me like it is.

Forty minutes later, I left my session with a feeling of resolution. I knew what I needed to do. I grimaced, hating to admit Dr. Killian's questions today might have helped clear my head. A little bit.

CHAPTER
Two

"**D**id you miss me?" Blake asked, wrapping me up in his arms for a quick hug as soon as he was through the door. We weren't alone. My dad sat on the couch in the front room, feigning interest in a book. Since I knew he wasn't really a reader, I wondered what he was up to.

"Maybe a little," I teased. "Glad you're back early this time." My heart ached, catching the scent of his skin. Knowing our words were being listened to, I asked, "How's your grandpa doing? Any better?"

With my family accepting Blake as my boyfriend, we had to come up with some plausible reason for why he traveled back to "California" so often. At first, it was Christmas break. No one asked questions. Then, as January started and with it, school, they needed some kind of cover as to why he left almost every weekend. The easiest one turned out to not be too far from the truth. Blake's grandpa was nearing ninety, and his health was deteriorating. He had always been close to his grandfather, so going to see him before he passed away made sense. Of course, my parents didn't need to know that Blake didn't visit with him long. They just thought the Knightleys were both thoughtful and very free with their money. Besides, Grandpa was a great code word for Jaxon.

"Grandpa's going to survive another week." Blake glanced over at my dad. "How are you doing, Mr. Campbell?"

My dad set his book aside and grinned. "Couldn't be better. I was wondering if you might lend me a hand today, Blake."

I cocked an eyebrow at my dad. Knew there was a reason he parked himself on the couch. Five minutes after he'd overheard me on the phone telling Blake I'd see him in a few minutes.

"Sure, be happy to."

"Great." My dad stood up, tossing the book aside. I caught a glimpse of the cover. Wuthering Heights? Really, Dad?

Still, I had to grin at the way Blake fidgeted with my hand as we followed my dad through the entry toward the garage door. It wasn't that Blake didn't get along with my family. He did, but there was always an underlying fear that my dad would one day forbid me from seeing him. I'd thought Blake had been joking about it before, but it turned out that he was quite serious. Not seeing me again terrorized him. I grappled with the fact Blake could love me so completely.

"Where are we going, Dad?" I asked as he opened the door and flicked the garage light on. "Don't forget it's freezing out there."

"I know. I think it's high time we put some of Blake's muscles to work." My dad patted Blake's shoulder before jogging down the three steps into the garage.

Blake visibly relaxed. "Sure. What do you have in mind?"

"Last night's storm left a few driveways and sidewalks in rough shape," he said, grabbing his winter coat off the power tool he'd strewn it on, probably when he got home from work last night.

One thing I'd always admired about my dad was the fact that he looked out for others. Every winter, he spent most of his Saturdays shoveling our neighbors' drives.

"You've got a warm coat on. Have any gloves?" my dad asked him.

Blake shook his head, and my dad tossed him a pair. "How about boots?" he asked, eyeing Blake's footwear.

"Got them on, sir," Blake said, holding up a foot. Sure enough, Blake wore a warm pair of hiking boots.

Sir? I wanted to ask Blake, catching eyes with him. Laying it on a bit thick, don't you think?

Blake grinned, ignoring the funny face I made at him, and grabbed a shovel from my dad. I glanced down at my bare feet and rubbed my arms with my hands.

"I'll be right back," I said, making a dash back to the door.

"Where do you think you're going, young lady?" my dad asked. "Blake and I got this. You go inside and keep warm."

"But Dad," I protested. "I've always shoveled walks with you."

"Yeah, I know, but I think it's time I find out what kind of stuff Blake's made of."

Dragonfly guts, I wanted to blurt. Instead, I met my dad's gaze. In other words, you want to get to know the young man dating your daughter. "Okay, I'll stay put, but if you aren't back by sundown, I'm coming to find you."

"Worried he'll turn into a vampire if we aren't, Samantha?" my dad asked, laughing at his own joke. Blake blanched, and I choked on my spit.

"No," I sputtered, "It's just that Blake's not usually here on Saturdays. I wouldn't mind going out tonight, that's all."

My dad chuckled, oblivious to our reactions. I mean, it's not like we're vampires, exactly. Just half dragonfly, half human. No biggie.

My dad waved his hand at me. "Sure, sure. Hey Samantha, mind hitting the garage door opener on your way in?"

I smacked the rectangular button and glanced over my shoulder as the door creaked to life, the pulley shifting into gear. I caught Blake's eye long enough to give him a reassuring grin. Dad ushered him out of the garage, both of them holding large shovels.

Four hours later, I had gone from amused, to slightly frustrated, to worried. Where the heck are they? They weren't answering their phones, and as tempted as I was to drive around to the usual houses we hit, I decided to wait. I'll give them thirty more minutes, and then I'm hitting the road. Or the skies...

I'd plopped myself on the family room couch, tucked in a warm blanket. Ironically, the book my dad had dropped earlier was the one I'd snatched up. Wonder whose this is anyway? My sisters weren't huge readers as far as I knew, and I'd only lately discovered the joys of getting lost in a make-believe world. Ever since the cabin, I needed things to help me sleep at night.

I felt my face flush thinking of what lulled me to sleep more often than not now. If my dad knew how many times Blake stole away to my room, tucking himself next to me and stroking my hair back until I'd fallen asleep, he'd wig out. Blake didn't stay all night though, as much as I wanted him to. I'd wake up in the morning alone, always wondering at what point in the night he'd left me. The smell of autumn mornings still lingered on my pillow.

The sound of someone walking toward the room had me glancing up from the book I hadn't really been reading. I could tell the footfall was too light for Blake or Dad. Krista was out with her boyfriend of the week and Mom had gone shopping... that left only one other person. I locked eyes with her as she entered the living room.

"Hey Jocelyn," I said, forcing a cheery tone.

She narrowed her eyes a tiny bit before she gave me one curt nod. Ugh. What is it with her?

Her gaze dropped to my lap. "Oh. There it is," she said as she walked over to me, her hand outstretched. "Hand it over, Samantha. It's mine."

I glanced down, a bit bewildered until I saw the book. "What? This?" I held it up to her. "Sorry, I didn't know whose it was. Here."

She snatched it quickly, pressing it against her chest.

"I didn't realize it meant so much to you," I said, not sure how else to take her reaction.

"It was a gift," she said before she bit down on her lip.

"Oh really? From who?" I untucked my leg, staring up from the couch. Jocelyn gave me the feeling she was about to bolt from the room. Realizing how tight my muscles had become, I almost laughed, knowing I was getting ready to chase after her. This is my sister, not a damsel, I reminded myself. If I'm not careful, my wings will bust out.

Jocelyn shrugged. "No one, never mind. You wouldn't understand."

"Try me. I'd love to know why that means something..."

"It doesn't. You just shouldn't be taking things that don't belong to you, that's all."

I sighed. "Joc, what's really wrong?"

She stared down at me. "What do you mean?"

"Did something happen... maybe something I don't remember?" I waited, hoping she'd open up. She continued tugging at her bottom lip with her teeth. "Did I do something?" I asked. "Or... did Sammy?" I had barely formed the word Sammy when she stiffened and turned on her heel to leave.

"No," she called over her shoulder as she practically ran away. "I've just got a lot on my mind right now, that's all."

Can't she even look me in the eyes anymore? My heart sank. We're sisters. Sure, it's never been perfect, but we're family. Judging her reaction to my mention of Sammy, I felt pretty confident of at least one thing. Sammy did something. Now I just have to figure out what.

CHAPTER
Three

I didn't follow her. My heart felt too heavy to do anything but remain on the couch. I tucked my knees against my chest, aggravated I couldn't remember what happened between the short time I'd left Tonbo and woken up in Jaxon's lair.

"Hey," Blake said softly, breaking the melancholy settling over me. I glanced up to see him in the doorway. "You okay?"

I nodded too quickly, and he was next to me in an instant. "What's going on? You look worried," he said, wrestling one of my hands free. "Sorry we were gone a long time."

I glanced over, surprised to detect no teasing.

"You can blame Blake for that," my dad said, catching me off guard as he entered the room. Blake gave my hand a squeeze and grinned.

My dad half laughed, half grumbled. "I had no idea he'd want to shovel half of Durango. Next time, I'll take you, Samantha."

I grinned at my dad, his face red, his neck wet with sweat. He had his back to us as he headed toward the kitchen.

"I need a drink," he muttered.

"I guess you showed off all of your muscles for my dad after all," I teased, glad for the distraction from Jocelyn. Being part dragonfly made one exceptionally strong and from what I'd seen of his upper body, Blake's muscles were more than adequate—dragon or not. I flushed, feeling the warmth of his hand covering mine, a thrill rushing through me.

The sound of my dad pouring himself a glass of water snapped me out of it.

Black chuckled softly when I jumped a bit. I swear, it sometimes feels like he can read my mind. Scary thought.

"No, I held back." Blake winked at me. "I didn't want you to feel bad, Mr. Campbell," he called out, loud enough for my dad to hear. He leaned back into the couch, pulling my hand into his lap. Guess hours of shoveling snow had made Blake more comfortable with my dad.

My dad mumbled something under his breath, and turned around to face us from the kitchen. He downed his drink and then held the empty cup out to Blake, pointing it out accusingly. "Better watch out, son. I'm going to steal you every Saturday now because of the way you showed off today."

"It'd be my pleasure," Blake said with a grin.

My dad sighed, trying to hide his smile.

"Hey, how about that date you owe me?" I prodded.

Blake ran his hand behind his head, scrubbing his neck. "I should shower first." To my surprise, he leaned over and planted a kiss on my cheek. "Be back in a flash."

I giggled as he jumped up from the couch to head home. My gaze followed him from the room, my heart aching to see him go, even if it was for a few minutes. I couldn't describe the longing I felt around him. I'd never felt it with any other boy before.

I turned and caught my dad gazing at me.

"He's not a bad kid, Samantha," he said with a shrug. "I was a bit worried with your track record."

"Hey, for the record, Mom loved Jeremy," I said in my defense, not really defending Jeremy. My dad had never cared for him that much. After I'd ended things with him, my dad had let me know how relieved he'd been.

"Yes, well, she's always had a thing for the tall, dark, and handsome." He grinned, gesturing to himself. "Not that I can blame her really."

I laughed. "Yeah, well, Jeremy is nothing like you, Dad." I paused. "Blake's not like any other guy I've dated, actually. Not that I've dated that many. But he gets me. All of me."

My dad's gaze softened. We both knew what I was talking about. He leaned against the doorframe and folded his arms. "About that... how are you holding up, kiddo? Still no more blackouts?"

I sighed. At least this much, I could share with him, as much at it killed me to not tell him about my new life as a damsel. Sammy was safer ground. "I'm good. It's just strange to know I could lose myself to her at any time."

He nodded, and it gave me an idea. Maybe Mack wasn't the only one who could help me learn who Sammy was. I felt like if I understood her better, perhaps I could piece together the missing holes in my life.

"Hey Dad, what was Sammy like? I mean, when she was around?"

He unfolded his arms and walked over to the couch. Sitting down next to me, he said, "She wasn't you." He smiled. "You're thoughtful and kind. Sammy, on the other hand, seemed hell-bent on making your mom's life miserable. Within minutes of her showing up, I'd hear the two of them arguing over something." He shook his head at the memory. "Maybe it's because she had such little control over her own existence, I don't know. She didn't like anyone telling her what to do or think."

I nodded.

"Luckily, you were the one around most of the time, Samantha."

"How would you know when it wasn't me, I mean? I know she didn't like to be called my name, but it seems like she could have fooled you sometimes."

"Mm..." He rubbed his chin. "Yeah, she could have, I suppose. But I would have seen through it, I think. Where you were pretty laid-back, Sammy always had an agenda. She seemed driven by something." His gaze shifted to the carpet. "She made it tough for you, with friends, school... boyfriends. She put a wedge between you and a lot of people because she said whatever was on her mind." He frowned. "Maybe I shouldn't be telling you this."

"No, really, I want to know," I begged. "It helps me to understand her. Please, Dad."

His brows furrowed as he met my gaze, but then he relented, "Well, after keeping it from you for so long, I suppose I owe you the truth now. I want you to know I was never happy with that therapist's decision not to tell you. When the normal medication route didn't work, they assured us it was the best thing for you. I'm sorry, Samantha. I never meant it to feel like we've been lying to you your whole life."

"I don't feel that way, Dad. I understand you only did it to protect me. And honestly, I'm glad you did." I wasn't going to lie, living with the knowledge that someone else hid within me, trying desperately to come out and take control, terrified me.

I gave him a reassuring smile, hoping he would tell me more.

"You know, if you really want to know more about Sammy, you should talk to Mack."

I swallowed hard. "Yeah, I will." Hearing Mack's name sent pain trickling through me. I missed my friend. I didn't care anymore that he'd lied about playing a hand in my changing. I knew he only did it because he loved me, not just Sammy. He didn't want my unfinished dosage to change me into something unknown, or even to destroy me completely.

"Or you could ask Jocelyn." My dad's words jarred me from my thoughts.

"Really?" I asked, my eyes widening.

"I wouldn't say Sammy and she were best friends, but Jocelyn spent more time with Sammy than the rest of us. She acted as a buffer of sorts at times. Maybe she can help you learn more... about your other half."

I hitched my lips into a smile, trying to act as if what my dad said was no big deal. Jocelyn and Sammy were friends? Or at least got along? My head spun with the implications.

Dad got up off the couch, giving my leg a friendly pat as he went. "I'll let you get ready for your hot date," he said with a wink before leaving the room.

I nodded woodenly, saying, "Thanks, Dad." But I didn't move from the couch right away.

So is that why she seems mad at me? She's upset I'm not Sammy?

CHAPTER
Four

I hated to tell Blake I'd hardly tasted dinner when he asked if my food was good. The restaurant we'd gone to was nice. The singer with the guitar in the corner added the right amount of ambience to the steakhouse Blake had picked. Everything was perfect, including the guy sitting across from me, so why did I feel sick inside?

I leaned across the table, taking Blake's hand into mine. He grinned at my touch. "Blake, I need to talk to Jaxon," I blurted before I lost my nerve.

His smile melted into a frown. "Sam, that's not a good idea."

"Why not? Is he still not doing well?" I timidly asked. I hated to hurt Blake and talking about his brother's lack of healing pained him.

He sighed. "No. Tonbo has tried everything he can think of." He hesitated, and then said heavily, "I thought maybe seeing his family would help, so I told Mary, his wife."

"Wait, what? You did? What did you say?"

"I showed her what I am."

My eyebrows rose. Blake never told anyone he was a dragon. Not even his parents knew the truth. "Did she freak out?" I asked.

"At first, she seemed relieved when I told her about Tonbo and the Dragon Fae. She assumed that's what Jaxon was too. With him disappearing more and more with only lame stories of where he'd been, she'd been convinced he was having an affair."

"Oh, that's terrible. Poor Mary."

Blake ran his free hand across his mouth, resting his jaw on his palm. "I wanted to stop there, not tell her more. But she had so many questions and... well, I'd still hoped seeing her would help Jaxon overcome this thing. So she had to know truth."

"How did she take it?" I asked, fearing the worst.

He frowned. "By the time I'd explained what Jaxon has become, she said she'd rather he'd been sleeping around." His voice grew quiet. "I don't think she understands how little control he has when he's the bug. As soon as she learned what Jaxon had done to others, she said they were finished. That she could never forgive him, and Noah would never see him again either."

"Oh, no." I groaned, not sure who I sympathized with more at the moment, Mary or Jaxon. "Poor Jaxon," I mumbled, realizing who had my true empathy. Not that I blamed Mary. Learning your husband had turned into a literal monster who couldn't control taking the lives of innocent people had to be completely devastating. I tried to imagine Blake suddenly turning into a monster—programmed to kill. I shuddered as a chill shot through me.

"Maybe with time, when Jaxon's better, she will feel differently," I said, squeezing Blake's hand.

He shook his head. "I hope you're right. But either way, I'm not telling Jaxon about Mary leaving him right now. And she swore she wouldn't say anything either. For now, she's just telling Noah that his dad is overseas doing charity work. Jaxon's done that in the past, so Noah's buying it."

When I heard Jaxon's son's name, I remembered how it felt to be in that small body with short limbs and a squeaky voice. Transforming into Noah had been the only thing to stop Jaxon from killing his brother. Or his brother killing him.

"Blake, maybe I can help Jaxon," I offered with a sudden idea.

His eyes widened a bit, and then he shook his head. "No, Sam. It's too risky. Jaxon—or the bug in him—still craves you."

My skin crawled, knowing what that meant. "But I'm also the only person, other than Noah, that Jaxon overcame the bug for," I pointed out. "In the caves, Jaxon pushed the monster away long enough to try to save me. Maybe seeing me will help him somehow."

Blake's lips twitched to the side as he considered my words. "You might be able to influence Jaxon, but the bug's cravings will overpower it."

I shook my head. "Blake, you said yourself, Tonbo has tried everything. Jaxon isn't getting better. We need to at least try."

He shook his head right back at me. "No. There's got to be another way for Jaxon to overcome this."

I wanted to argue, but he held his hand up. "I won't risk your life, Sam. It's not worth it."

We stared at each other. My frustration finally ebbed away with the realization of what my meeting with Jaxon would mean for Blake personally. Asking Blake to let me see his brother put him in a very bad spot. What if things didn't go well? What then? I sighed in defeat. Guess I'll have to figure out another way to get that information.

I tried to brighten up a bit, deciding to ask a different question. "Okay, but can you at least take me to the island to see Mack?"

I wasn't sure if it was hurt or confusion that flitted across his face. Either way, his shoulders slumped. "Alright, but don't think you can slip away and see Jaxon when my back is turned."

I bristled, wanting to remind him of how he'd been the one to slip away with Kory the last time we'd been there, but I didn't want to argue. I was finally going to the island. I didn't want him to change his mind now that he'd at least relented to that.

"Okay, so now to come up with a good cover story to get me there."

Turned out, coming up with an excuse was easy. I searched my phone for the next day off from school and discovered there was a teacher workday on January 16. Next Friday. Perfect, gives us a three-day weekend in 'California'. On the drive back to my house, I called my dad and asked if I could join Blake on his next trip back home, assuring him we'd be staying with Jaxon's family and in separate rooms.

I hung up and glanced over at Blake's anxious face. "Guess

your shoveling skills today won my dad over." I grinned. "He said yes."

Blake grunted. "Glad to know the blisters on my hand were worth it." He chuckled under his breath as he turned down a road that wasn't ours. I didn't ask where we were going. It wasn't exactly as if I was jumping up and down to go home anyway. I didn't want to face my sister yet.

When the car stopped and Blake shifted it into park, I glanced out my window. At first, I saw nothing but blackness. Once my eyes adjusted, I made out stars, the mountain's silhouette, and dark shadowy trees.

"Where are we?" I asked, unlatching my seatbelt.

"Somewhere private," he said, undoing his as well. He made no motion to open his door, only turned to face me.

The way his eyes danced, I had the feeling he wasn't thinking about the island at the moment. His gaze lingered on my lips. Funny how the world could seem so bleak and wrong, but right then, with Blake, none of that mattered. I gave him a crooked grin. This was the first time Blake had actually 'parked' us somewhere. It felt like such a normal teenage thing to do, despite how unusual our lives had actually become.

"What are you up to?" I teased.

"Well..." He reached over, grinning. I giggled as he easily scooped me up, pulling me across the console and into his lap. He released the seat to lean back, leaving me sprawled out on top of him, my long legs feeling like they were going every which direction.

Feeling awkward, I tried to support my weight with my hands.

He laughed at my attempts and pulled me down closer. "Stop that, you weigh nothing to me," he assured. "I figured it'd be better if we didn't get caught right before our big trip and—"

"And you don't dare make out in my room now that you and my dad are buddies, right?" I finished for him, while part of me wondered just how far he wanted this night to go.

Even with Blake sneaking into my bedroom, we never went

much past kissing. Blake would usually be the one to stop and insist on me getting some sleep. It'd become so much our routine that part of me began to wonder if maybe Blake just didn't really find me all that attractive. What eighteen-year-old could really be that in control of himself? Maybe he was with me out of pity; he felt like he had to watch out for me still.

"Maybe," he said with a grin, snapping me back to the present. I almost forgot what I'd even said to him, and his answer sent a shot of panic through me before I realized he couldn't hear my internal freak out. Shifting a bit under my weight, he let my body fall on to the seat alongside him. He tucked his arm under my head, my face easily pillowed by his chest. "That better?"

"Yes, thank you." I felt like I could breathe again. Being on top of Blake did weird things to me.

He leaned down, brushing my lips with his, and all my earlier fretting dissolved. My stomach dropped down into my toes, my insides tingling. I kissed him back, getting lost in how soft and warm his lips were. It amazed me that it didn't matter how many times we'd kissed—it always left my head spinning, my insides craving more of him. His hands wrapped around me, pulling me tight against his warm body. Next thing I knew, I was halfway back on top of him.

Okay, this scenario is way worse than being in my room. At least there, the fear of getting caught kept things to a minimum. Cradled in Blake's warm arms, completely alone, while his lips caressed my skin and lips filled me with the pang of desire. The intensity of the moment slightly terrified me, if I were being honest. This was uncharted territory for me, and being lost in the moment wasn't exactly the time to grapple with where the line to stop should be.

One thing I did know, my dad expected me to have a ring on my finger before I gave 'the goods' away. That's the line, I told myself as Blake's hands slipped under my shirt, crawling their way up my back. I shivered, his touch like fire, brushing the goose bumps shooting across my skin. I couldn't get enough air in; my head was spinning in an intoxicating fog.

When the tips of his fingers landed on my bra strap, I jumped, pulling back. Line crossed.

"Wait... I..." I stammered, my face flushing. In all the times he'd kissed me, he'd never tried to undress me. Did I admit to him the thought terrified and thrilled me at the same time? Maybe he really did want me after all.

Blake shifted back, readjusting the seat upright. With me sitting in his lap, he pulled me into a hug. "I'm sorry, Sam. I got a little carried away. I shouldn't have done that."

"No, it's fine, really. I guess I shouldn't be... embarrassed. You've probably done this with lots of girls," I said, dreading him confirming my suspicions. My love life had been simply kissing Jeremy, and I suppose Mack, even though I didn't remember it. That had been the extent of it for me. Or had it? I stifled a gasp from escaping me. I knew I was a virgin, but what about Sammy? I had no memory of what she did when she had the reins. My stomach felt sick at the thought.

"Sam, I'd be lying if I said I never kissed anyone else, but I've been in love with you for as long as I can remember. I guess the thought of you flashing through my head while being with someone else kept anything else from happening." He pressed a soft kiss to the side of my mouth.

It was a shock to know he might be more like me in the physical department after all. I assumed he'd have gone all the way by now. As I stared at him, I let a small laugh escape me.

Blake's brows rose. "What?" he asked.

"For so long, I thought what made me weird at school was the fact I've never," I flushed, "well, you know. But I have a split personality and can sprout wings, so being a virgin seems pretty normal right about now."

Blake chuckled. "Well, we have two of those three things in common. So you're not that weird," he teased.

My heart squeezed. For some reason, knowing Blake had never shared that part of himself with anyone else made me happy.

"I promise, I'll try to control myself around you better," he said, "Besides, hopefully, we won't have to wait much longer." He winked at me, and I could only stare at him.

"What do you mean?" I asked, leaning back a little so I could see his face better. I didn't want to move that much; his body was warm. Even with the engine idling and the heater vents blowing, the Colorado chill clung to the windows.

"January twenty-eighth, right?" he asked, peering down at me.

"My birthday?" I asked, still not sure I knew what he was getting at. Did he think that when I turned eighteen, I'd be free to do whatever with him?

He grinned and ducked down to nestle his lips under my chin, kissing my neck. I sighed, my skin tingling where he touched.

"Maybe we should skip this weekend's trip. I think I need to shovel a few more walks with your dad," he said, stopping his butterfly kisses. He glanced up and met my gaze.

"What? No way! We're going."

"Alright. We better get you home then. Don't want your dad mad at me," he said, lifting me up easily and helping me across the center console. I didn't want to leave his arms, but I knew he was right. It was late and time to get home. I angled the heater vents to hit me more directly, feeling the absence of his body.

I let the conversation slide around my birthday, even though I didn't have the heart to tell Blake that just because I was eighteen didn't mean my dad, or I, would be fine with me going all the way. Honestly, I secretly wondered if he meant something else. I hadn't forgotten the conversation in my room when he said he wanted to make me his Mrs. Knightly. The thought of marrying Blake sent my head spinning in a thousand different directions, and my heart in only one. I wanted to be with Blake in every way—that much I was certain. How my parents would feel about their eighteen-year-old daughter getting married was another matter.

I glanced over at Blake. By the way his brow line lowered, I had a hunch he wasn't thinking about marital vows right now. He seems nervous about bringing me back to Tonbo's Island. I got the feeling there was something else he wasn't telling me. Is it just his brother he's worried about?

CHAPTER
Five

Arriving at the island was different this time; I had bigger problems than the gawking eyes that still followed our every move. At least we flew directly to Tonbo's office headquarters. Mack wasn't here, but Blake told me Tonbo would skin him alive if he didn't bring me to see him first thing. When I thought of the impish man with bushy eyebrows and brilliant onyx eyes, I couldn't see him skinning anyone alive. Even with his oddities, Tonbo exuded kindness. I had to admit I was looking forward to a chat with him now that I knew about Sammy.

When I entered the building and felt the blast of icy AC, it sent my heart galloping. Every part of me screamed that Mack should be here with us now, like last time. The swirling blue-green color below my feet didn't help either. I'd seen those tiles before when I was Sammy. When Mack had brought her here...

I glanced at the circular desk, hoping for a distraction, but seeing the three beautiful damsels manning the phones only made me think of Kate.

I turned to Blake. "I'd like to see her while I'm here."

"Who?"

"Kate."

He glanced over, and I didn't miss the panic he tried to hide in his eyes.

Keeping me from Jaxon was one thing, but Kate too? I erupted. "You can't keep me in a bubble forever, Blake. I'm ready to talk to her. She could have answers."

He blew out air as his shoulders dropped. "It's not that. You'd be fine seeing her... if she were here still."

I stopped short. "What do you mean? Where is she?"

Blake glanced around before ushering me under the enormous breadfruit tree. He frowned. "She... escaped last week."

My mouth went dry. "What? And you didn't think you should tell me?" It was one thing to question the girl who'd done so much damage when she was 'behind bars,' but quite another to know she was free. Was she out there plotting something again? With Sammy?

"I didn't want to worry you, Sam. Her trial was scheduled for tomorrow. She'd been nothing but compliant, repentant even. Then one morning last week, she was just gone."

"And nobody saw anything? What about the surveillance cameras?" I asked, trying to swallow down the rising panic, but my tongue suddenly felt like it was too large for my mouth.

"Something tripped them out." Blake took me by the shoulders. "Sam, she probably just didn't want to stand trial for what she'd done. I'm sure she's long gone, and besides..." His face softened as he pulled me closer. "I won't let anything happen to you."

I knew now what he'd been trying to hide from me. Coming to the island had forced him to tell me that Kate had escaped. But he shouldn't be keeping stuff like this from me in the first place.

"You should've told me, Blake. The last time something tripped out the wires, Sammy and Kate broke into Tonbo's lab and stole serum," I reminded him. "Kate escaping... well, it can't be a good thing."

"I know," he admitted to my surprise. "I've wanted to tell you since I found out, but I didn't want to scare you. You've been through so much already."

The pain I saw in his eyes softened my rebuttal. His honesty with me was something we'd have to work on, but standing in the middle of a lobby wasn't the time or place.

"Come on, let's not think about her right now," he said, steering me away from the breadfruit tree. "There's someone dying to see you. Every time I come, he begs me to bring you."

I sighed and grumbled. "Oh, alright. Let's go see Tonbo. I've missed him too."

His smile grew as he stretched out his wings. I couldn't

help but be captivated by the way the light bounced off his blue-green, iridescent wings. He reached out a hand to me, his eyes expectant, waiting for me to follow after. I let my wings come to life and grabbed his fingers. We lifted up through the open lobby, stopping on the tenth floor. Like last time, we hadn't even knocked before the double walnut doors swung inward. Tonbo's face peered out at us, the wisps of silver in his round, black eyes as hypnotizing as ever. The smile and warm greeting I'd expected, however, were nowhere to be seen.

Instead, he shooed us in. "Come in, come in! No one out there can be trusted!"

With that, his little arms ushered us through the doors, practically shoving us into his private office. The doors slammed behind us. I glanced at Blake, thinking it was nothing more than another odd moment with Tonbo. My grin died on my lips as I saw Blake's concern.

"What do you mean?" Blake asked. "Tonbo, what's going on?"

Tonbo's onyx eyes widened, the silver streaking through the black pulling me in. "There are enemies in our midst, Blake," Tonbo announced. Glancing at me, he added, "Does she know about Kate?"

Blake nodded, and Tonbo continued, "Kate's not the only one to disappear. Others have gone missing too."

My stomach sickened. I wasn't sure which scenario was worse—Kate escaping or her being taken. Either way, it didn't bode well.

Blake's eyes were fastened on Tonbo. "Who else is missing?" he asked, his jawline taut.

"Ancients," Tonbo replied, his shoulders sagging. "Some of my dearest friends. Ones who would have never left on their own. Just gone. Someone is taking them."

Blake grimaced. "Do you think it's Kory?"

"It's the only conclusion I can come to," Tonbo said, sighing heavily. "As to why, I don't know. What would he want with them? They aren't trained soldiers. They're some of the kindest souls I know."

Although I hadn't met any of the ancients, I remembered Mack had mentioned them as being some of the first Dragon Fae. They lived in the Outskirts, the islands outside the main channel, surrounding City. They didn't leave because many of them couldn't morph back to human form or use camo to hide themselves. Tonbo spoke warmly of his friends, but for some reason, I had a healthy fear of the ancients. It was something Mack had said about them, though I couldn't remember what it had been.

"Why indeed?" Blake repeated, almost to himself. "You think his army has formed already? Maybe he's sending the bugs in after the ancients?"

Tonbo flinched. "I sure hope not."

"How many are gone?" Blake asked.

"Four so far. From different family clusters," Tonbo answered, rubbing his chin. "All of them taken while at the beach. No one has seen anything... but with camo, that isn't too surprising. What's more alarming is the lack of scents left behind."

"Do you think Kate's disappearance is related to theirs?" I asked, hoping her being gone really had nothing to do with Sammy.

"Perhaps," Tonbo said. "It has me thinking if Kory is behind all of this, he's got someone on the inside helping him out." Tonbo glanced at his doors leading out of his office. "Trust no one, Blake and Samantha."

I suppressed the ironic laughter I felt within. Trust no one is my life's mantra. Although, I thought, glancing at Blake, I do trust Blake. Even with his annoying habit of withholding information from me. And Tonbo didn't send my creep vibes into overdrive. The only other person I was still struggling to quantify my feelings over was Mack. But I refuse to believe he's the inside guy.

Blake met my gaze. "Sam, I think it's time we go see Mack."

Tonbo's lips twitched into a frown. "Ahh, my poor Mack. I can't make heads or tails to what happened between you and him, Samantha."

"That makes two of us, Tonbo," I answered as Blake stepped closer, taking my hand in his. "But I think it's time I talk to him again. I don't like the idea of him sitting in some holding cell." Tonbo threw his arms up. "Nor do I. He was granted full pardon for his actions. There's no lock on his room. He's free to go whenever he chooses."

"Does he ever leave?" Blake asked, his tone a bit too hard for my liking. I glanced over, wanting to know what he was thinking, but Tonbo sighed.

"No. That boy will not forgive himself." Tonbo scratched the back of his head. "I hate to admit it, but the last few days with your brother have kept me from seeing Mack. I'm glad you're going to see him. And will you be visiting Jaxon after?"

"No, not today," Blake answered before I could get a word out. I knew I shouldn't be disappointed, but I was. It's probably a really bad idea, anyway.

CHAPTER
Six

T he images I'd conjured of an actual prison cell were nothing like what I found Mack in. The cot bed and plain chair
gave it more of a mental hospital feeling than a jail. The
restroom was down the hall. According to the guard, that was the
only time Mack would leave his holding cell. The door was shut,
but through the rectangular glass window, I got a clear view of
Mack as we approached.

My stomach clenched. With his spiky hair turned into a
shaggy mess and no glasses, I hardly recognized him. He leaned
against the wall, where the headboard would've been if the bed
had a frame. He didn't notice us until Blake opened the door,
glancing first at Blake and then me.

His eyes widened and he jumped to his feet, running his
hands up and down his face before putting his glasses back on.
In that moment, I had to resist the urge to make a spectacle of
myself. I wanted to hurl myself past Blake and throw my arms
around Mack. Everything about this felt wrong. His eyes widened even further as I drew close.

"What are you doing here?" he asked. I tried to ignore the
frown he shot at Blake. "I told you I didn't want her to come here."

Blake shrugged. "I don't think anyone can tell Sam what to
do. She wanted to see you." To my surprise, Blake gave my shoulder a squeeze. "Hey, I'll be right outside the door when you're
done, okay?"

"Okay, thanks," I said, surprised he seemed to know what I
needed right then. I turned to Mack as the door clicked behind
Blake. We were alone. Maybe now he'll stop frowning.

Instead, Mack sat back down on his bed, his face contorting

into a grimace. It was so unlike the Mack I knew.

"Hey, I've come all this way to see you and this is how you treat me?" I asked, trying to make light of the situation.

As soon as I sat down next to him, I could feel him tense. I reached over and touched his shoulder. "Mack, hey, it's me here. What's wrong?"

He grunted. "What's wrong? You shouldn't be here. I don't deserve you coming to see me. I don't deserve Blake letting you." "Well, Blake doesn't get to say what I do or don't do," I said, annoyed Mack was under the impression he did. I ignored the fact he'd refused to let me see Jaxon. That's different...

"Of course I'm going to come see you. You're being ridiculous staying in here in the first place. No one's keeping you here."

"That doesn't matter, Sammy."

I let the name slide. Mack had been calling me that for so long, I wondered if he even noticed the difference anymore.

"I need to serve my time. I committed crimes. Against the islands, against Tonbo and Blake, and most importantly, against you." His voice softened a bit with the last statement. He cleared his throat. "I will do whatever Tonbo decides."

"But he already decided that you're free to go. The door's not even locked."

He glanced away from me and shook his head.

"Mack." I squeezed his shoulder. "It's time to come home. I mean, what do your parents think? Don't they miss you?"

"They think Tonbo's training me for something," he answered, his shoulder's slumping. "That's what Tonbo told them when they called him to find out where I went."

"Oh. Well, that's good."

"No, it's not. No one should be doing me favors. I'm the monster. Remember, Samantha?"

Back to Samantha again. "No, you're not. I am. I'm Sammy, and Sammy's me. In some freaky way, I'm my own monster. So stop moping around here. I need you," I blurted.

Mack glanced over at me.

I hesitated, and then let it all out. "It's not the same without you back home... I need my best friend back. My parents have me going to this creepy psychologist, trying to figure out Sammy, but you know her better than anyone else does. You're the one I should be talking to, not some doctor. I'm scared to death of her coming back. I don't know how to do this alone; I need your help."

I hadn't realized how much I needed Mack in my life until that exact moment. My words were a revelation. Mack's eyebrows lifted, the scowl disappearing.

"I'm so sorry, Sammy-er-Samantha," he stammered.

"It's okay, Mack. I'm used to you calling me Sammy. I'm good with it, really."

"No, I shouldn't call you that." He sighed. "You deserve better, Samantha. I guess I thought staying here was the best thing for you. I mean, I'm just a reminder of all the horrible things in your life."

"That's not true, Mack. Sure, I don't like to think about what happened, but Sammy could still be in my life right now. That doesn't change if you disappear on me."

"I guess I didn't think about that." He gazed back at me. "I just want to do whatever helps you."

"Then come home," I said, nudging his shoulder with mine.

He gave me half a smile. "Will that help, Sam..." He flushed before finishing, "—ster?"

I cocked an eyebrow at him. "Samster? That's what you're going to call me now?"

It made me happy to see Mack's face split into a real smile this time. "What? It's like hamster but with—"

"No way. I'd rather you call me Sammy."

"Hamsters are cute," he said, pretending to argue.

"Hamsters bite," I reminded him.

"True, but I'm pretty sure Sammy didn't add hamster DNA to your blend, so I'm not worried."

I slugged his shoulder, glad to have an excuse to laugh at the crud in my life.

He pulled my hand free from his shoulder. "Geez, your blend sure makes you punch hard, though."

"Oh whatever," I said, realizing he had yet to let go of my hand. I knew I wasn't in love with Mack, but there was a part of me that still longed for his closeness. Was it proof that Sammy was still in there somewhere? Or just the fact that Mack had been my first and only true friend for many, many years? Knowing Blake waited outside the door, I stood up and used our clasped hands to pull Mack to his feet.

"Alright, no more excuses. You're coming back with us."

Mack let my fingers go. "Like I said, the only reason I am is to help you."

"Fine. Sounds good to me." We made our way across the room, but before we opened the door, I glanced over at him. "You know, you're going to have to forgive yourself one day."

He didn't look at me, and I could sense he wanted to argue with me that it would never happen. I slipped my hand back into his. He shot a glance at me.

"I've forgiven you, Mack. We managed to be best friends with Sammy stuck in the middle of us before. Maybe we can again."

He rubbed the back of his neck with his free hand. "Sammy underestimated you—always thinking you were the one who needed saving. I think she had it backward."

I stared after Mack as he opened the door. Although the slump was gone from his shoulders, his stride still wasn't the confident one I knew. That was because there was one more person to face. Blake.

I couldn't help but think about what he'd said. Was I really stronger than Sammy had given me credit for? In the caves with Jaxon, I'd felt something claw at me, wanting to take over. It was the closest thing I had to knowing what Sammy felt like. That feeling had stuck with me ever since. I hadn't let her win that day. Did that make Sammy angry? Or did it make her go away forever?

My internal struggle was interrupted by Blake sizing Mack up and saying, "If there's anything you should tell me, anything you haven't already, do it now, Mack."

Mack didn't hesitate. "There's nothing, I swear."

"Alright," Blake said, capping Mack's shoulder with his hand.

"Let's get out of here and get some food. I'm starving."

I stared as the guys fell easily back into teasing one another, with Blake telling Mack he looked like a skinny girl with long hair. As I followed, I wondered if it could really be that simple with guys. I shrugged it off on the way back to Tonbo's office. Blake's seeming ease with Mack was a huge relief. Maybe things can get back to normal. Well, as normal as things get for me.

CHAPTER
Seven

"Nothing will be the same," Tonbo declared while pulling Mack into a hug. Not exactly the words I would have chosen for a welcome back, but Mack didn't seem to mind. "But that's okay. We're all in uncharted territory here."

For some reason, the words uncharted territory stirred up a memory of my dad talking to my mom. At the time, they'd been referring to me not being quite Samantha or Sammy. Since becoming a damsel, I wasn't either of the two. My parents weren't sure how to handle me.

"I know," Mack said when Tonbo released him. "And I'm willing to do whatever it takes to re-earn your trust, Tonbo."

"I know, my boy, I know. Come on. Let's have a nice meal together before you all retire for the evening." Tonbo patted Mack's back.

To me, Tonbo added, "With Mack's help, Samantha, I'll have a much clearer view of what you're made up of. That's part of the reason I've been begging Blake to bring you back to me."

Slightly jarred by Tonbo's ever-blunt words, I could only nod as Blake's hand slid over mine. He gave my fingers a gentle squeeze.

"That... and I'd like to have a talk with Sammy, if you don't mind," he finished. Blake's hand tightened reflexively, squeezing my fingers in the process.

"Tonbo, what are you talking about?" Blake asked, releasing his grip on mine when I gasped. To me, he mouthed, "Sorry." He'd misunderstood my gasp. Sure, my hand didn't feel great, but it was Tonbo's words that were making it hard for me to breathe. Talk to Sammy?

The anger I saw in Blake's expression led me to believe this was news to him. I glanced at Mack, whose chalk-white complexion and widened eyes appeared shocked as well.

Tonbo glanced at the three of us. "Oh, maybe I should've told you that after we'd eaten. I'd like to ask Sammy some questions, that's all."

"That's all?" Blake asked, folding his arms across his chest. "What are you talking about? Sammy's gone."

Tonbo scratched his temple. "Maybe she is, and maybe she isn't. Either way, I think I can access the parts of Samantha's brain where Sammy's memories are stored. They're in there; we just have to get to them."

"I don't know, Tonbo... that doesn't sound very safe," Blake said, his eyes meeting mine.

"The best thing would be to talk to Sammy herself," Tonbo continued as if he hadn't heard Blake at all. "And since Mack helped me map her genetic code, I feel confident that talking to Sammy will be quite safe. If she's still around, that is."

"Mack?" Blake cut in.

He immediately threw his hands up. "I had no idea about any of this, Blake. I only told him what I knew about the serum. I figured Samantha would want to know what Kate and... Sammy did to her."

Blake's jaw bulged as he took a deep breath in through his nose. I worried he'd blurt out, "You mean what you did to her," when he opened his mouth, but he didn't. "You're helping him bring Sammy back?" He glared at Mack.

Mack stuttered to respond.

"Now wait just a minute here," Tonbo cut in. "Everyone's getting all worked up for no reason. Mack only helped me with her DNA coding, Blake. No one is trying to bring Sammy back... at least not in the way you're thinking. I'm only proposing putting Samantha into a hypnotic state where I might be able to summon Sammy, if she still exists. If she doesn't, I can induce a deep relaxation. With the aid of a few pharmaceuticals, we can tap into her subconscious where Sammy's memories are stored."

"Hypnosis won't work," I said, my voice sounding flat and emotionless. I was amazed considering the wars raging within. Talk to Sammy? After the initial shock of the idea, I had to admit the thought of it both excited and terrified me. I had so many questions for her. So many things I wanted to understand better. She was a part of who I was and yet, she was a complete stranger to me.

Everyone's eyes were on me. I continued. "They tried it before, when I was a kid. My parents said it was to help me get over the drowning, but now I realize they were probably trying to get rid of Sammy. Either way, I never went under."

Tonbo grinned. "You would if I did it." Blake shook his head. "Tonbo, it's not going to happen."

"Why not?" I blurted, cutting off Tonbo's response.

Blake's eyes riveted on me, looking surprised that I'd even asked.

"Because, it's too risky," Mack answered for him, his tone sounding defeated. "Tonbo, you have to admit there's a chance that if you put her under and Sammy emerges, she might not go away."

I directed my gaze to the floor, trying to ignore Blake's direct stare. How could I explain to him the need I felt inside? He just didn't get how important it was to me to know what had happened. To know why Sammy did what she did... and more importantly, what she had planned for the future. Something inside screamed that even if she was gone, or suppressed for now, the plan she'd hatched and put into play with Kate was still in motion. The fact that Kate had suddenly disappeared only solidified the fears I had.

I need to know more... It's the only way I won't be the victim again. That I'll be the one in control.

"That chance is extremely small," Tonbo said.

"But there's a chance," Blake said. "So the answer is no."

I glared at him. Shouldn't this be my decision? Even the knowledge he was refusing because he feared losing me frustrated me. Why would he get the final say on the matter?

"I see I struck a nerve here," Tonbo said. I wondered why he had been so keen on it in the first place until he added, "We will find other ways to get answers to the ancients disappearing."

Blake's eyebrows shot up. "You think Sammy had something to do with it?"

Tonbo met my gaze. "I'm not sure. Just a theory at this point."

"Tonbo…" I took a step toward him. "What do you think happened?"

I felt Blake tense up next to me, but that was nothing to how pale Mack had become. He looked green, like he might puke at any second.

"Sammy appeared the last time you were here. As you know, she took over while we were in the theater. I didn't know about Sammy then, but if I had," Tonbo shot Mack and Blake accusing glares. "I never would have let you, or her, out of my sight. As it was, I sent you to your room. Thought you just needed some rest."

I nodded, holding my breath while my heartbeat seemed to speed up with each word he uttered. This was exactly what I wanted to know. What was Sammy up to? What did she do during that time?

"Sammy was left alone the rest of the evening," Tonbo continued. "We didn't check on you until the morning. By then, we discovered you were gone. Sammy had left a note behind, so we assumed you'd just flown home."

"Wait, she left a note?" I asked. "Do you still have it?"

Tonbo scratched his chin. "I don't think so… Well, actually, I might." He hurried over to his desk, rummaging through a few drawers. "I haven't cleaned out my desk in a while. Guess my bad housekeeping skills can come in handy." He straightened and held out a folded piece of paper. "Like today. Looks like we are in luck."

I rushed over, scared someone else might beat me to it. The paper felt cool to the touch. It was strange to hold something Sammy had created. It was concrete proof she had or did exist. The paper betrayed my shaking hands. Suddenly, I was terrified to see her handwriting. Would it look like mine? Blake touched my arm, letting me know he was near. His closeness gave me courage. I took a deep breath and unfolded it.

Tonbo, thank you for all your hospitality. It began. The handwriting was a tight cursive. Definitely not penned by me. I blinked and continued reading.

Please don't take this the wrong way, but I'm flying home. I have a lot on my mind, and I just need some alone time to sort it all out. I've been worried about my family's safety with the bug at large. I'd feel better if I was home with them right now.

I've asked Kate for directions back and feel confident I will make it fine. Please tell Mack and Blake to be careful destroying the bug. I won't rest until they are home safe.

I want to thank you for taking the time to run analytical tests on me. I hope you find the results insightful. I'm sure they will be easily deciphered by your astute mind. I look forward to discussing your findings when we meet again. I consider you one of the greatest minds of our time, and it was a pleasure to meet you in person.

-Sammy

I re-read the words. Seeing Sammy scrawled at the bottom made my stomach tighten.

Blake must have read it from over my shoulder because he grunted. "Do you even know what astute means?"

"Not really." I refolded the paper, tucking into my jean pocket. There wasn't much to the note, but they were Sammy's words. I wanted to keep it. "So you just assumed she went home?" I asked Tonbo.

He shrugged. "I had no reason to doubt her actions. If I'd known," he shot another glare at the guys, "it wouldn't have happened."

"Okay, you're right, Tonbo," Blake admitted. "I should've told you."

"So why do you think Sammy might have something to do with the ancients disappearing, Tonbo?" I asked, not wanting to get too far off subject.

Tonbo shrugged. "I don't have anything solid, really. Just curious what the girl's motivations really were. I have a hunch we haven't seen the last of her."

I wanted to blurt, "Me too!" but Blake wrapped his arm around my shoulders. I glanced up to see concern in his aqua eyes. He's worried I can't handle this. Part of me wanted to scream at him, But this is what I need to talk about! While the other half of me felt my knees go weak when I heard Tonbo confirm my own suspicions.

"You know, I think we'd all feel much better with some food," Blake said, his tone firm.

Tonbo glanced in my direction, hesitated, and then agreed. He and Mack led the way out of the office. I tried to convince Blake I was totally fine, but it was hard to hide the rush of adrenaline making my body shake and my teeth chatter.

He wrapped an arm around my waist as he steered us through the door. "Don't let Tonbo's words get to you, Sam. I think Sammy's long gone."

I knew he meant well, but the way he kept sweeping the reality of Sammy under the rug was getting irritating. I want answers. Not food.

CHAPTER
Eight

K ate's gone and Mack's acting weird. I chose to believe he wasn't hiding something, but that it was guilt eating at him. Either way, I was frustrated. The more I thought about Tonbo's proposal, the better it sounded to me. What could be the harm in accessing Sammy's memories? That wouldn't be like summoning her, so there should be no real risk. I'd used these very arguments with Blake after dinner, and he'd shot them all down.

He couldn't understand why I wanted to know what Sammy had done. He wouldn't even agree to ask Jaxon more about me. He felt it wouldn't help anything and would only cause me more pain. What did he know? It then led to me telling Blake in the middle of Tonbo's gardens that I was done with other people deciding what was best for me. Even with him assuring me that was not at all what he was trying to do, at that moment, my irritation won out. I cringed at the memory of storming off, telling him I needed a night alone, to sort things out. I grunted at the irony of using Sammy's very words from the note.

Now, lying in my bed alone, I couldn't decide if I wanted to throw something across the room or apologize. Other than when I'd accused him of being the monster, Blake and I had never quarreled like this before.

I glanced at my bed. The paper lay there, almost mocking me. The words themselves weren't notable, other than sounding like they were written by a professor, but something called to me in them. I flipped over on to my stomach and read each sentence over again. Was Sammy leaving this note just for Tonbo's eyes? Or could there be a message in there for me too? It seemed strange our penmanship would be so different. I guess I thought it'd look at least a little bit like mine, messy and childlike. Instead, her tight cursive seemed oddly out of place.

A soft knock broke my concentration. I quickly refolded the note and stuffed it into my pocket again. Even though it was past ten, I hadn't changed my clothes. I wiped my eyes, trying to hide the fact I'd been crying.

"Come in." I called, standing up. I figured it'd be Blake. Maybe he decided it was time we talked again. I wasn't sure where my feelings were. Would I be the one to say sorry first?

Mack's head appeared through the doorframe. "You sure? It's me."

"Oh." I cleared my throat, and then forced a grin, "Yes, of course." It wasn't that I didn't want to see Mack, but my heart was pretty torn up over my argument with Blake.

He shuffled in, his eyes never leaving my face. Not sure what else to do, I sat back down on my bed. Mack didn't hesitate to sit right next to me. Good. I wasn't in the mood for him to mope. I cringed. I'm the mopey one tonight.

"So what's going on?" he asked, bumping me with his shoulder.

"I'd rather not talk about Blake right now," I blurted, surprised he was here to play mediator in couple's therapy.

"I don't mean with Blake. With you. Why do you want to access Sammy's memories so bad?"

I glanced over at him, realizing what would come with Sammy's memories. Lots of personal time with Mack. I felt my flush face. That wasn't the reason I wanted to remember. Was it?

"I don't know. I just can't shake this feeling that whatever Sammy and Kate started when they changed me isn't over."

Mack flinched at my words, but he recovered quickly. "I don't think Sammy had any plans other than becoming a damsel. At least, Kate didn't tell me anything else."

"Well, not to be rude, Mack, but Sammy and Kate didn't always clue you in on their plans."

Mack relented with a tight laugh. "Can't argue with that."

"Don't you find it odd that Kate just happens to be missing now? Even Tonbo's wondering if Sammy had something to do with the ancients' abductions. He wants to talk to her, for crying out loud."

Mack grunted. "I think Tonbo's a curious man. He enjoys getting information wherever he can. Honestly, I wouldn't be surprised if that's why he wants to talk to Sammy. Just to see if he can do it."

I stared at Mack. "Are you serious? That's messed up."

He shrugged. "Maybe it is. I don't know. The line between right and wrong blurred years ago for me."

I didn't want him to ponder his own statement. Whenever he remembered the cabin events, he shut down on me. I couldn't have him do that tonight.

"I feel like something happened when she left Tonbo's theater that night," I said, directing the conversation back.

"What makes you think that? The note said she just went home."

"Yeah, but when you and I showed up that day, my mom acted like that was the first time she'd seen me," I pointed out.

"Yeah, you're right. But as a damsel in camo, Sammy could have easily stayed off your mom's radar if she'd wanted to."

"Exactly. So what was she up to? She left the theater, and then I woke up in Jaxon's cave. Aren't you curious to know what she did during that time?"

Mack sighed. "Actually, I'd rather not think about it."

"Because you know I'm right. Sammy can't be trusted."

He glanced over, but he didn't say anything.

"What's driving me crazy is the fact that the only ways I know how to figure this out Blake won't even consider."

"You mean with the hypnotizing?"

"Yes, or even talking to Jaxon."

"Well, seeing Jaxon isn't a good idea."

"Yeah, I know, he still craves me." I couldn't help the eye roll.

"No, Samantha. I don't think you really understand what that means." Mack's expression turned serious. "Blake's right on this one. Dragons, and especially bugs, never miss their target... like ever."

I stared at him. "What do you mean?"

"Dragonflies can predict where the target will be. They don't have to chase it down. They just calculate where to intercept it. Truthfully, that's probably how Jaxon got you so easily. He just bid his time, predicted your movements, and struck when you were most vulnerable."

My eyes widened. "So does that mean I can do the same thing too?"

He frowned. "Yes, you could. If you worked on developing that sense."

"You make it sound like it's a bad thing."

"Well, let's just say it wasn't by accident the Germans wanted to create a super army out of half-dragonfly men. If dragonflies were even three feet tall, they'd rule the planet."

I wrinkled my nose. "That sounds pretty far-fetched."

"No. It's true. They're hunters with a ninety-five-percent kill accuracy. To give you an idea of how insane that is, sharks only kill half of what they chase." Goose bumps shot up my arms. "Which brings up the whole issue of why changing everyone into Dragon Fae could prove fatal to mankind pretty darn quick," Mack continued.

"Like Kory wants to," I said.

"Yep. For the most part, dragons and damsels have learned to control their desires enough to live with it. But bugs don't have the same filter as us since they were the crude beginning. Jaxon was given DNA from one of those first monsters; he can't control it, Samantha. You can't blame Blake for not jumping up and down to dangle you as bait in front of his brother."

"But that's just it; Jaxon could've easily killed me. He had lots of chances. I was unconscious in his lair, for crying out loud. If the desire to hunt and kill is so uncontrollable, then how come he didn't?"

Mack seemed like he didn't like the answer, but he said it anyway. "Because Jaxon kept the bug from killing you, because he knew how much you meant to his brother."

"Exactly."

"Okay. Let's say you do talk to Jaxon, what do you think you'll even learn? I mean, he'll probably just tell you where he found you. How does that help?"

"I already know where he found me. A few miles away from my home. But I'm guessing he probably hunted me for a while, maybe tracked me while I was Sammy. He could tell me a lot more than you think."

"Hmmm..." Mack seemed unconvinced. "Has Blake asked Jaxon about all that?"

"No. He won't ask Jaxon about me anymore, and it's driving me crazy."

"Wonder why?" Mack asked, more to himself.

"Assuming Sammy wrote the truth in her note, and she did go home, she made sure my parents didn't see me," I said, changing the subject. I didn't want to think about Blake right now. It just made me mad all over again.

"Which isn't hard to do," Mack agreed.

"True. But I'm wondering if maybe Jocelyn saw her."

"Jocelyn?" Mack asked, his brows lifting up. "Why do you think that?"

I sighed. "My dad told me they were good friends before. For the past few weeks, Jocelyn won't stop giving me the cold shoulder. The only thing I can figure is maybe Sammy did something to tick her off. Maybe Sammy saw Jocelyn when she went home. Maybe something bad happened between them. I just wish I knew what was wrong with her."

Mack's eyes widened, and then he glanced away. *Maybe he knows something.*

"What?" I asked, forcing him to look at me by dragging his chin around.

He reached up, wrapping his fingers around mine long enough to set my hand back in my own lap. I wasn't sure why when he let my hand go, or why I felt a weird sense of loss.

"You're right about Jocelyn and Sammy being close. Maybe

Jocelyn's treating you bad because she's upset that..." He hesitated.

"That Sammy's gone?" I offered. "I thought about that too, but how would she know she's gone? How do any of us know she's really gone?"

"Good point."

"I'm wondering if maybe Jocelyn saw Sammy in the damsel form. Maybe that's why she's freaking out when she sees me now."

"Hmm, you might be right."

"What do you mean?" I hung on his every word.

"Once Sammy saw me as a dragon, she asked a lot of questions. I ended up telling her about Blake. How he saved you and loved you, but he still wouldn't change you. I even told her about Kory and how he and Blake parted ways. Sammy knew about Kate before she actually met her at the island. She knew a lot about the Dragon Fae world before you ever became a part of it."

I nodded along. None of this was shocking news to me.

"So maybe she told Jocelyn all about it too," he finished.

CHAPTER
Nine

I stared at him as the implications of his words sank in. It wasn't a far-fetched idea. If Sammy and Jocelyn were close, there was a chance Sammy told her about this part of her life too.

"When I changed into a damsel right before the Halloween dance, Jocelyn was fascinated by me, especially my wings. I was so scared she'd figure it out since she catches things pretty fast. It's hard to get one past her." I scrunched my eyebrows together. "I wonder how much Sammy had told her before. Did Joc make the connection that night? Realize what I'd become?"

"I don't know," Mack offered. "Maybe she's waiting for you to say something?" I shrugged. "If she is, she doesn't give me much chance. Most of the time, she rushes away as if I'm diseased. The last time, she accused me of taking a stupid book someone had given her. Like I'd steal a book from her in the first place. You should've seen the way she clutched it."

Mack glanced over at me. "Who gave her a book?" "I have no idea. She wouldn't say. She's been acting so strange lately."

"Well, maybe you should try talking to her again."

"What do you suggest? I just show up with my wings and be like, surprise."

"No." He grinned. "Maybe something a bit more subtle. Like, I know you were good friends with Sammy. Mind if we talk about her?"

"I guess it's worth a shot." I sighed and bumped his shoulder with mine. "Thanks, Mack."

He glanced over. "For what?"

"For listening to me. You don't know how much that means to me."

44

"Anytime, Samster," he said giving my shoulder a bump back. "You're really not going to give up on that one, are you?"

"Nope."

I giggled until a soft knock on the door made me stop. Mack jumped to his feet. His face flushed. Why's he so embarrassed? We were just talking.

"You can come in," I said, not sure if I should stand up or remain sitting. Mack was practically bounding to the door as it swung in.

Blake's eyes widened at the sight of Mack in my room. Mack greeted him casually, but the way he ducked from the room and disappeared so fast left a different impression.

Thanks a lot, Mack. You just made it look like we were doing anything but talking.

Blake remained in the doorway, but his body turned as if he were getting ready to leave too. "Sorry, didn't mean to interrupt," he said.

The way his expression fell made me panic. He's getting the wrong idea here. I'd been so furious with him all night, but seeing the pain in his eyes stirred something inside me. I didn't want to fight with Blake anymore; I just wanted him to understand where I was coming from. For him to acknowledge that my fears about Sammy could be true was important to me. We just need to talk.

I jumped to my feet. "You didn't." I tried to give him a reassuring smile. "I'm glad you came."

He didn't move. "You are?"

"Of course I am. Blake, I'm sorry," I blurted, deciding the best way to begin this talk was with an apology. "I shouldn't have blown up at you like that."

His eyes lit up a bit, but he still didn't move. Well, if he won't come to me, I'll go to him. As soon as I drew near, he reached out and took my hand.

"You have nothing to apologize for Sam. I'm the one who is sorry. I guess I didn't realize how much Mack meant to you."

"Mack?" I asked, taken back. "What are you talking about?"

Blake's eyes trailed down the hall, where Mack had dashed

away. "Sammy loved Mack, Mack loved Sammy. I guess I assumed that was the extent of it. But it's obvious to me now you have feelings for Mack. At least on some level. And if you need time to decide things, I'll give you some space. I'm sure it's got to be confusing."

My eyes widened. "You think that's why I'm upset? That that's why I want to tap into Sammy's memories?"

He nodded, eyeing me as if he was afraid I'd erupt on him again. Instead, I pulled him into the room and shut the door.

"That's not it at all," I said, frustrated he still wasn't getting it. "Sammy was in love with Mack, not me. I do care for Mack, but he's more like a brother."

He pulled me closer. I could feel my anger ebbing at his touch. Something about him always calmed me down.

"You sure?" he asked, "I've seen the way your eyes light up around him."

They do? I shook it off and jabbed him in the chest with my finger, halfway serious, halfway playful. "That's only because you keep making me scowl when I'm around you."

His eyebrows shot up. "I don't mean to. It's just this whole thing with Jaxon; it's not safe for you to see him, Sam."

"I know it's not safe for me to see him, but why won't you even ask him questions for me?"

"I did."

"Once. And you didn't push for details."

Blake considered me for a moment and then ran his hand across his mouth and chin. He sighed. "I don't like bringing you up, Sam, because every time I do, the bug emerges. Jaxon can't stop it. And then, all the progress we've made is gone."

I stared at him, stunned. "Oh. Why didn't you tell me that before? I don't want to make it harder for him. I wouldn't have kept pestering you to do it if I'd known."

"I didn't want to stress you out. I mean, telling your girlfriend that your brother's still dying to rip her to shreds isn't exactly on my top-ten list." Blake tried to smile, but his words were too near to his heart, even saying them as a joke.

I threw my arms around him. "I wish you'd told me, Blake. I'm so sorry. I won't pressure you about Jaxon anymore."

"Thank you." His voice was soft. I could feel his pain. He sat back a little, so he could look me in the eyes. "And I'm sorry I didn't explain myself better before. I need to work on being more open with you."

"Yes, you do." I jabbed his chest again, this time with a smile. He grabbed my finger and pressed it to his lips.

"So, what was Mack doing here?" he asked, his lips lingering on my fingertip.

"He was trying to make good on his promise to help me sort out Sammy." Not steal me away like you were thinking... At least, I don't think he was.

"Good to know," Blake said, leaning in to kiss my cheek, sending a little thrill through me. "I'm sorry I jumped to conclusions. I'm not usually a jealous guy, but you've made a mess of me."

His lips were inches from mine, and even though my heartbeat had gone erratic just being in his arms, I still needed to explain my side to him. "Blake, wait," I said, pressing my hand against his chest. "I need to talk to you about something."

"Sure, what is it?"

His question didn't feel defensive, so I dove in. "I need you to understand why knowing what Sammy has done, or might do, is so important to me."

"Sam, I think I do," His eyes softened. "I can only imagine how hard it is on you. The only reason I try to avoid her is to spare you more pain."

"No," I said, my voice firm. "You don't understand. You may think you do, but you don't." I half expected him to say he was only doing what was best for me. How he was only trying to protect me.

Instead, he simply said, "Then help me understand, Sam."

My heart warmed. I walked to my bed, leading him by the hand. When I sat down, he followed suit, pulling my hand into his lap.

"Okay, I'm listening," he said, giving my hand a squeeze.

I took a deep breath and told him everything. Even down to how much I detested my new psychologist. It didn't take too long and, true to his word, he listened without interrupting. When I was done unloading, I waited for him to respond.

I couldn't understand the tension in his eyes until he said, "I didn't know Jocelyn was being mean to you." His expression softened. "That must be tough."

I swallowed the lump in my throat and nodded. "It is, but mainly because it's driving me crazy. Blake, I can't describe it, but I know Sammy is up to something. I feel it in my gut. Until I know what it is... I'm scared. I'm scared I'll wake up one day and not be me. That Sammy will win. She'll be the one here, not me."

Blake pulled me into his lap. "That's not going to happen, Sam. I won't let you disappear. If you feel Sammy has plans, we'll figure out what she's up to, and we'll do it together."

I glanced up at him. "Really? You believe me?"

"Of course I do. I'm sorry I never gave you the chance to explain it all before. I guess I just got hung up on the idea of you seeing Jaxon being too dangerous. Then when Tonbo announced he could re-incarnate Sammy, all I could think was why on earth would we do that? She's only caused pain when she's around. I didn't want you to experience more pain. You've had enough to last two lifetimes."

He kissed my forehead. "Seeing how you were around Mack, and then you telling me you needed time to sort things out, I thought maybe you had other reasons for wanting to know more about Sammy. I thought you realized you really loved him more. I mean, you've known him your whole life. He's been there for you when I wasn't."

I couldn't bear to let him think I'd choose anyone over him. There was no question for me where my heart belonged. I answered him with a kiss, hoping to reassure him. He didn't fight me, but deepened the kiss, pulling me tighter against him. I knew I'd have to come up for air, but in that moment, I didn't care if I suffocated. All I wanted was him.

The desire shooting through my veins left me feeling disorientated. The firm grip of Blake's hands on my back pulled me closer to him. My entire body felt airy—like it was no longer attached to anything but him. His touch was the only thing my mind registered.

Somewhere in our kissing, we'd lain down next to each other, him leaning over me, his lips making their way down my throat. One second, I was in pure bliss, and then the next, a strange panic ripped through me. I didn't want him to go any further. Although we'd kissed plenty of times in my room, since Blake had always been the one to insist I get sleep, I'd gotten used to him being the guardrail against us going very far. Remembering the time in the car and feeling the urgency in his kiss now, I began to wonder how much of his self-control had been from being under my parents' roof.

I pushed against his chest. He leaned back immediately, his eyes searching my face. All I could think was how unattached to my body I still felt, the floating sensation overwhelming me. "Blake," I said, hating the out-of-body experience I was having. "I can't... we can't do this."

"What? Kiss?" he asked.

"No, I mean. We can kiss, but it's just... I feel really... strange." I felt my face heat.

He grinned, his eyes dancing a bit. "Are you losing control of yourself?"

I knew he was teasing, but I was serious. "I don't know. I've never felt like this before. I'm really dizzy. Can we just stop for a bit?"

His smile disappeared. "Of course. Are you okay? Sorry, I didn't mean to push."

"No, you didn't. I'm just feeling weird tonight, that's all." I tried to sit up, but I swayed to the side instead, falling back to the bed.

"Sam, are you okay?" he asked.

"I think so." I actually wasn't so sure. What I thought was mere hormones had turned into a very bad case of vertigo. Or worse, could it be Sammy trying to take over?

Blake scooped me up into his arms and leaned against the headboard. "No more kissing, I promise. Why don't you try to fall asleep?"

I let my head fall onto his chest, loving how his fingers felt stroking my hair back. "Thank you," I whispered. "I'm sorry I'm lousy company tonight."

He chuckled. "There's nothing else I'd rather be doing. Just try to relax. It's been a very long day. I'm sure with some sleep that you'll feel a lot better."

As I listened to his reassurance, I wondered if it wasn't for himself as well. Neither one of us had to say it. We were both afraid that if I had passed out, Sammy would be there.

CHAPTER
Ten

I was surprised to wake up to find Blake's arms around me. I'd grown so used to falling asleep with him, and then waking up to nothing, that the sound of his even breathing was a welcome change. We were facing one another with one of his arms tucked under my head, the other draped across the side of my body.

I couldn't help myself; I studied his face, even though it felt like spying. There were no worry lines to crease his brow. His forehead was smooth, and his lips were slightly parted. I was tempted to reach over and touch them. They looked so soft. Instead, I nestled my face into his chest. He stirred, his grip tightening on me as he pulled me closer.

"You awake?" he asked, his voice gravelly from sleep.

"Barely," I answered, loving how warm he felt.

He grunted and leaned over to kiss the top of my head. "Feeling better?"

"Yes, much," I said, happy the dizzy spell had ended. "Sorry if I freaked you out last night."

He leaned back a bit, so he could look me in the eyes. "I have to admit, you did worry me. Are you still feeling lightheaded?"

I shook my head.

He grinned. "Good. Because I think I have an idea about how we can figure out what Sammy may have been up to."

I sat back further, excitement pushing away all drowsiness. "Really? How?"

He let go of me so we could sit up. I tried to move and realized sleeping in jeans was so not cool. My legs were wrapped in bedding like a burrito. Tugging at the blanket, I tried to detangle myself. Blake watched me for a moment with a crooked grin.

"So, what's the idea?" I asked, finally getting rid of the blanket and kicking off the sheet.

"You know Tonbo mentioned the ancients were disappearing?" I nodded. "Well, last night, after you... er... left me, I decided to ask Tonbo more about them."

I felt my face flush at the memory of acting like a two-year-old and stomping away from Blake.

"Turns out they weren't just random ancients taken," he continued, like he hadn't noticed my embarrassment.

"Really? What do you mean?"

"The four taken were experts in different scientific fields. At least they were long ago. One was a renowned biochemist, one a biophysicist, another a genetic engineer, and the last studied under Mendel when Tonbo did."

My eyes widened. "Sounds like whoever took them knew what they were doing."

"I agree. Same goes with Kate too. She wasn't a mad genius by herself, but she helped Sammy develop your serum, which Tonbo considers groundbreaking. She could prove a valuable asset to someone trying to, let's say, build a new bug army they could control."

"Kory," I said, hating him more by the minute.

"That's what I was thinking, at least until last night. But now, thinking about what you just said, I'm wondering if Sammy is up to something."

"You think she's somehow involved with Kory's plans?"

"I'm not saying she is for sure, but there might be a way we could know if she had anything to do with the ancients' disappearances. Other than Tonbo's science experiments."

"How?"

"We could go to the Outskirts today."

I stared at him. "How will that help?"

"We could ask some of the ancients if they've seen you before. You've never been there, so if you look familiar, then..."

"Sammy's been there."

Blake nodded, seeming pleased with his idea.

"And even if they don't remember seeing me, I might still be able to tell. Remember when I went to Tonbo's office for the first time? Everything about it felt so familiar. Like the strongest déjà vu I've ever felt."

Blake nodded along. "So you might be able to sense it there too. Even better. So how about it? Up for a little field trip today?"

"Thought you'd never ask," I said, jumping from the bed.

Blake climbed off a bit slower. Smiling at me, he reached for my hand. "Sam, just one thing. Don't go too far from me, okay?"

"Why?" I asked, not sure if he was teasing or serious.

"Well..." He scrubbed at the back of his neck with his free hand. "Some of the ancients are a bit... intense."

"Okay," I drawled back. "Should I be getting worried now?"

"Not at all. If you stay close to me, no one would dream of touching you."

I didn't argue, worried if I kept harping on how potentially dangerous this could be, Blake might change his mind.

Instead, I squeezed his hand. "Okay, you have my word. I'll stay glued to your side."

I glanced over at Mack, happy Blake had asked him to come along. Every time I expected Blake to become catty about Mack's presence, he surprised me with how ready to forget and move on he was. Technically, Mack hadn't done anything wrong last night. He'd come to me as a worried friend, fulfilling his promise to help me sort through the Sammy thing. Sure, Blake had mis-read Mack's actions at first, but now watching him relentlessly tease him over his lack of prowess in the air, it felt like nothing had happened last night at all.

Other than me acting like a big baby. I sighed, pushing my wings faster. The guys were pulling ahead of me. I felt sluggish. What's wrong with me today? Guess I'm just wiped out.

"Is that all you got?" Mack hollered back at me.

Blake spun around in the air, half of his wings rotating the opposite direction to allow him to continue backward as his eyes studied me.

"Feeling okay, Sam?" Blake asked, slowing a notch.

I caught up and playfully pushed past him, putting quite a bit of space between us. "I'm great," I lied, hoping he wouldn't see through me.

He cocked an eyebrow at me and folded him arms across his chest. I pushed further away, trying to prove to him that I was just fine. He grinned as the distance between us grew. Then, in an instant, he was wrapping his arms around me, like he'd been right next to me the entire time.

I yelped. "Holy cow! Blake, you just scared me to death!"

"Oh, sorry. Didn't mean too. Are you dizzy?" he asked, his eyes filling with sudden concern. "Want me to carry you?"

With how hard I was breathing to get over my shock, I did feel a bit dizzy. I'd never seen anyone move that fast before.

"No, I'm good. Really. You can let me go," I said, playfully pushing against him.

Mack had flown over to see what was up. "Everything okay here?"

"Yes," I said as Blake reluctantly released me. He eyed me as if he still didn't believe I was okay. Trying to appear a lot stronger and steadier than I felt at the moment, I flew ahead of them both. It was Mack who caught up to me first. I was surprised to see Blake buzz past us. Not too far, but just far enough I wasn't sure if he was giving us a little space or not.

I glanced over at Mack, who gestured to Blake with his chin. "Remember what I was saying about being able to track and predict your mark's movements?" he asked.

"Yeah."

Mack glanced ahead at Blake, who was darting back and forth. Almost looking like he was scouting something out, but there was nothing but water below us. So far, there was no land in sight.

"Few do it better than Blake," he said.

My eyes widened. "Is that what that was?"

He nodded. "Who do you think killed the last bug? Sure wasn't Kory. Looks like that dirty weasel just stayed long enough to figure out how to get the bug's DNA. I wouldn't be surprised if that's the only reason he went on that hunting trip and got Blake all pumped up to go too."

I stared at Mack before glancing ahead at Blake, who had decided to dip down closer to the water. I wasn't sure why I was surprised by Mack's words; I'd known about Kory and Blake's hunting trip to kill the last bug. From what I'd seen of Kory's character, I wasn't shocked to hear he'd probably watched Blake kill the beast, only to take credit for it.

I gazed at Blake, who was now soaring extremely close to the swelling, black ocean. My heart warmed, watching him dip a hand in the waves. With his speed, the water shot up, leaving an enormous wake behind him. I was glad to see him enjoying himself. Things always seemed to be so serious in our lives; it was nice to see his playful side. Although he didn't say much about it, I knew his brother's condition weighed heavily on him.

I'd never met a guy like Blake before. In a world where I had a hard time trusting anyone, myself included, he tried to do the right thing. His sense of duty only seemed to waver when it came to taking over the island, but even there, he'd committed himself to something he didn't want to do for his brother. Tonbo promised he'd do everything in his power to save Jaxon, if Blake would finally relent in taking over for him when the time came.

I shook my head. "So in other words, with Blake around, I shouldn't be worried about a few ancients today, right?"

Mack glanced over at me, I expected him to laugh off my fears. Instead, he said seriously, "Well, as long as they see you with him, you should be good."

"Oh, great. Thanks a lot."

I was about to ask just what made the ancients so dangerous when Blake hollered back at us, "Hey, Mack, it's your girlfriend!"

Say what? I glanced around, seeing no one but us. Who is he talking about?

Mack let out a hoot and dove down to where Blake flew. He soared across the water's edge, his face pointed downward. What are they doing? Fishing or something? Is that the girlfriend Blake was talking about? Fish?

I gasped as a pair of slender, suntanned arms reached out from the water and wrapped themselves around the base of Mack's neck. A second later, Mack disappeared under the surface.

CHAPTER
Eleven

After I flew to the spot he'd gone under, I glanced at Blake. I couldn't understand why he just hovered there, grinning. Maybe I misread Blake's feelings about Mack.

I flew down, prepared to dive in, when Blake intercepted me, grabbing my waist. "Whoa there, partner. Mack's fine. You don't have to swim in after him."

I gaped at him, stuttering, "But someone's got him under the water!"

"I know." He chuckled. "Didn't expect Aster to pull him under so fast. I wanted to introduce you to her."

"Aster? Who's Aster? Is Mack in danger?" I fired off questions, still trying to get my brain to understand what just happened. Was Aster a damsel? Who could hold her breath for a very long time under the water... like me?

Mack burst out of the water. Catching the grin on his lips, my shoulders relaxed a bit. Oh good, he's all right. He shook his head back and forth, his hair flying everywhere, reminding me of a wet dog shaking his fur off.

"Darn, Aster, I'm drenched now," he grumbled, still smiling.

"That's what you get for making friends with them in the first place, Mack," Blake said. "You know how they love to play."

"They?" I asked. My eyes darting between the guys, I realized Aster had yet to appear. Glancing down at the water, I flew up a bit higher. With no land in sight, I could only wonder if Aster might be an Ancient.

"Oh sorry, Sam. Aster is part of the—" Blake began to explain, but his words were cut off by a loud splash from below.

I glanced down to see a beautiful, flawless face staring back up at me. I gaped at her eyes. And I thought Blake's were aqua...

Expecting her to fly up from the water with a pair of wings like us, I was shocked to see only locks of long, auburn hair covering her back and cascading down her front, floating in the water. With several braids woven through, as well as bits of seaweed and seashells, her hair was full enough to cover what might very well have been a naked chest.

She glanced at the guys. Before anyone could say anything, she burst up out of the water several feet, her hair fanning out, her back rounding, and her body arching as she made a perfect nosedive back toward the water.

I sucked in air, practically choking on my own spit. A silver-gray dorsal fin protruded from her lower back and a long, steel-gray tail followed after her.

I knew my eyes were saucers. "No way! Did I just see a mermaid?" I asked after the tail fins had disappeared under the water's surface.

Mack scratched his head. "Yep, and a crazy one at that."

Blake pulled me closer. "She's harmless, unless you're a wuss like Mack. She's part of the Irukas."

"The Iru-what?" I was having a hard time getting enough air in. It was like the world had just been turned on its head again.

"It's a group that was created a long time ago," Blake answered.

"Tonbo created mermaids? It wasn't enough he had flying people to worry about?" I asked, my eyes bulging. "What was he thinking?"

"Tonbo didn't actually create them himself. Some of the other dragons were in on the development of the program. It all happened a long time ago, so I don't know the details. They usually stay pretty close to the Outskirts, so they don't usually cause problems," Blake explained.

"Not unless we want to," a female voice said.

I spun around to see that Aster had emerged. My face flushed, realizing she'd probably overheard me expressing my opinion on Tonbo creating them in the first place.

I glanced down, meeting her gaze. Her aqua eyes raked me up

and down, a smile playing on her lips. She appeared to be around our age, but who knew with Irukas. If they were anything like damsels and dragons, she could be a lot older than she appeared to be.

With her chest just above the surface, I was relieved to see she did wear some kind of covering, even if it was barely adequate and showed far too much skin for me to be comfortable. The material was iridescent, blue-green in color, and clung to her breasts, leaving little to the imagination.

"So who is this, Mack?" Aster asked, gesturing to me with her chin.

"This is Samantha," he answered, grinning in my direction. "You know, the human girl Blake pined over forever and never did a thing about."

"Shut up," Blake muttered, smiling.

I thought it strange Mack called me human, like the rest of them weren't anymore.

Besides, I clearly had wings too.

Aster's grin turned mischievous. "Ooh... Blake's lover?"

I felt my face flush. I didn't know why the word lover made me squeamish. "Nice to meet you, Aster," I forced myself to say.

She giggled. "Pleasure's all mine. Not often our kind gets to see Blake, let alone his mate."

Now I knew my face was scarlet. I could feel the heat radiating off my cheeks. "Not often I get to see an," I stopped myself from saying mermaid, "Iruka." I hoped I said it right.

She laughed. "True." She winked, and I honestly wasn't sure who it was for. Her flirtatiousness made me uncomfortable.

"So," she drawled, pushing her long hair back behind her shoulders. With how the sun shone directly on her flimsy covering, I wished she hadn't. "Where are you off to today?"

"We're going to see the ancients," Blake answered. "Just learned some of them have gone missing. You Irukas wouldn't have anything to do with that, would you?"

Aster wrinkled her nose at him, frowning.

Mack jumped in. "What we mean is—do you know anything

about it? Perhaps seen something? Or noticed unusual visitors lurking around the Outskirts?"

Aster's frown melted into a grin as her gaze shifted to Mack, and she literally batted her lashes at him. "Nope. I only come up to play with fun dragons like you."

For some reason, her flirting infuriated me. Mack's flushing irritated me even more.

"How about Kory?" Blake asked. "You think he's fun still?"

Aster snorted, glancing back at Blake. "Kory is anything but. If I ever get my hands on him again, I'll pull him down deep, wrap him up in seaweed, and laugh at his water-bloated body." We all gaped at her as Mack responded, "Wow. Okay. What happened to thinking he could walk on water?"

She scowled. "Last time I saw that piece of scum, he wooed half of the Irukas to follow after him. Said he had a higher calling for them."

"Say what?" Blake asked.

She nodded back at him. "He sounded like a wanna-be prophet. The freaky thing is some of my closest friends actually bought it. He asked me to go too, but I told him where to shove it. I'm not joining his cult."

The guys chuckled as I asked, "So you don't know where they went?"

She glanced at me and shrugged. "Nope. Nor do I care. Kory's off his rocker if you ask me."

"What exactly was he promising them?" Blake asked.

"He said a war was coming. We just don't know it yet," she said. "According to him, everyone, Irukas and ancients included, will have to choose a side."

Mack ran his hands through his hair, muttering, "That crazy son-of-a-monkey's uncle."

"Guess we know Kory is looking for a fight," Blake said, frowning. "Only problem is, he's psycho enough to start one himself, just to justify what he's already done."

Aster cocked her head. "What do you mean? What did he do?"

Blake and Mack took turns filling Aster in. How Kory extracted DNA from the last bug killed, then experimented on Jaxon, and finally created a bug army.

"Which," Mack added, "is probably what he's going to use to start this war."

"You're convinced he's the one who will start it?" Aster asked. "That this army he's making is really not just for defending our kind?"

Blake sighed. "We don't know for sure, but I've known Kory a long time. And so have you, Aster. You can't tell me he hasn't ever been devious... slightly manipulative? After what he did to Jaxon..." Blake paused. "I don't rule anything out anymore."

Aster nodded. "Yeah, I guess you're right. Kory always had a bit of chip on his shoulder when it came to you, Blake. And even you, Mack."

"Me?" Mack said, grinning. "Naw. I'm a nobody."

"Not to me," Aster murmured as she openly blushed.

I could only gawk as Mack seemed to return that blush with his own nervous cough. Does Aster like Mack? And more importantly, does Mack like her? How the heck did I not even know about her until today? And, I thought with guilt, why am I so bothered by it?

"How many left with him?" Blake asked, cutting through my own thoughts.

"A lot." She frowned. "But not everyone. Most of us told him he was crazy and to leave us alone."

"Sad truth is," Mack said, "being left alone might not be an option for anyone if Kory has his way."

"No joke," I said, feeling the need to be part of the conversation. "So Kory never mentioned the bug army to the Irukas?" I asked Aster directly.

She glanced over at me, considering my question. "No, not exactly. He said he wanted to be ready for the coming war. Be prepared. He wanted our help because of what we can do."

Blake and Mack exchanged glances. "Crap," Blake said.

I wanted to ask what they were talking about, but Aster said, "So you're off to see what happened to the ancients, then? You think Kory recruited them too?"

"That's what we're hoping to find out," Mack answered. I was glad he didn't go into details about the other reason—my other half's possible involvement.

"Mind if I swim with you for a bit? Be nice to have some company. With Kory swiping so many, it's gotten a bit lonely down here," she said, her eyes fastened on Mack.

"Of course not," Mack said, grinning. "That is... if you can keep up."

"Ha. Just watch me, bird boy," she said, grinning.

"Whatever, fish tail," Mack crowed as he took off flying.

Aster immediately dove in, only to return moments later, soaring through the air like a dolphin. I was in awe of how fast she could weave in and out of the water. Blake and I followed them, not pushing to fly that fast, since it became obvious we'd pass Aster within seconds at top speed. Not saying she wasn't moving. It was insane how she seemed to skate across the water.

It was with mixed feelings that I watched Mack dip down into the water a few times, just as Aster would soar up and over him. Seeing how they never collided, only fell into an easy rhythm with one another's movements, I realized they'd done this before. Maybe lots of times before.

"So how come I never knew about Aster?" I asked Blake. "Clearly, you all go way back."

Blake glanced over at me. "Aster and Mack were best friends when Mack lived with Tonbo. Back when he was too young and had to stay at the islands until he could control his dragon. Remember?"

I nodded.

"They got pretty close. She was always coming to see him, so I got to know her too. When Mack moved away, Aster... well, she never got over him leaving her. She couldn't understand why he wanted to live on the mainland so badly. It took a while for her to forgive him."

"But," Blake said, glancing at Mack and Aster, who were now literally dunking each other in the water, laughing their heads off like a pair of kids. "Looks like it's all water under the bridge now."

"Oh. I feel terrible now."

"Why?"

"Because when Mack came back to Colorado, he watched over me. In the end, he fell in love with Sammy. He forgot all about Aster."

"Don't feel bad, Sam. It's not your fault. It's not as if Aster and Mack were in love. They were just good friends."

Watching how Aster kept wrapping her arms around Mack every chance she could get, I disagreed with Blake's opinion.

"Besides, even if they had been," Blake added, "it would have never worked between them."

"Because they're so different physically, you mean?" I offered.

"Yeah. She can't live on the land, and he can't live under the water. It's the classic Little Mermaid dilemma all over again."

I shook my head. "Just when I think I know which end is up."

Blake chuckled.

"So if Aster and Mack played as kids, that means she's our age too?"

"Yep. Aster is one of the—" Blake began, but the sound of singing stopped him. We both glanced down to see that Mack had lifted Aster out of the water, flying her up into the air as she sang to him.

The melody and tone of her voice sent goose bumps shooting down my arms and legs. It was beautiful, soothing... and slightly hypnotic. She clung to him, her tail wrapping itself around his torso. I swallowed, too shocked to be embarrassed by my own staring.

Blake squeezed my hand. "We're here," he said.

"We are?" I asked, barely registering what he said. I felt like I couldn't break my gaze, like my eyes had to see where that voice was coming from.

Somewhere in my mind, I heard Blake laughing at me. "You'll get used to it."

"Use to what?" I asked numbly, still gawking at Mack and As-ter. That was until Aster's lips landed across Mack's mouth.

I snapped back around to see Blake's amused expression.

"Irukas' singing," Blake said, answering my earlier question. One I'd forgotten I'd even formed.

I shook my head, realizing the strange pull was gone. It'd disappeared the moment Aster had stopped to kiss Mack.

"What was that?" I asked.

"Just one of the many ways the Irukas can be very dangerous," Blake quietly said. "If they choose to be."

I stared at him, realizing there might be more to these fish people than I'd thought. A loud splash caught my attention, and I glanced down to see Aster was once again in the water.

"Good luck!" she called out, giving us a wave. She dove under before any of us could respond back.

Mack caught up to us, his cheeks reddened, his hair all askew. He gave me a sheepish look, and I tried to shake off the feeling he'd just betrayed me somehow. Mack should be free to kiss whomever he chose. Why should I feel weird about it?

"Better be careful with that one," Blake said. Like a second thought, he slugged Mack's shoulder. "But it's about time you got some action."

CHAPTER
Twelve

T he island loomed upon us too fast. With all the Aster business, I felt even more ill prepared for meeting the ancients. We flew into what looked like a village straight out of a National Geographic magazine. Little huts complete with thatched roofs lined dirt roads.

"What in the world?" I breathed out as we finally touched down. "I feel like I just stepped back into time." "Not all the Outskirts are like this one. This is the oldest," Blake explained. "Each island usually has two or three clans living on it. They decide how it will be run. And what the living conditions will be like."

I gaped at Blake. "So some islands are more like City and some are like this?"

"Yep," Mack said.

Blake's hand brushed my arm. "Don't worry. These guys are peaceful for the most part."

"I don't really understand who the ancients are anyway," I said, my eyes scanning the area for any sign of life. So far, no one was out of their little huts. "I mean, I know they are dragons and damsels who can't do camo, and that some can't even morph back at all. Didn't Tonbo say he injected himself first? Wouldn't that mean he can't camo or morph either?"

"He couldn't at first, but he can now," Mack answered.

"So why can't the ancients? He must have figured out how to change himself to do it, why not them too?" I asked, rubbing my arms. The seeming emptiness of the place gave me the creeps. Where is everybody?

"They could if they wanted to change, but they don't," Blake answered, grimacing.

"What? Why not? Don't they want to be normal again? Able to live where they want?" I asked.

Blake's frown deepened. Mack shrugged. "They like living here," Mack said. "You see, when Tonbo first took the serum, he hadn't expected the wings to come with it. He'd always just been fascinated with dragonflies. There were so many legends and rumors of their healing abilities. Their strength, agility, long life, and incredible senses. As a scientist, he wanted to see what would happen if he combined it with human DNA. Like I said, he's a curious man."

"Sometimes too curious," Blake quipped, but it wasn't in a critical tone.

"Yeah," Mack agreed. "And we all know curiosity killed the cat."

"Which in Tonbo's case," Blake said, "his curiosity led to the Germans years later, forcing him to create super soldiers, who then turned into out-of-control bugs that hunted and killed his own family."

I glanced over at Blake. "If Tonbo was born in the 1800s, wouldn't his family have been long gone by World War Two?" I asked, but then it hit me. "Unless they took the serum too..."

"You're right. They did, but not right away," Blake answered. "When it became apparent that Tonbo's wings weren't going away, his family and some of his closest friends decided to take the serum and go into hiding too."

I glanced around at the village before me. "So the ancients are those who went into hiding with Tonbo?"

Blake nodded, turning down a side path that led to one hut that was set off from the rest. "Yes, most of them anyway. This island is made up of Tonbo's original followers. Remember I told you four ancients are missing?"

"Yeah."

Blake gestured to the small house before us with his chin. "This is Alek's home; he's one of the ones missing. Alek studied under Mendel during Tonbo's time."

"Did he help Tonbo with the serum?" I asked.

Mack answered. "He did, but Tonbo was the lead scientist. It was his work that had the final breakthrough. That's why the Germans came after him. They threatened to kill Tonbo's family and followers if he didn't comply."

"So why didn't the bug kill the other ancients when it killed his family?" I asked Blake as we approached the door. I'd turned to face Blake and didn't notice the small, wooden barrier opening.

"It did kill some of us," a female voice answered. I whirled to see a short, petite woman. Her gray hair was knotted in a bun, her body covered in a yellow sundress that left her golden-brown shoulders exposed. It was her wings that drew my eyes in. It was as if they'd been dipped in a glitter with every color of the rainbow bouncing back at me.

"Galina," Blake said, bending down to kiss both sides of the woman's face.

"Blake, it's been too long," the woman answered, a smile spreading across her face. She peered around Blake. "And Mack too."

Mack stepped up and followed Blake's actions, giving a swift kiss to the woman's face.

"Sorry for your loss," Mack said quietly as he pulled back.

The smile faltered on Galina's face as she shook her head. "Still can't believe he's gone, but I refuse to believe he's dead." She glanced over at me, and her face brightened. "But where are your manners, boys? Aren't you going to introduce me to your lovely new friend?"

I hadn't missed the opportunity to search Galina's face for any trace of familiarity while the boys had greeted her. I inwardly sighed. Nothing about her or this place gave me déjà vu.

Blake placed his hand on the small of my back. "You're right. Forgive me. Galina, this is Samantha Campbell."

Galina's smile reached her eyes, and I felt myself relax. With all the guys' vague warnings about the ancients, I didn't detect any malice in the woman before me.

"What a gorgeous damsel you are, my dear," she said, her eyes sweeping from Blake to Mack, "I see why you have captivated two of Tonbo's finest."

And just like that, whatever comfort I'd been feeling vanished. My face flushed as both guys stiffened next to me.

"Nice to meet you, Galina," I forced myself to say, unsure if I should kiss her face too. Instead, I reached out my hand. She clasped it, giving it a firm shake.

"Why don't we go inside for some tea?" she asked, pulling me inside her home by the hand she hadn't let go of.

I stumbled after her, glancing at Blake for reassurance. He nodded me on. Saying no to the woman was obviously out of the question anyway. As I entered her small home, I was surprised to see the level of comfort within. With how shabby the outward appearance of this village was, I expected dirt floors with some wooden furniture. Instead, I stepped onto a comfortable shag rug. There was a small kitchen, a living room with a couch, two armchairs peppered with bright floral pillows, and a hallway leading to what I assumed was a bedroom and bathroom. I hoped for the latter because I was not a fan of going in the wild.

Galina pointed to the couch. "Please make yourself comfortable. I will see to the tea, unless you'd prefer some cold water," she added, probably noticing how we were all covered in a thin sheen of sweat. I couldn't imagine drinking hot tea right now; nothing sounded more tortuous. I was boiling inside already.

"Water's great, Galina," Blake said, not sitting but ushering the old woman gently toward the couch. "But why don't you let me get it?"

She looked like she was about to protest, but then she sighed. "Oh, I suppose it wouldn't be too improper to let someone serve me for a change." She relented with a smile, settling onto the couch.

I decided to sit next to the woman, my eyes still scanning the room for any trace of familiarity. Nothing.

"You were saying some of the ancients died when the bug came?" I asked, hoping she wouldn't mind my prodding.

Her gaze dropped to the floor, staring at the rug below our feet. "Yes. We tried to defend ourselves, but it got to Tonbo's family first. You have to understand—none of us knew what Tonbo had created. All we knew was he'd been forced to go with the Nazis. We didn't know those things even existed. Then it's there... killing his family before they even knew what hit them."

She glanced over at me, the pain in her expression looking as fresh as if this had all happened yesterday, not years ago.

"The rest of us saw what was happening and fought back." Her gaze landed on her hands, which were clasped in her lap. Her thumb rubbed the knuckles of her other hand. It was then I noticed the slightly pink discoloration she was stroking. That's a scar with lots of history behind it.

She cleared her throat. "But the bug still killed many more of us. By the time Tonbo showed up, we'd ended it. It wasn't over for Tonbo, though. He swore he'd avenge himself of the monsters he'd been forced to create. From that day on, he locked himself in his lab, working night and day to improve his serum. One of the first things he wanted to change was the ability to morph back. He felt we needed to still be part of society, functioning as citizens in whatever country we might have been from."

"But the others didn't want that?" I asked, not wanting to be rude since she was one of those who'd opted not to change.

She shook her head. "You have to understand that when Tonbo gave us the choice to integrate back into society, the world was at war. Seeing what one evil leader did with such scientific advances made us realize it was safest for us and the rest of the world if we stayed separated."

Her gaze hardened. "Not that it did any good. So many Dragon Fae go around almost flaunting what we are, causing trouble for everyone."

"You're right," Blake agreed. "And there is one dragon causing a lot more problems than you think."

She glanced at him, her brows furrowing. "What do you mean?"

Blake sighed. "I'm afraid Kory's creating a bug army."

Galina gasped, her thumb rubbing her scarred knuckle a little faster. "What? How's that possible? Those creatures are long gone..."

Blake sighed. "I wish that were true, Galina." Blake then told her about Kory and Jaxon. I could tell by the strain in his tone that he didn't relish sharing the information.

With a tight jaw, Blake concluded, "We're pretty sure he's gathering supplies. Taking what he needs, which unfortunately, includes brilliant genetic engineers like your husband." Galina shook her head. "Alek will never go along with it. It's what they did to Tonbo all over again. What is Kory thinking?"

"Who knows with that looney," Mack grumbled.

Her face contorted with a rage that shocked me. One minute, she was a kind old lady, and the next, she looked halfway crazed. Instinctively, I leaned away from her a bit on the couch.

"He will pay for this," she hissed. "He doesn't even begin to understand what fire he is playing with."

Blake didn't seemed shocked by her display of fury. If anything, his face mimicked hers. "Trust me," he said, his tone dark. "No one wants justice for Kory's crimes more than I do."

Even knowing Blake had every right not to forgive Kory for what he'd done, I shuddered to think of what their next meeting would be like. I shifted in my seat, my wings suddenly itching to take off. I tried to ignore their pleading. There was no reason to bolt, was there?

Then it hit me why I felt so antsy. Everyone was furious with what Kory was doing; the hatred for him was palpable. What if Sammy is in on it all too? I mean, isn't that why we are here now? What if she played a part in Alek's abduction? Would Galina be so forgiving of her? Or me? Would Blake? How can I even live with myself?

"So do you think that's why so many Irukas went with him?" Galina asked, her lips set in a firm line.

Blake cocked his head to the side. "You guys know about that?"

"Of course we do," she said sharply. "The Irukas have watched over us for years. With over half gone now, we're exposed. Wonder if that's how Kory got to Alek and the others."

Blake and Mack glanced at each other, but they didn't say anything.

"You said the Irukas have watched over you? How?" I asked, hoping she wouldn't snap at me too.

Galina met my gaze. "The Irukas have always been loyal to us. They feel much the same about the world. Over the years, we've formed a symbiotic relationship. They protect us from unwanted visitors, and we take care of any physical needs they may have. We keep the waters pure and clean and make sure they always have adequate fish supplies."

I wanted to ask what the Irukas did with those unwanted visitors, but I held my peace. After feeling the effect Aster's song had had on me, I was almost afraid of the answer.

"We're aren't sure why they followed Kory," Mack said. "But Aster told us Kory fed them all a lot of crap about a higher calling and a coming war. Maybe the Irukas decided which team they wanted to be on."

Galina shook her head. "Seems strange to me. They've never wanted to be involved in the politics of man. That was why they chose to become the way they are."

"But some don't share the same sentiment," Blake said, folding his arms. "The newer ones have different ideas. Honestly, Tonbo has been worried about the growing restlessness he's sensed among the natural born."

I gaped at Blake. Natural born? Did that mean the Irukas could actually have children? That some of them were born that way?

I was dying to ask, but Blake had walked over to the closest window. Gazing out, he said, "Well, if Kory recruited the Irukas, we know at least one thing now." We waited as he continued to stare out. "Kory's operation is surrounded by water. Probably a remote island somewhere."

"And probably in the Pacific Ocean," I offered. "I mean, I'm guessing he wouldn't want them to have to swim across the world." As I said it, I wondered just how far they did go. Were there Irukas all over?

Galina nodded back at me. "You're probably right, Samantha. The Irukas don't care for long-distance swimming. Most of them have remained relatively close."

As Blake and Mack agreed with Galina, I inhaled. So far, nothing had pointed a finger at Sammy. Maybe all of my paranoia over her was really nothing. I mean, I had no hard evidence she'd done anything other than change me. Kate being gone and the ancients' disappearance could really all just be Kory's doing. Even the strain between Jocelyn could just be normal sibling stuff. For all I know, she's on too strict of a diet and it's making her cranky.

I let my wings relax and fall flat as the tension worked its way out of my shoulders. Everything's going to be fine. Kory's the bad guy, not me.

Galina glanced over at me. "You know, Samantha, now that I'm getting a better look at you, you seem familiar." She frowned in concentration. "Have we met before?"

Her words sent a jolt through me. My wings tensed as all my inner peace shattered.

CHAPTER
Thirteen

Fire raced across my cheeks as I stuttered to respond, "No, I don't think so." Really, I was trying not to hyperventilate.

"Hmm, I'm usually pretty good with faces. You must just remind of someone," Galina said with a shrug, dismissing the thought as fast as it had come, but it wasn't over for me.

Everything inside me screamed to leave this place, now. I exhaled slowly, trying to still my fluttering wings. Luckily, Galina didn't seem to notice my agitation. I glanced up to meet Blake's gaze, positive I'd see anger, betrayal, or even revulsion written there. Finally, he will realize I'm really part monster. That Sammy is a wicked part of me that I can't get away from. Here's the proof she's still messing with us all.

Instead, I saw concern, and perhaps a bit of surprise. Maybe deep down, he hadn't believed Sammy had anything to do with this. Guess we both know otherwise now.

I bit my lip as he walked over to me, holding out a glass of water. One I hadn't even noticed until it was inches from my face.

"Here, why don't you take a drink?" he offered. I could hear the worry in his tone as I took the glass from him. Guess he thinks hydrating will help. Really, I wanted to vomit. The truth of the situation felt like a billboard plastered to my forehead. Sammy's been here!

I tried to wrap my head around the possibilities. The only time I could see that being possible was during the small slice of time between Tonbo's theater and Jaxon's cave. Perhaps Galina had seen Sammy when she'd come to scope out Alek for Kory? Or had Sammy come on her own? Maybe to warn Alek? I could only hope the latter.

Blake continued talking with Galina, asking how things were going on the island. I couldn't really focus on their words. I just wanted to leave before Galina put two and two together and directed her fury at me. I glanced up to see Mack staring at me. He'd been sitting on the couch opposite of me. Catching my gaze, he offered me a grin.

He mouthed the words, "It's going to be okay."

I tried to smile back at him, but my lips stuck to my teeth. I finished my glass of water instead. Thankfully, we didn't stay with Galina too much longer. We'd gotten what we'd come for. After a quick farewell, we left the small home.

Blake immediately pulled me into his arms as soon as we'd taken off. I didn't fight him, letting my wings realign their flight pattern to match his. It was still strange to me, how quickly my body adapted to his. I didn't even have to think about what I was doing.

"I was afraid you were about to fly through her roof back there," Blake said, his arms not letting me go. He gave me a crooked grin.

I knew he was trying to make light of what we'd just learned, and I tried to take comfort in his arms, but I could only frown.

Like he sensed my need, he held me tighter. "Don't worry, just because she thought she knew you doesn't mean—"

"That Sammy's been there?" I cut in in disbelief. I stopped flying, forcing him to stop too. Pushing back on his chest, I looked him in the eyes. "Blake. Yes. It. Does. You're the one who came up with this idea in the first place. And now we have the proof."

Mack stopped next to us, hovering as well. "I'm afraid she's right, Blake," he said. "Looks like Sammy was up to something after all. You'd think with how much time I spent with her, I'd know her better, but she still blindsides me."

"Trust me, I know the feeling," I grumbled. I hated that Sammy's actions felt like a reflection of me. I mean, it's my body she's using to orchestrate her crazy schemes. Doesn't that make me somehow responsible?

"Very true," Mack said, giving me a sad smile. "So how do we find out what she was up to? I still have a hard time believing she would deliberately help Kory form a bug army. I mean, why would Kory need her anyway? He had the ancients, the next best thing to Tonbo himself. Unless..."

"Unless what?" I demanded.

The glare Blake directed at Mack seemed to be saying the same thing.

"Well," Mack said, his face flushing. "Sammy was... innovative. I know you question her motives, and frankly, so do I, but either way, her mind's still brilliant. What she did to you—" He stopped.

I reached over and touched Mack's arm, a gesture that brought a frown to Blake's lips. Forgiving Mack was one thing; it didn't mean any of us liked what Kate, Sammy, and he had done to me. I swallowed, trying not to let my own emotions take over. I had to be strong right now, not show how conflicted I felt at the moment.

"What she did to my serum was unique, I know," I said, finishing his thought. "So much so that Tonbo wants to study me." My throat closed up, my words fading. So much for being strong. Really, I felt like some kind of test tube. Everyone wanted to know what Sammy did to me—me most of all.

Mack's eyes shifted downward, and Blake frowned.

I cleared my throat. "It's okay; I know what you were trying to say. You think Kory wanted Sammy's help. Maybe he thought she could figure out how to control the creatures, since he'd failed with Jaxon." At the mere mention of his brother, Blake flinched.

No one said anything for a moment. I ran my hands up and down my arms, feeling a sudden chill.

"One thing I can't figure out is," I said, "what's in it for Sammy? So far the one thing I know about her is she's out for no one but herself."

Mack went to argue, but Blake's hard stare silenced him. I tried to be empathetic. I knew on some level Mack still had feelings for Sammy, but Blake held nothing but contempt for her, which left me in a befuddled mess on how I felt about it all. I mean, Sammy was still a part of me. I felt ashamed of my other half, wanting to hide it from Blake, afraid he wouldn't love me for what I really was inside.

Blake surprised me by actually answering my question. "Maybe a few more stops today will help answer that, Sam." I glanced over, and his gaze softened. "Are you up for it?"

I nodded, even though my insides screamed, No. As much as I was dying to know what Sammy had been up to, I was scared I wouldn't like the answer, and even more terrified Blake wouldn't either.

Blake scooped my hand up into his, giving me a crooked grin. "Okay, let's do this, then."

A few hours later, we'd visited with over a dozen different ancients. Out of those, a few more recognized me, but they couldn't remember from where. No one looked familiar to me, and we didn't learn anything to help us know why Sammy had been around the Outskirts in the first place.

Frustrated and exhausted, I was happy to hear this last island would be it. The sun was hanging low in the horizon, and even the brilliant colors streaking across the sky, mirrored by the water below, didn't lift the heaviness settling over my chest.

As we approached the shoreline, I could make out taller buildings. Coming in closer, I made out the boardwalk and the busy streets. Ancients were out and about here. As my feet landed on the sandy beach, I decided of all the islands we'd been to today, this one reminded me the most of City.

We walked a short pace, entering a street full of busy ancients. I glanced around, taking them in. From what I'd seen today, I couldn't understand why Mack and Blake kept warning me to not wander off by myself. The ancients didn't seem much different from the other dragons and damsels. They were older in years, and their wings tended to be larger and brighter than ours, but I didn't see why that suddenly made them dangerous.

Blake gestured to the tallest building. "Let's start there."

"What's that place?" I asked.

"The Science Center. If anything would've drawn Sammy in, it'd be that," Mack answered.

Seemed logical enough. Blake held the glass door open for me and added, "Plus, this is where the biochemist who disappeared worked. Can't hurt to poke around here a bit."

I nodded and ducked through the door into the building's lobby. The moment my feet hit the tiled floor, Déjà vu washed over me. I glanced down at the large, square tiles below my feet. Nothing about them jumped out at me, but something about this place did.

I grabbed Blake's arm. "I think I... Sammy's been here before," I whispered, almost afraid my own voice would burst the bubble of familiarity I was in.

His eyes widened, and he took a quick glance around. There was an information desk in front of us with an elderly Ancient manning the station. Small in stature, the Ancient's long, white hair and oversized, brilliant gold wings were all I could stare at. He reminded me of an angel, if angels had bug-like wings instead of the feathered ones often depicted in art.

Mack made a move toward the desk, quickly introducing us. Although, by the way his blue eyes kept darting toward Blake, I had a hunch he already knew who he was at least.

Blake gazed at the ancient for a moment, and then said, "I think we've met before... a long time ago when Tonbo was showing me around the Outskirts."

The Ancient smiled, obviously pleased Blake had taken notice of him.

"Tom... Tomas, right?" Blake asked.

Now the grin was ear to ear. Tomas bobbed his head up and down, his hair bouncing on his shoulders.

"Yes, sir." Tomas outstretched his hand to Blake. "A pleasure seeing you again, young master."

Blake firmly shook his hand. "Pleasure's all mine. Tonbo wanted us to come check on things," he casually added. "Make sure there haven't been any more problems after the latest disappearance."

"Oh, you've heard then, have you?" Tomas asked. "Such bizarre business. We've lived on these islands without any mishap for years. If you ask me, it's the Irukas leaving that started all this."

"You could be right," Blake answered. "Maybe you can fill us in with what happened to Otto, Tomas. Tonbo told me it wasn't that long ago that he disappeared."

Tomas's bare shoulders sagged a bit, revealing just how fragile the Ancient was.

"Otto was one of the finest biochemists I've known. A kind, generous Ancient if there ever was one," Tomas sadly said. "I'd be happy to help if I can." Scratching at his clean-shaven chin, Tomas turned his attention to me. His brows gathered, and then he snapped his finger, making me jump.

"Speaking of Otto, I know now why you look so familiar to me," he announced.

"Oh, really?" I asked, trying to mask a stifled gasp. This was different from Galina or the other ancients vague recollections. Tomas actually remembers me! My knees had turned to jelly as I waited for him to go on. What if he said something awful? Should I bolt while I still could? This is why we're here, I reminded myself. I could feel how tense Blake's body had become next to mine. Mack shifted his weight.

"Yes," Tomas said, not seeming to notice our tension. "You came to see Otto a few months ago. You spent some time in his office. I only remember this because Otto had commented on your brilliant mind after you'd left." Tomas smiled at me, pleased with recalling a memory. At his age, that was probably a feat. "And we don't get a lot of young visitors," he added with a shrug.

I tried to smile; at least, I hoped he believed it was a genuine one. Keeping the panic from creeping into my voice, I said, "Wow, I'm impressed. You have an incredible memory, Tomas."

Tomas nodded, accepting the compliment. Deciding he seemed to think Sammy's visit was amiable, I pushed it further.

"It made me so sad to hear of Otto's disappearance," I commented. "That's why I asked Blake and Mack if I could tagalong. Since we talked about so many things while I was here, I was hoping I could help in finding him somehow. We had such a nice time that day, but maybe Otto told you about that too." I forced myself to give a little chuckle. It sounded ridiculous to my own ears.

Tomas nodded in agreement. "Sounded like it from what I recall. Like I said, we don't get visitors to these parts often. The Irukas are very good at weeding out the unwanted, but sometimes, I wonder if they just keep everybody from coming here, dragons and damsels included."

"Isn't that what the ancients want, though?" I asked softly, hoping not to offend him. "To be left alone?"

Tomas shrugged. "Most feel that nothing but Tonbo's creations are worth their time, that the outside world is pure evil. Some even go as far to believe Tonbo's newer generations are too wild for their tastes."

So in other words, the ancients are a bunch of elitists. I wanted to say. How does that differ from Kory believing we're the superior race? One big difference popped into my mind right away. At least with the ancients, they wanted to be left alone, in isolation. Not hurting or bothering anyone else. Kory, on the other hand, did not. He's building an army for that very reason.

"Otto didn't agree with all that. It was why he was willing to see you that day. You are obviously not one of us." Tomas gave me a lopsided grin. I detected no contempt in it. "I think we miss out by being so separate, if you ask me." He glanced at Blake. As if remembering himself, he added, "Of course, the ancients always love seeing Tonbo and you."

Blake smiled, but I could tell it was strained. I think I'm beginning to see why Blake isn't jumping up and down to take over. The ancients were extremists, the Irukas were an entirely different group with unique needs to be met, and then on top of it all, Kory was the loose cannon running between everyone causing mayhem.

"Thanks, Tomas," Blake said. "We were wondering if we might check out Otto's office while we are here."

Tomas nodded. "Of course, Blake. Anything I can do to help. Although, he wasn't taken in his office. He'd been down by the beach."

"That's what we heard," Blake said. Blake kept a steady conversation going with Tomas the entire way up to Otto's office. Asking him questions about different Ancient's health, general island conditions, etc... I had a hard time paying attention to what they were saying. Knowing Sammy had been here made me want to drink in my surroundings. I hoped something would spark a memory, but other than the lobby, nothing felt familiar.

Unlike, Tonbo's office, this building didn't have an open lobby to the upper levels. It had an elevator. Climbing inside, I wondered if that was because the ancients were sometimes too old to fly. Tomas pressed number four, and the doors slid shut. I tried not to bump my wings into him as I stepped back next to Blake. Blake gave me a grin, slipping his hand into mine.

Tomas noticed this and his eyebrows shot up, but he didn't say anything. Guess Blake's love-life gossip doesn't make it to the Outskirts. When the elevator stopped and opened, he ushered us down the hall.

I didn't need to be told which one was Otto's office; I recognized it immediately. The wooden door leading into it wasn't an average door—a hand-carved dragonfly spanned across it. Not the type of thing you don't notice. As Tomas opened it up, I thought, Sammy obviously did.

CHAPTER
Fourteen

The office, though vaguely familiar feeling, didn't bring the onslaught of memories I'd hoped for. Fifteen minutes later, I rifled through Otto's desk drawers, frustrated and hoping to find something helpful. I was glad Tomas had the decency to leave us alone. We didn't waste time, each of us finding some corner to inspect.

The office wasn't overly decorative. No family pictures hung on the walls. A large desk, several filing cabinets, and a few chairs to sit on were about it. Not even a computer or laptop to pry through. I knew we weren't necessarily looking for clues to who took him. We all guessed it was Kory still, but I still hoped to glean why Sammy had been here.

Sighing, I tugged another drawer open. The contents shifted haphazardly within. Papers, pens, unopened mail. Nothing looked familiar. Nothing looked helpful. I growled and shoved it shut.

Blake, who'd been going through one of the filing cabinet drawers, glanced over at me. "Everything okay over there?" he lightly asked.

Mack, who'd been pouring over another filing cabinet, didn't even glance up as Blake made his way over to me.

"Just wish there was something here to help me remember," I grumbled. "I mean, was Sammy here to warn Otto? Or was she here to stage the abduction?"

"Maybe not finding anything means she was here to help," Blake offered. I knew he was just trying to reassure me. He, of all people, tended to think the worst of Sammy. I wished I could accept his statement at face value and leave it alone. Deep down,

I sensed my quest for knowing was going to end badly.

Mack called out to us, "You both should see this." He turned around, holding out the manila folder he'd been studying moments ago.

We rushed over. My fingers turned to ice at Mack's tense expression. Oh boy. Here comes the bad news.

Blake grabbed the folder and held it so we both could see. The detailed sketch on the paper glared back at me. I gasped, instinctively backing up.

I would never forget those black eyes, the small, pinched nose, the oversized mouth, the scar-ridden barrel chest, or the thick-corded wings. Even the patches of brown hair smattering the out-of-proportioned head. Blake cursed under his breath. We both recognized who it was. Jaxon. The bug version of him, anyway. Blake cursed under his breath.

"Why does Otto have a picture of Jaxon?" I asked. My heart was pounding hard enough in my chest that my ears had begun ringing. Figuring it was just adrenaline making me feel jittery, I tried to ignore it. "I thought the ancients didn't know about him. Galina acted shocked Kory had brought bugs back."

Blake's eyes raked the page. "Either she's a really good actress, or some ancients knew about Jaxon."

As Blake began flipping through the sheets of papers, Mack said, "There's more about him than just that sketch. His DNA sequencings, the exact formulas it took to modify the bugs DNA and form it into a serum to be injected, the test trials." Mack hesitated. "Maybe we've been looking at this all backward."

"No kidding," Blake agreed. "I'm beginning to think the four taken weren't taken at all, but willingly left to join Kory's quest."

"But if he left on his own, why on earth would he leave all this behind to be found?" I asked.

"Because no one would be looking for it or because he didn't care if everyone knew," Mack offered, "I don't know."

My mind was spinning with every new scenario placed in it. I grabbed on to the back of one of the chairs, the dizziness threatening my balance. The incessant ringing in my ears had gotten worse. I inhaled deeply, trying to fight off the disorientation. My fingers gripped the leather, my knuckles turning white in my effort to stay upright.

Blake was at my side in one of those crazy-fast movements I'd seen him do once before. If I hadn't been feeling so woozy, I probably would've yelped in surprise again. Instead, I fell limp into his arms.

He pulled me to his body. "Are you okay? You just turned chalk white. What's going on?"

"I'm just a... bit dizzy," I said, my head falling against his chest. The thrumming of his heartbeat soothed me, and I closed my eyes. I couldn't really tell if I was standing on my own, or if Blake was holding me up. My legs felt wobbly beneath me. Either way, I just wanted to fall asleep. Part of my mind screamed for me to stop giving in, but the other half of me felt too exhausted to care anymore.

"Sam," Blake said, and then he gently shook me. "Sam, can you hear me?"

I could hear the panic in his voice, feel his arms shaking as he held me, but I couldn't seem to form the words to reassure him. I couldn't even open my eyes. I felt myself being pulled away, like I was stuck in a river's current.

Mack's voice was right next to me. "Samantha, you can't give in to Sammy. She wants to come out, but you have to fight her!"

Sammy? This couldn't be Sammy? Could it? It felt too relaxing. Too peaceful. Too inviting...I gasped inwardly, hearing a low moan escape my lips. Crap! Of course this is Sammy! She's trying to take over, making me feel like it's the easiest thing to do. There was a small sliver inside me that reasoned her taking over right now might not be a bad thing. She'd be surrounded by Blake and Mack. They wouldn't let her go anywhere, and they could get the truth from her. If she's in on this whole thing with Kory, maybe they could even find out the secret headquarters for his bug operation. Would it be so bad to let her have a minute? With that thought, a whole new layer of relaxation settled over me. My eyelids became even heavier. A peace settled over me. I knew I was about to pass out, but it felt like the right thing to do. This is it. Sammy will be here. Everything will be okay now. I'll just be gone...

Gone? Gone for how long? Gone for good? I panicked. No, no, no. I struggled to open my eyes, and with the effort, my peace shattered. Panic seized me. I thrashed out, knowing somewhere in my mind, Blake was still holding on to me, pleading with me to come back.

Blake! I wanted to shout. I'm still here.

I fought against the weight holding me down, a crushing sensation spreading over my chest. I have to get out of this black place! Mentally, it felt like sprinting uphill with only humid, thick air to breathe. My lungs burned and I wondered if I was even breathing anymore.

"Sam," Blake begged. Somewhere in my mind, I felt his body's warmth. "Please come back to me." His words shattered the darkness surrounding me. The weight began lifting, and I hungrily sucked in air. My eyes flew open to discover Blake cradled me in his arms, sitting in one of the chairs.

His wet eyes met my gaze. The hand that had been stroking my cheek stopped mid-motion. "Is it you?" he asked, his eyes darting between mine.

"Yes, it's me." My voice sounded so weak. He pulled me to him, squeezing out the air I'd worked so hard to get in.

"I thought I'd lost you," he said, his voice thick. I could feel the tension in his entire body melt in my arms as a shudder made its way through his shoulders and back. When he sniffed, I realized how terrified he'd been that Sammy might have won.

He leaned back and searched my face, not seeming to care he had a few tears streaming down his own. "Are you okay now?" He held me tight, keeping me from falling off his lap.

I nodded. "I think so. Sorry I scared you. I didn't know what was happening until Mack told me." I glanced over my shoulder at Mack. "I think you were right, but it just felt so different this time."

"Different how?" Mack asked.

"I don't know. It felt so peaceful, like it was the right thing to do. At least, until I decided I didn't want to give in. Then it turned ugly." I couldn't help the shiver that shot through me.

Blake pulled me closer, giving my arms a brisk rub. It wasn't the cold giving me the chills; it was realizing that this place meant something to Sammy. I took comfort in his touch. It'd been his voice that broke through Sammy's hold on me. I inhaled deeply, chasing away the memories of how tight my chest had felt. One thing I couldn't shake though was how right it had felt to let her have control. That didn't make any sense, unless...

"Coming here triggered a lot more than just déjà vu," I said. "I think she was trying to tell me something."

Both guys stared at me, Blake's brow knitting together. "Why do you say that?"

I shrugged, suddenly not so sure why I'd thought that. "I just got this feeling her appearing was really important to her," I offered.

"Of course it was." Blake grimaced. "Sam, she wants to make you disappear for good."

I felt the terror behind his words. I knew then that his greatest fear matched mine. Maybe he'd been in denial before—maybe we both had been. Ironic, the moment he seemed to accept the reality that Sammy still existed, I suddenly felt the urge to defend her somehow.

I glanced at Mack, wondering what he thought. His frown matched Blake's. "I don't think it's a coincidence she tried to take over right when we learned the ancients might be in cahoots with Kory," Mack confirmed. "Maybe we were poking around too much for her liking."

I knew they were probably both right. Honestly, I had no idea why I was trying to give Sammy the benefit of the doubt. Her track record screamed otherwise. From what I knew of her choices, they were always self-serving, even if she claimed she was doing what was best for me.

So why did this time feel different? I tried to shrug it off and glanced back at Blake. The look of resolution in his eyes surprised me. He gently released his grip on me and helped me to my feet, keeping an arm tucked around me.

"I think we've learned enough here today," he announced. "Let's get back to Tonbo. I may not like the idea of it, Sam, but I think you've been right all along. Sammy's not gone, like I'd hoped. She's still fighting to take over. And from what we've seen today, she's involved with this mess somehow." His tone turned harder. "I want to know what she's up to, before we're too late to stop it."

CHAPTER
Fifteen

"You know, James Braid was really on to something when he developed hypnosis," Tonbo stated, settling into a chair placed near the sofa I was sprawled on.

When we'd gotten back to City, we first showed Tonbo what we'd found at Otto's office. Even with the papers in his hand, he had a hard time believing the ancients would willingly join forces with Kory. Seeing how agitated he'd become, Blake told him he'd changed his mind about tapping into Sammy's memories. That news had Tonbo practically bouncing on his toes with excitement.

Tonbo had insisted that we be left alone. He felt Blake and Mack hovering over me would be too much of a distraction. I needed to be able to relax fully for this to work. Tonbo had informed us there might be a way to do it without any drugs involved. Everyone had agreed to give it a try first before sedating me.

"You see, Braid knew there was something about the eyes," Tonbo continued. I knew I was in for a bit of a history lesson. Maybe that's how it works; he lulls me to sleep with a lecture. I stifled a grin. Truthfully, I didn't mind.

"There may be more to the eyes being windows to the soul then you realize, Samantha," he said in a hushed tone, like we were discussing a secret. "Braid would use a very bright object, hang it slightly above his subject's head, and then ask them to keep their eyes fixated on the object. Naturally, as they did, their pupils would at first constrict. It's bright. But as they studied it more, their pupil would dilate, and then constrict, and then dilate. Forming a beautiful wave of movement. Then, with his other hand, he'd move two fingers toward the subject's eyelids." Tonbo demonstrated, bringing his fore and middle fingers close to my face.

Not having a bright object for me to study, I wasn't sure if he expected this to work on me too.

"At this, the subject's eyes would shut and the deep sleep would begin. Amazing considering he developed this so long ago," Tonbo said, not seeming bothered that my eyes were still wide open.

"The eyes," he continued, leaning back into his chair, "take in everything around us. Details we aren't even aware of are gathered, processed, and stored. The interesting thing for you is that even when Sammy is in charge, your eyes are still gathering that information. Tucking it away, storing it. You may not recall it, but it's still there, buried in your subconscious."

"That's what my therapist kept telling me," I grumbled, remembering the sessions I'd rather forget. "It's just frustrating because most of us don't have ready access to our subconscious, but they all act like I should."

"They mean well, Samantha, but you are quite right. Tapping into the subconscious is tricky business. And with you having two tenants in that mind of yours, your brain has its work cut out for it," he added with a wink. "But as you're already experienced with the sensations of déjà vu and from what Blake said, recognizing Otto's very office, your mind is trying very hard to call it up. Or," he added with a shrug, "Sammy really wants you to know."

I stared at him, my eyebrows lifting. "You think Sammy might not be the bad guy here?"

Tonbo hiked his bony shoulders up until they almost reached his ears. I had to suppress the urge to laugh. He always reminded me of a little munchkin, and that movement didn't help the impression. Then his eyes widened as he gazed back at me. Staring into their blackness, taken in once more by the silver streaking through them, I remembered how hypnotizing he could be.

Maybe that's his method. He just says, Stare into my eyes. I think it'd work. Should I tell him?

"I'm not sure at this point, truthfully," he said, his somber tone chasing away my earlier facetiousness. "You know, I've learned a few things in my long years of life, Samantha. Never take something or someone for granted, never take something at face value, and never underestimate your enemy." He grinned. "And never forget to floss."

I smiled. "You do have nice teeth for your age."

He grinned back at me. "Thank you." He rubbed his hands together briskly. "Now, shall we get down to business? Time to find out what sweet, dear Sammy had to do with all of this."

"Sure," I said woodenly. I'd never longed to know something so much, while dreading its outcome at the same time. Wait, I take that back. I've felt this way before. The time Blake had begged me to listen to his side of the story when I was convinced he was my kidnapper. The time Mack had finally unveiled the truth, and I hung on to every terrifying word coming out of his mouth. This anxious pit in my stomach, I know all too well.

Since Tonbo continued to frisk his hands together, I began to wonder if that was his weird method of hypnosis. It was pretty captivating how much noise those little hands could make.

"Samantha, we aren't going to try hypnosis today," he announced, shattering my concentration.

"But..." I stuttered, "I thought that's what we agreed to try first." Fear crept in. Was getting me alone all a ruse so Tonbo could do what the heck he wanted with me? I knew I should give him some credit, but at this point, I was having a hard time trusting anyone, myself included.

Tonbo raised his hand. "Now, now, calm down, my dear. I'm not going to inject you or bring Sammy back. What I should have said is that I have a slightly different method I would like to use. Like I said earlier, Braid was on to something with the eyes. Have you heard of R.E.M., Samantha?"

"Uh, like the old music group?" I asked, trying to settle back down on the couch. My nerves were still fired up. I hated being so paranoid, but the last year of my life had proven to be a rough ride of never knowing, always fearing, and then discovering the worst.

Tonbo cocked his head to the side. "What? Oh no, not them. R.E.M. stands for rapid eye movement. Without boring you with too many details, I'll give you the skinny on it. During sleep, you go through things called R.E.M. cycles. During which time your eyes actually move rapidly back and forth. Hence the term. It's hypothesized that during such sleep phases, your memories are consolidated. Organized—tucked together if you will. There are theories saying the memories or information that's most relevant are strengthened and the ones deemed weaker, or less important, begin to disintegrate."

"Oh," I said, not quite sure what he was getting at. "So you want to put me to sleep and see if my memories open up while I'm in R.E.M.?"

"Very good. Yes, exactly." He grinned, and then added, "Well, not exactly. You don't have to be asleep. Just relaxed. I'm going to simulate R.E.M. by having you follow this ball."

He held up a long wand with what looked like a red marble at the end. With one flick of his wrist, the wand proved to be much more bendable than it appeared to be. It sent the ball flying back and forth, the marble becoming a red blur.

"You just have to track the ball with your eyes."

"Um, that's impossible. It's going way too fast. I can't even see the ball anymore."

"Even if your physical eye can't follow it, your subconscious mind will." He leaned in closer. "Just sit back, let your body fall into the couch. Relax and take a deep breath in through your nose and out through your mouth." I tried to listen, I really did, but this was just getting bizarre. How do you relax when a wand with a ball is being whirled in your face? I could barely look at it without nausea threatening my stomach.

Tonbo kept the wand moving nonetheless. His tone took on a deeper timbre. "I want you to let your mind wander while you keep your eyes on the ball."

I wanted to argue again that he asked the impossible, but I held my tongue. I needed this to work, so I tried to comply. Let my mind wander... to where? I tried to think of a safe place.

Ironically, that was what he said next. "Picture a place you feel warm, secure, and happy."

Blake's body wrapped around mine filled my mind, flooding my body with heat. Embarrassed by my own awakened desires, I tried to think of anything else. I can't daydream about Blake in front of Tonbo!

I tried to rack my brain for a new image.

Tonbo continued. "It can be anywhere. A place you've never been perhaps. But maybe only dreamed of."

Okay, I can do that. I pictured a warm, sandy beach. Gosh, can I get anymore cliché? Oh well. Don't have to win the imagination prize here... just play along.

I blinked my eyes rapidly, trying to lubricate them. Watching the blurry wand was drying them out.

"Good, good," Tonbo said. "Let your eyes do the work as you find your safe place. Where is it?"

Good thing it's not Blake's body anymore. "The beach."

"Wonderful. Describe it to me. Is it a rocky beach?"

"No, sandy. Lots of sand."

"Wonderful. Describe the water to me. Is it the ocean you're near? Are you lying on the sand? Are the waves calm right now?"

Better get answering before he gives me too many questions to remember. I wanted to close my eyes, to let my imagination take over more, but I knew I had to track the wand.

"It's a beach at the ocean," I said, "And yes, I'm lying in the sand." My face flushed as Blake's body was suddenly there, sidling up next to me, pulling me toward his naked chest. Crap.

"I'm alone," I lied, trying to force him to go away. The image of him in my mind cocked an eyebrow at me before vanishing from view. I glanced around, trying to take in more details of the beach, not wanting Blake's appearance to ruin the scene I was trying to create. "The tide is low. The waves are calm right now. I can see seaweed left behind. There are a lot of seashells scattered around." The details were coming surprisingly easy now.

"Excellent. How does the air smell to you?" he asked.

I inhaled reflexively, as if I could really smell it. "Salty. Like seaweed... and fish."

"Are you next to the seaweed?"

Funny he should ask that because I was. "Yeah, I'm playing with it. It's slippery and slimy." I was surprised to hear my own giggle. "It's fun to play with."

In my peripheral, I saw Tonbo nod. I kept my eyes fastened on the whirling, red ball.

"How does the water feel to your feet?" he asked.

How does he know I'm near the water now? I wondered as I felt my own feet sinking down into the warm, wet sand.

"It's cold, compared to the sand, but I like it. It tickles my toes as it comes up and down. It's pretty cold on my legs though."

"So you've entered the water? How far out are you?"

With each question, I immediately saw myself there. I'm in the water, I don't have my life jacket on... and my feet aren't touching anymore. Panic gripped me. Isn't this my warm, safe place? What am I doing out here?

"I'm too far out," I whispered. "The beach dropped off too fast. I can't touch." With each word, the octave of my voice raised higher.

"It's okay. Samantha, this is your safe place, remember? You don't have to be afraid of the waves. They can't hurt you."

"Waves?" I asked. My voice sounded strange to myself.

With the mere mention of the word, a rolling wave lifted me up higher and higher. I was carried on it, driven toward the beach with a frightening speed. I felt it crumble below my body as it met the shoreline head on. Sprawling downward, I smacked into the sand with hardly enough time to draw a breath before something was pulling me back again. Back toward the now-tumultuous waters. I was sucked into its undercurrent. I thrashed, clawing at the shore for something to grab. "No, no, no," I begged. "I don't want to go back!"

"Samantha, what's happening? Are you in the water still? Go back where?"

"The ocean, it's got me! It won't let go! I can't get away." The words rushed out. I knew logically that I wasn't there, but every part of me screamed I was. I wanted to break my concentration on the wand, I wanted the nightmare to end, but Tonbo kept on flicking it back and forth. Back and forth. I blinked, sucking in air, trying not to go under the water again.

"What's in the ocean you're so afraid of? Nothing can harm you there."

"I'm going to drown! I can't breathe!" I shouted back at him. What a dumb question!

"Are you under the water now?" he asked, his voice still calm. Obviously not minding I'd just yelled at him.

I was angered by his question, and my body was pulled under again. This time, I didn't come up. The blackness of the water surrounded me, pressing in. This is it. I'm going to die! I can't get out. I can't breathe!

"Samantha, if you are under the water, you don't need to be afraid. Nothing can harm you, remember? These are only memories. Memories tucked deeply in your mind. Now let your mind show you what happened next. Are your eyes open?"

I wanted to scream. If these are just memories, why do my lungs burn so bad? Instead, I tried to believe him. I forced myself to gulp in air, shocked it wasn't ocean water filling my lungs.

Slightly pacified, I answered his question, "Yes, I'm under the water... I don't see anything around me. It's just black. Cold and black." Something within me stirred as a strange peace settled over me. It warmed my core, surrounding me, holding me, chasing the fear away.

"She's here." My own words sent goose bumps shooting down my arms.

"She?" he gently asked.

"She's come to save me," I whimpered as tears sprung to my eyes. "She's not going to let me die. She can't. She's my savior. She will always save me."

"Is she saving you now?"

I searched the water, desperate to see her, but it was still just me. I closed my eyes, not wanting to see more, but then something grabbed my waist. The pressure on my hips made me want to scream. I withstood the temptation, knowing it would mean immediate death. As I held my breath longer, my lungs immediately protested. Wait, part of me reasoned, didn't Tonbo just tell me these were memories? I can breathe just fine.

But my body refused to comply. Instead, my mind screamed at me, I'm a survivor! I will save her! My eyes flew open with new resolve. Nothing but dark water surrounded me, but the hold around my middle didn't let up. I don't understand it.

"Something has me," I said breathlessly. The panic and fear from earlier had waned. Which makes no sense, I'm still underwater... I felt a strength within I didn't before. Cautiously, I reached down, wanting to know what held me. I stifled a gasp, shocked to feel a pair of hands.

"What is it? What do you see now?" Tonbo asked, his voice sounding like it was coming through a long tunnel.

"I don't know. I can't see anything. But I feel... someone." My words trailed off as I allowed my hands to travel up the ones holding me to find two arms and a pair of naked shoulders. Maybe I'm hallucinating. Maybe it's an angel of sorts. I skimmed up the neck, feeling the features. It feels so human. A faceless face. How is any of this possible? Maybe I really have died. Maybe this is what heaven feels like. The aching burn in my lungs let me know I was holding my breath again. That can't be right, can it?

The thing that held me didn't wait any longer, pulling me into it. Feeling a lean, muscular body, I knew it was a boy holding me. Now whether a human boy or an angel, I was still not sure. I didn't have time to process it more because he propelled us upward toward the surface with such an insane speed that I shuddered, my body feeling like it had collapsed on itself. I couldn't keep my eyes open. Ducking my head into the invisible chest, I blacked out, convinced an angel had just saved me.

I gasped, this time for real. Only then did I realize the wand was no longer in front of me. My body felt too heavy to move, but I managed a glance at Tonbo. He smiled back at me.

Understanding trickled through me, and I wanted to ask so many questions. I knew who the invisible boy in the water was.

This was the part of the story I'd always been missing. The part where Blake first entered my life.

Tonbo reached over, placing a hand on my shoulder. "You, my friend, just experienced Sammy's first memory."

CHAPTER
Sixteen

"So why did we stop?" I asked, surprised to hear how breathless I'd become. "Why did you stop the wand? It worked. I was seeing... her... I was her." I sank back into the couch as the reality of my words sank in. Sammy had come that day to save me. I felt it. Every part of her longed to rescue me, keep me safe. Suddenly, I felt guilty for my earlier statements about her only serving herself. She'd come into existence at a moment that could have meant immediate death to not only me, but also her. Yet, she still came. She wanted to save me. A strange, new ache filled my heart. A certain kind of sadness.

Tonbo squeezed my shoulder. "You did extremely well, Samantha, but I think you've had enough for today."

I wanted to protest, but at his touch, I became aware of something else. My shirt was wet. I glanced down, shocked to see I was drenched in sweat. Glancing back up at Tonbo, I didn't argue with him anymore. I felt like I could barely move, the exhaustion settling over me, letting me know I was done too.

"When can we do this again?" I asked instead.

"Depends on how well you rest tonight," Tonbo said, his lips twitching. "When do your parents expect you home?"

"Monday night. So we have all day tomorrow and most of Monday, since flying home doesn't take that long."

"Alright, why don't we get a fresh start in the morning? I think you've had a big enough day. I'm sure you're wiped out from just flying around the Outskirts, and now this." Tonbo held up the wand, glancing over at it.

I didn't want to look at the thing, even though it had provided a passageway into Sammy's memories. Tonbo's words had drudged up a different question, unrelated to Sammy.

"Yes, it's been a day," I agreed. "I even met one of the Irukas... or should I say mere-people?"

"Oh, how lovely! Who?"

"Aster. She was pretty upset with Kory taking away so many of them."

Tonbo frowned. "Sad, sad business. Kory keeps meddling where he shouldn't."

"Tonbo," I began, wanting to ask about the whole natural-born thing Blake had mentioned earlier, but a beeping sound interrupted me. I glanced around, not understanding where it had come from, until Tonbo pressed the ever-present long, silver piece in his ear.

"Yes," he said. He listened for a moment and then said, "Of course he may come in. Our session is done. I should've let him know—"

Tonbo didn't even finish his sentence before the door was opened and Blake rushed in. I could see the worry all over his face. One look at me, and his concern seemed to double.

"Are you okay?" he asked, dropping down to my side. I felt silly that I was still lying down on the couch.

I tried to reassure him. "I'm totally fine. Don't worry, Blake."

"She did great," Tonbo confirmed. "She connected beautifully and on the first try."

Blake's eyes widened. "It worked?" He peered down at me, his hands gripping mine. I tried to sit up, wincing slightly at the jabbing pain that shot through my skull.

"Are you hurt? What's wrong?" Blake asked, helping me up. He climbed on to the couch next to me, wrapping an arm around my shoulder. I think he noticed how wet my clothes were, but he didn't say anything. Instead, he shot Tonbo a withering look. "I thought this was supposed to be safe."

I must look as awful as I feel.

"I'm fine, Blake, really, I'm just tired. Tonbo said I need to rest tonight, and then we can try again tomorrow."

Blake's jaw tightened at the mention of doing this again, but he didn't disagree. For now.

"She's right, Blake. It didn't cause her physical pain. Just exhaustion. Nothing a warm bath and some good sleep won't fix," Tonbo reassured. "I'm very impressed with how well it did go, actually."

Blake seemed to consider his words as he glanced down at me. He brushed the hairs stuck to my forehead back, not seeming to mind my sweat.

"I did it, Blake. I connected with her. I was Sammy, in my mind anyway. It was like I could see and feel what she felt. I only saw one memory today. That's why we want to do it again. There's still so much to see."

"What did you see?" he asked.

I grinned up at him. "You. Saving me from drowning."

His brows rose up, and a smile spread across his lips. "You saw that?"

"More like felt it," I said, remembering how his hands had felt on my hips. We'd been kids then. He'd been a boy trying to save a drowning girl. Suddenly, it seemed profound or ironic, I couldn't decide which, that the second Sammy entered my life was the exact time Blake had too.

"I felt you under the water. Touched your face even." I stopped, brushing my fingers against his cheek, still remembering how his younger face had felt. "Then you pulled me up."

His smile grew as he leaned into my hand, kissing it with his lips. It'd been a defining moment for both of us—saving me had given him a purpose. From then on, he'd watched over me. Those small boy hands that had gripped my waist so long ago, pulling me from my own hellish nightmare, were still here, holding on to me, now. Trying to lift me from the hell that shrouded me. It felt right I should remember what happened in the water so long ago.

I didn't know if she could hear my thoughts or not, but I thought it anyway. Thank you, Sammy.

CHAPTER
Seventeen

"I don't think," Tonbo said, his words cutting through our intimate moment, "the next session will drain you as much. You have to remember what you experienced today was extremely traumatic. It marked the beginning of Sammy. It dredged up both your and Sammy's worst nightmare. Drowning."

"You think Sammy's afraid of drowning too?" Blake asked.

My nod matched Tonbo's. "Probably," I said. "I mean, she made sure I'd... or we'd, never drown again. Since I can hold my breath forever, being underwater is nothing to me now."

Blake seemed to consider my words, and then I felt Tonbo's gaze on us both. I glanced up to meet those crazy black eyes of his.

"Blake, I think we've done enough for one day. Why don't you take Samantha to her room, so she can rest?"

Blake didn't need to be told twice. He scooped me up in his arms before I could protest. "Yes, sir."

I grinned at his eagerness, not sure if it was worry for my health or the desire to have me alone that spurred him into action. Tonbo waved us off with an all-knowing smile. It still struck me as odd that he considered Blake mature enough to run not only his islands, but also to keep his people protected and in line. Tonbo obviously trusted him, thought of him as an equal even.

Knowing I was too exhausted to walk myself back to my room, I didn't protest to Blake carrying me. It felt nice being in his arms. Glancing over his shoulder, I watched how the lights reflected off his wings. I loved how they matched his aqua eyes. Not being able to resist, I ran one of my hands along the edge of his top set of wings. He surprised me with the shudder that rolled through him.

"Sorry," I said, withdrawing my hand.

He grinned. "You're fine. It just tickled."

I giggled and glanced around the empty hallway we were making our way down. My session must have run late. I'd halfway expected Mack to pop up somewhere, but he didn't.

As Blake opened my door and walked us through, I thought how different tonight was from last night. Still embarrassed I'd acted like such a brat, I leaned back into his chest, tucking my face under his chin. I couldn't resist planting a few light kisses on the side of his neck. He didn't say anything, but his grip on me tightened. As we neared my bed, a new tension worked its way through my body. My pulse quickened, adrenaline chasing away my earlier weariness.

Fully awake now, I glanced up at him. His eyes met mine. Suddenly, the silence between us felt palpable. I didn't wait for him to make the move, but pulled myself up higher and kissed him. Although he kissed me back, it wasn't enough for me. I wrapped my hands around the base of his neck, pulling his lips down harder on mine. He deepened the kiss as he laid my body down. I could feel him trying to pull back, like he didn't want to follow me to the bed. That wasn't an option for me tonight.

I tugged him down to me, wrapping my arms around his waist. A soft whimper escaped his lips as he allowed his weight to fall against my body, wings and all. The pressure filled me with a desire I'd never felt before. I knew I was in trouble, but I didn't care. This was the boy who'd saved me. This was the boy who'd loved me his entire life. Watched over me, protected me. Adored me. He was my world now. I'd never be normal again. The normal things like high school, college, and even marriage didn't seem to matter anymore to me.

Blake's kisses became frantic as one warm hand ran across my stomach, sending chills through me, the other getting tangled in my hair behind my head. When his fingers landed on my hip, I gasped. His lips were suddenly torn from mine. One moment, it was pure fire and desire, and then the next, he was just gone. I floundered at his sudden absence, trying to understand what had happened. Sitting up, I spotted him standing in the corner, breathing hard.

"What are you doing over there?" I asked, trying to still my own breathing while smoothing my hair down. I wasn't sure if I should go to him or not; panic was written all over his face.

Alarmed by the fear in his face, I glanced around. "What's wrong?"

"Nothing and everything," he said, giving me a crooked grin. "Just give me a sec; I need to calm down a bit."

"Oh." I felt my face flush. "Did I do something wrong?"

"No," he said, shaking his head and grinning. "You do everything just a little too right, actually."

"Then what's the problem?" I asked. Immediately after, I wasn't sure I wanted to know the answer.

Blake sighed and walked back over to me. Sitting down, he took my hand into his. "The problem is, Sam, I want this to be right with you. You aren't just any girl to me."

"And you aren't just any boy to me either, Blake."

"Exactly. I can't risk losing you because I want you so bad right now."

"Okay, you totally lost me there." Suddenly talking about why we couldn't have sex made me remember my own set of guidelines, which I had conveniently abandoned just moments ago. With my hormones dropping back down to a more manageable level, I became mortified I'd been the one egging this on.

"I mean, we have to be careful... What if..." he began.

"Blake, wait, stop," I said, ducking my face. "I don't know what came over me a bit ago, but you don't have to explain yourself to me."

"Sam, you're taking this all wrong. If you don't think I want you more than anything, you're wrong. This is killing me." He tucked his hand under my chin, making me meet his gaze. I saw no teasing in his eyes. "You're everything I've ever wanted. I can't wait to be with you, but I want it to be right."

I wanted to ask what right meant to him. Like after we're

married? Does he really have that high of a moral compass?

Then he added, "And safe."

"Safe?" I repeated like a parrot.

"Yes. What if you got pregnant?" His jaw hardened. "I don't want you to go through that."

I shifted in my seat, my insides squirming with nerves. My face flushed. "Hasn't the Dragon Fae world heard of birth control?" I asked. "And besides, I thought we couldn't have kids."

"Yes, we most definitely know what condoms are." He grinned and to my horror, he softly kissed my cheek. I wanted to shrink away with embarrassment. How can he be so comfortable talking about this stuff?

He leaned back and sighed heavily. "But just because we can't have kids doesn't mean damsels can't get pregnant."

"Wait, what?" I rocked back. "We can get pregnant?"

The fact he didn't even laugh at my blunder about the two of us having a baby let me know how unhappy Blake was sharing this information with me.

"Yes, we can. The pregnancies usually don't last long though, and even those who do end up giving birth, well, the... baby doesn't survive."

I gasped. "Oh, that's horrible!" My earlier embarrassment was replaced with an ache in my heart. "So what's wrong with them? Why can't any of them survive?"

The way he'd said 'baby' made me wonder just what kind of creature it was. Did it look human? Or did it come out with wings? Or a bug-like face?

His eyes met mine. "Sam, I'm so sorry. I never wanted any of this for you."

"Blake, I know, but it's better if you just tell me."

He ran his hand across his mouth before saying, "The baby doesn't look human."

My stomach sickened. What would I do if I gave birth to a bug? How would I feed it? Take care of it? Each question popping into my mind made my skin crawl. As much as I hated to admit it, perhaps it was a blessing they didn't live.

"So it's like a dragonfly?" I asked, trying not to freak out.

"Mm... more like a nymph, actually."

I stared at him. "A what?"

"Dragonflies lay their eggs under the water, and what hatches is called a nymph. Looks like a hairy beetle, with no wings, and it can breathe underwater. When it's mature and ready to morph into a dragonfly, it comes up on land, splitting open its body to let the dragonfly out."

"So it's sort like a butterfly coming out of a cocoon?"

"In a way, yeah. Anyway, when the baby nymph's delivered, it's not ready to transform into a dragonfly. It's still a baby, and the nymph is not ready to breathe air."

"Why don't they put it under water? And then wait until it's ready to hatch?"

Blake's eyes were pained when he met my gaze. "They've tried, Sam. It didn't work. What's inside the nymph isn't exactly human or dragonfly. It just doesn't know what to do."

My shoulders sank. Looking beyond the horror of having a beetle come out of me that actually housed another strange creature within it, the truth of it was—it was still a baby. With no chance of survival. My heart sank, sadness settling into me like a bad chill.

Blake grimaced. "Sam, I wish... I wish so much this wasn't your world."

"It's not your fault it is, Blake," I said, glancing to the floor, not wanting him to see the pain in my eyes.

"All I wanted for you was a normal life." His words were laced with such sadness, I had to meet his gaze.

I squared my shoulders, determined to make him see none of this was his fault. "Blake, normal escaped me the moment Sammy entered my life," I said, nudging his shoulder with mine. I grinned over at him. "And even with all of this, I wouldn't have it any other way because that's when you came into my life too."

He seemed to consider my words. Slowly, he smiled back at me. Bumping me back, he said, "Well, there's at least one thing I can make sure you get right still."

I wanted to ask him what it was, but I had a hunch it was what kept him from doing more tonight.

He chuckled to himself. "So weird. I guess I just realized how much I want you to have something normal in your life. You deserve better than this. We may not live traditional lives as Dragon Fae, but I can make sure I don't cheat you out of this."

His grin turned boyish as he glanced back at me. "I was letting you take the lead on how far we went with things, but tonight, you didn't seem like yourself." He winked at me.

I knew my face was flaming. "Whatever," I said as I slugged his shoulder, trying to mask my own embarrassment. When he pretended it actually hurt, I tried to hit him again. He pinned my arms down in a flash. It really was crazy how fast he could move when he wanted to.

"Call me old fashioned," Blake said, his face inches from mine, pulling all my thoughts back to him. "But I want your dad to like me."

I knew my dad would never know what went on between us here at Tonbo's place, and Tonbo himself didn't seem too worried that Blake never left my room at night. Maybe it was the lack of any rules here that had gotten to my head. Made me giddy with temptation. Blake's right. I'm not acting like myself. I'm usually a bit more reserved... at least, I think.

"I like that your old fashioned," I said honestly.

He chuckled and giving me a quick kiss, jumped to his feet. "You've had a big day today. I think I better let you get some sleep."

I knew he was right, but why was he leaving? "Can't you stay with me? Like you usually do?"

"I didn't say I was leaving, unless you can't keep your hands off me." He grinned, running his hands through his hair. As he glanced around the room, his wings disappeared. "Do you want to change into your pajamas first?"

"Yes, actually, I do. Waking up in jeans this morning was a nightmare." I climbed off the bed, realizing just how long the day had been. Grabbing my small bag, I rifled through for some shorts and a T-shirt.

After a quick change in the bathroom, I entered the bedroom to see Blake wearing nothing but gym shorts. I made my way to him, debating whether to demand he put a T-shirt on. How am I supposed to sleep with him half naked and looking so good?

He insisted I lie down, and I laughed when he even tucked me in. When he didn't settle down next to me, sitting down at the edge of the bed instead, I sat up, ready to protest. He could still sleep next to me; I wanted to promise I wouldn't even touch him, if that helped.

"Sam, I went to see Jaxon while you were with Tonbo," he announced.

His statement caught me off guard. For a second, I could only stare at him. After I swallowed, I asked in as casual a voice as I could, "Oh really? How did it go?"

He frowned. "Good, I guess. The bug never emerged."

I grinned. "That's great news!" I hesitated, unsure why Blake wasn't smiling too. "Isn't it?" Just means you didn't bring me up, I wanted to add, but I didn't.

"Yes." He inhaled deeply and said, "I even asked him about you."

CHAPTER
Eighteen

"You did?" I sat up straighter. "But you said the bug didn't take over...That's really good then."

I wasn't sure why Blake's frown just deepened. Jaxon stayed in control, even when he was thinking about me! Why isn't Blake happy?

"After what happened today, I have no doubts anymore that Sammy's not gone. It really freaked me how close you were to losing yourself to her. Makes me wonder if that time you got really dizzy when we were kissing was the same thing." He glanced at me.

"I don't know," I answered truthfully. "It might have been." Not wanting to get off track, I asked, "So what did Jaxon say if he remembered anything else about Sammy?" "Yeah. I should have asked him more questions before, Sam. I'm sorry I put my brother's needs above yours."

"Blake, don't say that! It wasn't like that at all," I argued.

"No, it was. I should've listened to you before. I just didn't want to make it harder on Jaxon, so I told myself there was nothing more he could tell us that would help you anyway." By the way his jaw hardened, I had a hunch there was something Blake dreaded telling me.

I reached over and touched his shoulder. "Blake, please don't look at it like that. I understand why you did what you did. And I don't blame you. Why don't you tell me what's wrong? What did Jaxon say?"

He took my hand into his. Meeting my gaze, he said, "Jaxon said he found you out in the woods, not that far from your home. That's when he'd picked up your scent and started hunting you down."

I nodded; this much we already knew.

"But by the time he got there, you'd gone into the house. He said he watched from the upstairs window. You were in your bedroom, alone, for most of the time."

"What do you mean? Who else was with me?" I dreaded hearing him say Mack. Although I knew Mack had been with Blake at this point hunting the bug, or Jaxon.

Blake grimaced. "Jocelyn."

I gasped, sucking air in too fast, and choking on my own spit. He patted my back, trying to make sure I was okay, but I held up a hand as I coughed.

"I'm fine. I'm fine," I managed between fits of feeling asphyxiated. Finally clearing my throat, I said, "I knew I felt something was off between us."

An ache settled over my heart as the truth sank in. Suspecting my sister was upset over something to do with Sammy was one thing, but knowing she might somehow be involved in this mess was quite another.

"Here I was just worrying about my brother, but I never considered how this might affect your family too." Seeing the pain in Blake's expression, I understood why he hadn't wanted to tell me this.

I tried to push the feelings that my sister may have betrayed me aside. I mean, we still don't know what Jocelyn even knows. For all we know, she thought she was just talking to Sammy for a bit.

"Was Sammy a damsel? Did Jocelyn see the wings? Does she know what I am now?" I asked, trying to focus on gathering information. I'll process what this means later.

"No, Sammy didn't have the wings," Blake said, giving me a smile. "So Jocelyn may not know anything about the Dragon Fae world. Jaxon said Sammy gave Jocelyn a large, padded envelope."

"What was in it?"

"He didn't know. Just noticed it was unmarked and puffed out like something hard was in it."

I bit my lip, curiosity getting the best of me. I'd have to ask Jocelyn about that.

"He said Sammy waited until Jocelyn left the room before she transformed and left. He tracked her for a while. He wasn't sure what she was doing. She kept zigzagging through the trees. Almost like she was searching for something."

"Why didn't he just attack right away?" I asked. "Why wait? He obviously had the upper hand."

"Because Jaxon fought the bug the entire time." I could tell by Blake's expression that this wasn't something easy for him to admit. Maybe he's afraid I'll beg to see Jaxon again. But why would I now? Blake was finally getting information from him. Information I'd been dying for.

"So where was Sammy when he, or the bug, finally won the fight? How did that go down?"

His face fell. "Sam, I'd really rather not talk about that."

"Why? You shouldn't feel bad, Blake. None of this is your fault, or Jaxon's. This just helps us…"

"No, this part doesn't. It just horrifies me… with how close…" His words faded as he winced.

Ready to argue that he was once again holding back when he shouldn't, I stopped. Seeing how much pain was in his eyes, I moved closer to him. Wrapping my arms around his shoulders, I said, "I'm here now. You didn't lose me that day, and you won't lose me now."

He glanced over at me, his hand reaching up to take my hand that dangled over his shoulder. "Jaxon said there was no fight."

"What?" I reflexively sat back.

"He said it was almost as if Sammy wanted to be taken. He said she just stopped, landed in the trees, and waited. He'd hovered above her for a long time, fighting himself. Almost like he did that day he'd come when Mack and I were fighting off those dragons. Remember that?"

"Yes," I said. I'd never forget the day I'd discovered the bug Kory had warned me about was real, and worse, I was his target.

"But the bug won. Jaxon said he flew down and scooped you

right up."

"Why on earth would Sammy want the bug to take us?" I demanded, knowing Blake didn't have the answers. No one does. Because this doesn't make sense!

"I have no idea," Blake said. "Jaxon did say she'd been carrying a small bag with her. But when they took off, the bag fell down into the trees."

At this, my head snapped up. "We need to find that bag."

Blake forced a grin. "We can go home tomorrow. Skip out on your next session with Tonbo."

I hesitated, trying to decide which option was better. "No, I need to meet with Tonbo. At least one more time." When I saw Blake's face fall, I knew he'd rather I not. I wondered what he was so afraid of. Was it just seeing things that might bring me pain that worried him? I shrugged it off for now.

"After tomorrow's session, we'll go. Do you think Jaxon can describe the exact place he grabbed me?"

"I'll ask him tomorrow while you are with Tonbo."

"Good. Because I don't know about you, but this has felt like the longest weekend of my life. I'm ready to go home."

CHAPTER
Nineteen

This was not what I wanted to see. As the wand blurred in front of me, I tried to backpedal out of the memory I'd just been thrown into. After seeing a few precious moments in the child version of Sammy's eyes, I was beginning to really enjoy spending time in her shoes. Seeing how she'd jump to defend me at school, telling the kids who teased to bug off, I couldn't deny Sammy's protective feelings toward me. Everything I'd thought I'd known about her was shifting. Her interest in studying all stemmed from understanding what was happening to us. She wanted to fix us, both of us. Make us one somehow.

In my mind, Mack's hand brushed the hair back off my face, his fingers tickling my skin. I tried to hide the shiver that rolled through me, not because his touch repelled me, but because my entire body gravitated toward him. It felt natural. This is Sammy's memory. Not mine. It felt weird, and now very wrong, to live in her shoes.

That didn't matter to my heart, or the way my pulse pounded as he glanced at my lips. Mack understands me. He finds me fascinating... He's one of the few who actually knows me. Not just Samantha.

Suddenly, I knew we'd never kissed before. The way his eyes darted uncertainly between mine. The way his hand shook while touching my face. In that moment, I wasn't seeing Mack as he was then, but as the little boy who'd gone out of his way to talk to me, who'd stuck up for me on the playground, and who felt just as fiercely as I did that Samantha needed protecting.

When Mack finally leaned in, his lips pressing down on mine, I was not prepared for the fire that spread through my body. I wasn't ready for the intense yearning I had for him. I saw myself wrapping my arms around his neck, kissing him back, my back arching.

I bolted up. "I don't want to do this anymore!" I exclaimed.

The wand stopped immediately. Tonbo peered over at me. "Everything alright? Are some of the childhood memories too painful?"

The last thing I'd told Tonbo aloud was when I was about ten years old, asking Mack if he'd ever dissected a frog before. Tonbo didn't know where my mind had leapt to, and I wasn't about to tell him. I'd known this might be a possibility when poking around in Sammy's memories, but I hadn't realized how much I'd feel what she had felt. I was beginning to see why Blake wasn't in love with this idea. It connected me to Sammy, yes, but it also formed a deeper connection between Mack and me.

I didn't want to make eye contact with Tonbo. The guilt felt like it was written all over my face. This was worse than simply knowing about Mack and Sammy. I had actually felt it.

And what I felt, Mack felt. And he remembers too.

"I'd rather not focus on the past anymore. I want to see what happened with Jocelyn," I said, not really answering his question. I knew that was why we had been digging around in the past, trying to establish what Sammy and Jocelyn's relationship had been. But all Sammy seemed fixated on was Mack. Every memory seemed to only show me how deeply Sammy had cared for both Mack and me.

As I realized how desperate she was to fix us, the cabin and all its charades didn't seem so much like a horror film anymore. When the layers I'd built around my heart began to peel away, I felt a baseline of trust building in me. It was possible Sammy hadn't been the bad guy. Maybe she'd just been misguided. Her intentions could have been altruistic after all.

Tonbo seemed to consider my words. Tilting his head to the side, he asked, "Want to give it one more try? I will try to guide you a bit more toward Jocelyn. How does that sound?"

After a moment's hesitation, I nodded. We needed this to

work. I knew when I got home I was going to confront my sister, but with how she'd been treating me lately, I doubted I'd get a warm welcome. Or that she'd tell me anything at all, for that matter.

I settled back down into the couch. Blinking several times, I readied myself to stare at the red blur before me. This time, I noticed I wasn't dripping in sweat. That's because all the memories Sammy are letting me see are happy ones so far. Truthfully, I had no idea if Sammy was even aware of what we were doing, and if she was, how much control she had over it. But some part of me felt like she decided what played out across my mind's stage.

Tonbo's words pulled me back into a relaxed state. As my body began to drift into the pleasant scenery he was describing, I settled down deeper into the couch.

"You are in your bedroom now," he said, guiding me away from the cozy mountain scene he'd created to my real home. "You just got home from mountain biking, and your body is feeling heavy and relaxed. What do you want to do now, listen to music, read a book?"

"No music. I need..." I stopped, trying to figure out what it was I sought. "I need another book on biogenetics. Mack thought he had a copy somewhere at his house, but he can't find it. He said he'd try to stop by the college today and grab me a few more textbooks." Even as I said the words, a very small part of me was aware we'd tapped into another one of Sammy's memories; the rest felt like I was actually living the moment. I felt anxious, desperate for the books Mack had promised me.

"Mm. Sounds interesting. What are you hoping to learn from this book?"

I hesitated to answer. My mind reeled on how to phrase it. Logically, I should just be guessing what Sammy would say. But being in the moment, being in her very shoes, it was like I knew her thoughts. I struggled within myself, unsure I wanted to tell Tonbo everything while at the same time, wondering why I felt like I'd betray Mack if I did. These are Sammy's memories, not mine, I reminded myself.

I let the words just form on their own, even knowing in some part of my brain that Tonbo already knew. "I don't know if you'd believe me, if I tell you."

"Try me," Tonbo replied.

"Okay. Mack's a genetic anomaly. He's part dragonfly." As I said it, a new memory flashed through my mind of me kissing Mack. His hands holding me, our bodies so close. Feeling my face turn scarlet, my cheeks burning with embarrassment, I was about to tell Tonbo I was done for the day, when in my mind, Mack gasped and jumped, no more like flew, away from me.

Inside the memory, I gaped at Mack, who stood before me with two beautiful, orange-red wings.

Knowing I'd just seen when Sammy had first discovered Mack's secret, I tried to focus on what I was telling Tonbo.

"It's the most incredible thing I've ever seen," I said, once again falling into Sammy's thoughts, my words sounding more like her words. "Mack can heal faster. He's stronger. I keep telling him it might be able to fix Samantha and me, but he won't change me."

Anger bubbles up within me. "He told me who created the actual formula, but he won't take me to meet him, either. His name is Alois, but he goes by Tonbo. Apparently, he has his own islands, off the coast of California somewhere."

Somewhere in my mind, I hear Tonbo's gasp, but I ignore it. I don't want to lose what I'm seeing, feeling. I don't want to shatter the connection.

"If Tonbo could just hear my story, I know he'd help me. He'd fix our broken pieces. He'd make it so Samantha wasn't so introverted and depressed all the time." Was that what Sammy thought? That I was depressed? "He'd help me not be so angry and frustrated. Samantha and I need to be one. That's the only way we will both be truly happy."

I almost pulled myself out of the delusion I was experiencing. Sammy's statement hit me upside the head like a two by four. Is that true? One thing I did know was that Sammy believed it. Were Sammy and I like two halves of a soul that needed to be welded back together?

"Does Mack bring you the book you need?" Tonbo asked, breaking my line of thought. "Are you alone in your bedroom?"

I refocus on being in my room. I'll think about all this later. I need to gather what I can from this memory.

"No, Mack hasn't come yet. But someone is knocking on my door," I said, hearing the knock in my mind. My heartbeat sped up as the memory played out before me. The door opened, and my sister walked in.

"It's Jocelyn," I told Tonbo. "She likes to come to talk when it's... me."

"What do you talk about?"

"Mainly, how mom drives us both crazy," I said with a sigh. "That's how Jocelyn always knows she'll find me, and not Samantha. Mom's usually in a tyrannical mood. Joc comes to vent out her frustrations."

"Why does Jocelyn have a hard time with your mom?"

"Most of the time, she doesn't, but lately, Mom's been scheduling more and more modeling gigs for her. Wanting her to live the dream she didn't get to because she had kids. I think the pressure to always look skinny and perfect is really getting to Jocelyn. I worry about her. She goes on too many crazy diets, if you ask me."

"So is Jocelyn venting about your mom today?"

"No, actually, she's not. She wants to tell me about her new boyfriend."

In my mind, Jocelyn was smiling ear to ear. I knew I should tell Tonbo what I was seeing, but for the moment, I wanted it to just play out. Tonbo must have sensed this because he stayed quiet and didn't pry.

⦚⦚⦚⦚⦚⦚

"Sammy," Jocelyn said in a hushed tone. "He is the most amazing guy I've ever met. It's just been so crazy how it's all worked out. I mean, I never would have thought in a million years I'd fall for him... because... well, he's a bit younger than I am. And I don't usually like guys younger than me. It's weird, but I don't think I even care anymore!" She giggled, throwing her hands up like she'd surrendered her heart to this guy. I noticed then that there was a book in one of her hands.

"How much younger are we talking?" I asked, a little alarmed to see my somewhat serious sister acting like a giddy schoolgirl.

"Just a few years," she said offhandedly.

I suppressed the urge to call her a cougar. Somehow, I knew she wouldn't appreciate the joke.

"He's just so sweet. He makes me feel so special. Look," she said, holding out the book. "He even gave me this. It's his favorite copy, but he wanted me to have it. Said I'd understand him better if I did."

I reached out for it, curious more than anything. The large tree on the cover niggled at my mind, reminding me of something. Reading the title, I asked, "Your boyfriend's favorite book is Wuthering Heights?"

"He said he read it when he was younger, when he used to be pretty sick and lonely. It's about a boy who is taken in by a man with a daughter and a son. But when the man dies, the son starts bullying him. Eventually, the boy leaves his home, even though he's secretly in love with the girl. Anyway, years later, he gets his revenge as an accomplished and wealthy man."

I stared at Jocelyn, wanting to tell her that her boyfriend sounds messed up, but I don't. "I'm glad you found someone who makes you happy," I said instead, handing her book back. "Does this young mystery guy have a name?" She hesitated, her smile faltering a bit. "Okay, if I tell you, promise you won't freak out?"

Now I'm more than curious about who this guy was. "I won't freak out. Unless it's Mack."

Jocelyn waved that off. "Of course it's not Mack!"

"Then I don't care who it is. Come on, just tell me."

"Okay," she said, her eyes meeting mine. "It's Kory."

CHAPTER Twenty

Now it took all of my willpower not to bolt up and gasp. Kory? Jocelyn is dating Kory? I tried not to dwell on my own reactions. I needed to see how Sammy felt about this. I let her memory continue to play out. Sammy's inner thoughts came with it.

"Kory? Wait, is he the guy I used to go to school with?" I asked. I only knew of him because Samantha's friend Jen had a huge crush on him. I'd been unhappy to take over a couple times and discover I was in Jen's trap of never-ending school gossip. I couldn't stand girl talk. From what I could tell, neither could Samantha. It was why Jen's friendship had always been an anomaly to me. I shook this off.

"I thought he moved away a few years ago."

"He did, but he's back now. We stumbled into each other on campus. He was there signing up for some classes he's going to take during his senior year. We got to talking and, well, one thing led to another." Jocelyn grinned again, lighting up her pretty features. "I mean, he doesn't look like he's still in high school, but I haven't really told anyone because it is embarrassing."

I shrugged. "You just barely turned twenty-one, Jocelyn. Isn't he eighteen? That's not that big of a deal."

"True," she said, her grin turning a bit mischievous. "He doesn't act like any of the guys I went to high school with, that's for sure. He's so smart, Sammy. He's developed this stuff that makes you feel so amazing, at least that's what he's told me. It can..." She hesitated, her words fading.

Now my interest was piqued. "What kind of stuff? Hey, he's not into drugs, is he? I know everyone thinks it's so great that marijuana is legal here, but—"

"No," she said, waving me off. "It's nothing like that. He said it's more like a diet pill, but it's a shot. You know how so many people take those vitamin B shots or the hormones to help them lose weight."

"Jocelyn, you're crazy if you think you need to lose weight," I countered. My sister was too skinny if you asked me.

"I wouldn't use it to lose more weight," she argued. "It would just be nice to be able to eat every once in a while and not gain a gazillion pounds."

I wanted to say she should just quit modeling. That she should tell Mom to leave her alone about it all.

"Anyway, he hasn't given me any of it yet, so stop stressing yourself, Sammy. I'll make sure it's safe. You act like I've never taken diet pills before."

"Taking a little caffeine pill is one thing, Jocelyn, but taking something your eighteen-year-old boyfriend is concocting in his basement is quite another!"

Jocelyn wrinkled her nose at me. "I knew I shouldn't have told you. You don't understand. Kory's been taking the stuff for a long time, and he said it's totally natural. He said it only made him healthier and stronger."

I gaped at her. Just what kind of shots is she talking about here? "I thought you said he's still developing it? Now you're saying he's been using it for a while? This is sounding a lot like drugs to me."

"It's not drugs like the kind you're thinking. I don't do drugs, Sammy, and I'm not about to start now. Do you know how bad they age you? They make you look awful. Kory's still perfecting my blend. It takes time to get it just right for each person."

Now all I saw were red flags. Mysterious shots that made you strong and healthy? I couldn't deny how similar that sounded to what Mack had just told me about what it took to become a dragon or damsel. There was no way Kory was mixed up in all that too, was there?

"I haven't even told you the best part, Sammy. It's an anti-aging serum too!" Jocelyn exclaimed, grinning again. "So I can stay young and wrinkle free for a very, very long time."

I could only stare at her. Time to talk to Mack.

"Kory's dating Jocelyn," I blurted to Tonbo as the memory I'd been so immersed in snapped shut.

The red blur before my eyes stopped. For a second, I found it extremely satisfying to be able to focus on the red marble. It helped to clear my head even further.

"How much does she know? Has Kory revealed himself to her?" he asked, leaning in toward me.

"I don't know. I didn't see that part. Just her telling Sammy about dating Kory and how he has this magical formula." I let my words sink in. "He's going to give it to her to keep her from aging or gaining weight."

I met Tonbo's heavy gaze and said, "I think we both know what the magical formula is, but I don't know if Jocelyn knows. What I saw must have happened right before the cabin. Sammy didn't know Kory was a dragon then, so I'm guessing she talked to Mack about all of it after this."

Tonbo nodded. "So the question still remains. What side of the fence is Sammy on? With her sister in the picture, maybe her allegiance was swayed toward Kory a bit easier."

"Maybe," I said, "But if she did side with Kory early on, why didn't she go to him to be changed? I'm sure when she talked to Mack and he told her Kory was a dragon, the thought must have crossed her mind. That she could ask him for the special stuff he was telling Jocelyn about, I mean. Especially since Mack wouldn't do it himself."

Tonbo leaned back in his chair and folded his arms. "You're right. There must have been a reason she didn't. Do you think she mistrusted him?"

"I don't know. The one thing all this has shown me, though, is that Sammy really did believe she had to put us back together again, for us to be happy. She didn't want to take over when she became a damsel. She thought becoming a damsel would finally make us one."

Tonbo seemed to consider my words. "And perhaps it did. You are not the same person you were before, Samantha."

I stared at him, taken aback by his statement. I would know the difference, wouldn't I? When I remembered things as Sammy, it felt like I was thinking and feeling those things.

"No, I'm not the same," I answered thoughtfully. "But I'm not her, either. I don't have free access to all her thoughts and memories unless I'm doing this." I pointed at the wand Tonbo held.

"If we were finally one person, shouldn't I remember what Otto and I talked about in his office? Or what was in that padded envelope Jaxon saw her give Jocelyn? I should know what she dropped in the woods when Jaxon picked her up."

Tonbo moved forward, leaning his elbows on his knees. "Maybe you are still separated. Or maybe she's not letting you see those memories. I guess, at this point, we don't know for certain."

I wanted to argue how wrong he was, but my mind had gone in so many different directions, my emotions tugged along with it, that I felt too exhausted to think about whether Sammy and I were truly one now. The only thing I could focus on was the fact that Jocelyn and Kory had been, or were still, together. I needed to know what my sister knew.

"I think it's time I talk to Jocelyn."

"Probably a good idea. Perhaps after that, we can resume this. I feel there's much we can still learn from her memories. If you are comfortable doing this again, that is."

I felt myself flush. Too much of this was just that—uncomfortable. Every memory seemed to dig me deeper into something I wasn't sure I'd be able to get back out of.

"Of course. I'll try to get back here as soon as I can, Tonbo." I stood up, pushing away the lingering effects of deep relaxation. I needed to feel my feet underneath me.

Tonbo walked me to the door, his hand patting my arm as we went. "Just remember the Chinese proverb, Samantha. A diamond with a flaw is preferable to a common stone with none."

I glanced at him, unsure what he was getting at.

He opened the door for me. Giving my arm a gentle squeeze, he said, "You may feel having Sammy there within you makes you broken. But you aren't seeing how truly magnificent the two of you are together. What you've both created. There's no one quite like you now, Sam."

I stared at him, wondering if he could be right. Should I embrace who I was? Both sides? Accept that Sammy might take over at any moment and trust that it was just fine? That she wouldn't put me in jeopardy? That she truly had my best interest at heart?

I leaned down and hugged Tonbo. "I'll try to remember. Thank you for everything." Surprised to feel another hand fall on my arm from behind, I straightened up quickly. Turning around, I fully expected it to be Blake.

I failed to hide my shock. "Mack."

His quickly dropped his hand. "Sorry, didn't mean to scare you."

"No, no. You're fine," I flustered to recover, feeling my face redden. "Just jumpy from my session." It wasn't entirely untrue. I wasn't about to admit to him how his touch fired up Sammy's old memories a bit too much for my liking.

CHAPTER

Twenty-One

I didn't miss the way Tonbo stared at me as we said our farewells, but I tried not to pay attention. Breathing deeply, I tried to shake off my jitters. It's just Mack, my friend. No need for anything to be different. Or to act weird.

Moving away from Tonbo's office, Mack asked with a grin, "So, learn anything useful today?"

I blinked back at him. I knew it was an innocent question, but I had to swallow and clear my throat before I could respond. "Apparently, Kory's dating my sister."

Mack groaned. "Seriously? Which one?"

"Jocelyn." I shot him a glance. "So I guess my hunch wasn't too far off, huh?" I told him about my encounter with Jocelyn as Sammy, and how Sammy had wanted to ask him about Kory in the memories I'd seen.

He didn't say anything at first, staring at the floor as we walked. I waited, sensing there was something behind his frown.

"You know when I told Sammy all about Kory and Blake's history, she could've mentioned the fact that Jocelyn was dating Kory," Mack said at last. "Why didn't she say anything to me about that? Was she trying to hide something else from me?"

I didn't miss the pain in his words. I hadn't fully appreciated Mack's suffering until today. His feelings for Sammy hadn't been real to me before. If anything, they'd irritated me. Made me feel like he was on her side, not mine. They even made me a bit jealous, if I was honest with myself. Mack was my friend. Not hers. He saw me through some rough years. Was always there for me. Now I knew I wasn't the only one Mack had done that for. He'd been that for Sammy too. She was just the side of me that reciprocated his feelings for her.

Now seeing the way Mack frowned, I felt the need to reach out and comfort him. Finding an empty office down the hall from Tonbo's, I pulled him into the room and shut the door. He glanced over at me, his frown melting into confusion.

"Mack, Sammy loved you," I said, surprising myself, but feeling like he needed to know.

He snorted in disbelief and let go of my hand. "I used to believe that, but she used me, Samantha. Played me like the fool I am. I was a means to an end for her. Nothing more."

"No, that's not true, Mack. She really cared for you."

"Ha. Everything I thought I knew about her has turned into lies. She never told me what she was really up to. How do you think it makes me feel to keep learning how deep her lies go? Like what the hell was she doing with Otto in the first place?" His jaw hardened, anger making his face taut.

I wanted to scream right back at him that her secret agenda impacted me way more than him, but I kept my voice level. It had been a long day for both of us, and it wouldn't do any good to let our frustrations out on each other.

"I have no idea, but I know she loved you. That wasn't a lie."

He looked like he might argue back, but then with a long sigh, he shook his head. "I appreciate you trying to make me feel better, Samantha."

"I'm not making this up to make you feel better!"

"Then how would you even know what Sammy thought and felt?" he asked, his tone taking on an edge I wasn't used to. We'd never been this open with one another. I knew we were both feeling raw and vulnerable. We'd never been in this much pain. Well, Mack always was, but I hadn't realized it until today. Until I felt those deep feelings for him. Sammy's feelings.

"Because that's all she wanted to keep showing me today!" I blurted. "Every memory I saw, you were there. It's like you were all she thought about, next to how to fix me! I kept trying to learn about Jocelyn, but instead, I'm reliving every intimate moment the two of you had together!" I growled out the words, frustrated

I had to feel those times. They confused me. Made me want to draw nearer to his heaving chest. They made me want to throw my arms around him and press my lips against his.

Instead, we stared at each other. Mack's eyes widened as my words fully sank in.

"Sammy." He slipped with the name, but I didn't care. "I'm sorry. I had no idea how hard it would be for you... to see that."

"It's not," I lied. "And you have nothing to apologize for." I rubbed my hand across my forehead, trying to shake off the emotions swirling inside me. The desire to kiss Mack was about to make me crazy. Maybe Tonbo wasn't so far off after all. Maybe Sammy and I are together now. That would sure explain this. I sighed. Just my crappy luck Mack showed up to get me after today and not Blake.

Thinking of Blake, my heart lurched painfully. It was like a sleeping giant finally awoke. Slowly the longing for Mack began to ebb.

"Listen, Mack, I just want you to know that after what I saw today, I feel for what you are going through. I know you and Sammy had real feelings for each other. Those don't just go away."

He lifted one eyebrow, but he didn't say anything for a moment. Slowly, he reached over and took my hand into his. For a second, I felt like I couldn't breathe right. His touch sent a thrill through me. I wanted to draw closer, feel more of him. His eyes darted between mine. I sensed he was holding his breath too.

Time stood on its head. I wasn't sure how long we sat there, just staring at each other. Finally, he used his other hand to open the door.

Turning to meet my gaze again, he said, "Look, let's not talk about Sammy anymore. At least, not about that. I shouldn't have vented on you. I'm sorry. It won't happen again. This is kind of confusing... for both of us."

With the way my heart fluttered when he glanced at my lips, I almost pulled him to me with our clasped hands. Instead, I made a rash decision and practically bolted from the room, dragging him along with me.

If he noticed the way I fidgeted or didn't answer his proposition, he made a point not to let me know. Instead, he gave me a reassuring smile and began walking down the hallway, swinging my hand and arm with his. Part of me knew it was all a show, that he was really dying inside and didn't want me to know. The other part reasoned, If he can pretend that just didn't happen, so can I.

"So, Kory's dating Jocelyn, huh?" he asked.

Glad to change the subject, I finished telling him everything I'd learned, which looking back, wasn't that much. He nodded along as he listened. When we reached the outside of Tonbo's office, I realized I had no idea where we were heading. Or where Blake was for that matter.

"Is Blake still with Jaxon?" I asked, worry filling me.

Mack frowned. "Yeah." He rubbed the back of his neck. "He... asked me to come get you. Help you get ready to leave."

I eyed him, sensing there was something he wasn't telling me. "Spill it, Mack,"

He grimaced. "It hasn't been a good visit today."

"What? What's going on? Is Blake okay?" Now panic gripped me.

"Blake's fine. He's not hurt. He just... Jaxon can't get the bug under control yet. Blake doesn't want to leave him like that."

I bit my lip. "Oh." I felt awful inside. "This is my fault. I'm the one who asked Blake to talk to Jaxon about me again."

"Don't blame yourself. This is something Jaxon has to overcome—somehow."

"Well, maybe I can help."

"What? No way." Mack shook his head at me, like he already knew what I was thinking.

I sighed in defeat. I hated to admit to Mack that in some strange way, I felt drawn to Jaxon. Logically, I really didn't need to see him. So why was I always pushing to? It just felt like we had unresolved issues between us.

Yeah, he wants to kill me. I frowned. Great, I'm even more messed up than I thought.

"Okay, fine. I give. I won't try to help," I grumbled. Feeling irritated and too wiped out to argue more, I pointed in the direction Tonbo's estate was. "Hey, I think I'm going to head back and take a bath while I wait for Blake."

"Alright," Mack said, moving to follow after me.

I held up my hand. "I know the way. Why don't you go check on Jaxon's progress and let me know in a bit?"

He hesitated, and then nodded. "Sure thing. Go try to relax."

"Okay, I will. See ya, Mack." Purposefully taking off before him, I peeked over my shoulder, waving back at him. He waited until I'd gone a distance before he rose up and flew in the opposite direction.

As soon as I felt I could, I tucked in an alleyway, my heart galloping in my chest. I knew picking up Mack's scent would be easy. I could follow him in camo. Just see where they're keeping Jaxon. What can the harm in that be?

CHAPTER

Twenty-Two

It had turned out to be extremely easy to track Mack. His lingering scent of spices filled me with a strange excitement. I didn't even have to think about it. My body took over as soon as I had camoed out. Zigzagging through City's buildings, I wasn't too surprised to see Jaxon wasn't being held downtown. After five minutes of flying, I'd entered the more secluded side of the island. There weren't many buildings or houses. Probably better to keep a caged, wild killer out where no one lives.

Heading toward the green-carpeted mountains that made up the center of City's island, I dropped down lower to the ground, not wanting to miss Mack's scent. I scanned the area, seeing only rough rock outcroppings, green moss, trees, swaying vines... nothing manmade around. A little worried I'd messed up, I slowed my pace. Breathing deeply, I identified Mack's scent through the tropical flora surrounding me. Good. They're out here somewhere. To get a better vantage point, I rose up higher. It was then I spied a flash of metal off to the right through the canopy of trees, up higher on the mountain. Moving closer, I could tell it was a rooftop.

There you are. A thrill shot through me. With eyes alert, senses heightened, I carefully made my way toward the building. I had no idea what kind of security measure Tonbo might have taken. I didn't want to set off any alarms. I just wanted a closer look.

Even with the lush vegetation surrounding it, I could make out the general U shape of the building. Painted white, there were few windows or doors that I could see. Following Mack's path, I dropped down to the left wing of the building. Seeing there was a manned guardhouse, I realized I'd foolishly assumed I could just peek through some window and see Blake and Jaxon. I sat back against the tree I'd landed in, debating what to do.

I should just turn around and head back now. That's what I should do. But something in me wasn't satisfied. There was a courtyard past the guardhouse, stone pavers leading up to the white building. The final obstacle to get through was two massive steel doors. Glancing around, I was surprised to see there was only a low block fence surrounding the place, looking like it was more for decoration. When you can just fly over, what good is a fence anyway?

The place didn't really scream prison. Not with flowers, small palm trees, and manicured bushes landscaping the courtyard. There was even a large fountain in the middle of it all. I bit my thumbnail, my insides screaming to take action, but I needed some kind of plan. Or a reason to get the dragon in the guardhouse to let me pass, without alerting Blake I was here.

My way in presented itself as two dragons flew up to the guardhouse. They were both dressed in cargo shorts, carrying large boxes. As the guard dragon gave them a curt nod, probably recognizing who they were, I zoomed forward. Carefully sidling up next to the two, I prayed my scent wouldn't be a dead giveaway. Immediately, the dragon closest to me glanced in my direction.

"Hey, you smell that?" he asked the other two.

"What?" the one bearing a box asked. I could tell what they were delivering wasn't light; both of their foreheads were glistening with sweat. Guess when you hide up in the mountains, driving deliveries up isn't really an option.

"Smells like... flowers," he said, his eyes searching where I was. Blake had said most dragons and damsels couldn't detect you once you were in camo. They relied solely on scent to identify others once invisible. I was an anomaly, my eyesight just sharp enough to see the faint outlines of others.

"We're in the middle of the freaking jungle, idiot," the other grumbled. "Everything smells like flowers. Let's get rid of these supplies. My arms are killing me."

Seeing how well built the two were, I had a haunch those

boxes probably weighed a ton. The guard chuckled and waved us on. As we made our way through the courtyard, flying lower to the ground, I continued to hold my breath. It wasn't just the sense of smell that was heightened. If these two heard me exhale, I'd be found out. I stayed as close as I dared without touching either one of them.

The guard must have pushed something because as soon as we drew near, the two metal doors opened like French doors. Once inside the brightly lit building, I waited until the delivery boys veered off, making their way down the left corridor. Only once I was sure they were far enough away, I inhaled deeply, hoping to decipher Mack's scent over the smell of the two new dragons.

Identifying it, I shot to the right. Knowing it had a relatively simple layout from the outside, I was slightly surprised at how large it felt inside. With white-tiled floor and white walls, it reminded me more of an old hospital wing. Deciding to walk instead of fly, I passed closed door after closed door. Having no windows to peer into, I was more than curious as to what was behind them. But that's not why I'm here, I reminded myself. Mack's scent carried me down the hall, where I could see it dead-ended with a large pot of flowers sitting on a side table.

My adrenaline spiked. Jaxon's behind one of these closed doors. Wonder which one? I got my answer when the door at the very end of the hall opened, and Mack stepped out. I froze, once again holding my breath. He hadn't looked my way yet. He shut the door behind him, his lips downturned. I glanced around in panic. Suddenly, this whole idea of mine seemed ludicrous. What am I thinking? They're going to figure out I'm here. There are not a lot of places to hide if all these other doors are locked.

Mack didn't move. He only leaned against the wall. Removing his glasses, he shut his eyes and began kneading them with his knuckles.

I wanted to draw nearer, but I didn't. Mack knows my scent, unlike those delivery guys. Too late, I remembered Blake had said that Mack had an uncanny sense of smell. His eyes popped opened. Throwing his glasses back on, he flew right for me before I could backpedal fast enough.

He grabbed my arms and wordlessly dragged me back. Opening a side door that was apparently empty and unlocked, he pushed me into the room. Not used to Mack being so forceful, I could only stare at him in shock.

He paced the floor, his mouth working, but no words coming out. Finally, he turned on his heel and faced me. "Samantha, I know it's you, so you might as well ditch the camo." He ran his hands through his hair, exhaling loudly. "Sorry I was so rough. But if Jaxon catches your scent, these walls won't be strong enough to hold him back. Not today, anyway."

"Oh." I didn't know what else to say. I didn't want to be visible; I knew my face was flaming red with embarrassment. *I'm such an idiot. What am I doing here?*

I ditched the camo anyway. As soon as Mack laid on eyes on me, his face softened. "Sorry. I didn't mean to scare you... it's just... this is the last place you should be. What are you doing here?" he asked, echoing my own sentiment.

"I wasn't going to go any closer; I just wanted to see where Jaxon was... see how it's going." I knew my reasoning sounded ridiculous. Somehow, I didn't think telling Mack that my insides were itching to come here would help my case.

"Listen, I know you don't like being left out," Mack said, folding his arms. "But Blake and I aren't trying to hide things from you anymore. Jaxon's dangerous, plain and simple. Sure, his holding room keeps him in place. Most of the time, Tonbo's got him strung out on different serums, trying to undo the damage that's been done. But lately, the bug has gotten pretty fed up. And then with Blake bringing you up this morning... Well... let's just say the bug's winning today."

I opened my mouth to respond, but the sound of a door crashing open down the hall reverberated down the tiled hallway back to us. Two seconds later, the sound of glass shattering pierced the air. Mack cursed, pushing me back.

"Stay in here, no matter what," he commanded.

He bolted through the doorway, leaving me standing in the middle of an empty room, unsure what to do. Instinctively, I switched to camo, my heart galloping in my chest.

"Jaxon..." Blake's voice carried back to me. "I don't want to hurt you. You have to control this thing!"

I gripped the doorframe, trying to keep myself from leaving the room. My insides screamed to go to Blake, but I knew seeing me would only make it worse for Jaxon, and in the end, Blake too. Still wanting to know what was happening, I carefully peered around the wall I clutched.

I slapped a hand over my mouth to keep from crying out. Right in the middle of the broken floral arrangement, Blake was pinned against the wall, the bug holding him up by his throat. Mack didn't waste time. He flew straight for Jaxon, grabbing hold of his neck from behind.

"Jaxon, if you can't stop this, we'll have to knock you out again. Come on, man, fight this!" Mack yelled.

The bug roared, no coherent words coming out. With his free hand, he swiped at Mack like he was an annoying fly on his back. Seeing how purple Blake's face had turned, I no longer cared if the guys got mad at me. If I don't do something, the bug's going to kill him!

I didn't stop to second-guess myself, flying into the hallway. Instantly, the bug spun around, dropping Blake and throwing Mack's body off him. It didn't matter that I was invisible—his black-bug eyes honed in on me. He knows I'm here. Somewhere in the background, I saw Blake scrambling to his feet. I spared him a glance to make sure he was all right. His confused stare in my direction crumbled into disappointment. Blake knows I'm here too.

I froze, seeing how the bug wasn't trying to kill Blake anymore. For a split second, no one moved. The bug's barrel chest heaved up and down as he peered right at me, Blake's aqua eyes glared at the back of his brother, and Mack... I glanced around. Where did Mack go?

My heartbeat felt like it was the only thing moving; everything was at a dead standstill, like we were waiting for the penny to drop. All of us knew we might not recover from the ripples of this one moment.

I ditched the camo. For a split second, Blake's shoulders fell, and then his entire body straightened, his muscles tightening. He's ready to do whatever it takes to stop his brother. I can't let that happen. This is all my fault. I should never have come. Why did I? I wanted to transform into Jaxon's son again, but something inside me told me not to.

I shocked myself when I said, "Jaxon, I'm here."

"Finally," the bug growled. "I've been waiting."

CHAPTER
Twenty-Three

Blake sucked in air, his eyes wide as he stared at the monstrous form of his brother. He grabbed on to his brother's back, even though the bug hadn't moved. The words the bug had said were terrifying, but the lack of movement on the bug's part was confusing everyone. Me, most of all. Now what? I got his attention... what do I say to stop this?

"Well, I'm here now, so let Jaxon come back," I said, hoping no one heard the way my voice shook.

A low rumble shook through the bug's frame, echoing down the hallway. It ended in a horrible cackle.

"Jaxon?" The bug roared with laughter. "He's done fighting me. I've won. Jaxon's gone."

"No, he's not," I argued, but it didn't matter. His words had enraged Blake. He pulled back on the bug, wrapping his arms around his throat, putting him in a chokehold.

"You're lying. Jaxon was just here," Blake hissed into the bug's ear. "He's the one who wins this, not you."

The bug only laughed harder. "You fools. Nothing can stop me. Unlike Jaxon, I have no weaknesses."

"You're wrong," I instinctively said. "You do have one weakness."

The bug's black eyes squinted in my direction, ignoring Blake's tightening grip on his neck.

"It's me," I declared.

The bug wailed and rushed forward, the thrumming from his heavy wings making the entire hall vibrate and whip with air. Blake yelled for me to get out of there as he pulled back harder on his chokehold, twisting the bug's neck at a horrible angle. I shot away from them both, pushing my wings to their limit.

The bug was mere feet away from me when he stopped his pursuit long enough to wrestle with Blake. Reaching back over his shoulders, the bug grabbed onto Blake's wings, flipping him over his head and hurling him across the room.

"Blake!" I cried, seeing how mangled his wings were when he hit the wall and slid to the ground like a dead weight.

The bug grabbed onto me, his arms and legs snaking around mine. "I need you," he croaked, his nasty face inches from mine. There was something desperate in those black eyes. "I need you to..."

I didn't even see Blake move. One second, he looked unconscious on the floor, and the next, he was tearing me from the bug's grasp. I stumbled back, falling to the ground. Blake didn't stop charging his brother. Shoving him back, his forearm pinning the bug's throat to the wall, Blake brought up a shard of glass he must have picked up from the broken vase. The veins in Blake's arms and neck were bulging. I knew this was it. The final blow to kill his brother. By the rage I saw in those eyes, I knew the dragon in Blake had taken over.

"Stop," the bug croaked. "Blake, wait."

I gaped at the bug, the sudden change in tone shocking me.

Blake hesitated. The broken shard remained frozen in his hand, which I noticed was now trembling.

The bug groaned. "I don't want to kill you. Just get out of its way. She's the one it wants." Although still in the bug form, we both knew it was Jaxon pleading with Blake.

"Like hell I don't! I need answers. She has answers!" the bug immediately roared.

"If you want her, you go through me," Blake shouted, his muscles tightening again. His knuckles turned white with how hard he griped the broken glass. It was then I noticed the blood streaming down his hand.

"Wait, Blake. Let me talk to him," I begged. I knew I should flee, but I couldn't.

"Get back, Sam!" Blake commanded through gritted teeth.

"What answers?" I quickly asked. There was something in those black eyes, something the bug wanted from me, and I was starting to believe it wasn't just my life anymore.

"What did you do to us?" the bug hissed, thrashing his head side to side while still pinned. A shudder ran through the bug's body. "What did you do to us?" he repeated, this time with a wail.

"What? I didn't do anything!" I said, but despite my better judgment, I drew nearer.

"Your special blend!" the bug gurgled out as sobs began racking his frame. "Should have been smart about it, but I was so curious."

Blake's grip had slackened slightly, allowing the bug to speak more freely. The glass was still ready, poised in the air.

"What are you talking about?" Blake demanded.

"Sammy's so special," the bug slurred. "Had to know. Had to try."

Was it just me, or were his words slowing down? I flew closer. "My blend? You mean because you took my blood that it changed you somehow?"

The bug chuckled mirthlessly. "If only I had been satisfied with the taste of your blood, but I went back... back to the woods... when you were unconscious... in my cave... and found... what you dropped—" The bug's head slumped to the side, his enormous black eyes shutting.

"No!" I cried, rushing forward. Blake released his hold on his brother, his eyes wide with bewilderment.

"I didn't do anything," Blake said almost defensively to me. As the bug's body slumped down, Blake carefully laid him on the ground, making sure his head didn't smack the tile floor.

I dropped down to my knees, mesmerized by the bug's form changing before us. Within seconds, a half-naked Jaxon was curled up on the ground. Blake's fingers ran down his brother's arm, pulling out the dart that was now clearly visible.

Mack's voice from behind made me jump. "I got the tranquilizer gun as fast as I could. Everyone okay?"

So that's where he went. Mack's eyes scanned me up and

down, making me flush. "We're fine, Mack. The bug was telling us something."

"Oh." I heard regret in Mack's voice. "Sorry."

Blake straightened up. "No need to be; you did the right thing."

Mack nodded, still seeming unsure. "Did you learn anything before I... knocked him out?"

I ran my hands through my hair, exhaling. "Sounds like Jaxon, or the bug, went back into the woods to get the bag Sammy dropped when he took her. And whatever was in it is freaking him out now."

CHAPTER
Twenty-Four

Both guys stared at me, Blake's expression hard to read. Blake hadn't wanted me anywhere near Jaxon. And what did I do? Snuck in here and said, 'Here I am, Jaxon.' My insides squirmed. I put Blake in a horrible position, one that involved choosing my life or his brother's. I knew what decision he'd made today, and I could only guess it had to eat at him.

"I better get Jaxon back into his room," Blake said, his eyes lingering on me for half a second before he carefully swooped his brother up into his arms.

We followed him down the hall, as Mack asked, "How did he get out anyway? The door has a lock on it."

"I had to get some air, and Jaxon rushed me before I could get the door shut. He's never really tried to escape before, so it took me by surprise. He had me shoved up against the wall before I even knew what hit me," Blake admitted. "I guess he'd sensed you were here, Sam."

I cringed. I'm such an idiot. Why on earth did I come here today?

I was saved from responding because both Blake and Mack ducked into Jaxon's room. I remained planted in the hall, feeling too ashamed to move. When the guys emerged a few moments later, Blake's hand was bandaged from where the broken vase had cut him. I knew he only did that to keep blood from going everywhere while the wound healed itself.

I couldn't miss the look of defeat in his eyes. I wanted to comfort him, but I was so afraid I'd been the one who'd made things so much worse for Jaxon.

"You think the bug took something that was in Sammy's bag?" Mack asked, rubbing the back of his neck.

I nodded. "That might be why he got so agitated today when you asked about it, Blake. Whatever was in that bag, it's bothering him now. I think that's why he wanted to see me today. The desire to know what Sammy had done to him outweighed the urge to kill me." Blake frowned. "I'll wait until he wakes up and try to ask him again. Maybe Jaxon can tell me about it before the bug takes over again."

"No," I said, reaching out to touch Blake's arm. "Don't ask Jaxon. I don't think he remembers any of it, or he would have told you about it the last time you'd asked him. Besides, it will only make the bug come back. Let's give Jaxon a break. I think there are other ways we can find out."

"You mean Tonbo's therapy?" Blake asked, and my face heated. After today's session, I really didn't want to do it again. The lingering effects of it still had me feeling funny being near Mack and Blake at the same time. I knew Mack didn't know exactly what I'd felt and seen today, but after our earlier encounter, I think he had a hunch.

Mack's eyes sought out mine, but I ducked my head. "No. I mean, I can do it again, if that's what it takes, but there might be someone else I can talk to."

"Jocelyn," Mack offered.

Seeing Blake's confusion, I quickly filled him in. As soon as he heard my sister was dating Kory, a frown etched its way across his face.

"Jaxon saw Sammy give Jocelyn a package," I said, reminding them, "Maybe if we know what was in that package, we can figure out what was in Sammy's bag too," I offered.

Blake sighed. "That may work, but only Jaxon, or the bug, knows for certain what was in the bag he snatched. We should stay here and ask him when he comes to."

I shook my head. "I can't stay, Blake. I need to get home to my sister, find out what she knows. Besides, I only make it worse for Jaxon." I knew I just reminded Blake how stupid I was to come here, all over again. He'll be glad to get me away from his brother.

I was shocked when Blake pulled me to him instead.

"I'm so sorry, Sam," he whispered. "Of course you want to talk to Jocelyn."

I hadn't realized how much I needed his touch. My body melted into him, my lungs feeling like they could finally breathe again. His embrace chased everything else away, even if it was only temporary. I wished I could stay here, leaning against his chest, forever, letting the thrumming of his heart soothe me, but the desire to get out of this place won out.

Glancing up, I caught Mack quickly averting his eyes from me. I felt a twinge of guilt. Darn it. I shouldn't feel guilty. I've done nothing wrong. I'm with Blake. Not Mack. Still, even as I justified it, my heart hurt to see the sadness in his eyes.

Mack cleared his throat. "Why don't you both go home? I'll stay here and check on Jaxon, make sure I didn't use too much tranq," he added with a wry grin.

Blake separated himself from me, so he could look Mack in the eye. "No, I'll stay. You and Sam should go home. Jocelyn knows Sammy and you were together, Mack. She might open up more with you there."

My insides seized up when I heard Blake say Sammy was with Mack. The images of kissing Mack filled me with an odd longing again. Uh-oh. I can't fly home with Mack. I need you, Blake.

Mack held up his hand, almost as if he knew my inner turmoil. "Blake, you could use a break. You've been here all morning. I've got this. I'll wait until Jaxon is up and feeling good. Then I'll question him."

Seeing the dark circles under Blake's aqua eyes, I knew he was right.

Blake's lips twitched as he considered the offering before he finally relented. "Alright, but don't question him alone. Have some techs here with you to help out if needed."

Mack patted the tranquilizer gun that hung from his hip. "Don't worry; I'll keep this baby handy too." He gave us a lopsided grin. I was sure it was meant to reassure us.

As we passed, Blake reached out and gripped Mack's shoulder. "Thanks, man. I appreciate this."

Mack nodded. "Sure thing." Mack's eyes met mine, and his smile grew.

"Be careful," I said. "I don't think the bug's going to like the fact I'm gone and he didn't get answers."

Mack gave my arm a squeeze. "I'll be fine. Go talk to your sister."

I gave him a nod, trying to give him the same reassuring smile he was giving me, and then followed after Blake, swallowing down the lump lodged in my throat.

Mack's going to be fine, I told myself as we cleared the compound. As if sensing my turmoil, Blake's hand found mine. Wordlessly, we flew back to Tonbo's City. It didn't take us long to gather up our things. We exchanged a few small pleasantries, but neither of us brought up anything of importance. The undercurrent of strain between us felt palpable to me. I assumed him not bringing up me going to see Jaxon behind his back meant he was upset enough to be weighing his words.

As we left the room we'd stayed in, he reached for my arm.

"Wait," he said, stopping me in the doorway. "Before we take off, I want to talk to you about something."

I met his gaze and admitted, "I messed up today, Blake. I'm so sorry."

Panic flitted through his eyes as he hesitated. But then, he said, "No, don't be sorry, Sam. I understand. I'm sure it has to be so confusing for you."

"I wouldn't say confusing," I answered, my brows gathering. "More like frustrating. But I shouldn't have... done what I did. I feel bad for the pain it caused you. You shouldn't have to choose like that."

Now his brow line matched mine. "I'm not the one who has to choose, Sam. I made my decision years ago. You'll always be the only one for me."

"But you shouldn't have to choose me over your brother!" I countered, my bottom lip trembling. "I'm so sorry that you had to fight Jaxon again today because of me."

Blake's eyes widened. "You think I'm upset you came to Jaxon's holding cell today?"

"Y-yes." My voice cut out on me. Clearing it, I added, "Aren't you?"

"Going to Jaxon's is what you meant by messing up then?" he asked, his expression eager.

"Well, yeah. What else would I be talking about?" I asked, completely confused.

"You mean, you and Mack didn't kiss?"

"What? No!" My faced flushed.

Blake didn't answer me. He just pulled me to him, his lips meeting mine. It didn't take me long to realize by the way he gripped my body tightly against his that he'd feared he'd lost me again. But why? Why would he assume anything? It's not as if he knows how tempted I'd been. Does he?

I pulled back a bit, wanting to know why he'd jumped to conclusions. "Why did you think something happened between Mack and me?"

He frowned. "Before your session this morning, I went and saw Tonbo. I just wanted to make sure you'd be alright while I was with Jaxon. I'm not wild about this whole walk-in-Sammy's-shoes business. Honestly, it makes my skin crawl for some reason. I'd hoped Tonbo would reassure me. Instead, he told me how you actually feel each memory like it's your own. It got me thinking about who Sammy spent the most time with. Mack. When I asked Tonbo about it, he said there was chance that reliving her time with him would make those dormant feelings real to you."

Blake's face was expectant as he peered back at me. He wanted me to say that nothing could be further from the truth, but I couldn't.

"Would've been nice if Tonbo had given me that warning before I did today's session," I murmured.

"So the weirdness I detected between you and Mack just now was because you've fallen in love with him?"

I stared at him. "If you were so worried I'd fallen for Mack, why were you insisting he go back home with me now?"

"Because I wanted you to have time to figure things out, without me there. I don't want to be the third wheel, Sam. If you're feelings for me have changed, you can tell me." "My feelings for you could never change, Blake," I leaned in and kissed his lips once, hoping to reassure him of this. "I'm in love with you."

"But you have feelings for Mack too?" he asked softly.

I rubbed my forehead, wanting more than anything to simply lie. However, Blake deserved the truth. "Seeing Sammy's life, her memories, opened parts of me that I don't understand. It's like for those few minutes, I'm her. Everything she felt, I'm feeling. I wish I could tell you I didn't experience feelings today. But I can't. I don't want to hide things from you. I saw, or felt, Sammy and Mack's first kiss. I didn't even want to be in that memory, but it was like Sammy just kept pushing me to see how much she loved him."

I didn't miss the pain growing in Blake's expression.

"And how much she loved me," I added. "Sammy was convinced that she and I could never truly be happy unless we were one again. That's why she wanted to change us. Not so that she could be the dominant one and make me disappear, but so we could finally heal. Not broken anymore."

I stopped, waiting for Blake to say something. I could tell the Mack subject wasn't over for him, but he seemed to be considering all of my words.

"If what you say is true, and Sammy really wanted to heal you both, then why did she tie you up in that cabin?"

"I don't know," I admitted.

"She didn't have to do it that way. Jocelyn was dating Kory, and Mack told Sammy about him being a dragon too. She could've gone to him for help."

"I don't think she trusted Kory."

"Well, even still. She and Kate stole the serum. Why play all the charades? Why not just start the injections then? Why did Sammy think she had to terrorize you?" I had no answer.

Blake hesitated before taking my hands in his. "I hate to be the one to say this, Sam, but I think it's because she wanted to win. She needed you to be afraid, so she could take over."

I didn't want him to be right. Thinking of Sammy more as my savior brought peace. Made me feel like I could trust myself again. I hated that she could be my own inner demon, living within me, waiting for the perfect time to break free.

I took a breath, squaring my shoulders. "Well, let's go find out. Time to talk to Jocelyn."

CHAPTER
Twenty-Five

My house was quiet. We had no intention of letting anyone else know we'd returned home a day early, so we stayed in camo as we crept through my bedroom window. It was Sunday evening. Everyone should be home. By the smells wafting through the house, dinner had probably just ended. My stomach wasn't the only one gurgling. I glanced over at Blake's silhouetted form.

"Hungry?" I whispered.

His stomach growled back at me, and I giggled.

"Dang, that roast smells good. Maybe I can sneak down to the kitchen while you interrogate Jocelyn," he said quietly, his hand finding mine. "Dig us up some food. Feels like we haven't eaten for days."

"With the weekend we've had, I don't think we've stopped long enough to eat," I murmured in agreement. "Let's go find Joc. If we're lucky, she's alone in her room."

Blake didn't answer, just silently turned my bedroom door handle. Ever so slowly, the door cracked open. I knew Blake was peering through the opening to see if the coast was clear. Even with being invisible, it wouldn't do for my mom to see my bedroom door just fly open on its own.

"We're good," Blake whispered.

I followed him through my door, shutting it quietly behind us. Jocelyn's room was at the end of the hall. As we moved past Krista's room, I was grateful she'd left her door open and her stereo on. Though the music wasn't loud, it helped mask the sounds of our movements.

Still, I couldn't help holding my breath as we inched closer to

Jocelyn's closed door. I glanced over at Blake, and then realized he wouldn't be able to see me looking at him. I leaned in closer to his ear. "What should we do? Just open the door and slip in?" I asked.

I felt him shrug. Turning to face me, his lips brushed against my cheek. "Maybe you should go first, in case she's not dressed or something," he whispered.

"Okay," I agreed. My fingers had just wrapped around the door handle when I felt it turn on its own accord underneath my palm. The door swung inward, taking my arm with it. I gasped, my body falling into my sister's.

Jocelyn's eyes widened, her lips opening. Blake threw his hand over her mouth. Within seconds, he somehow pulled all three of us back into her bedroom. I shut the door behind us and then whirled to see my sister thrashing around, her eyes bulging at the invisible thing holding on to her.

Not sure what else to do, I ditched the camo. I held my hand out to her and said, "Jocelyn, it's okay! It's just me."

Now I was sure Jocelyn's eyes were about to pop out of her head. I'd never seen the whites of her eyes before. Maybe she didn't know as much as we'd thought.

Blake dropped the camo too, and Jocelyn honed in on her captor, her eyes narrowing. As her body jerked about in Blake's arms, she grumbled against his hand.

"Blake," I said. "Let her go."

"She's going to scream," he warned.

When Jocelyn growled into his fingers, I sighed. "You're right. She might. We can't talk here. We're going to have to take her somewhere private."

Jocelyn shook her head at us, her wailed 'no' heavily muffled by Blake's fingers. I sickened. This wasn't how I wanted this to go down, with my sister scared out of her mind.

"Jocelyn, we're not going to hurt you, I swear. I just need to ask you some questions. I'm not sure how much you knew about this…" I paused, turning so my wings were visible. Jocelyn didn't seem as taken with the wings as I'd thought she'd be. Maybe she's seen these before. "But I have to know what you know."

Jocelyn eyed me for a moment, her expression hard to read with half her face covered. I bit my lip, debating the best course of action. There was no turning back now since she'd seen me as a damsel. I had no guarantee she wouldn't blab this to my parents the minute we left. I'm committed now. Better get this over with.

"It'll be dark soon. We'll have to just risk no one seeing us fly her out of here," I said to Blake, realizing we should have come ten minutes later so the night could give us a way to hide my sister.

At my statement, Jocelyn stopped wiggling and said something into Blake's fingers. It didn't sound like a protest this time. I met Blake's gaze, both of us debating if we should let her speak.

"Jocelyn, I'm sorry. Blake and I aren't trying to scare you," I said softly, moving closer to her. "I know you and Sammy were close. Trusted one another, confided in each other. Did Sammy ever tell you about us," I pointed at Blake and myself, "being Dragon Fae?"

Jocelyn glanced at Blake, and then back at me. After a moment's hesitation, she nodded her head.

"Okay, great," I said, smiling. "That's a start. So Sammy told you about how she, or we, became a damsel?"

Again, Jocelyn nodded her head. I hated to see Blake's fingers still clamped across her mouth, but I wasn't sure what she'd do if he took them away.

"So you knew Sammy was the one who orchestrated the abduction and the cabin? That she was the one who changed me? With Kate's help?" A muffled, "Yes."

"Did you always know?" I demanded. How could she keep that from me?

Immediately, she shook her head.

Slightly pacified, I asked, "Do you know anything about Kate's disappearance now?"

Jocelyn's eyes narrowed, but she didn't respond.

"Alright. Well, let's talk about Kory then," I said, switching tactics.

Now Jocelyn's eyes were slits. If her mouth weren't covered, I had the feeling her lips would be scowling at me right now.

"I know you're dating Kory," I said, my voice flat. Seeing the way her eyebrows shot up, I added, "Sammy told me. Anyway, I know Kory's been promising you a shot that makes you not gain weight or even age. Guessing you know now this is what he's really been peddling, right?" I turned again, letting my wings flutter.

When Jocelyn didn't respond, I threw my hands up and growled, "We need answers, Joc. Too many lives are at stake." I glanced at the window, relieved to see it was finally growing dark. "I think we can risk it now, Blake. Let's get her out of here."

Jocelyn shook her head, muttering something into Blake's hand. He lifted his fingers ever so slightly and asked, "What was that?"

"I won't scream, I swear," she said, her words rushing out, "You can't take me. Not tonight."

My eyes narrowed at the way she said tonight. "Why? What's happening tonight?" I asked.

She bit her lip, Blake's hand still hovering inches from her mouth. She grimaced. "Nothing. Fine. I'll talk. I'll tell you everything I know, but you need to promise me you'll leave me alone if I do."

Blake and I met eyes, and then he turned to look at my sister. "Wish we could promise that, but you're involved in something a lot bigger than you realize."

She scowled. "I know more than you think, Blake," she spat back at him.

"Great," Blake dryly said. "You won't mind sharing it with us then."

She seemed to consider him for a moment before meeting my gaze. "To answer your question, yes, I know what Kory's serum will do to me, that I'll be like you, but I didn't always. Sammy didn't know either, but she found out through Mack. Of course, she didn't bother to tell me then." She frowned. "She decided to keep all of that to herself. I had no idea what really happened at the cabin. I swear, Samantha. It wasn't until that dance, when I saw your wings, that I knew something was definitely up with you. But Sammy didn't seem to be around anymore, and the last time we spoke before the cabin, she just kept warning me to be careful around Kory."

"Why?" I asked.

"Because she's a freaking hypocrite," Jocelyn muttered. "Warning me that Kory's serum might not be safe, while planning on taking it herself."

I could see how she would see it that way. Sammy had been plotting how to transform herself.

Jocelyn swatted Blake's hand away from her face. "Do you mind? I'm not going to scream."

Blake relented and gave her a little bit more space. Knowing how fast Blake could move, I wasn't too worried.

"If you ask me," Jocelyn continued, folding her arms, "they're a lot more alike than she thinks."

"Who? Sammy and Kory?" I asked, not liking that idea.

"Yeah. They both wanted to change, to become more than just human. That's all that Kory wants too. To improve humanity, make it better."

Blake and I exchanged glances. How much Jocelyn knew of Kory's real designs, we had yet to determine. But this is good. Jocelyn is talking freely with us. For some reason...

"So if Sammy never showed you what she was, how did you find out?" Blake asked.

"Oh, I didn't say she never did, just not then," Jocelyn admitted. "But it was Kory who showed me. He transformed for me." A smile tugged at her lips, despite us being there to see it.

"When?" I asked.

"It wasn't long after that Halloween dance you went to. In fact, I'd been the one to bring it up to him. I couldn't get over how real it looked on you. There was something about it, I just couldn't let go. And well, one thing led to another with Kory, and then he was transforming before me. Telling me what you both were now. He kept asking me who'd taken you to the cabin. Like I knew then."

My mind tried to put the pieces together. I'd gone to the dance. Blake had left for what I'd thought had been California. It'd been during his absence that Kory had stolen away to my bedroom. He had insisted that Blake had been the one to change me, so much so that I'd been scared to death of Blake when he'd returned from Tonbo's Island. I guess Kory really did suspect Blake.

"So when did you learn it was really Sammy and Kate, and not me?" Blake asked.

Jocelyn shifted her weight, her eyes darting to her window. "Sammy told me," she answered, wringing her hands together. "Now, I've answered all of your questions. Will you please go, now?" Her eyes darted to her window again, and a wave of understanding hit me.

"What's the rush, Joc?" I asked, forcing a smile. "Worried you might miss something?"

"No, I'm not worried, just annoyed. As fun as this is, I have other things to do." She tried to scowl at me, but there was no hiding how pale her complexion had become.

"You haven't answered all our questions," I said evenly. "Not even close. Like for starters, when's Kory coming over?"

CHAPTER
Twenty-Six

Blake's surprise was almost as comical as Jocelyn's shock. "He's not," she stammered, but the sudden blush in her cheeks said otherwise.

"Oh good, so we can keep talking then," I insisted, watching my sister squirm under our glares. "So has Kory made good on his promise yet? Are you one of us now?"

She seemed to be weighing her options. Finally, she shook her head. "No. I'm not like you." The defeat in her tone was hard to miss.

Blake tilted his head to the side. "Seems like he would have changed you by now. Wonder what he's waiting for?"

She made a face at him. "I had to give him what he needed first. You can't just change someone without the right DNA." She said it like we should've known this.

Blake snorted, and I suddenly felt sorry for my sister. It was apparent Kory was stringing her along for some reason. The worst part was that she seemed to genuinely care for the jerk.

"Jocelyn," I said, drawing nearer. "If Kory wanted to change you, he would've by now. He's been lying to you. He doesn't need to make your formula different for it to work."

"You're wrong," she said, backing up a step. "He warned me you'd try to stop me, to keep this world from me, like you have the right to decide. Kory's making sure things are just right for me. He doesn't want me to suffer because," she hesitated, "because he loves me."

"Okay, let's say Kory does love you," Blake said evenly. "And who knows, maybe in his own twisted way, he does. What does he mean by the right DNA?"

Jocelyn sighed, rolling her eyes at us. "Again, he needed a good match for me. So the transition would be smooth and painless." She glanced at me and said, "He told me yours was extremely painful, and I don't want that."

I scowled. "Since when does Kory know what I felt?"

Blake's disbelief matched mine. "So Kory needed your DNA to make your own special serum?"

Jocelyn's haughtiness slipped as her eyes darted to the window again. "Not mine," she said, her lips twitching.

I frowned. "Then whose?"

Her eyes shot to the carpet. "Yours," she admitted.

"Mine?" I asked, gaping at her even though she refused to meet my gaze. "Kory wants my blood?"

When she didn't answer right away, Blake said, "Well, he's not getting it. Ever."

The way Jocelyn shifted her weight didn't bode well with me. The mysterious padded envelope Sammy had given Jocelyn tugged at my mind. It couldn't possibly have been that, could it?

"I think he might already have it," I said, my stomach falling.

Jocelyn's eyes met mine, and she nodded slowly.

"What? How?" Blake demanded.

"You said Sammy showed you her wings. Let me guess, back in November, right?" I asked, piecing it all together. The time between passing out in Tonbo's theater and waking up in Jaxon's cave. That short time period that had haunted me for months was finally falling into place. I'd left the theater, stopped at the Outskirts, chatted with some ancients, and then gone to see my sister.

Jocelyn's eyes went out of focus as she said, "It was the first time I'd seen Sammy since, you know, the kidnapping and all that. She just showed up, started telling me how I should break up with Kory. That the shots he was promising me weren't what I thought they were. We had a pretty... heated discussion. I mean, who was she to tell me to break up with him? She just disappeared on me. Completely gone. Then she comes barging into my room, demanding I break up with my boyfriend because the shots will change me? Make me like her? I told her Kory was going to make sure it was easy on me, not like how Blake changed you."

Jocelyn's eyes darted to Blake. "That's when she had the gall to tell me she plotted it out herself! That you had nothing to do with it! How could she tell me not to do something she herself went to great lengths to do? Hypocrite," she muttered.

Well, that explains all the hostility I'd been sensing around my sister lately. She's been mad at Sammy.

"So you asked Sammy for her DNA after that, and she just gave it to you?" Blake incredulously asked.

"Well, no, not exactly." Jocelyn bit her lip. "I knew she wouldn't do it because she didn't want me to change. She kept telling me how it's not what I think. That I would be giving up too much for it. I just kept reminding her—didn't she just do the same thing? Talking about family, telling me how I'd lose Mom and Dad, Krista, never have children of my own."

Jocelyn snorted. "Again. Didn't she just throw our family away when she changed? Didn't she decide being a damsel was more important than being my sister?" Hearing the hitch in her voice, I realized how deeply Jocelyn had loved Sammy.

"You're right," I said, my voice somber. "It does seem like she threw it all away, but you aren't understanding why she did it. She believed it was the only way she and I could have the life we were meant to have. She hoped it would heal us, make us one. I don't think she ever meant to hurt you."

She shook her head at me. "You can keep telling yourself that all you want, but Sammy never cared about anyone else, you in-cluded, Samantha. She only looked out for herself."

"Why do you think that?" Blake asked when I stiffened.

"Because all of her fussing about Kory was a ruse to keep me from becoming a damsel. Like I said, she's a lot more like Kory than she lets on. Just drives me crazy that she acts so high and mighty about it all, when in the end, she wound up in cahoots with him after all."

Even though we'd suspected Sammy might be involved in Kory's schemes, hearing Jocelyn confirm it made my stomach turn.

I crossed my arms. "If that's true, why aren't you mad at Kory too?"

She narrowed her eyes at me. "Because Kory's the only person I trust anymore."

I was temporarily speechless. Her frustration with Sammy was one thing, but why was I getting the brunt end of it too? Blake took a step closer and wrapped an arm around my shoulders. Seeing the contempt in her eyes for him, I wondered what horrible lies Kory had filled her head with.

She threw her hair over her shoulder. "I find it ironic that you both keep acting like I don't know what's really happening, like Kory's keeping things from me, but he's the only one who's been honest through it all."

Seeing how she kept defending him with almost crazed eyes, I felt like my sister had been brainwashed. This can't be my sister. It just can't.

Trying to give her the benefit of the doubt, I said, "I don't think you know about everything. If you did, you wouldn't be saying—"

Her laugh cut my words off. "You think Kory hasn't shown me his plans?" She smiled at me, throwing her weight to one hip. "I know about all of it."

Neither Blake nor I said a word. Jocelyn's vanity was proving extremely valuable. If she wants to boast about what she knows, all the better for us.

"The transformation of the world into Dragon Fae is inevitable," she said, giving Blake a long look. "Honestly, Kory can't see why you keep fighting it. It's the superior race. It's only a matter of time until it takes over completely, and when it does, there needs to be some order to the chaos that will come. That's why he's creating a force that will be able to govern, keep the peace."

Hearing my sister rattle off Kory's propaganda made the hairs on the back of my neck stand on end. Can't decide if I'm more freaked out she bought it or the fact that Kory just might be delusional enough to believe his own bull crap.

"So Kory's told you about his bug army then?" Blake asked, staying focused. I couldn't seem to say anything; my insides were raging. I wanted to scream at Jocelyn, tell her how stupid she was being. Don't think of her as your sister right now.

"It's not a 'bug' army," she said, scowling at him. "He calls them Dragon Defenders because they fight for what's right."

I felt my own eyes bulge out, an almost hysterical laugh bubbling up, shocked with how blind love had made her.

"What's right for who? Kory?" Blake asked. "If it's his sense of right and wrong that governs our future, I'll pass."

She made a face at him.

"So where does Kory keep his bugs... or the Dragon Defenders?" he asked, putting emphasis on his last two words.

"I don't know, but..." She stopped short, her eyes widening.

She's trying not to tell us something. I could sense my sister's predicament. She wants to cooperate so we'll leave. Kory must be coming soon. At the same time, I could tell she was fighting herself on how much to divulge. Seeing how anxious her face had become, it dawned on me.

"But," I finished, "Kory's going to show you tonight, right?"

Her eyes shot the floor, her silence answer enough.

"So how do you know Sammy and Kory are working together again?" Blake asked, still staying focused on gathering information.

My mind shot in an entirely new direction, a plan hatching within me. A plan that just might work. Jocelyn's words cut through my thoughts, though.

"Kory told me Sammy's blood, or yours, would be a close enough match," she said, looking at me. "So I tried to think of how to do it without it seeming strange. Luckily, it wasn't too long after that when Sammy showed up in my room. When I saw how adamant she was that I not change, I knew she'd never willingly give her sample. Since Kory had already told me about his plans for the future, how we needed something to protect us, I changed my tactics. I told her I needed her blood sample to help make the Defenders stronger."

Blake and I glanced at one another.

"So Kory told you about his plans before he'd sent me on that goose chase to kill my own brother?" Blake asked, his brows gathering.

For the first time, Jocelyn's haughtiness faltered. Her bottom lip stuck out a bit as she asked, "What are you talking about?"

"Your precious boyfriend convinced me there was a bug," Blake said through a tight jaw. "And despite what he told you, bugs are not defenders of truth. They're killers that the Germans developed in the hopes of making super soldiers. Kory injected Jaxon, my brother, with the DNA of the last bug killed. But the one thing Kory hadn't counted on was Jaxon being out of even his control. So he hatched a scheme that sent me after my own brother."

My sister's blank stare relayed her ignorance. "I don't understand."

"What don't you understand? That Kory lied? Or that he's not the man you thought he was?" I sarcastically asked. "Kory's the real monster if you ask me."

"If that were true, why did Sammy go along with it then?" Jocelyn countered, seeming to have recovered from her moment of uncertainty. I stared at her, the memory of the padded envelope mocking me. "Why would Kory want to kill one of his Defenders? He's been so careful to develop them. He's had a team of experts helping him get it right."

"Guess we know who that team was now," Blake said to me. He glanced back at my sister and asked, "What do you mean by Sammy went along with it?"

"When I explained everything to Sammy—about the Dragon Defenders, how they're necessary to keep the world safe from the future that's coming whether or not we like it, she suddenly changed her mind. She said she could appreciate what Kory was trying to do. She told me to give her an hour and she'd bring me what I needed. After that, she left."

"Let me guess, she came back and gave you a vial in a padded envelope," I muttered.

My sister nodded, and another piece of the puzzle fell into place.

CHAPTER
Twenty-Seven

By the way my sister began fidgeting with the hem of her shirt, her eyes darting to her alarm clock, I knew the appointed meeting time was almost there. Even though I probably had another hundred questions to ask her, they could wait. This was a golden opportunity, and I wasn't about to miss it.

"So you gave Kory my blood sample and then what? Why haven't you been transformed yet? What's Kory waiting for now?" I asked.

Jocelyn bit her lip. "He's wanted to... He just got so busy with his Defenders. You see, when I told him what I'd done to convince Sammy to give it to me, he'd said I was a genius. That the entire world would be grateful to me, for my vision of the future. He said he had to hurry back and start using the sample right away. That it couldn't wait. But he promised me that as soon as everything was working right, he'd take me to see the Defenders, and then he'd change me. It'd be safer that way."

I folded my arms. "So you haven't seen him since? He just took the sample and left you?"

"No, he hasn't left me." She huffed. "He's been here several times."

"So how are you so sure he's going to ever make good on his promise?" Blake asked. The glint in his eye let me know he was trying to bait her.

"Because he told me the last time he was here that tonight's the night!" she yelled back at him.

Bingo! That was all I needed to know. I turned to Blake. "You should take Jocelyn away from here."

He stared at me before shaking his head. "No way. I know

what you're thinking, Sam, but it's too risky."

"Blake, it's perfect! Don't you see how perfect this is?" I didn't say more; I didn't want Jocelyn to know what I could do.

Jocelyn's eyes narrowed as she pointed to her door. "I've told you everything I know. So you both better go now!"

My gaze pleaded with Blake, who still looked like he wanted to argue. Running his hands through his hair, he grumbled something under his breath.

"I hope you know what you're up against," he said with an exhale. In an instant, he was sweeping me up in his arms, kissing my mouth soundly. The next, he grabbed hold of Jocelyn's body, leaving through the window so fast that all I heard was one stifled yelp from my sister.

Just like that, I was alone in my sister's room. I didn't waste time, transforming into the exact replica. I glanced down at the shirt Jocelyn had been tugging at just moments before. The only thing left to do was to decide how Jocelyn would act around Kory.

Opting for confident, I squared my shoulders and waited. It only took moments until I could make out mint and musky cologne in the air. Wow, we cut that close.

Making the rash decision to pretend to be Jocelyn had been easy; now the reality of it crashed down on me as questions of how to act like my sister barraged me. Starting with should I go open the window? Should I be the forward one, trying to touch Kory while invisible? Or do I wait until he appears and act surprised he's already in my room? Jocelyn wouldn't be able to detect his scent after all....

Luckily, my bedroom window opened and Kory appeared almost simultaneously as he climbed through. My stomach dropped to my toes as I remembered Kory and Jocelyn were not just friends, they were together.

He didn't waste time, closing the distance between us. I had to force my legs to move toward him, plastering a smile across my face. Really, I wanted to knock him to the ground and beat the tar out of his white teeth. How could he trick my sister like this! Jocelyn was only his latest victim. I wanted to kill him for what he'd done to Jaxon and Blake. Tearing two brothers apart, destroying Jaxon's life.

I swallowed back my rage, trying not to tremble under the hands that reached for me. Unfortunately, being in Jocelyn's form didn't act as a buffer for how Kory's arms wrapped around me made my skin crawl. I knew I would lose it if he tried to kiss me.

"I've missed you," Kory whispered into my ear. He dropped his lips to my collarbone. Inhaling deeply, he murmured, "Mm... you always smell so good."

I forced the words to come out. "I've missed you too."

He planted light kisses along the base of my neck, working his way up to my jaw.

I can't do this! my mind screamed. I pushed him back a little. "Kory, you promised me tonight was the night," I said, forcing what I hoped looked like a flirty grin.

Even as I said the words, I realized I hadn't thought the other part of that equation out. Would I actually let Kory inject me? There was no telling what he had concocted for my sister. The object of this charade was to find out where the bugs were being kept. That was it. It wasn't to become another science experiment.

"I know I did." His brown eyes didn't leave my face. For a moment, we just stared at each other.

Panicked he wasn't buying my act, I leaned in and forced myself to plant a few light kisses on his cheek. "Sorry, I just can't wait to finally be like you. I want to be on your side when the world changes."

I felt Kory's body relax with my last words. He pulled me back into his arms, tightly squeezing me. "There's nothing I'd like more." Hating every moment he touched me, I was relieved when he let me go.

Glancing around my room, he asked, "So did you get everything prepared like I asked you to?"

Sure hope so. I bit my lip. Figuring my sister would have done everything for this night to be right, I said with confidence, "Yes."

"Perfect," Kory said, moving toward the small carry-on leaning against my sister's dresser. He picked it up, adjusting the strap to be longer. "Then it looks like there's nothing keeping us from leaving. Are you ready to go?"

I nodded, trying to act eager and excited. Really, I felt like a buffoon smiling back at him. He must have attributed my odd behavior to nerves because his gaze softened as he drew nearer to me.

"Don't worry. It will be like when I flew you over the lakes. Only this time, the ride will be longer. Just relax and let me do the rest, okay?" The way his eyes swept up and down my body, I couldn't help the quick glance down to make sure I was still my sister.

"Okay, sounds good," I said, relieved to see I hadn't changed back. Looking up, I caught Kory's arched brow. Maybe Jocelyn would have said something different. He recovered quickly from whatever he'd been thinking, slinging my bag over his shoulder. The carry-on wasn't exactly made to hang around someone's neck, but it didn't seem to bother Kory to have the luggage banging against his hip.

I took a step closer to him. I'd had Blake carry me enough times to know he would probably hold me like a bride being carried over the threshold. I wrapped my hands around the base of his neck, more of a gesture to get going, but Kory didn't lift me up.

Instead, he cupped my face with his fingers. "Thank you for being patient with me, Jocelyn. I know it's been hard waiting. I want you to know how much I appreciate you believing in me. In my vision for the future."

I could only stare at him, conflicted on so many levels. For that split second, I truly believed Kory had feelings for my sister, and that maybe deep down, he really believed his actions were justified by some greater good he envisioned for the future.

On the other hand, I still wanted to beat the tar out of him for being such an idiot.

"You've been worth the wait, Kory." The words tasted foul coming out of my mouth. "I'll do whatever it takes to be with you forever."

I must have said the right thing because Kory closed the gap between us, kissing my mouth hard enough that I staggered back. Instantly, his arms snaked around me, pressing our bodies close, keeping me from falling. I realized he was airborne when we were both horizontal, with nothing below me. Who needs a bed when you've got wings? It took all of my willpower to not let my own wings rescue me from the desperate situation I'd thrown myself into. One thing I did know for certain, my sister would have no qualms about this scenario going too far.

Crap! I racked my brain for a plausible reason to halt his progress, his hands moving with confidence around my body.

"Kory," I blurted. "Why don't we get out of here first? My dad has gotten all paranoid lately. You should've seen the way he grilled Krista the other day because he thought she'd had a guy in her room."

Kory grunted, setting me back down on the ground. "Honestly," he said, catching his breath. "I don't know why you still live at home. Such a hassle."

I grinned up at him. "I won't be for much longer."

He smiled back at me. "True." Finally, he swept me up in his arms. "You're right. Let's go somewhere a little more private."

I wrapped my arms around his neck, leaning into his chest, commanding myself to look pleased about it.

"And I know just the place," he added with a wink. "But first, you're going to need a jacket."

CHAPTER
Twenty-Eight

It didn't take long for me to be inwardly cursing the fact Kory had insisted I bundle up as if I were going sledding. For whatever reason, Dragon Fae didn't seem to feel the weather around them as much, which most of the time proved convenient. I tried to ignore the sweat dripping into my eyes, smashing my face against Kory's chest to wipe it away. Misinterpreting my gesture, he pulled me even closer, probably trying to warm me up. Just what I need. More warmth.

We'd been flying for over three hours now. I'd seen enough to know we'd passed over California and were now somewhere in the Pacific Ocean. Past Tonbo's Islands.

I tried to take in every detail I could. Unfortunately, with miles and miles of dark, swelling water below us, there wasn't much in the way of land markers.

"Kory," I said, tipping my chin up so my lips were against his cheek. I knew it was the only way to get his attention. The roar of the air passing around us made hearing one another difficult.

He immediately slowed down, tilting his head to make eye contact.

"How far are we going?" I asked, purposely keeping it vague.

"Another three hours to the halfway point. We'll stop and rest there."

Another three hours is only halfway there? I hadn't counted on his secret base being quite so far away. Six straight hours of being stuck in the same position was going to drive me crazy.

"Oh. That much further?" I asked. Calculating the distance we'd already covered, I added, "I'm no expert on geography, but it feels like we should be hitting Hawaii soon." I gave him the best flirtatious smile I could muster, "I wouldn't mind stopping there."

"Today's your lucky day then, my love." I cringed at the term of endearment. "Because I just so happen to know a great place for breakfast on the island of Kauai."

So Hawaii is the halfway point. Good to know.

Concern flooded his eyes as he peered down at me. "Are you comfortable enough? Want me to carry you differently?" he asked.

I wanted to say I was fine, but my legs were asleep and my lower back ached. I'd give anything to straighten out my knees. "I'm okay; you're the one I'm worried about. How are you carrying me this long? You don't even seem winded."

"Don't worry, you weigh nothing to me."

Gag me. I was sure that comment probably made Jocelyn go all giddy. I forced a laugh.

"Here," he said, letting go of my knees. Instantly, my legs whipped out below me. I yelped in surprise as panic gripped me. Not because I feared falling, more from feeling my wings itching to save me.

"Sorry, didn't mean to scare you," Kory said, pulling me in against his body. Even though it felt wonderful to stretch my legs, being face to face with him was not ideal.

"That better?" he asked.

Hoping to avoid further eye contact, I ducked my head against his chest. "Yes, thank you." Really, it was so much worse.

I hated to admit to myself, that one thing was for certain. From what I'd seen so far, Kory did seem to care for my sister. I didn't know if I should be comforted by the fact, or disturbed.

I wanted to lose myself in the way the moonbeams danced off the water, bathing the white sand in a surreal glow. I could see why Hawaii was the destination of lovers, and the island of Kauai was no exception. Exhausted from almost seven hours of flight, I stretched my legs into the cool sand, loving how it felt on my bare toes. I'd stripped off my winter coat and rolled my pant legs up, wanting to enjoy the night air on my skin. The soothing sound of water lapping against the beach was almost enough to block out the guy sprawled out next to me. Almost.

I glanced down to see his chest was still heaving from catching his breath. As soon as we landed, Kory had crashed down, at first making to pull me down next to him. I'd quickly made the excuse of him needing to rest and that I wanted to see the beach for a minute. He must have bought it, or maybe he was too wiped out to argue. With his arm draped over his eyes, his breathing settling down, I supposed I should feel some remorse he had to carry me the entire way.

I felt only a smug satisfaction. Still, seeing his body stretched out next to me, his wings twitching as he rested, I had to admit that Kory wasn't unattractive. Even though I hadn't given him much thought over the years, I knew my friend, Jen, was still obsessed with him. What would she give to trade places with me now? Not to mention, my super picky sister. She can have any guy in Colorado for crying out loud, and she picked Kory? It didn't matter that Kory's features were handsome; his actions repulsed me. His personal agenda made it hard to sit next to him and act as if I were in heaven.

I felt a heavy hand land on my thigh; it took all my willpower not to fling it off me. Why didn't I think this through better? In the split second I'd taken to hatch my plan, I hadn't processed what these scenarios would be like. I figured I'd discover where the base was, make my escape when Kory wasn't looking, and get back to Blake with vital information. But now... I'm stuck on an island over three thousand miles off the coast of California, and we are only halfway there! And every minute it takes for us to get there, I have to pretend to be in love with this creep!

I groaned inwardly as Kory slowly sat up, pulling me into his arms as he did.

"Sorry about that; I just needed a second to recharge," he murmured, kissing my neck.

"I didn't mind. Just sorry you had to lug me here," I said,

swallowing the bile creeping up my throat. My pulse was racing, my mind working hard to find some way to escape his hold.

"I'm happy to carry you," he said, his lips working their way behind my ear. "I love everything about your body."

Ugh. "Well, you won't have to carry me much longer," I said, purposely trying to break up his kisses. He'd made his way to my jawline, his lips making their way to my mouth. I'm going to die!

To my surprise, he sat back a little. "True," he said. Scratching the faint stubble at his chin, he added, "Hey, about that."

His tone warranted me sitting back a little too. Sounds like he's about to stall some more.

"Mind if we go see the Defenders first?" he asked. "Before I change you?"

"No, not at all," I said, probably too quickly. That would be perfect!

He glanced over at me, a question forming on his lips. Realizing Jocelyn might have made a stink about waiting any longer, I added with a forced laugh, "I guess I'm a little nervous about the whole shots thing, so I don't mind seeing your operation first. Besides, I want to know how Sammy's blood helped you out."

His shoulders relaxed a bit as he chuckled. "You and needles. I promise you won't feel a thing. I have everything prepped for you."

"Thank you for making it easier for me. So... should we get going?"

His eyes widened. "What? Now?"

I nodded and he shook his head, laughing at me. "I'm still part human, Jocelyn. I need a few hours of sleep before I fly another seven. Besides, it's after one AM. Aren't you a little bit tired?"

"Yeah, I guess I am. I've just waited for this day for so long. I don't want to waste any more time." My words rushed out.

"Well, time's the one thing we have more than enough of now," he drawled out, pulling me back into his arms. "I made sure everything will be perfect for you. Besides, your mom's so thrilled with the modeling gig I got you in LA that she shouldn't bat an eye when we tell her your week trip turned into a longer opportunity. We don't have to rush this."

I stared back at him, piecing together what he was telling me. Guess I know Jocelyn's cover story now. So what, they were going to just tell my parents she got a permanent job in LA and wouldn't be moving back? They better plan on taking some actual pics of Jocelyn because Mom won't be satisfied until she sees proof of this job. Like a freaking billboard of her daughter.

"I know, thank you for that," I murmured back at him as his lips crept their way back to my mouth. "So," I said between his kisses, "Are we going to sleep on the beach then?"

He rocked back a bit. "Why, want to?" he asked, his voice deep. "Could be magical out here."

The sensation of ants crawling up my legs saved me from answering right away. Reaching down with my free hand, I scratched my skin, desperate to rid myself of whatever critter was there. "Would be great if I wasn't so itchy," I mumbled.

He glanced down at my calves. "Mm... sand fleas," he said, standing up and reaching down to pull me up as well. "Luckily for us, I've made other sleeping arrangements." He gestured to the house nestled in lush island flora above the beach we'd landed on. I wouldn't have even been able to see it if it weren't for the lights on in a few of the windows.

"Come on," he said, walking up the sand, pulling me along with him. "You're going to love Malekesi and Lamani."

I glanced over at him. "Who are they?" "They own the home I always stay in when I go to and from my facility. Don't worry, they know all about us. And," he added, squeezing my shoulders as we walked, "Malekesi makes the best food. You'll love it."

Dread trickled through my entire body. Dumb me! Of course we'd have to spend the night somewhere. Can't expect Kory to fly me fourteen straight hours.

"Great," I lied. All I could focus on was the way Kory's hand was massaging my shoulder as we moved closer to the house.

This is bad. Real bad. There's no way I'm spending the night with Kory. Never mind the kisses, I'll switch back to me for sure.

CHAPTER
Twenty-Nine

I could have kissed Malekesi for not only stuffing me full of the most delicious food I'd ever tasted, but for insisting Kory and I have separate rooms to sleep in after our stomachs were ready to pop. Kory had rolled his eyes in amusement, but he didn't argue with her. What Malekesi lacked in height, she made up in girth. Her commanding presence had more to do with her infectious smile than with the stern finger she wagged at Kory when he had tried to follow me into my room.

"No sir, not in my house," she'd said, ushering him to the room next to mine. "I see no rings on your fingers. You treat her with respect."

Kory had opened and shut his mouth several times, but in the end, he'd shrugged. I hurried into my room before he could come up with some excuse to follow me. Glad to have my sister's suitcase, I flipped open the lid and rifled through her belonging. Seeing the amount of clothes she had packed, I had a hunch my sister hadn't planned to return from this trip. A lot of opened-back shirts.

A small part of me felt bad. I took away what she's been looking forward to for months. Feels like I crashed her wedding or something. I had no doubt now Kory cared for her on some level, but the jury was still out on whether he was using her.

Trying to find something decent to sleep in, I was horrified, but not surprised, by all the sheer and skimpy nighties I found. Sighing, I settled on an open-backed T-shirt. If I have to choose between my front or backside being covered, I'll opt for my front. Relieved to find jogging shorts, I quickly changed, snapped the light off, and slipped into bed.

A few seconds later, someone slid into the bed next to me. Although not visible, the hint of mint and musky cologne was a dead giveaway. Hands wrapped around me from behind, pulling me toward him to spoon. I tried not to stiffen. Great, now what?

"Kory," I whispered to the dark room, "Malekesi is going to kill you if she finds you in here."

He snorted. "Since when do you worry about getting caught?"

Crap. My brain screamed to find a solution to this precarious situation. There was no way I was letting him do more than the kisses he'd already planted on me. Not to mention what might happen if I fell asleep...

"Since I met a Hawaiian woman," I responded, half serious.

He chuckled. "Relax, no one's going to know."

"Uh, Kory... I..." I stammered as he begin planting kisses along the back of my neck. "Would you hate me horribly if we just slept tonight?"

His lips withdrew from my skin. With the sudden silence that followed, I was half tempted to turn around to see his expression.

"Not at all," he said, his tone definitely strained. "Everything okay?"

I rotated to look him in the eyes; I couldn't afford to blow my cover now. "Yes, I'm just really tired. I had no idea how wiped out flying would make me."

His gaze softened a bit. "So," he said, his voice almost hesitant, "it's not because you're having second thoughts about... us?"

"What? No. Why would you say that?"

"Well, you just haven't seemed like yourself today," he said, "I mean, you've usually already jumped my bones like three times."

I couldn't help my face flushing. This was getting to be too much for me. I shouldn't be living my sister's intimate moments!

"Kory, that's not it, I swear. I'm just a pile of nerves. I think I'll feel better once we get all settled in. Maybe after I've seen your Defenders and I see how you're going to change me, I can relax more."

He cocked his head to the side, his arm still draped around my body. "Sorry, I guess I didn't realize how stressful this must be for you." He leaned down and kissed my cheek. "I promise you have nothing to be worried about. The transformation will be painless. I will be there for you every step of the way."

"Thanks," I said, praying he'd stop kissing my neck. To my relief, he did. To his credit, he settled down, still holding on to me, but not groping me.

"Goodnight, my love," he whispered, nestling his lips against the back of my neck.

"Goodnight," I said, hoping it didn't sound too stiff. I waited in silence. I wasn't sure if he was upset or falling asleep until his breathing slowed down and deepened. Only when his arm went slack around my middle did I dare scoot further away from him. Once there was some space between our bodies, I commanded myself not to fall asleep.

Shouldn't be too hard right? Who needs sleep? Just think about tomorrow. We'll finally know where the Defenders are. Then all I've got to do is slip away when Kory's back is turned, fly as fast as I can home, and pray no one follows me. Like Kory... or all those Defenders...

I frowned. My escape plan was looking a bit bleak, if I was honest.

CHAPTER
Thirty

"**N**ever been so happy to get somewhere in my life," I muttered in complete honesty. Traveling to Kory's secret base had taken almost two full days of fast flying. Even with leaving Kauai early, the seven hours it took to arrive felt never ending. With my feet sinking into white sand, I glanced around, seeing nothing but tropical green trees hugging the beach.

"Where are we?" I asked, stretching my arms above my head, hearing my back pop in several places. Dying to be me again. I knew now that being in my sister's form for this long straight was a huge risk. The night had proven to be a long one. Luckily, for me, the one time I did succumb to sleep and awoke to discover I'd morphed back into my own form, Kory had been sound asleep. What would I have done if he'd seen me? The adrenaline rush after that made it easy to stay wide awake, counting down the minutes until sunrise. I knew I was much of the reason we had such an early start. Kory's grumblings had let me know he hadn't been thrilled to 'hit the road' as the sun rose.

Now, walking on the beach, my feet sinking into the sand, I was grateful my own nervousness kept the adrenaline pumping. I needed it.

Kory grinned at me, all signs of grumpiness gone. "It's a small island in the Vava'u Islands."

"The where?"

"Tonga," he said.

"We're in Tonga?" I repeated, wanting to make sure I knew exactly where we were. I had to find my way back here someday, hopefully with a small army.

"The Vava'u Islands are a group of islands in Tonga. I think there are like seventy small islands in it. This one," his hand gestured to our surroundings, "is known as Ofu Island." He glanced over at me. "To the rest of the world, anyway." I lifted an eyebrow. "But not to the Dragon Fae world, I take it?"

"Nope," he said, his grin spreading. "It won't be long until Ofu becomes the new world capital."

I could only stare at him, not sure if I should laugh or be horrified at the absurdity of his statement. "World capital? You think this small island will be the Dragon Fae's headquarters?"

He nodded. "Not just this island, but all of Tonga. All of Polynesia, in fact. But Ofu will always be special because this is where the Defenders were born."

Kory's arm draped around my shoulders was the least of my worries. Kory's a delusional maniac. Since we remained on foot, it allowed me to ask questions. When we were flying, it proved difficult. I wasn't about to waste any time.

"So why here? Why Ofu?" I asked. "There doesn't seem to be much around. I don't see any buildings."

He chuckled. "Yes, well, don't expect a lot of air-conditioned rooms here either. I learned there was a parcel of this island for sale a while back. When I inquired further, it turned out a corporation in trouble owned not only the parcel, but also the entire island. They were in a tough spot financially, so I bought it."

"The parcel?"

"No, the island. This is ours, Jocelyn."

I swallowed. My sister would be knocking Kory down with kisses right now, that much I was sure. All I could manage was a smile in his direction. I saw the hurt flash through his eyes.

"That's amazing," I said. Not wanting to blow it all before I'd actually seen the Defenders, I leaned over and kissed his cheek. "You are incredible, Kory. I don't deserve you," I gestured to the island, "or any of this."

My words must have appeased him because he pulled me closer and kissed the top of my forehead. "Of course you do. You aren't just anyone to me, Jocelyn."

Apparently not. I hated seeing this sincere side of Kory. It made everything I needed to do that much harder. My sister, through no real fault of her own, fell in love with a psychopath.

"What do the people on the other islands around here think? Do they know about the Defenders?"

"Oh, they know about them."

I glanced over at him as we made our way further into the tropical juggle. So far, I'd seen nothing manmade. Every step felt like I was leaving civilization further behind. Reminded me a lot of some of the Outskirts we'd visited.

Kory met my gaze. "Who do you think made up the Defenders?"

I gasped, despite myself. "You changed Tongans to make them?"

"Yes, mostly Tongans, a few Samoans."

"I... did they even want to be changed?"

Kory glanced over at me and laughed. "Of course they did. I didn't force anyone. They simply saw the appeal like you did."

"Yeah, but I just want to be a normal damsel. From what you told me, the Defenders are created to fight. There's a big difference," I said, glad my point was a valid one. I couldn't imagine anyone in their right mind choosing to become what Jaxon was. No one would. Kory must've have lied to them...

He nodded along. "True, but that's just it. Did you know the Pacific Islanders are over represented in the military, especially the Navy Seals? I heard somewhere that taking in their smaller population numbers, they are over two hundred percent over-represented in fact."

I stared at him. "So because they like to sign up, that makes them..." I had to force myself not to say the word 'killers'. Instead, I managed to ask, "Want to be made into super fighters?"

Kory shrugged. "I'm not sure if more islanders sign up for the military as a means to escape island life, or if they do feel an innate desire to defend and protect their family more than others. Who knows the reason? It's just a fact. I saw an opportunity here, and I took it." He grinned at me. "Their natural athletic build didn't hurt either."

So in other words, Kory made bugs even bigger than Jax- on. I couldn't stop the shudder that rippled across my shoulders. Luckily for me, Kory didn't seem to notice because he was gestur- ing to the small village now popping out from among the trees.

"Come on. I want you to meet a few of my Defenders."

"Okay," I said as my stomach knotted. What if these 'Defend- ers' craved me like Jaxon? What if they could see through my charade?

Within moments of Kory mentioning the Defenders, a large Tongan man approached us. Standing several inches above Kory, his shoulder width was probably double mine. I gaped up at him. Since Kory had told me on Kauai, I knew the wraparound, Hawai- ian-looking skirt was a called a lavalava. Lamani had been wear- ing one too.

I saw no wings on his brown, bare back. The man smiled, dimpling his cheeks and revealing a row of white teeth. With curly, black hair and deep-set eyes, his features were more attrac- tive than menacing. His barrel chest, massive biceps, and thigh muscles were another story. I didn't even want to imagine his humungous body in bug form.

"Jocelyn, this here is my right-hand man, Kalepe."

"Mālō e lelei," Kalepe said, his voice as deep as the ocean itself.

"Ah. Hello," I said, unsure what he'd said to me.

"Mālō e lelei means hello," Kory explained as Kalepe reached out to shake my hand. I placed my hand in his, feeling it swal- lowed up in warm, calloused palms.

"Don't worry, I speak English too," Kalepe said, giving my hand a vigorous workout. When he released me from his iron grip, I could only stare back at him. "It's a pleasure to finally meet Miss Kory."

"I've been looking forward to finally meeting you, Kalepe, too," I answered, slightly weirded out to be referred to as 'Miss Kory'.

"Kalepe was one of the first ones to get Sammy's DNA," Kory stated in a matter-of-fact manner.

I swallowed hard, my face flushing.

Kalepe beamed back at me with pride in his eyes. "I'm honored. Thank you for making it possible."

"Ah... you're welcome," I said as he pumped my hand with his again. There was no doubt that Kalepe seemed to be in control of his Defender side. Makes me wonder...

"So, you think having Sammy's blood helped?" I asked Kory.

His eyes widened as he nodded. "Yes, most definitely."

"How so?" I asked.

"Maybe it'd be easier if we show you. Everything ready for us, Kalepe?" Kory asked, wrapping an arm around my shoulders and steering me toward the village again. We commenced on foot, which made me wonder what would happen if Kalepe morphed. Would he be as ugly as Jaxon? Would his wings be thick and corded, his head bald, his eyes too wide and black?

"Yes, sir," he said brightly, snapping me out of my dark imaginings. "Everything has been prepared, like you asked." He pointed to the left where I saw a simple lean-to structure. Without walls, logs formed its shape. Vines and large leaves made up the thatched roof. Two men were covering a large stack of stones with broad-leaved branches. Smoke curled out from under gray stones. The aroma of cooked bacon filled the air.

Kalepe continued, "The umu is cooking pigs for tonight's feast. The Defenders want to honor your return, Kory, and we have something special planned for your ceremony, Miss Jocelyn."

Kory nodded along. To me, he explained. "See those rocks over there?"

I nodded quickly as dread trickled through me. What was the ceremony Kalepe referred to? Surely not changing Jocelyn into a damsel, right?

"That's an underground oven," Kory explained. "It's where they cook their food on special occasions, like today."

Staring at Kory's grin, I could only think one thing. I needed to get out of here and fast. I was in enemy territory.

Another Tongan bounded up to us, his grin from ear to ear. Seeing how tightly he embraced Kory and then turned his delighted eyes back to me, I sickened, realizing something else.

Swooping in and destroying the Defenders might not be as simple as we'd hoped. These Tongans aren't the enemy—no more than Jaxon is. Kory's using them. Brainwashing people to accommodate his hidden agenda.

CHAPTER
Thirty-One

This was the moment I'd dreaded and longed for since I'd set out on this crazy ride with Kory. Finally, I get to see the Defenders' headquarters.

After chatting with several more Tongans who were busy setting up the area for the night's festivities, Kory had informed Kalepe that he wanted to show me the progress they'd made first-hand. Kalepe had told us he'd meet up with us in a minute; there were a few last things he needed to oversee.

It had only taken us a few minutes by flight, with Kory holding me, to stop in front of the only real building I'd seen on the island. Kory told me he needed a state-of-the-art facility. Walking through the front door of the squat, stucco building, I was surprised at how hot it was inside, though.

Kory glanced over at me as I lifted my hair up, tying it into a knot. "Sorry about no AC. Don't worry; it's something I'm working on for us."

I shrugged. "I don't mind. Besides," I glanced up at the ceiling, "there are nice fans everywhere."

Kory seemed pleased by my response, giving my shoulder a gentle squeeze. I was glad he didn't try to make a romantic moment out of it. Perhaps the island's humidity and heat was enough of a deterrent. I didn't want anyone to touch me. Being indoors, you lost the nice island breeze.

Kory led us down a short corridor that opened up to a square space—one entire wall covered in clear glass. I stepped closer, my curiosity getting the better of me. I had to know what lay on the other side.

I couldn't help the gasp that escaped me. It looked like I was staring into an old army hospital wing, with dozens upon dozens of white beds forming straight lines across the floor. Only there were no war soldiers filling the beds, only Polynesian men. Hooked up to IVs. All seeming asleep. I saw no monstrous forms, no bug-like faces, no wings...

"I don't understand. Are these the ones being changed into Defenders?" I asked.

"They are already Defenders. These are some of the last ones to receive Sammy's DNA. They've all been sedated, in case you're wondering, so they aren't in their defender form right at the moment. Once they have completed the process, they will be like Kalepe. Free to roam around and be normal, until they are needed to transform."

"And then what happens?"

"When I need them, they will be ready," he said, not really answering my question.

"So they don't just fly around like us?" I asked, wondering just what these Defenders were really like. Maybe they had less control than what Kory was making it out to seem. Maybe they were a little more like Jaxon after all.

Kory gave me a strange look, and I realized my blunder. "I mean, like you do. And I will soon," I quickly added.

"No, they don't," he said with a tight jaw. His face brightened a bit. "But that part has gotten better, thanks to your contribution from your sister."

"What do you mean?"

He seemed to hesitate. "Well, one drawback to being a Defender is that they aren't quite as human as you will be as a damsel. Or what you see me as now."

"Less human, how?" I loved that as Jocelyn, I got to ask questions without him getting suspicious.

"You and I still look like ourselves—are roughly the same shape and size. Defenders get much larger. Their wings are different. Their faces are... not quite the same."

So in other words, I wanted to say, they are every bit the monster Jaxon is.

I stared out the glass, getting a rough estimate of how many beds there were. Three rows of twelve. Makes thirty-six. Thirty-six bugs. I wanted to puke.

"So Kalepe and the rest of the islanders are already Defenders, just not in their form then?"

Kory nodded.

"So how many are there total?"

"Kalepe was part of the first batch. I only did it to twelve with him. Wanted to make sure it'd work and have no adverse reactions. When I saw how well it worked, we set up this room. I think we've filled it three times now already."

Three times thirty-six, plus twelve. My head was spinning. There were over a hundred bugs! How many more did he plan to change? Time to find out.

"You said these aren't the last ones. How many more do you need to change?"

"There are still twenty more Defenders I need to give Sammy's DNA to. They will be next in here, after these guys are done. Then everyone will be back to normal." Normal. Ha. Hardly. "Can I see them?"

"Who?" he asked.

"The ones you haven't given Sammy's DNA too, yet. You said it made a big difference. Just wanted to know what they were like." I pointed out the glass. "Before this."

Kory's lips hitched to the side. "I was planning on showing you, but now I'm not so sure." "How come?" I turned to face him.

"I don't want to freak you out since they are very different from what you'll become."

"Are you worried that I'll change my mind?" I tried to give him a reassuring smile. Really, I was dying to see these raw Defenders. Were they more like Jaxon? Because what I'd seen of Kalepe, he seemed a lot more in control of his inner demon. Did my DNA really make the difference? If it did, why hadn't it worked on Jaxon? I more than remembered how he'd already sampled my blood, deep within his cave.

I tried not to shudder at that memory and took a step closer to Kory, hating I had to reach out and caress the face I wanted to slap. "Nothing could change my mind. I want to understand the world I'm going to be part of, that's all."

Kory leaned into my hand and kissed it. Ugh...

"Okay. But promise me that you won't freak out, kay?"

"You have my word."

He pulled my hand down from his lips and led us from the room, back into the corridor. This time, we veered to the right. A few paces down, he stopped and turned toward a metal door. It seemed out of place, since the rest of the doors in the place had been made out of wood.

Seeming like he came out of nowhere, Kalepe was suddenly standing behind us. Sweat beaded on his forehead, his chest heaving as he tried to catch his breath. Did he run here?

"Didn't want you going in alone, just in case," Kalepe explained quickly, swiping his forehead with a handkerchief.

Not noticing any pockets in his lavalava, I wondered where the cloth had even come from. When he tucked one edge of it in at the side of his clothes, my question was answered. Seeing how tight Kalepe's muscles were at the moment, the danger of the situation weighed down on me. Twenty bugs were on the other side of this door. Maybe I will be seeing Kalepe in his Defender form after all.

"Thanks, Kalepe, but I'm sure we will be just fine." Kory proceeded to pull a key from his pocket. With a few twists, he unlocked the door.

He pushed it open, and I sucked in my breath. Here goes nothing.

Even expecting to see a barrier between the Defenders and us, I was still shocked at the cell-like cages before me, two rows of ten, with a narrow walkway between them. Within the barred-up up cages, monstrous, brown, winged bodies lay sprawled out. Most appeared to be asleep or resting. Some gazed about with boredom. One look at their oversized heads and bulging, black eyes caused adrenaline to tingle through me. It was unearthly quiet.

Kalepe wasted no time and stepped further into the room, between the cages. The Defenders stared back at him with little interest. Kory pulled me in as well, licking his lips and fidgeting with my fingers. For all his show of bravado, the way his eyes darted to the cages and back at me, I could tell he wasn't as comfortable in this room as his comrade was.

I squared my shoulders, telling myself there was nothing to be scared of. They were all in cages after all. I'd passed the first few when Defender heads began popping up. Necks turned my way. One by one, their nasty black eyes honed in on me.

I gulped back the panic. It was like seeing twenty Jaxon's, only bigger, blacker, and with even more fanged teeth. Almost in unison, heads reared back and a fever-pitched roar ripped through the room. Instantly, the Defenders were on their feet, grasping through the bars with clawed hands, all trying to reach me.

Kory jumped back immediately, pulling me back with him, cursing as we went.

Kalepe doubled back too, muttering, "Wow, wonder what's got them all fired up today?"

I had a hunch I knew what it was. Sensing the bugs' lust for me, I didn't protest as Kory led us out of the room and back into the corridor. I hadn't realized how badly I was shaking until he wrapped his arms around me. I caught the funny look he tried to hide when I met his gaze.

"I'm sorry, Jocelyn. They don't usually act like that."

I wanted to say, Wanna bet? Instead, I said, "I'm fine. It was just a little freaky, that's all."

"It was freaky," Kalepe confirmed as he joined us. "They are settling down now, sir."

Kory nodded back. "Good. We're going to my hut to rest before tonight's activities."

"Good idea, sir. I will stay here and make sure they all calm down." Kalepe rubbed the back of his neck. "It will be good when this is all over. Nice to have my friends back again."

I stared at him, realizing how true his statement was. Those weren't just monsters to Kalepe. Just like Blake with Jaxon, Kalepe was anxious for his friends to overcome the beast within them.

Kory cleared his throat. "I hear you there, Kalepe. But thanks to Jocelyn here, we are that much closer to the end."

Thanks to Sammy, you mean. Now, I just need to figure out what the heck she did.

CHAPTER
Thirty-Two

As the light of day faded, the small hut Kory called home darkened. He rose up from the hammock bed we'd been resting in. Luckily for me, he hadn't pushed too much more than kissing. The way his eyes kept darting to me, questions forming but dying on his lips, I hoped the deepening frown on his lips meant he was truly concerned over my sister's welfare. Not that he'd become suspicious of me somehow.

Kory lit several kerosene lamps with his back toward me. "The electricity here is spotty. Best to always have a few of these handy."

"This island is gorgeous, but it's pretty remote. Seems like hardly any electricity would make it harder for your operations."

He turned around, bringing his lamp with him, the light bouncing crazy shadows off his face.

"We don't need as much technology as you think. Once the serum was perfected, the actual process of administering it is pretty straightforward. Just need some beds and IVs. And a backup generator in case the power shorts out."

"So how did you perfect the serum? You didn't do it here, then?"

One brow shot up before he sat down next to me, laying a heavy hand across my stomach. "Why the question all of a sudden? You never wanted to know about this stuff before."

"I don't know. I guess being here makes it all so real. Since I'm about to take the plunge, I want to know more." I prayed he'd buy my reasoning.

He stared at me for a minute, and then slowly grinned. "Don't get me wrong, I like you wanting to know more about what I've created." He dropped down to let his lips brush against mine.

I suppressed my gag reflex. You've created something you don't know how to control, Kory, I wanted to shout at him.

"So tell me more about it," I urged, trying to escape his lips.

"Well..." He leaned back a bit to my relief. "I didn't do it alone. I had some help from amazing scientists. I have to be honest; they had a lot more to do with the actual developmental phase. I simply brought them the original bug DNA I'd gotten before." I said nothing at his slip in terms, calling his precious Defenders bugs. It was the bug he and Blake had killed.

"I'd done one test before, and it... didn't go as planned," Kory continued.

Yeah, no kidding. Poor Jaxon.

"So, I recruited some experts to make sure that didn't happen again. You get to meet them soon, at tonight's party."

The missing ancients and Kate? I sat up a little. "Oh good. When does the party start?"

"We could head down to the beach now, if you're feeling up to it. Shouldn't be too long until the food is ready."

"Great. Let's go," I said, jumping to my feet, pushing past Kory, who laughed at my eagerness. "I'm starving."

Before I could get too far, he wrapped his arms around me from behind. Kissing the back of my neck, he murmured, "I must say, Jocelyn, you're like a different person here. I think the island brings out the best in you."

I shrugged off the pang of guilt, knowing Kory believed me to be my sister. I forced a laugh. "Thanks, I think." Grabbing his hand, I pulled him forward. "Come on, all that island food's calling my name."

He chuckled. "Since when has food called your name? Normally, I can hardly get you to eat anything."

I swallowed hard, realizing how right he was. Jocelyn wouldn't be clamoring to get to dinner. "Um... since I know I can stop dieting for good once I get that shot," I said with a grin.

He stared at me, and then relented. "You're right, there."

He led us out of the hut, while my mind focused on one

thing—find out how involved Kate and the ancients were in all this, and then get the heck out of here.

The island was anything but quiet tonight. Torches lit up several paths leading down to the beach, where bonfires were already lit and roaring with life. The evening tide provided the perfect backdrop to the festivities. Tongans were everywhere, mostly male, but I did spy a few women bustling around the food huts lining the beach. I recognized the outdoor cooking ovens Kory had pointed out earlier. The piles of rocks had been removed, leaves cast aside. Long sheets were spread out over the ground, piled high with not only cooked pigs, complete with snout and tail, but also an array of colorful, steaming food. As we passed, I recognized yams, coconuts, and some fish, but I had no idea what most of it was. I just knew it smelled delicious.

Kory pointed at the food. "That purple stuff is taro, tastes like a potato. That green, spinach-looking thing is called Lu Pulu. Its taro leaves with corn beef, onion, and coconut milk inside. I know it sounds strange, but trust me, it's delicious."

I nodded back at him. "Sounds great to me. When do we eat?"

He grinned. "Soon, I promise."

Kalepe suddenly appearing right in front of us made me jump a bit. Amazing how quiet he can be for how huge he is.

"We are ready for you," he announced, his grin dimpling his cheeks.

"Perfect," Kory said. "Guess soon is now."

***

If I hadn't been so distracted by the four ancients, I probably would have enjoyed my dinner a lot more. As it was, the food passed through my mouth hot, delicious, and severely underappreciated. Really, I was dying for Kory to introduce me to them. They stuck out, even with suntans, their creamy complexion a dead giveaway amongst the deep brown of the Tongan. Once everyone had found their seat on the long, spread-out 'tables,' I was disappointed to see the scientists were far down the long line, too far to strike up a conversation with them.

The other distraction was trying to find Kate among the feasting group. Even with the torchlights leaving deep shadows, I was fairly confident she just wasn't here tonight. I wondered why. Maybe she wasn't here at all; maybe she never had been. Kory had only mentioned scientists helping him. Maybe we were all wrong by thinking Kate had been involved in this in the first place.

After I'd eaten way too much, and my stomach truly refused to hold anymore, I leaned back a little.

Kory glanced over. "Told you that you would love it," he said contentedly.

"It's all amazing. I've never tasted food so good."

Kory gestured to what was before us. "This is all in your honor, Jocelyn."

"Mine. Why mine?"

"For what you did for the Defenders. This entire village wanted to thank you."

"But it wasn't me, really. It was my sister's DNA that made the difference. She should be the one here, receiving the honors."

Kory shook his head a bit. "I would have invited her if I could've, but it's hard with... Samantha... and all."

I bit my lip. "I know. I hardly see Sammy at all anymore. Makes me sad."

"Oh, really? So you've forgiven her then?"

Crap. Guess Jocelyn confides in Kory more than I'd thought. "Yes. Well, if we are both going to be part of this strange new world, it seems silly to hold on to a grudge."

Kory just stared at me. "Okay, who are you? And what did you do with my Jocelyn?" he asked, grinning.

I flushed, stammering to respond. He couldn't possibly know, could he?

He pulled me into his arms. "Relax, I love the new you. I never thought you'd forgive Sammy, that's all."

I went to respond, but someone else had drawn near. "Kory, may I introduce myself to your lovely friend?" the man asked.

My pulse jumped with excitement. Finally! An Ancient! Now, which one are you? Average height and build, a hooked nose, and silver-streaked eyebrows greeted me. His most notable feature by far was the fact that his eyes were flecked with the same brilliant gold that made his wings shimmer in the moonlight.

"Of course, of course! Excuse my manners," Kory said, jumping to his feet. He helped me to mine as well.

"Jocelyn, this is Alek, one of the brilliant scientists I told you about. He helped make this possible."

Alek grinned and reached for my hand as I made the connection. Alek was with Galina, the woman who'd invited us in for tea and told us her husband would never willingly help Kory. Yet, here he was, pumping my hand with a grin on his face, not chained in some cellar.

"Pleasure to meet you, Alek," I said. In a moment of compulsiveness, I added, "I think Sammy might have mentioned you in fact."

Both Kory and Alek's eyes widened. Kory's was more a look of surprise, while Alek's was one of horror. Oh boy, no turning back now.

"Yeah, I think it was you she mentioned. When she told me about the Outskirts. She said she went to see some of the ancients, I think she called them. I could have sworn she'd mentioned you and... Otto, I think it was." I knew I was taking a huge risk, but there was no turning back now. Time to shake this bag and see what cat fall's out.

I knew Sammy had left Tonbo's theater and gone to the Outskirts before she'd come to see Jocelyn. Sure, I didn't know what Sammy had told Jocelyn when they'd met that day, when Jocelyn had convinced Sammy to give her the DNA she wanted, but Kory didn't know that. And neither did Alek. This can work, I reassured myself.

"Why yes, that's correct," Alek stammered, clearly trying to recover from his earlier shock. "Your sister did come to see me, like you said." Alek's words seemed strained, his expression pinched. "It wasn't long after she'd left me, and the others, that

Kory approached us with this opportunity," Alek finished, giving Kory a glance.

By the way Kory gaped at him, I got the feeling he had no clue about Sammy's visit with the ancients.

"Wonderful, well, I'm glad you decided to help," I said, trying to smooth out the little bump I'd thrown at everyone. "From what I've seen, it looks like the Defenders are doing great. Hard to believe they are any different from you and me." I gestured to Kalepe, who smiled back at me. "I mean, except those Defenders I saw today in the cage, that is, they all just look normal to me." I let my words tumble out, hoping it came across like friendly babble.

Kory frowned. "Sorry you saw that."

Alek nodded, sadness entering his eyes. "The DNA from those early super soldiers Alois developed was pretty volatile."

"So what was it about my sister's blood that made such a difference?" I asked, angered that Alek made it out like this was all Tonbo's fault. "I mean, why does it make the Defenders not look like what was in those cages?" I asked, sensing Kory's eyes on me.

Alek opened his mouth but another man, who had sun-kissed wrinkles and a long, white beard, answered for him.

"Your sister's DNA is quite unique," he said through his thick beard.

I glanced over to see who had joined us. No doubt another Ancient.

"Jocelyn, this is Otto, another one of the masterminds behind it all," Kory stated.

"Nice to meet you, Otto," I said, remembering it was in his office we'd found the blueprints for Jaxon. Wanting to stay on topic, I asked, "You said it's unique, how so?"

Otto cast a quick glance at Kory, who gave a curt nod of approval. "Well, let's put it this way, Sammy or Samantha, whichever you prefer to call her, would have made one hell of a bartender. She knew how to mix the elixirs, if you will. It's as if she hand-picked the specific genomes she wanted replicated from a variety of species and stuck them all in her. She was ahead of her time in so many ways."

Another vague answer. I wanted details. "So it's not enough that she has wings, doesn't age, and can turn invisible? What kind of genes are we talking here?" I figured it was okay if I sounded ticked. Knowing my sister, she would be.

Kory shifted his weight as Otto answered, "From what we extracted from her sample, she has not only dragonfly but also sperm whale and the mimic octopus, of all things."

This was not news to me, but I had to act as shocked as Jocelyn. "What? Why those?"

Kory shrugged. "We have no idea. Sammy never mentioned it to you?"

"No. Like I said, she kept a lot from me when it came to her damsel life," I let contempt riddle my words. Kory must have bought it because he wrapped his arm around my shoulders. "So is that what helps with the Defenders? Whale and octopus DNA?" I asked, wanting to glean more from Otto.

Otto shook his head. "Honestly, we aren't exactly sure. There a few other strains we are still trying to determine."

"One of which appears to be bee DNA," Alek chimed in, his silver eyebrows rising.

"Bees?" I repeated, this time with genuine surprise. Both Otto and Alek nodded back at me. "So, what, Sammy can make honey now?" I asked, purposely playing dumb. Kory gave me a patronizing smile as two more men approached.

After quick introductions, I met the other two missing ancients. Ulrich and Rupert. Both were aged, with smiles as bright as their wings. I just couldn't fathom why these four ancients would join Kory's cause on their own volition. It made no sense. They purposely shunned the rest of the world, living in the Outskirts. Why would they now be part of creating an army to so-called govern the new world Kory envisioned?

Kory turned to Ulrich and Rupert and asked, "So Jocelyn was just saying how Sammy had visited with Otto and Alek before giving Jocelyn her blood sample. Did she come see you two as well?"

I didn't miss the way Otto's eyes widened. Pretty obvious these guys didn't want Kory to know Sammy had seen them.

Ulrich and Rupert glanced at each other before Ulrich answered, "No, but I wish I could have had the opportunity to meet Sammy. I wouldn't mind talking to her about her findings."

Rupert quickly nodded in agreement. "We could only have been so lucky. What an honor that would have been."

Kory harrumphed and muttered something under his breath. Apparently, he did not like being the last to know—on anything.

"Sammy had come to see me, but I'm afraid the topic of the Defenders had not been brought to my knowledge at that point. Kory," Otto said, looking at him directly. "You came to me not long after her visit. If I'd known what I'd be involved with, I would have had a lot more questions for her."

"So what did you talk about?" Kory asked, his jaw hard.

Now I was wishing I could take my earlier statement back. I had no doubt now the ancients didn't want Kory to know about Sammy's visit at all. It made me wonder just how loyal they really were to Kory's cause. Maybe them playing along with it was just an act.

"Sammy wanted to know if there was anything we," he glanced at Alek, who nodded back at him, "could do to help her and Samantha be one again. She said she'd hoped transforming into a damsel would have been enough, but it wasn't. She came to us when she was in control."

Alek caught my gaze and firmly said, "She was looking for a cure."

CHAPTER
Thirty-Three

I knew my mouth gaped open, but I couldn't help it. I didn't know what to believe. Had Sammy really stolen away to the Outskirts in the hope of curing us? And then what, she gave up and went home to warn Jocelyn to stay clear of Kory? After which, she willingly handed over her blood to make the bug army stronger? None of this made any sense. Just when I thought I was getting it, finally understanding Sammy better, I felt like I was starting completely over again.

Kalepe, who'd stood back listening, stepped forward, motioning to Kory. "I think we are ready for the ceremony now."

Alek and Otto's explanation must have appeased Kory's earlier anxiety because a grin spread across his face.

"Wonderful, Kalepe," he said, "Shall we continue this down on the beach? The Defenders have something special planned for us tonight."

Now my anxiety heightened. Just what kind of ceremony were we talking about? Surely, Kory wouldn't try injecting me now, right? Knowing how jumpy Jocelyn felt about this, he wouldn't dream of making a public display of her injections... would he?

Kalepe let out a loud whooping noise as we wound down the fire-lit path to the beach. I was surprised to hear several other Tongans match the sound. It reminded me a bit of wolves in a pack, howling to one another. Not sure if it was an island or Defender thing, I stepped a bit closer to Kory. For some reason, the mild-mannered Kalepe was giving me a different vibe now. There was a manic energy about him, a wildness in his gaze when he glanced back at me. The grin that had dimpled his cheeks, giving him an almost boyish feel all day, now left me feeling sick with adrenaline.

Kory gave my arm a squeeze. "Relax. They have some songs they want to sing and dance to; it's nothing too scary."

"Okay," I said, noticing how more and more Tongan men were crowding around us as we waded through the soft sand. They still wore their lavalava skirts, but now I noticed they wore some kind of grass skirt around them as well, adding color and fullness. All were bare chested, and a few of them sported flowered leis around their necks.

The bonfires from earlier were now raging, three total, one definitely larger than the others. It was at this fire that we gathered around. Two old lawn chairs stuck out like sore thumbs. When Kory beelined for them, I supposed they were meant for us. With the others sitting directly on the sand, it felt funny to be the only ones sitting in chairs. With a yelp from Kalepe, all the Tongans were on their feet, and we were the ones being dwarfed.

Somewhere, drums began to droll out. I found the source quickly as bodies moved to clear our view. I could only stare. One monstrous Tongan was in the forefront, manning four drums by himself, each drum easily five feet high, three feet wide. Three more Tongans were behind him, forming a line, each one drumming furiously on one tall drum. I'd never heard such a rhythm before. My entire frame shook with the reverberations.

With the drumming, the energy around the fire spiked. I watched in wonder as Tongans began catcalling out different sounds and rhythms, their bodies beginning a slap dance like I'd never seen before. The drums didn't stop, just increased in speed and force, and the Tongans frenzied movements sped up too.

Kalepe danced around in and around the other men, calling out commands I didn't understand. Then, as the drumming reached the pinnacle, the fire leaping around, lighting up the bodies leaping and bounding around us, Kalepe let out a call that I did understand.

"Defenders! Transform!"

I gasped, my eyes darting to Kory. His eyes danced with the

same manic energy Kalepe's had. This was the big ceremony? The sound of angry flesh being torn away, along with roars and screaming, assaulted my ears. I couldn't help but jump to my feet, readying to bolt. Really, I wanted my own wings to burst out and take me from this.

Kory grabbed on to me, shouting to be heard above the insane noise surrounding us, "Don't worry! These Defenders are perfectly safe!"

Kory's crazed stare was enough to make me look away and meet the horror before me. No longer men, the Defenders' enormous heads turned, black, bug-like eyes all gazing back at us. One stood out from the rest, and from the shredded remains of his lavalava, I knew it was Kalepe. Though not as scare-ridden as Jaxon, their heavy-corded wings, oversized frames, hunched shoulders, and elongated claws reminded me of the bug Jaxon tried to overcome within himself. To my shock, none of them rushed us. If anything, they continued in their chants and half-slap-half-jumping around the fire. With monstrous roars, Kalepe seemed to be calling out commands still.

"See?" Kory called back to me. "The Defenders are completely in control of themselves!"

I sickened at Kory's pride—at the impossible feat we had before us. How can we stop this now? We can't just destroy them. If they could be reasoned with, maybe I could convince Kalepe he was being misguided. That Kory didn't have their best interest at heart.

Maybe I could...

My thoughts were shattered by a long, high-pitched wail making its way through the dancing and beating drums. The timbre was definitely female, the note surprisingly on key for how loud it was. The drums suddenly stopped, and with it, the dancing. The Defenders suddenly appeared restless, more black eyes glancing my way than I'd like.

Kory stiffened and turned to stare at the shoreline, swearing.

"What was that?" I asked, my nerves already frayed by the sight of the Defenders slowly meandering closer to me. Why didn't Kory notice them?

"The Irukas," Kory muttered. The feminine cry sounded again. This time, the melody was haunting.

Knowing Jocelyn wouldn't have a clue what that meant, I asked, "The what?"

He didn't answer me, just marched away, motioning for Kalepe to follow. I shrunk back, almost tripping against the lawn chair as Kalepe went to pass me. I didn't trust bugs, no matter what you called them. Kalepe glanced my way, inhaling deeply. His black eyes gave me a questioning look before he hustled to catch up to Kory, who had made his way to the shoreline. Being away from the light of the bonfire, they may as well have disappeared for all I could tell.

Something brushed my arm, and I jumped, spinning around at the same time. An enormous black head peered down at me, the eyes too far apart and the nose too small.

"Hi... you're a... one of the Defenders? Right?" I asked, trying to dodge the lawn chair and move back a step or two.

The Defender nodded, its mouth splitting into a wicked grin as it inhaled deeply through its pinched nostrils. "Yes," he purred back at me. "And you are not what you seem."

I wasn't sure what terrified me more, his proximity or the fact he knew I was a fraud. How can he possibly know?

I was surprised to hear Kory crow loudly, and thankful I was saved from the Defender bearing down on me. He moved back quickly, perhaps not wanting Kory to see him pressuring me. Kory made his way back toward me, the fire lighting up the whites of his eyes and teeth with how big he was smiling now. What could possibly make him happier than seeing his Defenders dancing around the fire?

My answer came with arms and wings pinned back by Kalepe's monstrous Defender form. His head was held high with his blond hair wet and curling at his neck.

Blake.

CHAPTER
Thirty-Four

I bit my lip hard enough to draw blood. I can't cry out to him. Not here, not now. What was he doing here? Had he come searching for me and the Irukas caught him?

Blake met my gaze. In the light, I made out a blackened eye and a bloodied lip. I had jumped forward a few steps before remembering Jocelyn would not show kindness for Blake's predicament. Jocelyn's disdain for him was pretty clear in her bedroom two days ago. Or had I been gone longer?

I couldn't blame Blake for coming after me; I would've done the same thing in his shoes. Reading relief in his expression, I knew he'd been worried over my safety. If only he'd waited a bit longer to come! I was going to make my escape tonight. Although, seeing how the Defenders kept casting glances at me, I began to wonder just how easy escaping would've been after all.

"Well, well, well. What have we here?" Kory drawled out as a few of the Defenders hooted.

"Kory, this is madness," Blake said firmly, not seeming to mind the Defender holding on to him.

"Madness? You showing up here is madness. I must say, I thought you'd come a bit more prepared. I mean, what did you expect to find?" Kory's laugh was mirthless. "I knew you'd figure out what needed to be done, eventually. See the wisdom in my plans. So I'm going to assume since you came so... unarmed... that you must be ready to join our great cause."

"Do you even hear yourself?" Blake demanded. "You're creating monsters! Why on earth would I want to be a part of that?" Blake shot the four ancients who hovered near Kory withering looks.

They dropped their heads, refusing to meet his gaze.

"Because, my dear, old friend," Kory drawled, "this is all inevitable. Dragons are the superior race. We're stronger, faster, and live so much longer. Humans will be a thing of the past. And when this new world begins, there will need to be some kind of order to the madness. I don't know why you refuse to see it. I'm not creating monsters; I'm creating trained soldiers who can help keep things from unraveling. You can't keep sticking your head in the sand. When are you going to man up?"

Blake's eyes narrowed. "Man up? Is that what you were doing when you injected my brother? Tricked him into becoming something you knew nothing about? Now he fights a demon within himself. Then you had the gall to trick me into killing him for you! Was that all you manning up, Kory?" he retorted. His words caused a ripple through the crowd.

Apparently, the Defenders knew nothing of Jaxon. Still, the four ancients would not meet Blake's piercing gaze. Amazing how he could command so much authority with his arms still pinned behind him.

"I agree with you on one thing," Blake continued as Kory shifted his weight. "I won't stick my head in the sand anymore. I can't pretend the Dragon Fae world doesn't exist. Because it does, and I'm proud to be a part of it. But," his word rang out over the crowd, "creating super soldiers from bug DNA is not the answer. We can't control them. We will never be able to control them."

The Defenders looked to Kory, their black eyes widening.

"Oh," Kory crowed, "that's where you're wrong. These are good men. They want to defend the innocent. I'm sorry, truly, for what happened with Jaxon. I never meant for it to turn out like that." Kory frowned. "Jaxon came to me, begging to be able to help watch over you, his kid brother. I thought the desire to protect and fight for something he loved would be enough to keep the monster at bay. But I was wrong."

"You never told him there was a difference! You never gave him a choice. Which makes me wonder—did you even give these people a choice? Did they know they didn't have to become bugs?

That they could still fight and be warriors as dragons? Why give them the extra demon to fight within themselves?"

As the argument moved between the two, I noticed how the Defenders' gazes would shift, listening to both intently. Maybe this was the moment we needed. Maybe Blake could reason with the Defenders, make them see whose side they should be on.

"They've overcome their demons, and now they have the strength of thousands of dragons. And yes, I did give them a choice," Kory retorted.

"How?" Blake demanded. "If what you said is really true, how did they do it?"

Kory snorted. "Your precious girlfriend helped us. Or didn't you know that already?"

Blake shook his head. "Samantha has nothing to do with this."

"Not Samantha—Sammy. I must say, Blake, you're one dirty dude. Got yourself two girls for the price of one. That's the thing of daydreams, right?"

Seeing Blake straining to lunge for Kory, his wings a blur of movement, I hauled back and punched Kory in the arm—hard. Kory whirled around, shock in his eyes.

"Hey, that's my sister you're talking about," I hissed back at him, praying Jocelyn would have had enough decency to defend my honor.

Kalepe's monstrous form had easily stopped Blake's struggling, holding him in place. Hearing no cry of anguish, I hoped the popping sounds I'd heard weren't Blake bones. Maybe Kalepe wasn't trying to actually hurt Blake. Not yet, anyway.

Kory seemed to consider me for a moment, his eyes sweeping my frame, leaving goose bumps across my skin. Can he tell? Maybe the gag is up.

"You never cared what I said before," Kory muttered under his breath, but then he shrugged, pointing to Blake in Kalepe's arms. "Well, I can't just let you go, now can I, Blake? You know where my Defenders are. I can't risk you running off to tell Tonbo." He gritted his teeth. "I can't stand how you worship that man."

"Don't kid yourself; you only wish Tonbo still held you in high regard. You're nothing more than a spoiled brat," Blake sneered.

Kory grimaced as his eyes narrowed. "You're a bigger damn fool than I'd thought. I couldn't care less what that old man thinks," he growled. "You leave me no choice, Blake. If you aren't going to join my cause, you'll only get in my way." He scowled. Looking at Kalepe, he commanded, "Do what must be done."

"No," I gasped, shrinking back at Kory's hard stare. He waited, and I stuttered, trying to formulate my thoughts. "Maybe he will change his mind if he sees what these Defenders can do. He's only been around his brother. He hasn't seen how different they are from what his brother became." Funny how the straight-up truth was the best answer I could come up with at the moment.

Kory's lips twitched, his eyes darting between Blake and me, a smile spreading across his face. "You know, you're right, Jocelyn. Take him down to the cages, Kalepe. Maybe spending some time by the unchanged will help him see how different my Defenders are."

"Yes," I agreed, even though I wasn't so sure anymore that I'd saved Blake from a worse fate. Hoping to convince Kory he'd want Blake alive, I added, "Blake could influence Tonbo's followers. Get more on your side."

Kory glanced over at me, his expression hard to read in the fire-lit night. "Perhaps he can." There was something in his tone that sent the hairs on the back of my neck on end, but I couldn't focus on what it was. Kalepe forcing Blake away captivated all of my attention.

Two additional Defenders had to manhandle Blake's struggling form before he was contained enough to fly away. It sickened me, but it delighted Kory, who clapped like it'd been the evening entertainment.

CHAPTER
Thirty-Five

J ust have to make some lame excuse to Kory when he gets back, and then get down to those cages, I told myself. I'll free Blake, and we'll get the heck of out here. This undercover idea had turned into a full-blown mess. Instead of getting a sneak peek and coming back, we were thrown into a battle we were ill equipped for. Although, I thought with dread trickling through me, how could we possibly have prepared for this? We can't just wipe out the Defenders. They aren't evil killers. Dangerous beasts who appeared to be in control of themselves, yes. Malicious murderers, no.

The only hope I had was to figure out how my blood helped them and do the same thing for Jaxon. Then try to persuade all the Defenders not to follow their creator, Kory. Should be easy enough, right? I inwardly groaned. One glance at the Defender staring down at me, and I could sense the hopelessness of it all. There was something manic in their devotion to Kory.

Shortly after Blake had been taken away, we'd returned to Kory's hut, where Kory had excused himself, saying he had some business to attend to. I could only hope that didn't mean torturing Blake. Anxious to finally have a moment alone, I had been readying myself for ditching Jocelyn's form so I could fly out of there, when a Defender had entered the room. Apparently, either Kory doesn't trust me, or he doesn't trust the rest of this island. Either way, an enormous bug staring down at me made my skin crawl.

The Defender, who up to this point had remained silent, cocked his head to the side and said, "I know your scent." His voice rumbled from deep within his chest.

"Oh, really?" I asked with forced brightness.

"You are not what you seem," he continued, echoing the other Defender's sentiment from earlier this evening.

Crap. They must be able to tell I'm not my sister.

Kory re-entered the room and saved me from responding, but the blank expression written across his face only deepened my dread. He mumbled something quietly to the Defender, who promptly left, shutting the door behind him. Kory's eyes met mine, the intensity in them setting me on edge. Suddenly, coming up with any excuse to leave seemed impossible. Perhaps I can pretend my appendix has burst...

He wasted no time and marched across the room to me, yanking me by the wrists, pulling me to him.

"Oh, Kory," I yelped, not entirely sure if this was an attack or merely a passionate gesture.

When his lips crushed mine, I decided the latter. Even though I was never fond of kissing the enemy, there was something different in the way he pressed his mouth on mine this time. I felt no love in how he pinned my body against his, his unshaven face scraping my skin while he refused to let me come up for air.

I struggled to find any excuse that wouldn't blow my cover. When he shoved me up against the wall, almost knocking the air out of me, I snapped, thrashing to free myself.

I don't care what he thinks anymore. He's acting psycho!

Managing to pull my lips away from his long enough, I shouted, "Kory, stop it!"

He chortled, "Aw... come on, baby. Thought you liked it rough, Jocelyn."

I sickened at the way he said my sister's name. Does he know? Either way, I had to get away. Twisting, I attempted to knee him in the crotch, but our bodies were mashed too tight for me to get the right angle or leverage. Leaves only one last weapon to use.

I turned abruptly, my mouth seeking his. After I felt him stiffen with surprise, I bit down on his lips, hard. The metallic taste of his blood entered my mouth, turning my stomach.

He gasped, his head rocking back, but he still didn't let my body go. He grinned, blood lining his teeth. "Oh, come on, Sammy, I know you want to come out to play."

"Sammy? What are you talking about? You're scaring me!" I screamed back at him, trying in vain to shove him off me.

"That's the whole point. I have to scare you, so Sammy will rush in to save the day. So," he hissed, leaning in too close, "let's stop pretending you're Jocelyn because I know you're not. Question is—are you Sammy yet?"

"I'm not Sammy!" I spat, feeling validated to say the words aloud. "You're crazy! Let go of me!"

Did I see a flicker of doubt flash through his eyes? Maybe I can still pretend...

He threw me back, my head smacking the wall with such force that it left my vision swimming.

"You're nothing like your sister," he growled, his hands finally releasing me. I fumbled to make a run for it, but found myself falling instead. With ears ringing and my equilibrium swaying, I blinked rapidly, trying to clear the horrible fog encasing me as my body hit the ground with a thud.

"There you are." Kory knelt down next to me, and to my horror, brushed the hair back off my face.

I couldn't stop him; the room was spinning too hard, too fast. As my wings burst through the back of my shirt, I knew the gig was up. I was me again, no longer my sister. Was that why Kory had knocked me nearly unconscious? So I'd transform?

Rubbing his mouth with the back of his hand, he cleared away the remaining blood from his lips. "So who do we have? Samantha or Sammy?"

"How could my sister ever love you? You're a monster," I mumbled back at him. Still unable to climb to my feet, I massaged my throbbing head with my fingers. The pain was nauseating.

"Ha. I'm not the one pretending to be someone I'm not. Tell me, Samantha," he leaned close, his voice dropping to a whisper, "did you enjoy kissing me?"

I groaned, trying to pull myself to my knees. "Don't flatter yourself," I spat. "You disgust me."

He chuckled. "I seem to recall you getting into it."

He reached out toward me, and I smacked his hand away. "Don't touch me!"

Finally managing to get upright enough to kneel, I became aware of my quivering wings. Trust me; I want to get out of here just as bad, I thought.

Kory jumped to his feet. Before I could stop him, he grabbed me under my arms and scooped me up with him. I didn't care if his hands were the only things holding me upright at the moment. I'd rather fall to the floor again than have him touch me.

"Let go of me," I growled through clenched teeth.

To my shock, he complied, even backing up a few steps. "Okay, okay, but just know, Samantha, that hurting you was never the end goal. I just need Sammy here. Not you. It's nothing personal."

I snorted back at him. "So what... the plan is to torture me until she arrives?"

He shrugged. "If that's what it takes."

"You are a monster. Why do you need Sammy so bad, anyway? You already got her blood. You have your precious Defenders now."

He sucked in a breath. To my surprise, he walked over to his hammock and sat down. This was it, my chance to escape, but sensing he was about to actually answer my question, I couldn't leave. I had to know. What was the connection between Sammy and Kory?

"I have questions for her," he simply said.

"Join the party," I grumbled.

He grunted, giving me a crooked grin. "Must be frustrating not to know what your other half has been up to."

"You have no idea," I said, realizing the longer we kept talking, the more my head cleared. Better for flying. "I just can't figure out why on earth she would ever help you?"

His grin widened. "I like your tenacity, Samantha. You aren't afraid to fight back, even though I have Defenders standing outside this door, ready to rip you to shreds if needed."

I swallowed. Okay, that wasn't the answer I was hoping for. I tried to act brave. "You still didn't answer my question. Why did Sammy give you her blood? What's in it for her? And don't try to feed me your propaganda crap."

"You might think it is propaganda crap, but it's not. The need for an army is real. Sammy saw that too, obviously. Why else would she offer her blood to me so readily?"

His words stirred something within me. A question lingering in my mind... Yeah, why else?

"So what are your questions for her?" I redirected, not wanting him to think on his own rhetorical question. "According to you, your Dragon Defenders are submissive and perfect. Why do you need Sammy now?"

"Because your little stunt has opened a whole new world to me." His eyes lit up, and my stomach turned. "I had no idea you could transform yourself like that. I admit, everything about you has thrown me off, but your scent most of all. Jocelyn's scent is so different from yours, and I know yours, Samantha. But I couldn't figure out how she could possibly be you. I mean, no one has ever been able to do camo like that. Luckily for me, I wasn't the only one with doubts. My Defenders, with their heightened senses, knew you were a fraud when they transformed. Don't ask me how that works, but as soon as Kalepe told me down by the beach when the Irukas brought Blake to me, I knew. Blake would only have come to rescue his precious Samantha."

Crap... this was a bigger mistake than I'd thought.

"Of course, I wasn't entirely convinced so I went and talked to the ancients about it. They said it was plausible with the octopus DNA they found."

So that was why he had left me with a babysitter. At least that means he hadn't been torturing Blake all night.

He pinched the bridge of his nose as he frowned. "Just wish I could find that blasted Kate. She's the one who helped make Sammy's original formula, for crying out loud."

Taken aback by Kory's seemingly honest statement, I asked, "Wait, she's not here with you?"

He eyed me for a second, and then said, "No, why? Did you

think she was?"

"I figured she busted out of her holding cell to join your forces, like the four ancients had."

"No. I should've grabbed her while she sat like a sitting duck, but I had the ancients. I didn't think I'd need her. Then this past week, with... what's been happening... I went to find her and discovered she was already gone."

"What do you mean? What's been happening?" I asked, not really expecting him to tell me.

"Nothing," he murmured under his breath, taking a step closer to me. "Look, nothing against you, Samantha, but I really need Sammy right now."

I didn't like the way his eyes raked me up and down. What does he think? Sammy's hiding somewhere on my body right now?

"Well, in case you haven't noticed, I don't exactly have control over when Sammy decides to pop up," I said with forced calmness as my muscles tightened. My wings screamed for release. Even knowing Defenders stood outside this room, I readied myself to bolt. Now or never.

I met Kory's gaze. "So I guess you're stuck with me, Kory."

With my last words, my wings jumped into action and I shoved past him, flying toward the door. Pretending to be Jocelyn for so long had left them feeling stiff and unused.

Kory didn't even bother to follow me, only laughed at me. "Go ahead. I was going to hand you over to them anyway to see if they might be able to scare dear Sammy out of you. You just made my job that much easier."

I didn't open the door, scanning the room around me for anything that could be used as a weapon. Maybe I can force my way out there with Kory as my prisoner. I knew it was a ridiculous hope, but it was all I had left.

The door swung inward before I had the chance to grab anything. Within seconds, Kalepe's monstrous form was wrapping his arms around me, squeezing the air out of me.

CHAPTER
Thirty-Six

I struggled against Kalepe, although it did nothing but leave me feeling bruised. Finally deciding he wasn't actually going to squeeze me to death right then and there, I stopped fighting and let him fly me away. At this point, I'd prefer anywhere over being in the same room with Kory. I hate him! If Blake doesn't make him pay for all he's done, I will. Thinking of Blake, my heart throbbed. What had Kory's goons done to him while he'd messed around with me?

I cleared my throat. Trying to be heard over the roar of air surrounding us, I shouted out, "Kalepe!"

The dark, enormous head turned to peer down at me. He said nothing, but I knew he'd heard me at least.

"Where's Blake? Is he... okay?" I asked. When he didn't say anything, panic shot through me. "Kalepe, he didn't do anything wrong! He just came to check on me!"

Again no answer, just black eyes peering down at me with the strangest of expressions. It wasn't exactly hostility I sensed, more curiosity. I could only hope some part of Kalepe could still be reasoned with. Being alone with him now, flying, this felt like my only hope.

"Please," I cried, my voice breaking as tears sprung to my eyes, "Please tell me Kory didn't turn you into a real monster... a murderer."

A deep rumble came from Kalepe's chest as he said, "He's not dead." I couldn't stop the sob that racked through me as the reality of almost losing Blake crashed down on me. Of all the places to have a breakdown! I should be acting strong—in control. Instead, I'm bawling on a bug's shoulder...

Kalepe's eyes glanced down at me for a second, and then he was back to navigating through the thick trees we'd entered. I sniffed back my tears, peering around. I wasn't too surprised to see the squat, stucco building up ahead. Kory had said to put Blake with the unchanged Defenders. Just hope that doesn't literally mean in their cages.

Since the building wasn't large, it didn't take us long to fly down the short corridor that led to the open room with one entire wall made of glass. Kalepe didn't stop to gaze at the Defenders still hooked up to IVs, just continued to where the unchanged Defenders still sat, caged up, waiting their turns.

He veered to the right. Within seconds, the metal door loomed before us. Even though Kalepe had said Blake wasn't dead, bloody and mutilated were still very real possibilities. My insides constricted, nerves tightening the muscles across my neck and shoulders as Kalepe gave the door a push with one monstrous palm. The weight of the door was no obstacle for him and swung in with a bang.

With our noisy entrance, Defender heads popped up from within their confines. A roar issued from the imprisoned as my eyes sought out Blake. Where is he? Did Kalepe lie to me?

My panic to find him outweighed the monsters trying to reach me from within the bars. I hardly noticed my clothes being yanked on until Kalepe let out a horrible growl. When it ended, the room went dead silent.

His eyes honed in on the beasts surrounding us, shouting, "Dragon Defenders, back off! This one is not for you!"

Did that mean Blake was? I tried not to overanalyze Kalepe's statement and took their calming down as a chance to finish my search.

That was when I saw him. He was in the back of the room, in a cage by himself. I wanted to cry for joy, but the stillness of Blake's body lying on the ground, curled in the fetal position, made my mouth go dry.

Still, I managed to croak, "Blake!"

There was no movement from the last cage.

Kalepe landed down. With my body still held tightly against his, he marched me toward the empty cage next to Blake. I went willingly; I needed to be near Blake. I had to make sure he was okay. Passing the quieted, but hardly pacified, Defenders, the hairs on the back of my neck rose. Chills shot down my arms. Unlike Kalepe, whose eyes even in bug form had the look of reasoning behind them, every pair of these black eyes had only one thing written on them. Destroy her.

Kalepe didn't shove me into my cage, which I was grateful for. My body was still sore from Kory's manhandling. In fact, it seemed the longer I'd been held by Kalepe, the gentler his grip had become. I guess he sensed I wasn't going to make a run for it.

I didn't pay attention to Kalepe. Somewhere in the back of my mind, I heard the scraping of the key, locking me in. All my focus was on Blake. I scooted as close as I could to his body, reaching through my bars, hoping I could span the space that separated our two cages.

"Blake!" I hollered. "Wake up! Come on... Blake, wake up!"

Nothing. I scanned his body. There was dry blood on his clothes, where I could only assume injuries had already healed. His wings appeared unharmed; nothing seemed to be broken from where I sat. So why isn't he waking up?

"Blake!" I yelled louder. "You've got to be okay! I need you! Please! Please wake up!"

Still nothing.

Sensing someone watching, I glanced up to see Kalepe still stood over me, his black eyes once again taking on a very quizzical, almost confused gaze. It reminded of someone... someone else who'd given me the same look. Jaxon. When he'd been begging me tell him what I'd done to him. I was sure it had to mean something, but right now, I didn't care. I didn't care that Kory's damn bug army was going to wreak havoc on the world. I didn't care what Sammy had done, or might still do. I didn't even care if she took over, if only it meant Blake would be okay.

He's the only thing that matters to me. How did I ever lose sight of that? I should never have insisted on going on this crazy, hair-brained scheme of mine.

"What's wrong with him?" I asked, my voice shaking as my eyes welled up. "Why isn't he waking up?"

Kalepe glanced over at Blake, and then to me. He seemed to consider his answer. Finally, he said, "He's been drugged. Kory wants him out of the way, not dead. We aren't the bad guys here."

Relief whooshed through me as I quickly said "And neither are we, Kalepe! We don't want to hurt you, or the other Defenders. We just want to make sure," I paused, weighing my words, "you aren't being led by someone who can't be trusted."

"Kory can be trusted," Kalepe growled back at me. "He's our creator. He takes good care of us."

"Why didn't he tell you about Jaxon, then?" I asked. "Did you know you aren't the first ones?"

Kalepe remained silent, rubbing his jaw with his clawed hand. It seemed strange to converse with him while he looked so inhuman.

"I heard what Blake said, at the beach, about his brother. I'm sure Kory did what he thought was right. He's merciful and kind."

"Merciful? Tricking someone into killing their own brother is not merciful! Kalepe, you don't know Kory like I do... like Blake does! He lies. He manipulates people into doing what he wants. He—"

"Enough!" he roared back at me, his black eyes hardening. "I won't let you speak of him in such a way!"

I scooted back, away from the bars, startled by his eruption. "It's the truth," I said flatly. "Sorry if the truth hurts. Kory's not what he seems. He's ruthless. The fact that we're in cages because we don't agree with what he's doing shows how insane he is. What's he going to do to the rest of the world? Huh? Going to torture them too? Put them in cages if they don't want to transform into dragons and damsels?"

Kalepe, to my surprise, didn't argue, but seemed to be listening.

"Look, you're not a bad guy. None of you are. You signed up to be Dragon Defenders. Defenders of the right. You thought you'd be the super heroes of the world. I'm telling you right now, Kory has different plans for you."

"You say all this, yet you are the one who pretended to be someone else. You have been the deceptive one since you arrived on our island. Why should I listen to you? Kory's never lied or tricked any of us."

I shrugged. "I guess you can't know for certain. Not yet, anyway. But you can't tell me something about all this doesn't feel off to you. I can see it in your eyes, Kalepe."

He rocked back on his heels, his large, black eyes narrowing. "Tell me then, if Kory is as wicked as you say he is, then why did you sign up to help him?"

I snorted. "That wasn't me."

"It was Sammy, right? She's still a part of you."

"No." I rose to my feet, grabbing the bars that separated us. "She's not. She's done things behind my back my entire life. I never even knew she existed until just months ago. She's the reason I'm even here... that I'm part of this crazy world." "Then you have her to thank," he evenly said. "She's as much a part of you as this Defender form is a part of me. I've come to accept it. Embrace what it has to offer. I think you should do the same, Samantha."

I huffed, unable to respond, not sure if I was more shocked by Kalepe turning into my therapist, or the fact his advice might have some merit to it.

"I'll leave you now," Kalepe said, turning to go.

"Wait, aren't you going to torture Sammy out of me like Kory asked?" I said a bit sarcastically. If I was honest, deep down, there was a twisted part of me that actually wanted him to try. If Sammy's so dang smart, like everyone seems to think she is, maybe she can see a way out of this. I wasn't really sure how Sammy would play the cards if given the whole deck, but seeing Blake's still form next to me, I felt certain she'd do a better job than I had. At this point, who cares whose bloody side she's on? Maybe, just maybe, she's on both our sides.

Kalepe hesitated, frowning. "No," he said. "Torturing you so Kory can get some questions answered does feel off to me."

Shocked, I stared at Kalepe's retreating monstrous form. No doubt in my mind now. These... well, not the ones right next to me... but the Defenders given the extra DNA are different. They have a conscience. They can be reasoned with. And, I thought with elation, glancing over at Blake, that means there's finally hope for Jaxon!

CHAPTER
Thirty-Seven

"**S**am!" a voice hissed in the darkness.

I stirred, rubbing my eyes. My shoulder and hip ached from the hard floor I'd been sleeping on. This was my second night in here. Slowly sitting up, I glanced around, but the room was too black to make anything out. After spending the entire day before waiting for one of the howling beasts to finally break free and tear me to shreds, I decided Kory's idea of scaring Sammy out of me was simply to leave me here. Surrounded by vicious bugs and an unconscious Blake.

Trying to muffle out the awful bug noises, I'd wrapped my arms around my head and apparently fallen asleep. Now, straining to make anything out in the lightless room, I wondered if I'd only dreamt of someone calling my name. With only eerie silence greeting me, I weighed out my options. Either those bugs finally crashed after tormenting me all day, or they aren't in here anymore.

At the last thought, I clutched at the bars and whispered, "Blake."

"Sam? Is that you?" he immediately responded.

"Yes, it's me!" I practically shouted back in my excitement. "You're awake, finally!"

"Are you okay?" we both asked each other at the same time.

As soon as we'd both established that we were both unharmed, Blake asked, "How long have I been out?"

"Since last night. I was freaking out; I thought you'd never wake up!"

"No kidding. Wonder what they knocked me out with... Where are we anyway?"

"You don't remember anything?"

"No. They injected me with something as soon as we left the beach. I'd been prepared for a butt-whipping, not to wake up two days later in some kind of a cage."

"Oh. Well, you got the cage part right. Here, reach through the bars." I extended my hand out and was elated to feel his fingers grasping for me in the dark. We grabbed one another's hands.

"We are locked in with..." I said, letting my voice drop. In all my excitement to discover Blake awake, I'd forgotten about the fact the Defenders might be listening in right now. "The bugs Kory hasn't given Sammy's... or... my blood to."

"I don't understand. What do you mean the ones Kory hasn't injected?"

Realizing I had a lot to explain, I rushed into what had happened, trying to fill him in with every detail I could. From the difference between the unchanged Defenders and Kalepe, to how the ancients were here and Kate was not. When he asked what went wrong with my cover, I hated admitting that the Defenders had figured it out and told Kory, who then tried to torture Sammy out of me.

"I'm going to kill him," Blake growled in the dark.

"Maybe Kory's right. Sammy should be here, not me," I admitted, giving into the feeling of defeat. Our present predicament did seem pretty dismal.

"What on earth are you talking about, Sam?" The anger behind his words was hard to miss.

"Blake, look at us. We're in cages. Kory's psychotic. I don't know; maybe Sammy can find a way out of here."

"Sammy wouldn't help any of us if she were here. She'd probably go off and develop a new serum, leaving us with a thousand new problems to solve. She doesn't care about you, Sam. She's just as psycho as Kory."

Blake's words felt like he'd reached across the bars and slapped me. Gasping, I shrunk back, pulling my hand away. Logically, I knew he was probably right, but Kalepe's words had stirred up the desire to trust Sammy all over again. Was it so wrong I still wanted her to be the good guy?

"Sam, what happened?" he asked, not understanding my actions.

"Nothing," I said, trying to rein in the sudden anger flooding me. Ironic, since just yesterday, I'd decided nothing mattered more to me than Blake, including Sammy. Frustrated with myself, I took a deep breath and went to try again.

"Sorry," he said before I could get a word out. "I wasn't trying to hurt your feelings. You know I'm not talking about you, Sam, right? Sammy is different than you."

I swallowed back the desire to repeat what Kalepe had said to me. Surrendering myself to her was not the answer. Besides, last I checked, bugs weren't exactly sages of wisdom.

"I know, Blake. Sorry I got upset. I'm just so confused right now. Nothing makes sense. Like where is Kate in all this? Kory made it sound like she's never been involved at all. And," I added, "the ancients acted really weird when Kory found out they'd seen Sammy."

"Yeah, maybe they weren't as happy to comply as Kory thought," Blake whispered. "Think Sammy really went to see them about healing the both of you?"

"Honestly, I don't know. But one thing I do know from being here, Sammy's blood made all the difference in these bugs. Kalepe isn't the same, Blake. Kory told him to basically torture me to get Sammy to come out, and he refused."

Blake let out a low whistle. "Really?" he asked.

"Really. Which makes me wonder if Kory got mad at him since I haven't seen him since he brought me here. Other Defenders came to bring us food."

"Wait, there's food in here?" Blake croaked. "Why didn't you start with that?"

I laughed, realizing how ravenous he must be. He'd been unconscious for almost two full days. I could hear him rummaging around his little cell.

"There should be a tin bowl, near the front of the cage," I offered, just as the sound of metal ricocheting to the floor sounded.

"Crap," he muttered. "What the hell, I'm starving."

Poor guy. He's probably licking the spilled taro and yams off the floor.

"So you know what this means, Blake, right?" I asked, hearing the sound of him licking his fingers.

"Mm?" he hummed back at me as I heard the sound of the bowl scraping against the floor. "Just trying to get some of this back into the bowl. I don't even want to think about how disgusting this floor is," he muttered.

I grinned, wishing I could see him, but sure he'd be embarrassed if I could. "It means," I continued, "that we can do the same thing for Jaxon. He can be in control again." His rummaging stopped. "I've seen it, Blake. Kalepe isn't the same. The Defenders down by the beach, the ones who've brought the food, they aren't the same."

"Sam." There was something defeated in his tone. "Jaxon has had your blood already. Remember? And it hasn't helped."

"Then there's something more to it. We just aren't seeing the bigger picture yet. I'm telling you there has to be a way for Jaxon to behave like these Defenders do."

"These Defenders," Blake spat the word out, "aren't as innocent and wonderful as you think, Sam. They follow Kory."

"Not all of them do," I retorted.

"Okay, so maybe one or two don't, but most of them follow Kory with blind devotion. They could be made to do anything. Which is why..." He stopped short, and I waited. "They have to be destroyed."

"What? No! No way, Blake."

"Sam, I know it sounds horrible, but it's the truth."

"No. They can be reasoned with. They're still people! They just wanted to do the right thing. Be soldiers to help keep order. You can't just kill them. It'd be genocide!"

"You're sounding like you believe Kory's crap, Sam."

"Not even close. Kory, on the other hand, you can have. He's the one pulling the strings here, Blake. Don't destroy the puppets, kill the puppeteer." Even as I said it, I knew my analogy sounded ridiculous.

"Kill the puppeteer?" he repeated, and then chuckled softly. "Sorry, couldn't help myself. Okay, so say we do off Kory, you think that will solve everything?"

"Uh... well, no. But it'd make me feel a lot better."

Blake's laugh deepened, and then he sighed. "Me too."

We both sat there for a moment, perhaps not ready to argue with each other again. I was still so relieved he was alive. I wished I could throw myself in his arms, instead of hackle him about what we should do about Kory and his bug army.

Killing the Defenders was wrong. That much I was certain of. What drove me bonkers was that I couldn't shake the feeling the solution to this was somewhere in the back of my mind, niggling at me. Tickling my conscience, begging me to listen.

Sammy, if that's you, you better just show up, because I'm pretty much out of ideas.

A little shocked at my own willingness to let her in, I cleared my throat. "Well, I guess you and I can argue for the rest of our lives, however short they may be, about what's best to do with the Defenders. Because we can't do a darn thing about it stuck in here."

"That's where you're wrong."

"What do you mean?"

"I mean..." Blake's voice dropped to where I could barely hear him. "It's not by accident we're in here. I've got a plan."

"You do?" I wished I could see his face, gauge if he was being serious or just trying to make me feel better.

"Yes. Did you think I'd really sit around and wait for you to come back after you left with Kory?"

I stared at the blackness between us, frustrated the room had no windows. "Um, I guess I did. You really have a plan?"

"Of course I do. I'm seriously offended you think the Irukas could catch me that easily."

Hearing the cockiness in Blake's voice, I couldn't help but laugh. Maybe he's telling the truth! Maybe all hope isn't lost! "Okay, okay. Just tell me what's going on. How are we getting out of here?"

"We're not," he said.

CHAPTER
Thirty-Eight

"Ok... that doesn't sound like much of a plan to me," I said, frowning.

"Well, not yet, anyway. We need to sit tight for a bit longer... let things play out. Perhaps things already have. Either way, we have to wait and see."

"Blake, you've totally lost me. What are we waiting for? Is Mack coming to get us out?"

"Yes. Once the Irukas are done."

"Irukas? Aren't they the ones who captured you in the first place?"

"I let them get me."

"Okay, so you let them get you. Either way, aren't they on Kory's side?"

"Not all of them."

I let out a whoosh of air, ready to explode if Blake didn't stop giving me cryptic answers.

He must have sensed my frustration because he said, "Alright, let me start at the beginning. Get you up to speed."

"Thank you. That would be nice," I grumbled back at him.

"So like I said, I didn't just sit on my thumbs after you made your grand exit with Kory. I followed your scent all the way to Tonbo's Islands. I knew you didn't stop there, but I decided I needed Mack. He's an amazing tracker."

"What about Jocelyn?" I asked, interrupting.

"That was my other reason for stopping. I figured leaving her with Tonbo might give her a fresh perspective on this whole thing."

"Good idea. Okay, so you got with Mack and just followed me

here?"

"Well, not right away. First, I wanted to know what Mack had gotten out of Jaxon while we'd been gone."

"Oh," I said, my stomach tightening with nerves. "Did he get anything?"

Blake exhaled. "Yes. Some we'd already guessed on our own. I guess the bug being so upset helped Jaxon remember more. Anyway, he told Mack that when he'd captured Sammy, she had dropped a bag, which he'd gone back to retrieve while Sammy was unconscious, like we'd thought. He said he found an unmarked vial of blood in it, which he'd then, like an idiot, straight up injected himself with when he'd got back to his cave. He didn't run any tests on it, didn't even know whose blood it was. Jaxon said the bug was obsessed with it, so there was no stopping him. He said nothing felt different from it. He didn't notice any new or special abilities. So then, when you woke up, he decided to get blood directly from you. Which I'm sure you remember all too well."

"So why did Jaxon ask me later what'd I done to him? He must have started feeling differently."

"You're right, he did. After he'd begun treatment at Tonbo's facility, he started feeling this insane need to see you. And it wasn't just because he craved you like before." Blake's tone dropped lower, and I knew this was hard for him to talk about. "He said it felt like..."

"Like what?"

"Like he had to protect you."

"Protect me from what? Him? Maybe Jaxon's winning after all."

"I can only hope that's what it means, but Jaxon says he feels the need the strongest when he's the bug, not himself. I guess the bug in him is furious for sampling your blood in the first place. He's convinced it's changing him somehow, and the bug doesn't want to be changed... not like that anyway."

"If he's so worried about changing, what's he doing sampling my blood in the first place? Not just once, but twice!" I shook my head, even though Blake couldn't see me. "Blake, I know you're scared to have hope, but it sounds like Jaxon might be becoming more like the Defenders after all. He's gaining more control over the bug in him."

"Even if that's true, why's it not working the same? Do you think Kory and the ancients altered your DNA more after you'd given it to them?"

"Got me, but I do think the ancients are holding back on us. They know something, and they aren't sharing it with Kory."

"Which could be good news for us," Blake confirmed.

"Yes, it is. So, tell me again how staying in these cages is all part of your plan?"

Blake chuckled. "Yeah, I guess I better get to the good stuff before things start happening. Before Mack and I took off to track you, we stopped by Tonbo's and let him know what was happening. After he'd calmed down about me letting you go in the first place, he suggested we go ask the remaining Irukas for help. They weren't real receptive at first, but with Tonbo and Aster's convincing, we got a lot of them to agree. We'd need them to even get close to this island."

"I don't really understand. Aren't all the Irukas in the water? Why couldn't you just fly over them?"

Hearing Blake chuckle again, I wished the room wasn't so black. Not only was it annoying to not be able to see his face, but I also didn't like the fact I didn't know what the rest of the bugs were doing. Why were they so silent?

"You'd be surprised the amount of mischief those fish people can cause. Remember the feeling you had when Aster sang?"

"Yeah? What was that?" I asked, and then I gasped, "Don't tell me they can hypnotize people with their songs just like real sirens?"

"Not exactly, but close enough. The Irukas are part dolphin. Which, I don't know if you know much about, they are excellent communicators. They're able to make all kinds of different sounds, one of which is a frequency modulated whistle. For some reason when the two DNA's mixed, the Irukas seductive song was the byproduct. It's hard to ignore and can lead people to do unexpected things."

"So in other words, they can brainwash people with their singing?"

"Pretty much."

"Okay. That's totally freaky!"

"Yep. Then add to that the fact dolphins are extremely intelligent and protective, you can see why Kory was so keen on recruiting them."

I nodded, even though Blake couldn't see me. I remembered watching a program on dolphins once where a survivor of a shark attack said dolphins had come to his rescue, fighting off the shark and surrounding the man until he made it to safety.

"So what happened when you got here?" I asked.

"When we got close enough, I pretended to be Aster's prisoner so Kory's Irukas would buy Aster and the rest changing their minds. That's why I keep telling you, I let them have me."

"Why the bloodied face then?"

"It needed to be convincing so I let Mack punch me before we got here."

"What?" I gasped.

"I wouldn't have gone down without a fight. Besides, it's not that bad."

I could only stare at the space between us. "So where's Aster and Mack now?"

"That's the good part. Aster is still with the Irukas, waiting for the right time to make her move, pretending she's on Kory's side. For all I know, that moment might have already happened. Mack snuck on to the other side of the island. With the huge party down at the beach the other night, most of the island had been deserted. And with the excitement over my capture, no one should have noticed his arrival."

"But you don't know for sure?" I asked, dread filling me.

"Well, from the looks of it, if they had, they'd have thrown him in here with us, don't you think?"

"I guess so, assuming Kory decides to keep him alive." I

frowned. "Blake, maybe we shouldn't be talking about all this now. I mean, what if the other bugs hear us?" "There aren't any other bugs in here with us."

"What? How do you know? They were here all day yesterday."

"Because when I first came to, I heard a lot of commotion. Sounded like cages being opened and people, or things, being rounded up. When the door opened briefly, I made out the silhouettes of all of them leaving, but I was still too groggy to put it all together until you told me what had been in here."

"Oh. Wonder why I didn't hear any of that." I couldn't imagine sleeping through the bugs leaving the room. They would have been more than a little noisy.

"You were asleep," Blake said easily, as if that were even plausible. "Honestly, it's so black in here that I didn't even know you were next to me. You probably were sleeping pretty hard. It's been an exhausting few days. Are we underground? I swear I feel like I'm in a cave right now. What I'd give for my cell phone or a flashlight."

"No, I don't think so. I never went down any stairs. This room just doesn't have any windows, and I'm pretty sure it's night again. Hey, if they took the others out of here, wonder why Kory's just leaving us alone? Doesn't it seem strange? Like he should have been torturing us or something?"

"Actually, them coming to grab those guys might be proof our plan is working," Blake said.

"Really? You know you still haven't told me what this great, big plan of yours is yet, Blake. Like what's Mack doing?"

"Okay. I know. Let me explain something first. When we went to Aster, she told us something interesting. After we'd left her to go to see the ancients, she said all the talk over them disappearing got her thinking about some of the Irukas that had gone missing over the past year. Most of them were natural borns around our age. Because it was a group of guys and girls, most of the Irukas chalked it up to teens running away together."

"But Aster doesn't think so?"

"Not anymore. She's convinced Kory took them, just like he's taken everything."

"But why only a few of them? It's not like they could protect the island by themselves."

"Exactly. When Kory came to recruit, he did it visibly. But Aster said if someone took the teens, it was done in secret."

"Why would Kory?" "Aster thinks he is experimenting on them."

"What? Why?"

"One of the biggest downfalls to the Dragon Fae world is the inability to have children. It's the one thing that could threaten us with extinction. Our population grows only by injecting new victims. The dolphin and human DNA mix didn't have the same side effect. Maybe because dolphins are mammals, the gene code is more compatible. Who knows? Either way, they can have children. They won't die out."

I knew my eyes were as big as saucers. I'd heard Blake mention the natural borns, and I'd been dying to ask him if it meant what I thought it did.

"So... you think Kory is experimenting on them so that... what?" My voice barely carried. I didn't like where my mind was jumping to. "He can have a baby or something?"

"Aster is convinced of it. She said either Kory's strung them up, taking their blood, or he's tried even worse things. He's done something to those Irukas he took. And Mack is on the island, trying to see if he can find out what. Once he has proof of what Kory's done, he will return to Aster, who will then convince all of them to join us."

I felt a strange feeling washing over me, starting at the top of my forehead and working its way down, leaving the hairs on the back of my neck standing on edge.

"Join us, to do what, exactly?" I asked, afraid I already knew the answer.

"Destroy Kory." He hesitated a moment before adding, "And his bug army."

CHAPTER
Thirty-Nine

"**B**lake, we can't just destroy the Defenders!" I argued again, this time jumping to my feet. "This is madness! They haven't done anything wrong! You're talking straight-up murder!"

"Sam, listen to me."

"No. I won't be part of this, Blake. It's wrong, and you know it!"

"Sam! You have to listen to me. You don't understand. The Defenders are still bugs. You want to release a hundred monsters out into the world? And just hope humanity survives?"

I wrung my hands together, pacing the small confines of my cell. There had to be another way!

"Kory's army of bugs will change the world as we know it. Dragons are bad enough, but this? They can't hardly be stopped, Sam. They are drawn to blood and violence. Even if Kory's subdued their inner animal for now—"

"He has! I've seen it! They aren't the same. I can't understand why you refuse to see it when it means hope for your own brother!"

I heard Blake inhale sharply.

"Sorry, I don't want to drag Jaxon into this, but I just don't get it. Why can't you accept the fact that Jaxon might be able to live with the bug in him? Why are you so against everything the Defenders stand for? Even when it means a chance for Jaxon?"

Blake didn't say anything, and for a moment, all I could hear was the sound of our heavy breathing. We'd reached a crossroad. If Blake pulled the trigger on this... killing the Defenders before giving them a chance... I didn't know if I could forgive him. It felt wrong on so many levels.

And yet, even as I sat there, my breath slowing down, I could see his side to it. He didn't trust Kory, which meant he didn't trust anything Kory had been a part of. Including the Defenders. In his mind, they were trained killers merely waiting for their master to give the green light.

"There's a lot more to Kory and this operation then you realize," Blake said in a deep voice. "Like what happens if Kory did find a way to fix our reproduction problem? What then, Sam? The Dragon Fae will take over the world. Not to mention the bugs. They're monsters. Hell, we're monsters. The world has enough with just us, don't you think?"

He sighed. "You act like I enjoy this. Like I want to be the one who declares genocide on a group of people! I never wanted any of this on my shoulders."

I dropped down to my knees in front of the bars. "I know. Where's Tonbo in all this? Shouldn't he be the one making this decision and not us?"

"He's the one who hatched this entire plan. Once Mack gets the proof needed to convince all the Irukas to join us, the singing begins. It will draw the bugs out toward the ocean, where they will follow the Irukas all the way back to Tonbo's islands," he said, his tone sad.

"Tonbo has a large storage shed, not far from one of the beaches. He's preparing it now. When the bugs come, they will be led into it. Then the doors will be shut and locked. Tonbo's gathering enough dragons together to make sure we get everyone in there."

My stomach sickened. "And what? Gas them or something?"

Blake didn't answer.

"Are you serious? This is way too much like World War Two! Who's next, the Irukas? Because from where I'm standing, they're potentially lethal too! I mean, they can convince an entire group to march into a gas chamber, for crying out loud! What if they decide they want to take over the planet next? Are you going to kill them off?"

"That will never happen. Tonbo has ways to keep them in line."

"You've got to be kidding me."

"Sam, I don't like this anymore than you do! The whole thing makes me want to puke. But do you have a better plan?" There was desperation in Blake's voice.

I squared my shoulders, even though he couldn't see me. "Yes, as a matter of fact, I think I do. Or at least, I know someone who does."

"Who?"

"Sammy," I called out, not really answering Blake's question. "I know you can hear me; I know you are still somehow aware of what's happening. I give. Okay? I surrender! You can have me!"

"Sam? What are you doing?" Blake barked at me, but I ignored him.

I held my hands out, closing my eyes. "You can take over, Sammy, because I trust you have a plan. Better than killing a hundred islanders who had no idea what they were signing up for."

"Sam!" Blake pleaded with me in the dark. "Don't do this!"

"Blake, I can't stand by while you help kill Kalepe and others like him. I won't do it. I'd rather Sammy win because... I don't know if I can be with you if you kill them all like this."

The words felt heavy and horrible, filling my mouth with acid as they came out. I wished I could take them back, but I couldn't. It was the truth. Blake had shown more compassion for his brother Jaxon this entire time. And Jaxon had done horrible, rotten things. These Defenders hadn't done anything. Not yet, anyway. But that did not justify killing them first and asking questions later.

For a minute, there was nothing but silence between us. Then I heard something that sent me jumping back. A female laughing.

"Well played, Samantha," she drawled out from the blackness.

"Sam? What's going on?"

"I don't know," I answered truthfully, trying to place not only where the voice was coming from, but also whose it was.

There was a soft tsking sound. "I must say, lover's quarrels are so tedious. Both of you are so passionate about your own standpoint, while scared to hurt the other one's feelings."

"Who the hell are you?" Blake yelled.

"Ever so demanding, aren't we, Blake?" the girl answered, growling out his name. "Like I have to answer to you."

Confused, my eyes continued darting around the room. Who was in here with us? Had she been in here the entire time? I was pretty sure there were no female Defenders.

He groaned. "I should've known. Just like you, Kate, to hide so no one can see the piece of garbage you really are."

CHAPTER
Forty

"Kate?" I blurted, my stomach filling with nerves.

"Call me every name in the book, I don't care. I'm not the one proposing genocide." Her voice carried across the room. "I suppose since you know I'm here now, there's no point in keeping you both in the dark."

Immediately, light flooded the holding cells, temporarily blinding us. Eyes watering, I took in everything, all the empty cages, Blake jumping to his feet, and Kate's smug grin as she squinted back at us. With her brunette hair hitting her lower back in soft waves, her long, lean body with curves in all the right places, for half a second, I wondered why Blake never fell for her. Minus the whole manipulative, backstabbing part, she'd be quite the catch.

"There, that's better," she said easily. "I really don't have time to be groping around in the dark."

"So why were you?" Blake asked sharply, his eyes narrowing.

Kate made her way over to my cage. To my shock, she produced a key, which she promptly slid into the lock.

"Because," she answered, not looking up as she released the lock and pulled my door open. "I had to make sure Samantha and Sammy were finally on the same page."

I could only stare at her.

She gave me a crooked grin. "So typical of guys," she said easily, like we were the best of friends. "To think killing and violence is the answer to everything."

"Yeah, you're one to talk," Blake countered. "I seem to recall you tying Sam up in a cabin and using horror tactics to scare Sammy out of her. I wouldn't exactly call that non-violence, would

225

you?"

I could only gape at the pair of them, too shocked to formulate my own words.

Kate rolled her eyes at him. "We never would have hurt, Samantha. Besides, I seem to recall you forgave Mack pretty readily. Seems a bit odd, seeing how he played just as much a roll in Samantha's transformation as I did. So what, Mack gets to be one of the good guys, while Sammy and I are left to be the villains of this story?"

I knew my eyes were saucers and my mouth probably could have caught a fly or two. Did Kate and Sammy really want forgiveness?

"This isn't some freaking fairy tale, Kate. You and Sammy need to quit messing with everyone's lives. Sam's most of all," Blake retorted.

My brain finally registered that Kate was staring back at me, completely ignoring Blake's comment.

"Well, you coming or not?" she asked. "As much as I'd love to stay and talk with lover boy, we're actually on a tight schedule."

"Oh…" I stalled, my mind a muddled mess. "We've got to let him out first." I rushed over to his cage, where Blake grabbed my hands through the bars.

"Didn't I just hear you say you didn't want to be with him?" she asked, marching over to me.

My face flushed. "No. Well, I only said that because I can't… I mean… I couldn't if he—"

"Killed all the Defenders?" she finished for me. "Yes, well, news flash, sister. We let him out, and that's exactly what he'll do." She gave Blake an icy stare. "Come on, Samantha. We've got to hurry."

"Sam, don't go!" Blake said, pulling me closer to him through the bars. "You can't trust her. She's a liar. We still don't even know whose side she's on."

"I'm on Sammy's. Which translates into, we don't kill all the Defenders today because we have another solution."

I glanced over my shoulder at Kate, for some reason believing her. Blake tugged back on me.

"I don't know what she's planning, but it's never good. Sam, I don't want to lose you. Please." Blake's voice caught. "Don't go. We can figure this out together. Maybe we can talk Tonbo into—"

"Now who's the liar?" Kate cut in. "You can't talk Tonbo into anything. Trust me, Sammy already tried."

I rocked back. "What are you talking about?" I asked. When did Sammy talk to Tonbo?

"Bugs remind him too much of what killed his family," Kate answered, clearly not misunderstanding my question. "He never took the time back then to see if those soldiers could be saved. He only saw them as monsters and didn't stop until every last one was destroyed. What makes you think he will feel differently today?"

"Jaxon," I blurted, still dying to know when Sammy and Tonbo supposedly had this heart to heart. Blake was unusually quiet, his lips pressed in a frown. "He hasn't destroyed Jaxon. He's been trying to help him get better, even," I added.

Kate gave a bitter laugh. "Yes, Jaxon. My point exactly. Just why isn't Jaxon getting better? Sammy made sure he got what he needed to be "cured"." She threw up quotations. "So why isn't he like the other Defenders? What makes you so sure Tonbo's helping him, anyway?"

Because why on earth would Tonbo sabotage Jaxon?

Blake's eyes narrowed. "What are you saying, Kate?" he asked through a tight jaw.

"I'm saying I don't have time for this. Sam, you need to come with me now if you want to stop this. Story time can happen later."

Blake didn't release my hands. "I'm coming with you."

"So you can run back and warn Tonbo? No way."

"Then Sam stays here." Blake wasn't kidding either. I didn't think I'd be able to escape the grip he had on my wrists, even if I tried.

"Aw, come on, Blake. Don't you trust me?" she asked, moving even closer to us.

"About as far as I can throw you," he muttered.

"Well, in that case, you shouldn't have a problem letting go of your girlfriend and letting us take care of business," Kate hissed, grabbing on to one of my arms, tugging me toward her.

I winced as Blake didn't release his hold. "I'm going with you," he repeated.

"Not going to happen, Blake, so I suggest you let go of her before you leave her in bruises. Or worse."

I felt like a rag doll caught in between two stubborn forces. I knew Blake was terrified of letting me out of his sight and yet, I also somehow knew Kate really did have a plan. Something deep within me begged me to trust her, to trust Sammy. Just this once.

"Kate," I said firmly as both of them continued to argue over me, pulling painfully on my arms. "I'm not leaving without Blake, so if we're in such a hurry, why don't you stop wasting time fighting and let him out?"

Kate scowled as Blake grinned.

I turned to him next. "But Blake, we're going with Kate. No one's running to Tonbo. Not until we know if we can trust him. If he's really the reason Jaxon's not getting better, then we owe it to Jaxon to find out. If you can't agree to this, then I'm leaving with Kate now, alone."

Now Kate grinned back at Blake. His mouth snapped shut, the argument he'd been ready to give me seeming to die on his lips.

I tried to give him a reassuring smile. "Nothing has been adding up, Blake. We've hit too many dead ends. This might be our chance to get it right. Just this once, I'm begging you to trust me, Blake."

His eyes widened. Glancing down at his hands still gripping mine, he slowly let go. Meeting my gaze, he said, "Of course I trust you. It's her that I don't trust. But you have my word. I'll go with Kate. Because if what she says is true," his jaw bulged, "I want to know."

Kate rolled her eyes, sighing heavily. "Fine. Let's just get this show on the road." Unlocking his door, she added, "Better buckle up, Blake. You may not like me, but trusting Sam means trusting Sammy too."

Blake wasn't smiling, but he gave Kate a nod that he understood. To me, he reached over and brushed the hair back off my face. Leaning over, he kissed my lips.

"Oh my word! We so don't have time for that now!" Kate huffed, throwing the door open and peering down the corridor. "Coast is clear. Let's go."

Kate may not have had the time for a kiss, but I needed it. Having Blake by my side, I felt stronger. Like we could do this, maybe even win. Blake gave my hand a quick squeeze as we took off, flying through the now-empty building.

"I should just find Mack and call this whole thing off," Blake said as we came up to the glass wall. We had stopped long enough to see the beds were all empty now. There didn't seem to be any Defenders left in the building.

"No," Kate said. "Let them finish carrying out Tonbo's orders. Rounding up all the Defenders into one place will actually make this a lot easier. Let's just hope we can make it before anything else happens."

"I don't get it," Blake said as we took off again, carefully weaving our way through the building, keeping a look out for bugs. "You say you have a plan, Kate. But how did you know about Tonbo's plan in the first place? I mean, no one's seen or heard from you in over a week, and suddenly, you have all the answers?"

"I guess it would seem like that to you." Kate stopped short, peering around a corner. Since she'd taken the lead, we both stopped next to her. "Main doors look free and clear," she said, glancing back at us. "Those little Irukas must be singing their hearts out. Kory's got to be in stitches over it. Here..." She pulled something out her pocket. "You'll need these for the rest of the way."

"What's this?" I asked, taking the small pieces of foam from her.

"Ear plugs. Let's just hope they're enough. I haven't exactly tested this out beforehand." She shrugged and stuffed one into her ear.

"Ear plugs," Blake repeated, following her example. "How did you know about all this again?"

"Because," she said, her voice becoming muffled and distant sounding as I finished putting my earpieces in. "Tonbo's plan wasn't just hatched to deal with Sam running off to the island with Kory. Tonbo's known how he would handle Kory's bug army for a while. He just didn't know where it was yet. Guess he was just too lazy to do it himself. He was happy to let you guys do the leg work in finding it."

We'd flown to the main front doors. Blake out flew Kate and beat her to opening them. At first, I'd thought it was a strange moment to be chivalrous, but then seeing how much Blake struggled to open one of the metal doors, I realized we probably needed a code to open them automatically.

Blake opted for the manual, brute force method. It worked.

We flew through and entered the jungle beyond. The night was black, lit by the stars and the half moon. A light breeze rustled the canopy of trees overhead. We flew low, keeping our eyes out for anyone.

"So saying Tonbo had this in mind, how did you know about it then?" Blake asked, not wasting time harping on Kate. "I'm guessing he didn't just tell you during visitor hours while you were being held there."

"No. He didn't. In fact, I found it quite insufferable how differently he treated me from Mack, but I guess you wouldn't be bothered to notice things like that. Shame too. Maybe if you'd seen the fraud Tonbo is instead of worshipping the ground he walks on, we wouldn't be in this mess now, Blake."

"What are you talking about?" Blake demanded. I knew he got defensive when others spoke ill of Tonbo. I didn't like it either, but I also knew things were off. Something wasn't right.

Kate stopped flying. "Listen, we need to switch to camo and shut up so no one overhears us. So I suggest we wait on all the questions."

He was in her face instantly, grabbing her by the shoulders.

"Blake!" I cried

He ignored me. "And I suggest you give me one damn reason not to tear you to shreds right now."

"So much for trusting Sam." She scowled at him.

"You're not Sam," he growled back at her.

I flew toward them, tempted to bang their heads together. "Stop it! Both of you! You're wasting time. Blake, we'll get answers later. We have to stop Tonbo from killing the Defenders. Because they aren't here anymore, which means they are flying across the water right now!"

Blake's chest was heaving. I'd never seen him so angry. For a moment, I was worried he'd give into his dragon side completely.

Then he exhaled through his nose and shoved Kate away from him.

Seeing a smile creeping on her lips, I said sharply, "Kate, you will answer every question we have after we stop the Defenders from being gassed. Understand? Or I may just let Blake have his wish."

Both Kate and Blake stared at me. I guessed my threat had been believable because with one last disgusted look at each other, we took off again without another word.

CHAPTER
Forty-One

It didn't take us long to catch up to them. Not being in camo, they were a horrific sight. A hundred monstrous, black forms flew through the night as even more Irukas weaved through the water below them. From a distance, the Irukas' bobbing fish-tailed bodies reminded me a bit of the salmon run along the Animas River. My dad had taken me fishing enough to know how driven the salmon were. They were going to make it upstream, no matter what the costs.

Mack must have found the proof they'd needed because I had no doubt the Irukas were driven now. They were protecting their own.

Since we were in camo, no one stopped us as we sped alongside the massive, moving army. Although, I could swear a few of the closest Defenders seemed to stare right at me. The earplugs only muffled the melody rolling along the waves; the tantalizing desire to join the throng was as strong as the ocean's tide itself. After Blake pulled back on me more than once to keep me from being sucked in, he'd insisted on all of us holding hands. Kate had made a silent fuss, but in the end, she'd relented, grabbing on to my other free hand. I'd seen Blake's outline shrug. Wordlessly, we continued.

At the front of the procession, I spied Mack, gripping Kory's arm. Not that it mattered; it didn't look like Kory was fighting back. In fact, even Kalepe, who flew next to Kory, seemed totally compliant.

Man, those Irukas pack a punch when they want to. Right below Mack, Aster swam. Each time she soared out of the water, her lips moved along with the song. It was eerie and beautiful at the same time. Her tailfin would flip, and back into the water she'd go. I held my breath, waiting for the split second until she emerged. Because of the mass numbers of Irukas, the song never ended but continued rolling out. It reminded me of a choir staggering their breathing while holding a particularly long note. Aster came back up, adding her voice to the choir again.

Blake pulled me back toward him—again. Oops. Better keep my eyes on the road.

It felt weird to pass Mack. Shouldn't we tell him something? Let him know we're free? I could only guess the plan had been for Mack to take the lead, getting the Irukas to woo the Defenders away, and then once they were in Tonbo's cage, he could come back and free Blake and me.

Kate must have sensed my very thoughts because I saw her shake her head vehemently as we shot past Mack and Aster, leaving the army behind.

Now what? I wished we could ditch the camo, but we'd agreed we'd keep it until we arrived. Kate had insisted it would be safest since Tonbo had spies everywhere. Blake had snorted back at her, but he'd gone along with it. Now that the army was well behind us, and the sucking pull of the Irukas melody had finally ebbed, I half expected Blake to break his word and appear. To my surprise, he didn't, but that didn't stop the questions.

"Since no one will hear us now..." Blake said as we all continued flying tightly together. I felt Kate try to release my hand, but I didn't let go. "You can start explaining yourself. I want the straight-up truth. No more half answers. How did you know about Tonbo's plan? You said Sammy talked with Tonbo. When? Is that how you know?"

We heard Kate sigh. "I suppose I have to tell you everything now, huh? Can't it just wait until this is all over?"

"No. It can't. Because I have to make sure you really have Sam's best interest at heart. How do I know this claim to save the Defenders isn't a ruse to get Sam alone so you can get Sammy to come back?"

"Oh," I said, my breath catching, Blake was right. What was I thinking telling Kate I'd go with her? She wants Sammy here, not me. She could have all sorts of things waiting for me wherever we are going. I shook my head. What had come over me back there? It sank in even deeper. Pretty sure Sammy came over me. She wants me to trust Kate, but why? So we'll save the Defenders? Like some kind of PBS special on save the killer whales? Or does she really have other ideas for me?

"I swear, Blake, you're so aggravating sometimes," Kate muttered, "Alright. I'll tell you what I know. Then maybe you will stop wasting your energy hating me. And Sammy for that matter. Heck, you might even like us."

"I wouldn't go that far," Blake said darkly. "I don't know if I can ever forgive you for what you did to Sam."

"Why not?" she asked with a laugh. "Like I said, you're all chummy with Mack again. Not that we mind, really, since Sammy cares for Mack. She's happy you've forgiven him. She's a bigger person than I am."

"You know it's really creepy how you keep talking about Sammy," Blake said, "Like you two have regular phone chats all the time. Because I'm pretty sure Sam has been the one in charge for a while now."

"Hello... It's really creepy how you both keep talking about me like I'm not even here," I blurted. No one said anything. I sighed, sensing both of their gazes. "You guys have no idea what it's like to hear you talk about Sammy... when I'm her. It's my body she uses. You both carry on like you should decide what's best for Sammy and me. I'm getting kind of tired of it, truthfully. I think it should be my choices—my decisions."

There, I said it. I knew they were staring now. Oh well, it needed to be said.

"Sam, I'm just trying to protect you from psycho people like Kate," Blake said, obviously not caring if he offended her.

Kate didn't say anything, but I could tell by the way she abruptly pulled her hand free that she didn't like it.

I didn't fight her. I was done fighting. Besides, holding hands while flying was tedious and a bit awkward. We could use scent to keep track of one another, and I could still make out the rough outline of Kate's form.

Still holding Blake's hand, I drew nearer to him. "I get it, Blake. I do. But I'm done with being sheltered and protected. In my experience, it has meant one thing. People I love have kept things from me. Like I'm too fragile to handle anything."

Blake went to say something, but I cut him off. "Anyway, we've gotten off topic. Kate, you have a lot of explaining to do. We've got a few hours before we get to Tonbo's Island, and the army is behind us. So there's no better time than now."

Whatever he'd been about to say to me, he let drop. "I agree. So how about you start at the beginning, Kate?"

"Alright, but I'm warning you. You may not like what you hear."

"I already don't like it," Blake mumbled.

"Trust me, it gets way worse."

"Spill it," I said, tired of waiting.

"Where to begin? How about with your transformation? The truth of it is, Sam, Sammy really did want to heal you both." Blake snorted, but he didn't interrupt. "She came to you at a time you needed help, when you were drowning. After she and Blake here saved you, she realized she wasn't really… a normal person. She said she always felt like half a person, almost like a ghost. Saving you gave her purpose."

I felt Blake's body stiffen in surprise. I knew he'd felt the same way about saving me from drowning too. Who knew that Sammy and Blake might actually have something in common?

"She decided she'd find a way to heal you, since she realized her very existence meant you were broken. She spent a lot of time defending you, telling all the stupid people who made fun of you to bug off. She really had no patience with school drama." "I saw that with Tonbo," I admitted.

Kate grunted. "We will get to Tonbo in a sec. For now, I want you to know that what you saw was real, Sam. Sammy may not be perfect. She tends to be a bit bossy and a know-it-all at times," she said with a laugh. "But she really did all of this to help you and her become one."

"If she was so selfless and wonderful, couldn't she have found a way to just go away? I mean, Sam didn't need her. All this being one sounds great, but I think Sammy was afraid of not existing. I think she wanted to be one so she could have more control."

"You know what? I don't really care what you think, Blake. You're so hell-bent on seeing the worse in Sammy, and that's fine. All that matters is what Sam thinks. So just shut up, will you?" I felt Blake moving toward Kate, so I pulled back with all of my strength on his arm to keep him from moving. "Please, Blake. Just let her talk. I need to hear what she has to say," I pleaded. I'd seen some of those memories Kate referred to, and I'd felt Sammy's intentions. Even with all that had happened, they had started out altruistic.

"I'm not saying I will buy every word, but let's stop fighting long enough to see what her side is," I added.

Blake sighed and nodded. I'd never seen him so quick to violence, except when around his brother, but that was defending me. I glanced over at Kate's outline. Blake sees Kate as the enemy. Probably how I should see her too, really.

"So the cabin happened," I said, "Let's keep going."

"Yes, the cabin happened. It was a botched mess," Kate grumbled. "It wasn't supposed to be like that. We never wanted it to go on that long, but we needed Sammy to come out at least once during the process. Sammy felt like if both her conscience and yours were present during it, that with the DNA injected, you'd emerge out of it, melded into one. For a bit after, I wasn't sure if it had worked. I mean, I wasn't exactly one of your best buds, Sam. We'd never even met. So I had to take Mack's word for it. Honestly, he was so torn up from the entire thing that he wanted to avoid you at first. He said he couldn't tell who you were anymore. You'd slipped into such a deep depression. He'd been terrified we'd ruined you permanently."

I had to squeeze Blake's arm, so he wouldn't jump in. I knew he wanted to bark out, 'You did ruin her!'

"But then that all changed when lover boy here moved in.

Suddenly, you came back to life."

Blake gasped softly. Obviously, her words surprised him.

"You're right," I said. "I did. I had a reason to live again."

Blake pulled me closer to him. "So did I," he said, kissing my forehead. To Kate, he asked, "So when did you figure out Sammy and Sam were still separate?"

"It didn't take long after you showed up, Blake. Mack had been waiting for you, Sam, to make the connection. To remember him as more than just a friend. Then when it was obvious you had feelings for Blake, Mack knew you didn't share Sammy's memories. The only thing we weren't sure of was if Sammy was still around at all, or gone forever."

Poor Mack, I thought. That must have been so hard.

"You didn't pass out after that, and with the hunt to figure out who'd changed you, Mack and I decided to keep a low profile."

"I bet," Blake muttered, but to his credit, he didn't flare up at her.

"Then, I started getting the letters again," Kate said nonchalantly, taking us both by surprise.

"What letters?" I asked.

"Sammy's letters," she said, easily, while I nearly choked on her words.

CHAPTER
Forty-Two

"**I** don't remember writing anything!" I blurted. "And until that night in the theater, I never passed out either. So when did she do it?"

"At night, when you were asleep," she explained. "Sammy's always had more control at night when your subconscious relaxes. So once things settled down a bit, she started writing me again."

"Wait a minute. I'm Sammy every night?" I can't breathe. Am I breathing right now?

"Oh, not every night. She doesn't always take control, just some nights when she needs to," Kate rushed on.

"That's disturbing on so many levels," Blake mumbled, and I realized he was so right. I mean, what did that mean for our future? How could I relax at night knowing someone else got to use my body for a few hours? Oh my gosh! Has she been there some nights when Blake and I were together?

"I don't know why you are both freaking out. You've known Sammy can possibly show up at any time. So what's the big deal?"

"The big deal? You just told me that when I sleep, Sammy gets free rein. It makes me never want to go to bed again." Suddenly, all the restless nights with Sammy plaguing my dreams made sense. She had been there. Those dreams weren't so farfetched after all.

"Like I said, it's not every night. And besides, Sammy's not going to hurt you, Sam. When will you believe me on that?"

I knew Blake wasn't happy about this new development, but we didn't have time to waste either. Kate had a lot more to say.

"Okay, fine. What did the letters say?" I asked. I'll freak out about my need to become an insomniac later.

"At first, she just said how sorry she was things hadn't worked as we had planned. She let me know she was still there and was still working on a way to solve the problem. Then the letters got more interesting. Apparently, Sammy decided it was time she learned more about her sister's boyfriend, Kory."

My mind scrambled to piece together my Kory-Sammy timeline. It all got so confusing. Trying to keep it straight how much I knew versus what Sammy knew at any given time was almost impossible. It would be so much easier if we could just meld our consciousness together.

"So at this point, Sammy knew Kory was a dragon," Blake asked. "She also knew that Kory was dating Jocelyn, and that Kory was developing his own serums, right?"

"Right. She knew about Kory and Jocelyn before the cabin even happened," Kate said, confirming what I'd seen in my Tonbo-induced 'vision'.

"About that, why didn't she just go to Kory for the serum since Mack kept refusing to do it?" I asked. "I mean, seems like that would have been the easiest thing."

"Yeah, maybe she would have, but thank heavens she'd already met me by then," Kate said.

"Oh, that's right. You mean when Mack took Sammy to the island," I said. "You said before she started writing letters again, so I'm guessing after that visit, you started corresponding through letters, right?"

"Yes. Looking back, it was foolish. But how else could we do it? We could hardly call each other. That's too easy to trace. Letters can be hidden."

What I wouldn't give to see those letters now! After this was all over, I'd make Kate show them to me.

"So Sammy and you plotted the cabin out through letters?" Blake asked.

"Yes, basically. After the transformation happened, and the letters started up again, I knew Sammy was still there. Being a damsel only seemed to amp her need to fix you, Sam. She became obsessed, which led her down Kory's path. She wanted to know what he was up to. She was always too curious for her own good, if you ask me. I never wanted to be dragged into Kory's melodramatic war. Kory's a spoiled brat. Always wanting to be the center of attention."

"Finally, something we can agree on," Blake muttered.

"Told you that you might like me in the end," she teased, and I felt a stab of guilt. Kate did like Blake. She loved him. What must this be like for her now?

"Kory didn't know about Sammy's existence at first, but he found out about her before you did, Sam," Kate continued. "Jocelyn told him after the Halloween dance, when Kory let her in on the whole Dragon Fae world. Even though Kory knew about her, she kept a low profile when she followed him at night. He never knew she was basically stalking him. There was one night the tables were turned, but that'd been you at Lemon Reservoir, not Sammy. Remember that?"

"Yes," I said. "How could I forget? That was when I'd found out I wasn't the only winged creature out there. I'd tried to catch Kory, but he'd been too fast. And then there was that night he'd come to my room." And accused Blake of being my kidnapper, I left that part unsaid.

"Yeah, and in the meantime, while Sammy shadowed Kory, she'd write to me about what she'd discovered," Kate said. "I read about the last bug's DNA and what Kory had done to Jaxon. When she wrote me about the plans for the Dragon Defenders, something changed. For the first time since I'd known her, her letters stopped obsessing about fixing you two. Instead, she focused on a much larger problem."

Blake's silence was palpable. He didn't argue, but seemed to be listening.

"You mean, Sammy didn't just join forces with Kory like Jocelyn said she did?" I asked, scared to have hope.

"Heck, no. She's no idiot." Kate hesitated, and then added, "But she did make one big mistake. She trusted Tonbo to do the right thing."

Hearing Blake gasp, I knew this was where it would probably

get unpleasant between the two of them again. I braced myself for it.

"But Tonbo didn't even know about Sammy until recently," he countered.

"He'd sure like you to think that. Why do you think Tonbo kept me in a holding cell with no visitation rights, while Mack was free to go, huh?" She grunted. "Since Mack wouldn't tell Tonbo about her existence when she was trying to change into a damsel, she asked me to do it. It was a bit tricky, seeing how I couldn't admit I'd been the one to change Samantha in the cabin."

"When was this?" Blake asked, his tone sharp.

"Before you took Sam to the island to meet Tonbo. Before you left to hunt down Jaxon," Kate firmly answered. "Sammy asked me to tell Tonbo everything. She wanted you to know who you were really hunting, Blake. She thought he would warn you."

Never mind we were getting close to the Outskirts, Blake suddenly ditched the camo.

"I need to see your face, Kate," he commanded when we stopped abruptly to stare at him. "If you're going to tell me that Tonbo knew full well I went after my own brother, I need to know you're not lying." His chest was heaving.

I felt Kate's inner struggle. We were getting close. What happened if an Ancient found us out? Finally, with an exhale, she appeared.

"Fine," she relented. "Look me in the eyes when I tell you this, Blake. I went to Tonbo. I told him what I was about to tell him sounded crazy, but that it was true. Blake's girlfriend, Samantha, had an alternate personality. Started way back from the freak drowning accident she had when she was young. I told him Samantha's split personality had reached out to me since I worked with Tonbo and was Blake's friend, wanting me to warn everyone about Kory's real plans."

"You didn't tell him about the cabin? How convenient for you," Blake said darkly.

"The only reason I didn't then was because I knew I'd be imprisoned. And Sammy needed me to be her hands. She needed me to finish what we'd started."

"I'm surprised he bought it at all. I mean, how would Sam even know who you were, Kate? She'd never even heard about you until Kory's making up a bunch of lies about what happened between us."

"Um, that's not entirely true," I slowly said. Blake shot me a glance. "Your sister Anna told me about Kate, at least that she was your girlfriend before." I felt my face flush. It felt horribly awkward to be the one to point out their obvious history.

"What?" he blurted, and then shook his head. "Either way, why did Sammy reach out to someone she didn't really know? Without telling Tonbo about your history together, Kate, it seems like a weak story, at best."

She shrugged. "You know, at the time when Tonbo shoved it under the rug and pretended he didn't believe a word I was saying, I'd be inclined to agree with you."

"There's one thing I don't understand," I interrupted. "It would have been a lot more believable if all this had come from Mack. I mean, he knew about Sammy for years. He never told Tonbo about her at all? Why didn't she just reach out to Mack? Confided in him? Or..." My stomach sickened. "Maybe she did. Maybe Mack has known about this all along too."

"No," Kate said, her voice absolute, when Blake stiffened. "Sammy didn't want to hurt Mack anymore. When she realized the treatment hadn't worked and saw what the whole cabin thing had done to him, she knew she'd made a mistake."

"How do you know?" I asked.

"She told me in her early letters. She didn't want Mack knowing she was writing me at all. She didn't want to involve him anymore. She felt he needed his friends to trust him again. The less he knew, the better, in the end."

"Maybe because she feared Mack would have the gall to stop her this time," Blake said.

"Or maybe because she really did love him, Blake." Kate frowned at him. "You'd be surprised what people are willing to do for love."

Another awkward pause.

I cleared my throat. "Okay, so we don't have much time. Why don't we just skip to what matters. You told Tonbo, he may or may not have believed you, but then what? I came to the island with Blake and Tonbo's theater happens. Please, please tell me you know what Sammy did during that time."

Kate's lips twitched to the side. "I do know. Question is—are you ready to find out?"

CHAPTER
Forty-Three

"Stop stalling, Kate. Just spit it out," Blake demanded, clearly as irritated as I felt.

"When Sammy took over in the theater," Kate said, looking at me and ignoring Blake, "Tonbo either knew or realized then what was really happening. He told you he'd had you brought to your room to rest, Sam, but what he didn't tell you was he came to see you soon after. Only you were Sammy, so you don't remember."

Thankfully, Blake didn't interrupt, so she continued. "Sammy again told Tonbo of Kory's plans, pleading with him to keep you from killing your own brother, Blake." She glanced over at him. "But he wouldn't budge, accused her of making it all up. He thought there was no way it was really Jaxon, and even if it were, that there was nothing to be done but to kill him. Said it was too late for Jaxon."

Blake's frown deepened, but he still didn't stop her.

Kate sighed and rubbed her forehead. "That's when Sammy spilled the beans and told Tonbo there might be a way another way of dealing with Kory's Defenders. She'd found something that could help them control their urges. She needed time to make sure it worked right. Time she didn't have sharing her body with you."

It felt funny hearing Kate put it that way. Suddenly, I felt bad for Sammy. Although, to be fair to myself, I had no idea about any of this. Heck, I didn't even know she existed at this point.

"Tonbo became adamant that under no circumstances was Sammy to experiment on the bugs. He felt the results could only make things worse,"

"A valid argument," Blake commented in an even tone. "So what happened? Obviously, Tonbo and Sammy didn't see eye to eye."

"Nope. So Sammy did the only thing she could do. She pretended to faint."

"Oh," I said. "So Tonbo would think it was me coming back. Right?"

"Exactly. Tonbo got you back in your bed and left the room fast. As soon as he was gone, Sammy took off for the ancients."

"What about the letter she wrote and left for Tonbo?" I asked.

Her eyes widened. "What are you talking about?"

Luckily for me, when I transformed back into myself from Jocelyn, my same clothes came too. I pulled the folded-up piece of paper from my pocket.

"Tonbo said this note was left from… er… me. But if what you said is true, Sammy wouldn't have left a note at all for Tonbo saying she was leaving."

"Let me see that," she said, holding out her hand.

I hesitated and gave it over. For some funny reason, I didn't want to part with it.

"Sammy didn't write this," she said after a glance. "I'd recognize her handwriting anywhere."

"Then who did?" I asked, taking the letter back from her.

She shrugged. "Who knows… maybe Tonbo did after he discovered she was gone. To cover his tracks."

Blake frowned at Kate. "You said Sammy went to see the ancients next. Why?"

"In all their heated discussion, Tonbo had mentioned a few of the ancients who had been there during the bugs' terror. He had been using them to prove his point, saying, 'Just ask Alek or Otto if a bug is worth saving!' Well, Sammy decided if Tonbo wasn't going to help her, maybe they would. It was a huge risk, but she did it anyway."

"So that's how Otto had Jaxon's plans in his office? Sammy had shown them what Kory was up to?" I asked, trying to piece it all together. "Why would they agree to help her? I mean, they are pretty loyal to Tonbo. And the bugs' had killed their friends and family long ago too," I said, remembering how Galina had said not just Tonbo's family was lost that day.

"Good point," Kate said, "But Sammy knew a few things from her own research that maybe Tonbo hadn't shared with everyone, including the ancients. Since she knew Otto and Alek, with a few other key scientists, had helped Tonbo develop the original Dragon Fae serum, she thought it was worth a shot to at least present them with the facts."

"What facts?" Blake asked, his eyes narrowing. "I find it amazing that Sammy can find out things that no one has known for a hundred years. I mean, she must have an amazing search bar on her computer. Oh wait... she shares her computer with Sam. And come to think of it, most of her days are shared with Sam's consciousness."

"You can make all the snarky remarks you want, Blake. I'm not making any of this up. Just stop me now if it's not at least answering some of your questions."

He grimaced but didn't say anything. Clearly, he was going to let her finish as he promised me, and then we'd see where the chips fell.

"Okay, then. Where was I? Oh, yeah. The ancients. Man, are they a mess if I've ever seen one. Good luck governing them, Master Blake." Kate laid the title on thick.

Annoyed with how slow Kate was going about this, I squinted at the horizon. There was something out there, far in the distance. Were those Outskirts? Were we that close already?

Crap! Kate has so much to tell us. Like what we're going to do to stop all this! All we'd really learned was that Sammy thought Tonbo was a ruthless killer who saw no good in the Defenders' lives, Sammy supposedly had some cure up her sleeve after all, Tonbo may have lied about knowing about Sammy, which put the whole, I need to speak with Sammy, into a new light, and Tonbo might have been the one who was keeping Jaxon from getting better.

That last thought sickened me. If that proved to be true, I

didn't know if I could ever forgive Tonbo.

"Kate," I said in a sharp voice. "We are getting close. You need to speed up this explanation!"

Kate glanced ahead and spied what I saw. "Okay. So long story short," she said quickly, "Sammy went to the ancients. She pleaded with them to understand that just because something is different, or maybe doesn't fit the mold, doesn't mean it's a monster. She got them to see that even the bugs—a byproduct of science gone wrong—still had lives worth saving."

"Wow," Blake said, clapping his hands like Kate had just given a speech. "You know, this all sounds wonderful. Too bad it's not real life. The super soldiers were stone-cold killers. I should know. I killed the last one, remember? There was no humanity left in it. I can barely see humanity left in my own brother! He was a good husband, the most devoted, loving dad I've ever seen. A doctor, for crying out loud—dedicated to saving people! Now, I barely recognize what's left of him. So sorry if I don't buy the whole, let's save the bugs because they are still people speech."

Hearing Blake's torn words, I felt how deep his pain really ran. His love for his brother was the only thing keeping him from finishing him off.

"The bugs Tonbo developed for the Germans long ago aren't so different from you and me, Blake. They were given the same dragonfly DNA, but Tonbo added lots of testosterone and adrenaline. Enough that it would have killed any normal man. But with the dragonfly DNA, it created huge, out-of-control dragons, or bugs, as everyone calls them. I always hated that term. Seems so juvenile."

"Kate," I snapped. "Who cares what they're called! For us being in such a hurry, you'd think you'd explain what we are about to do!"

She frowned at me, slowing in her flight. "But that's just what I'm doing! You have to understand why and what Sammy did. The history of this is important. Or Blake is never going to go along with what we have to do now."

CHAPTER
Forty-Four

"Just tell us," Blake practically growled out. "I haven't liked a word you've said so far anyway."

Kate frowned. "I was hoping you'd see that Sammy really isn't the bad guy here."

I licked my lips, trying to decide what I should say. Part of me really liked to think Sammy had the master plan, that her motives were really good after all.

Kate must have taken my silence as a good sign because she shot me a sympathetic smile. "Samantha, maybe one day you'll get to know Sammy like I have. When this is all over, I'll show you the letters. Then you'll see."

"I'd like that, actually. Thanks," I replied honestly, even though Blake didn't look happy about the idea.

Kate took a deep breath and faced Blake. "So to answer your question. What we have to do now is get to your brother."

"What? Why?" he asked.

"Because when Sammy went to the ancients, they didn't just sit around sipping iced tea. They developed a new serum, with Sammy's... or well, your blood, Sam. Sammy had the theory that if the bugs were given something to help them come together and work as a team for a common goal, their out-of-control desires to hunt and kill could be channeled into something better. With the ancients' help, she added honeybee DNA."

"Yeah, that's what Alek told me back with Kory," I told Blake. "So Sammy and I don't actually have the bee DNA then, she just added it to what she gave Jocelyn?" I asked, hoping I was keeping this all straight.

"That's right. Sammy got the serum ready and told the few ancients who had agreed to help that they should try to find where Kory was and join him. Pretend they were on his side, whatever it took to gain his trust. She felt they should be there to alter the Defenders without Kory really knowing. In the meantime, Sammy wanted to test her new serum out on Jaxon. She figured since Jaxon was doomed either way, it couldn't hurt to try. She knew you were hunting the bug, so she knew she had to move fast. Get to Jaxon before you did," Kate told Blake as goose bumps shot up and down my arms.

Blake might not like what Kate had to say, but too much of it was making sense to me. Like puzzle pieces snapping into place.

"So she flew home to warn Joc about Kory first," I said.

"Yes, she'd hoped if she told Jocelyn the entire story, that she'd see why Kory was so evil," Kate said, nodding.

"But Jocelyn just felt like Sammy was a hypocrite since she had been the one to change herself in the cabin, not me," Blake added. "Jocelyn told us about this part."

"Oh good, so then you know how she asked Sammy for a sample of her blood. Sammy told her she'd need some time and left. Really, she needed a minute to think. She knew this was the perfect opportunity to get the new DNA serum into Kory's hands and into the Defenders' blood, but she'd wanted to test it out first on Jaxon. In the end, she knew she didn't have much time left. She divided the sample into two vials. One she gave to Jocelyn, and the other to Jaxon."

"So that's why Jaxon said it seemed like she wanted to be caught," I said. "Sammy did. Only she probably didn't mean to drop the bag. Lucky for her, Jaxon went back for it."

"Actually, I bet she dropped it for that very reason," Blake said, scratching his chin. The hazy outline of the Outskirts was all too clear now; we'd need to be switching to camo soon.

"What do you mean?" I asked.

"Sammy," he said, for the first time with no contempt in his voice, "knew the bug in Jaxon would have been more cautious if she'd had it with her, maybe even tested it out to make sure it wouldn't hurt him. But since she'd left it behind, almost like she didn't want him to have it..."

I laughed. "It only made him want it that much more. No questions asked."

Kate cocked an eyebrow at Blake. "Told you Sammy knew what she was doing."

"So Sammy gets the new serum into Jaxon's blood and hopefully Kory's new army, and then I wake up in the cave. Her job's done," I said with a little bit of awe. "All those times I was so close to passing out, Sammy was really trying to come back to tell us what she'd done, so we could finish it," I said more than asked.

"Exactly." Kate grinned at me.

"Which I'm guessing has to do with Jaxon," Blake said, his tone surprisingly void of argument. "I'm still not seeing how the bee thing fits in. So you're telling me he wants to work with other bugs now, or something?"

Kate didn't have a chance to respond because something fast and invisible knocked into her, sending her body catapulting backward. Blake swore and shot after Kate's cartwheeling form. As soon as Kate got herself reoriented, the invisible dragon must have put her in a chokehold. I got a glimpse of her gasping for breath, clutching at something across her neck, before she disappeared.

Blake yelled over his shoulder, "Sam, camo now!" and then he was gone from view as well. I quickly switched and shot after them. At least, where I hoped they were.

Why do they always want to fight invisible? It makes it so hard to tell what's happening! Wouldn't it be easier to not have to just use scent and sound? I mean, one of the huge benefits to be being part dragonfly is that we have insane vision!

Remembering how fast Blake could target his prey and attack, it dawned on me. Maybe that was the exact reason they did camo out. Perhaps it leveled the playing field a bit more. Not being able to use super-human sight to stalk prey was the price paid to not have the prey use that same skill in return. Either way, I couldn't stand not knowing what was going on. All I could hear was grunts, gasps, and a lot of cursing. They were moving too fast for me to tell whose outlines were whose. I so need to work on my sense of smell! All I could make out was Blake's warm amber scent, Kate's lilac and spring floral, and something new that was a bit too sweet to be pleasant. Almost like watermelon-flavored candy. How any of that information could help me fight was beyond me.

From the outlines, it appeared Kate had been freed. I drew closer to her. No one had touched me, but that didn't mean we weren't surrounded right now.

Blake gasped, and then suddenly appeared, looking like he held someone by the neck.

"You've lost, so you might as well show yourself," he commanded.

Kate and I both followed suit, dropping our camo.

When our attacker appeared, it was my turn to gasp. Without her hair in the ever-present tight chignon and thin-rimmed glasses perched on the edge of her nose, I almost didn't recognize her. When she smiled at me, the way it didn't reach her eyes had my mind registering that it was really her.

"Dr. Killian?" I asked.

CHAPTER
Forty-Five

"Hello, Samantha, or is it Sammy today?" she asked, tilting her head to the side, not seeming bothered by Blake's chokehold. I halfway expected her to produce a pad of paper at the same time. Not wearing the business apparel, but clad in tight black pants and a black tank top, I couldn't wrap my brain around what she could possibly have to do with any of this.

"Wait, you know her, Sam?" Blake asked, his brows knitting together.

This day could not get any weirder. I threw up my hands in mock surrender. "Yeah, she's my psychologist!" I gaped at her, refusing to believe she was not only a damsel, but was also here attacking us too. This is impossible!

Blake's eyes widened, probably trying to wrap his brain around the implications. He tightened his hold on Dr. Killian. "What are you doing here?" he demanded.

She only gave him her heartless smile.

"Who cares? Just get rid of her, Blake," Kate stated, hand on hip.

"Why are you here?" he repeated, ignoring Kate and restricting her air even more. "Who sent you?"

She shot him a dirty look, but the way her hands scrambled to free herself gave away how panicked she must have really been feeling.

"The army isn't far behind us, Blake. We don't have time for the doctor," Kate repeated.

Dr. Killian struggled to speak with Blake's tight hold on her throat. "You'd like that, wouldn't you?" she managed to hiss out. "For them to follow you blindly and not ask questions, but they need to hear my side so they can decide for themselves."

"Actually, I'm kind of tired of everyone's long-winded stories today," Blake interrupted. "This is your last chance—tell me why you're here now, attacking us, or I swear I will end this, and it won't be pretty."

"He who controls the army will rule the world," she gasped out.

"What?" His hand loosened on her neck, and I saw the color wash back into her face. "What are you talking about?"

"Why do you think Kate's obsessed with saving the Defenders? I mean, come on. Don't tell me you really buy Sammy as the warmhearted savior and Kate the devoted helper to the end? They want the army for themselves!"

"Shut up!" Kate shouted back at her. "That's not it at all!"

"I don't understand," I said, shaking my head. "Even if what you say is true, why are you here? I mean, my parents were looking for a psychologist... and they just happened to get you? You knew about me being a damsel the entire time I saw you, didn't you? What was your angle? Huh?"

Dr. Killian cleared her throat. "I've never lied to you, Samantha. Yes, I'm a damsel, but I'm still your psychologist too. It wasn't hard getting the right people to recommend me to your parents. Your mom was upset about your nightmares. At least, that's what she thought they were, and since you and Sammy were practically celebrities in the Dragon Fae world, I recognized your dreams for what they really were. Sammy. I even told your mom. I wasn't trying to keep secrets. She became quite distraught and decided to keep tabs on you more at night. She's never really trusted Sammy; always felt in her gut that Sammy had something to do with the cabin. Guess she wasn't that far off, really."

Dr. Killian shrugged, and I could only stare. Who knew! My mom was watching out for Sammy to show up again...

"That's when your mom discovered Sammy leaving at night. Lucky for you, you have a large tree outside your window, or she would have had a lot more questions."

"Argh," Kate interrupted, grabbing Blake's arm that wasn't

holding Dr. Killian. "Believe me or don't, either way, you can't just trust her! She said herself the importance this army could play. What makes you think she's not after it for that very reason? If we don't get to Jaxon now, all of this is for nothing! Even you," she shot Dr. Killian a withering look, "know no one wins if Tonbo destroys the Defenders."

Dr. Killian not countering her statement made me think Kate might be right. I had so many questions I wanted to ask still. Like how did she know we'd be out here right now? Why was she really here? Even with Dr. Killian throwing a monkey wrench into everything, deep down, I still believed Kate. We need to fix Jaxon, and then somehow everything will work out. No idea how, yet.

I glanced over at Kate and nodded. "You're right, let's go."

Seeing her look of relief, I switched to camo and immediately took off, not glancing back to see if Blake would follow. Kate was by my side in an instant, her body a mere silhouette against the sky, her camo matching the blueness surrounding us.

Blake, of course, did follow us, with my psychologists in tow. I was shocked to see that once they'd caught up to us, she'd been willing to switch to camo when Blake did. It would have been easy enough to refuse and us be easily spotted as we passed the Outskirts.

"Got to make a pit stop before we get to Jaxon," he informed us as we passed over the last island. "Can't have the doctor giving us away."

Kate and I didn't object. Even with his hand over her mouth, we could clearly hear her complaints. I guess she's not too happy about being our prisoner. I was a little shocked on the lack of planning on her part. She attacked us, odds three to one. What did she hope to accomplish? Realizing she had really only targeted Kate, I supposed she'd hoped we would have been a bit more sympathetic to her cause. Which was what again?

I tucked that question away for later; we were under a time crunch. City was fast approaching, and with the preparations for the arrival of the big bug army, the hope was no one would notice our little groups' semi-silent entrance.

Dr. Killian began wailing against Blake's fingers. Kate mumbled something under her breath. I caught the words, 'silence her for good.'

My heart was beating so hard and fast in my chest that I was glad Dr. Killian was causing a fuss. It distracted me from what we were about to do. We entered the island from the southwest side. The beaches here weren't as sandy as up north. There were more rocks and trees breaking up the oceanfront, and since we didn't want to march right up the boardwalk in downtown City, it was a great place to sneak in.

We needed somewhere to stash the noisy doctor first. And, I thought with rising panic, I need Kate to be a bit more specific on what we're going to do with Jaxon.

Tonbo's large storage container was further south of us on the southern tip of the island, Blake informed us as we slipped under some trees. It felt great to have my feet on solid ground again. Long flights were exhausting, even as a damsel.

"So," Kate said in hushed tones. "Where should we leave the doc?"

"At my place," Blake stated.

My head whipped in his direction. "Your what?"

He chuckled. "Did you think I lived with Tonbo when I'm here?"

"Well, yeah. If you've got your own apartment, why did we stay with Tonbo this whole time?"

"It's a house," he corrected me, his voice drawing closer to me. "And as much as I'd love to have you stay with me, Tonbo insisted on you being his guest."

I heard Kate snort. "Yeah, I bet he did. So he could keep close tabs on Samantha."

Dr. Killian made a noise, I wasn't sure whether she was trying to agree with Kate or not. Either way, Blake must have thought better of arguing about what Tonbo's motivations really were.

"I'll be right back," he said, surprisingly close to my ear. "Let me go drop her off."

"We'll go with you—" I began.

"No, it'd be better if you wait right here. Give me two minutes." He brushed his lips against my cheek.

He was gone before I could disagree. Really, I was dying to see where he lived. I mean, what eighteen-year-old high school senior has his own digs, already? I didn't care about the size; I just wanted to see what it was like. Was it messy or meticulously clean like his car? Would it be nicely furnished with an entertainment center, couch, dining room table, etc? Or would it be like sitting on a folding chair while I get you a TV tray to eat on?

The thought of staying with him at his own house sent a thrill through me. I bit my lip, embarrassed by my own desires firing up. We might be on the brink of a full-blown war if things don't go right... and I'm thinking about making out with Blake!

I was about to ask Kate if she'd been to Blake's place, but then remembered they had history together and maybe I didn't really want to know what she'd been doing at his house anyway.

Blake was true to his word and returned moments later, rescuing me from the weird feeling of jealousy in my chest. I caught his scent before he even touched me, yet I was still surprised when he pulled me into his arms.

"When this is all over, I promise I'll show you everything," he said, his voice huskier than normal.

I returned his embrace, even though I knew Kate was growing impatient and perhaps uncomfortable.

"I'm going to hold you to that," I murmured back, kissing his cheek. I leaned back a little, hating the camo, wishing I could look him in the eyes. "Don't worry. Everything's going to be fine. You'll see. Now let's get to your brother."

CHAPTER
Forty-Six

Sneaking into Jaxon's compound proved to be a little tricky. After Blake informed me there were air sensors surrounding the short fence that would go off if we flew through them, I was glad I hadn't tried to the last time I'd been here. I'd been lucky the delivery boys had shown up when they had.

Which was why I was now waving at the gatekeeper, wearing cargo shorts and carrying a large box. I'd impressed myself with fabricating from memory; I was one of the guys I'd seen before. Kate and Blake remained in camo, silently following me.

As soon as the double doors shut behind us, Blake whispered. "Change back. I can't handle you being a dude anymore."

Five seconds later, I was me again and back in camo.

Blake's fingers wrapped around mine. "I wasn't about to hold your hand while you looked like Fabio."

I giggled. "Yeah, that would have been weird for me too."

The building wasn't large, and it didn't take us long to wind back to where Jaxon's holding cell was. As we got nearer, I could hear Blake's breathing speed up.

"Kate, what exactly happens now?" he asked.

To my surprise, she appeared before us holding a syringe with a bright yellow label on it. Glancing around and seeing the coast was clear, I opted to become visible too. Blake sighed and did the same.

"An EpiPen?" he asked, frowning. "Pretty sure that's the last thing Jaxon needs right now."

"That's where you're wrong. When Tonbo created the bugs, he pumped them full of epinephrine, but not enough norepinephrine. So when Sammy altered the serum, she added more."

"I don't understand," I interrupted. "What's the difference?"

"Well epinephrine, or adrenaline, whichever you want to call it, targets the blood vessels and the heart, leading to the constriction of certain blood ways and the opening of others, all in order for your body to have the fight-or-flight response to stress. Your heart will be beat faster, your lungs get more air, etc..." Kate's words came out fast.

I nodded along; I knew how an adrenaline spike felt all too well. I was having one right now. Felt like all my blood was in my heart, leaving my fingers, toes, and the tip of my nose cold and numb.

"Norepinephrine stimulates the heart too, but it also acts as a neurotransmitter. Which basically means it arouses the brain. Making you more alert. Spikes the reward centers. Adding the extra norepinephrine to the serum makes it so the Defenders can be reasoned with, which in turn, helps them control their appetites more."

"So if Jaxon got that same formula, why isn't it working on him? Why does he need more adrenaline?" Blake asked, pointing at the EpiPen.

"It is working, but not all the way. Jaxon's is being suppressed."

Blake just stared at her.

"Your brother's on Prozac," she explained. "Or some other anti-anxiety medicine. Who knows which one, but all he needs is a little jump start."

"How do we know it won't make him worse?" he cut in. "Tonbo said Jaxon would only have control when he was relaxed, not shooting up adrenaline."

"Of course Tonbo would say that! When are you going to get it through your head? Tonbo doesn't want Jaxon to get better!" Kate shouted back at him.

I winced. Someone might hear us! What's she thinking?

Turned out that someone did. There was a loud crashing sound from the other side of Jaxon's door. It was followed by a horrible wail.

"Jaxon!" Blake didn't hesitate. He punched the code into the door lock and bolted inside. When Kate dashed in after him, I steeled myself for the worst and followed after. If Kate's wrong, this could get ugly fast.

It took my mind a second to register that no one else was in the room attacking Jaxon. The noise we'd heard must have been when Jaxon transformed. I'd never been in here before to know if the bed was usually flipped on its side, with the bedding sprawled across the floor, or if it was just when the bug took over. Next to the torn-up bed, an IV bag hung from a pole, the lines still dancing around from where Jaxon must have just ripped them out.

Blake was in his face, pushing back on his barrel, scare-ridden chest. "Just calm down, Jaxon. We're here to help you."

Kate glanced at me, giving me a subtle nod as she tucked the EpiPen behind her back. I knew then why she'd gone to so much trouble to bust me out of Kory's holding cell and have me here. She needed a distraction to get close enough to inject Jaxon, and I was the perfect bait.

Well, I swallowed hard. Here goes nothing. I took a step further into the room.

The bug's neck snapped toward me. He let out a roar of triumph, spitting as he spoke. "Finally! You're here! My witch friend." His corded wings spanned as he charged forward, taking Blake along with him.

To my shock, Blake didn't try to put him in a chokehold. He only remained between the bug and me, his hands pushing hard against his chest.

"Jaxon, stop! We can help you," Blake pleaded.

"I'm here," I said, trying to keep my voice steady as Kate maneuvered at my side. She was trying to get out and around Jaxon. "And I can tell you what you want to know."

The bug stopped advancing abruptly a few feet in front of me, Blake still planted between us. Kate froze at the bug's side. So far, he'd paid her no mind, but that could change at any moment. I needed to draw him closer, give her a chance to get him from behind. Should be easy enough since his eyes were fastened on me. Those horrible black holes—so dead that no light would even reflect off them.

"I know what's happening to you now, why you feel different," I said, taking a step toward him.

The bug greedily matched my movement, closing the gap between us, just as Kate slipped behind him unnoticed. The bug tried to swipe Blake out of his way, but Blake's grip was iron as he wrapped his brother up in his arms. "Now, Kate!"

She didn't need to be told twice, lunging forward and crashing into the backside of him. The horrible wail that followed let us all know she hit her mark. Jaxon collapsed at my feet, convulsing, screaming, and looking like death itself.

Blake dropped down to his brother, trying to gather him up to keep his head from smacking against the floor. "I thought this was supposed to help him!"

"It will," Kate yelled to be heard over Jaxon's horrific sounds. "Just give it a second. He's been half alive for too long."

If the bug version of Jaxon was only half alive, I'd hate to see what Kate thought was whole. Seeing how badly he was seizing, panic shot through me. Had we put our faith in the wrong person? Why had I trusted Kate, of all people, over Tonbo in the first place? I trusted Kate over Blake, for crying out loud! No wonder Blake had been at her throat the whole time.

Amidst Blake swearing and shooting accusations at Kate, the bug stopped shaking in his brother's arms as his eyes rolled shut. Unlike last time when Mack had given him a tranq, Jaxon did not reappear. The enormous, grotesque bug form remained. Motionless.

Oh my gosh! What did we do? I dropped down next to Blake as he shook the bug's broad shoulder.

"Jaxon? Can you hear me? Come on, big brother! I need you to pull through this."

Nothing. Blake dropped down to check for vitals. He rocked back, his eyes glaring. "He has no pulse. What the hell did you do to him, Kate?"

Kate backed up. "I swear, it should have worked! Blake, I didn't mean to hurt him! He should have..." Her words faded as her gaze shifted to the bug.

Glancing down to meet the black eyes staring back up at me, I yelped, making Blake jump. The bug bolted to his feet, leaving Blake and me on the ground, staring in disbelief.

The bug lumbered toward Kate, looking half drunk in his movements. "What did you do?" he slurred as Kate backed up fast. "What's happening to me?"

Blake and I were immediately on our feet.

"She didn't do it, I did, Jaxon," I blurted, and Blake grimaced. At this point, I think he'd be glad to have Kate take the fall for this. Especially if the bug decided to get violent.

The bug stopped and riveted his eyes on me. In an instant, he had me in his arms. Blake tried to intercede, but I waved him off. We could go round and round in circles all night with Blake trying to hold his brother at bay.

"We have unfinished business, you and I," I said firmly, acting as if his crushing hold didn't terrify me. "Now, listen. We don't have a lot of time. Jaxon, if you can hear me, listen in too. What I did healed you both. You and the bug can coexist. You don't need to keep fighting one another." The words tumbled out, almost feeling like they weren't my own. If I didn't know any better...

"No, no, no," the bug complained. "You made us weaker! You made us... feel again. I don't like it!" he growled, and yet, his hold didn't tighten.

"I gave you a conscience. I reminded you that you're still part human, not just a monster," I snapped back, surprising myself at the force behind my words.

The bug reared his head back a bit. "Why ruin what I was?"

"Because you're miserable! Because it's never enough for you! No matter how many hunts, how many lives you take, it's never enough. Even me. You know deep down your obsession with me was only a fleeting thing. Once I was gone, what would you have to live for? You have no purpose. No family. Nothing!"

Was I really saying these things? What had come over me?

The black eyes stared hard at me. "How can I want to kill and protect something at the same time? It makes no sense. Why...

why did you change me?"

"I just told you. Now you have to decide if you want to find true happiness or if you'd rather continue for centuries with an emptiness inside that terrifies you. Lie all you want to us, but I know the truth. I know what it's like to be half a person. A shell of what you could be. Stop fighting who you really are. Let Jaxon be a part of you. Let him influence your decisions. You will be happier and stronger if you do."

"Sammy?" Blake whispered, drawing closer but not interceding. As much as I wanted to glance over at him, reassure him it was still me, I didn't want to break eye contact with Jaxon. It was too critical that the bug understand this.

Yet the way he said, 'Sammy', sent goose bumps crawling down my arms. The words I'd just told Jaxon felt so confident, so full of truth, and yet... I had never even considered the bug's happiness coming in here. But as I said the words, I knew they were the right thing to say. How would I know that?

I'm still me, right? I can't be both people, can I? For half a second, I racked my brain, trying to conjure up memories with Mack. I had to know which ones came to mind. Would I see things only Sammy knew? Memories flashed, but only the ones I'd seen during Tonbo's therapy and my own version of history. Nothing new flew across my mind's stage. I tried to picture Jocelyn, and once more, I had the same result. How can I know?

I had no idea how long the bug held me, both of us staring hard at one another. Strangely, the advice I'd just given him was the exact thoughts buzzing through my mind now. Was it possible I'd somehow finally let Sammy in now? Was I capable of that? Were we now one... like I told the bug to be with Jaxon?

Kate touched my shoulder and I jumped, realizing then the bug had released me. Yet, I couldn't look away from those black eyes. I was too scared to face Kate or Blake. Whose memories would I see? What version of me was I?

The bug nodded back at me. "You feel it too, don't you?" he asked. "The confusion, the temporary loss of self." The bug's shoulders relaxed, his wings falling to his sides.

My mind was spinning in a hundred different directions, thoughts shouting at me that weren't there before. Foreign thoughts. *It's okay. Relax, Sam. We'll get through this.*

I shuddered. *Sammy? Is that really you?* I heard nothing back. *Okay, I've lost it. I'm officially crazy. Maybe I need Dr. Killian after all!*

I felt Blake holding my hand, and Kate tugging on my shoulders.

"Come on,"

"We've got to!"

"Sam?"

"Sam, are you okay?"

I ignored them, unable to look away from those black eyes. There was something in the dead, yawning holes that hadn't been there moments before.

A light danced off Jaxon's pupils. I clung to it as if it was my last hope.

CHAPTER
Forty-Seven

Funny that it took Jaxon, or the bug version of Jaxon, to snap me out of my stupor when he grabbed my hand and said, "You didn't give up on me. Thank you."

I wanted to respond, but my emotions got the better of me. I could only nod. Jaxon let me go and turned to face Blake, whose eyes immediately glanced at me first. I could see the panic written all over him. He wasn't sure if I was Sammy or me. That makes two of us.

Blake's aqua eyes shifted to his brother when Jaxon extended a hand.

"I know it doesn't look like it, but it's me. Jaxon," the bug said in a deep voice. "I'm in control now."

Blake stared back for a moment. Ignoring the hand, he threw his arms around him instead. Hugging the enormous, hideous form of his brother, Blake wept on his shoulder. The tears I'd fought off earlier sprang back up. Sniffing, I brushed them back with my fingers.

Kate cleared her throat. "As much as I love warm family reunions, the Defenders are probably in the cage by now."

Blake sat back, swiping his own tears away. "You're right. Come on, Jaxon. We're not done for the day. One battle down, but a huge one to go."

Jaxon, of course, had no idea what Blake was talking about, but luckily for us, he was willing to be caught up while flying.

Listening to Blake rattle off what'd been happening while Jaxon had been basically living in a drugged stupor, I focused on how Blake's hand felt on mine. He hadn't said anything when he reached for me when we took off. I knew by the electricity racing through my veins at his touch that I was definitely drawn to him. I aligned my flight to get even closer to his warm body. If he noticed, he made no sign. He continued to stroke my hand with his thumb as his grip remained firm. Feeling the warmness spreading through me, the desire to snuggle up even closer to Blake overwhelming me, I decided I had to be me still. I mean, Sammy wouldn't want Blake, would she?

With how few dragons and damsels were out, we opted to remain visible. At least until we got closer to the large containment shed. Where we were sure the whole island was buzzing with excitement, dread, or maybe both. It made talking so much easier when you could see each other. Blake didn't waste time explaining either. So far, Jaxon had listened, quiet and composed. It felt out of place. Where was the fighting between the brothers? Where was the stuff that gave me nightmares?

"So I have the right amounts of adrenaline now to help me control what's inside me," Jaxon said, "but you're saying Sammy added bee DNA too?"

His question was directed at Kate, who opened her mouth to respond.

To my own shock, I replied, "Yes. I did." Blake's thumb stopped stroking, but he didn't let go of my hand.

"Er... I mean, Sammy did," I stuttered, trying to recover. "She felt that even with the added thought processing, the danger with the Defenders, or bugs, was they'd crave a purpose, and if they didn't have one, or someone to follow, they could still grow restless. You have to understand, in your bug form, you are a hot mess of adrenaline. You need a thrill as bad as a junkie needs a high. But with the bee DNA, you can channel all that energy and drive into a purpose."

Blake and Kate stared at me while Jaxon, oblivious to the fact that I shouldn't be the one explaining, nodded along.

"Makes sense," he commented, more to himself, while I tried to deal with Blake's penetrating gaze. "So what do we need to do now?" he asked.

Kate just stared back at me, waiting as Blake's brows gathered. He still hadn't released my hand yet.

"We need to get to that container and get the Defenders out. It won't be easy since they are under the Irukas spell, for lack of a better word, but the bee DNA will help us," I said, the words coming easily. While my mind screamed, I have no idea what we're supposed to do! Kate's the one with the plan!

Where do you think she got that plan, huh? my own voice said in my head.

My stomach sickened. Oh no. Not again. I'm not me, am I?

Let's just say, neither of us are right now. But let's worry about this after we put out the major fire, okay?

"Sam?" Blake asked, and I blinked.

"Huh, yeah?" I asked.

"You okay?" he gently asked.

"Yes, why?"

"What Blake really wants to know is are you Sammy or Sam?" Kate bluntly asked. "Truthfully, I wouldn't mind knowing too."

"I'm... me," I said lamely.

Jaxon chuckled, but being a bug made it sound menacing. "I know exactly how you feel."

Blake's grip tightened on my hand. He pulled me closer, brushing his lips against my cheek. A shiver raced through me. I liked it.

"You sure you're okay?" he asked again.

I gave him a reassuring smile. "Yes. Don't worry. I'm Sam."

Not totally true, the voice reminded me.

Really? Of all the times for you to suddenly appear! Why now?

You think I like this anymore than you do? Look, I know you've got questions. Heck, I do too. But we don't have time to...

Blake leaned over and pressed his lips against mine. Fire raced through me, and I had to resist the temptation to pull him in for a deeper kiss. Not a good time, Blake, I thought with panic, even though I enjoyed his closeness.

Tell me about it. Why don't you tell your lover boy to hold off, will you? You've got Jaxon awaiting his orders. Trust me, you don't really want a bug to grow impatient, the voice inside my head snapped.

I pulled back, mustering the best smile I could, hoping Blake wouldn't see right through me. Really, my sanity felt like a bad craft project held together with white glue. Everything was sliding and if I wasn't careful, I just might fall apart in front of everyone.

"I'm glad you're okay," Blake said, ignorant of how not okay I really was.

"Me too." My voice sounded strange to myself. Alright, Sammy. What do I tell Jaxon?

Open your mouth. I'll do the rest.

"Jaxon." This time my voice was steady and sure. I turned to face him. "There's more to the bee DNA. The one thing every hive needs is their queen. The worker bees will fight to protect her. That pheromone she gives off can trump almost anything, including the Irukas' song."

I stopped, letting my words sink in.

"Wait. Are you saying I'm their queen?" he slowly asked, sounding confused.

Kate nodded, and even Blake looked pleased with this idea.

But I had to go and say, "No, I am."

CHAPTER
Forty-Eight

"Say what?" Kate blurted, flying up to me. "Sammy, you can't be the queen. You don't even have bee DNA in you."

Obviously, I didn't tell you everything in my letters, my mind muttered.

I was too stunned to respond to Kate's question. I could only echo her sentiments in my head. What in the world, Sammy? You better explain how I'm the queen right now! Or I'm going to tell everyone that... you are... um...

This ought to be rich.

Oh, shut up! How can you drop a bomb like that on me! Why not Jaxon, huh? He's perfect! That had been the plan with Kate, right? Why'd you change it?

Jaxon had no idea about the thoughts raging inside me when he crossed his chest with one arm and bowed his head toward me.

"I understand the feelings I've had to protect you now, My Queen. I will do whatever it takes to keep you safe. You have my word."

I wanted to tell Jaxon to stop acting as if I were some kind of royalty. Instead, I gaped at my own arm reaching out to touch the side of his face.

"Good, because I need you to help me rescue your brothers. Those Defenders are your family, Jaxon." My voice sounded foreign to my own ears. "You'll find your purpose together."

Jaxon's black bug eyes narrowed. "I will do whatever it takes to rescue them, but I will not let anything happen to you, either."

My mouth fell open, shocked over the strange turn of events, confused over what or who I even was. My stomach was spinning, my face felt hot, and my fingertips were like ice.

Blake shook his head with a look of disbelief. "Glad to see we are finally fighting on the same team, Jaxon." To Kate, his expression darkened. "I don't understand all that's happening right now, but once we stop the genocide, you and..." His eyes flicked toward me. "Well, you better explain to Sam and me what the blue blazes is going on."

"I think Sam knows more than me at this point," Kate said sharply. It was clear by the way she stressed my name that she didn't think I was even around anymore.

To me, Kate leaned closer. "Sammy, I thought the plan was for Jaxon to lead the Defenders out of here. Take them somewhere safe until we can convince Tonbo not to kill them. Why are you the queen?"

Yeah, Sammy, why are we the queen, huh? You owe me that much too! I demanded. I had no idea what to say to Kate, who was waiting for an answer. I wanted to shout, Stop calling me Sammy!

But instead, I said, "Kate, calm down. It was the only way Tonbo won't hunt down Jaxon and the Defenders. You think Tonbo will stop just because one Defender is in charge of all of them? Tonbo doesn't see them as human anymore at all. He won't stop hunting until they are all dead, just like he did before. But maybe if I can show him I can control them, maybe he will show mercy."

For as much I was dying to have Sammy's side of everything out in the open, her taking over, saying what she wanted to say, was straight creepy. I felt a total loss of self. One glance at Blake showed me how far gone I really was. He was searching my eyes, pain etched across his forehead in worried lines.

I reached out to him, wanting to comfort him, to let him know he hadn't lost me, but instead, my words rang out. "Look, I'm done explaining things. We have to act now."

I'd thought the container would be more like the Knightley's barn, large enough to house a few toys, maybe even an RV, but the long, rectangular building looked more like an abandoned plant or warehouse. With no windows, a flat roof, and an enormous sliding door in the front, I could only wonder what in the world Tonbo built it for in the first place. I didn't like that it reminded me of a containment facility, where one might house dangerous chemicals or drums filled with radioactive waste.

It was as if he built this for the just-in-case scenario. I shook my head as Sammy purred into my thoughts. *You aren't that far off. What did you think Tonbo did with the really naughty dragons, huh?*

I shuddered at both Sammy's sentiment and the scene before us. We'd switched to camo the moment all talking had ceased. At least, all the outward talking. Sammy had insisted on conversing with me the short distance down to the south tip of the island. Once we caught sight of the container, she'd finally shut up.

I knew now what she wanted me to do.

The army was here. We'd taken far too long getting here. Too much time talking. Half of the lumbering, still-hypnotized group was already filing into the white building. Kory and Kalepe were nowhere to be seen, and neither was Mack.

Thinking of my friend deep inside that horrible, windowless building, I panicked. *We've got to get him out of there before it's too late!*

Don't worry. Tonbo won't kill Mack, Sammy thought back, but I detected the tiniest bit of worry laced through her words. *There's no time to waste. Time to go.*

I didn't need to be told twice. This was it. Jaxon was at my side, the heat from his enormous frame radiating out to me. As I glanced over, I detected his silhouette's outline. I knew he was facing me.

"Jaxon," I said in a low voice, "We've got to get in there and find Kory and Kalepe. Up till now, the Defenders have treated Kory as their queen because he created them. But he doesn't have the right pheromones, so sometimes their loyalty has swapped to Kalepe because he's more like them. We need to get Kory out of the way, and Kalepe on our side. He can help sway the rest of them faster to follow me."

Blake was directly behind me, listening, but he wasn't touching me. Every time I spoke, it only seemed to solidify for us both that Sammy was running the show right now.

He sucked in air at my instructions. "You can't go inside. What if Tonbo seals the doors before you get back out? Can't you just call to the Defenders from out here?"

I turned around, facing him. His warm, amber scent made my heart ache with a sad longing. I touched his face, my fingers cupping his cheek. He leaned into them, his hands wrapping around mine, clutching as if he were afraid I'd let go. I wanted to promise him everything would be fine, that Sammy knew what she was doing, but I couldn't shake the feeling I was somehow saying goodbye to him.

My hand withdrew too quickly, and I felt him stiffen in surprise. "Blake. I need you to stop Tonbo from gassing us. Do whatever it takes. I can hold my breath for a very long time... and so can the rest of the Defenders, but if we are sealed into that building, at some point, we are going to need to breathe."

Blake shifted back. Even without seeing him, I could feel the tension rolling over him.

I berated Sammy. Stop it! Just let me be myself with Blake! He's hurting!

Sammy shouted right back at me. There will be time for that later! I need you to stay focused. Honestly, you're a mess of hormones right now!

The power struggle between us was pushed to the side because Kate was grabbing my arm, gasping. "Look! They're all almost inside!"

She was right. There weren't as many Defenders left anymore.

There were no more arguments. We took off, holding on to one another's hands once more, trying to block out the Irukas' song. It had faded since they remained at the shoreline, singing up the beach, guiding the Defenders to their own death sentence. Even still, the pull to do what they asked in their lyrical tones was hard to ignore.

Yes... let's go inside. We'll find peace in there...

Really? Sammy snapped at me.

I shook my head, trying to clear the haze I was in. Feeling Kate's hand pull away from me, I thought with smug satisfaction, At least I'm not the only one. I gave her a yank back and we continued on, me holding both Blake and Kate's hands. Sadly, this time, he didn't stroke my skin.

When we got up to the container's opening, Blake leaned in toward me and whispered, "I'm not giving up on you, Sam. I love you." He pressed his lips against my forehead, and then he was gone before I even had time to respond.

I felt his absence, the loss of his strength next to me. I wanted to fly after him, tell him how desperately I loved him too. How my life was empty without him, but it was too late. He was gone, and even with Kate and Jaxon flanking my sides, I'd never felt more alone. Sammy knew what to do, not me. I was scared. Terrified. The Defenders should want to protect me, not kill me, but what about the bugs who hadn't gotten the latest injections? Where were they? Had they succumbed to the Irukas singing? Were they inside too?

I bit my lip, my resolve slipping. Then I felt it. A warmness settling around my chest, stilling my breathing, focusing my vision.

Sam. Don't be afraid. We've got this.

I squared my shoulders, Sammy's strength filling me with new courage, and I dove inside the white building, Jaxon and Kate following after me.

CHAPTER
Forty-Nine

It was chaos inside. The further back we moved, the more the Irukas' influence had faded. Defenders were disoriented, restless, and looking for answers. The building we were in offered little to clue them in as to where they were and what they were doing—cement floors, plain metal walls, and track lighting. I noticed there were way too many overhead sprinklers in place in case of a fire. My stomach sickened.

This is really made for gassing people, isn't it? I asked Sammy, not really wanting to know the answer. We were weaving toward the back as fast as we could. The volume of complaints seemed to be greatest in the rear. I couldn't help but notice the way Defenders stared after us as we shot past. We remained in camo, but I got the feeling they could see us anyway.

Yes. It was a huge mistake confiding in Tonbo. I'd hoped he'd see the opportunity in fixing what Kory started. Instead, he told me what he'd do if he found them.

Put them in here? Did he build this for that very reason then?

No, he already had this as a precaution. Dragon Fae's have their enemies. Usually themselves, sadly.

I wanted to ask her so much more, but we'd found the source of the biggest commotion.

Kory. His eyes were bloodshot, his hair slicked back, probably from the amount of times he'd run his hands through his hair.

"What the hell!" he shouted at no in particular. Then to Kalepe, he threw his arms up. "Why is nobody moving? Let's get out of here!"

Kalepe didn't respond to Kory's urges. Instead, he turned to face me. I didn't shy away from his pointed stare.

He can see us, I told Sammy.

I know. Ditch the camo. It's time. I did as I was told, and a collective gasp followed.

Kory's eyes bulged, his mouth stuttering, "Impossible!" He shot a dirty look at Kalepe. "What's she doing here? I told you to end her!"

Kalepe's black eyes darted back and forth between Kory and me, panic written all over them. My heart swelled; he had disobeyed Kory's orders to save me. His sense of right and wrong solidified what we were fighting for.

I took a step forward, Jaxon and Kate, still invisible, moving with me. "Kalepe," I called out. "You felt the need to protect me, didn't you?"

He didn't answer, just shifted his weight. Kory folded his arms and scowled at me. "You shouldn't be alive."

"Funny," I said, moving even closer. Kalepe's eyes widened. "I thought you were dying to talk to me. I mean, you tortured poor Samantha trying to get to me."

Kory gaped. "Sammy? How do I know it's you and not just Sam pretending?" Even as he said the words, I could see the eagerness in his gaze, the way his eyes raked up and down my frame.

"Think whatever you want, Kory, I'm not here for you." I turned toward Kalepe. "I need you to get everyone out of here, now! We're all in danger!"

Kalepe shook his head. "No, we have to stay here. They promised us that we'd be safe."

Kory growled. "See what've I've been dealing with? I've been trying to get them to budge, but they won't get out of this damn building!"

"Clearly, the Irukas' song is still swaying them," I muttered.

"What?" Understanding dawned on Kory. "Is that what happened? Why on earth would they turn on me?"

"Oh, I don't know, maybe because you've been experimenting on them," a voice said from behind me. I whirled around, my heart hammering in my chest.

"Mack!" I cried out. Despite everything, I threw my arms

around him. "You're okay!"

"Of course I am." He returned my embrace, and then rocked back, looking me in the eyes. "Question is—are you? Sam, what are you doing here?"

I wanted to gush so many things to him. A strange tide of emotions were swirling within, and I had a bad feeling Sammy was about to take full rein of my body by the burning desire I had to plant a kiss on Mack's lips. But a sudden movement in my peripheral made me jump. Kory was lunging toward us.

A whoosh of air sent my hair flying as something invisible sent Kory soaring backward. Then in an instant, Kory was dangling, his face turning purple as he grasped what held him by the neck. Jaxon.

Seeing Kory in danger, Kalepe roared into action, lunging for Jaxon, who'd dropped his camo just as Kalepe and him collided. They all went skidding across the floor, the ground shaking at the impact. Somehow, Jaxon managed to still grasp Kory's throat with one hand, while blocking Kalepe's attacks with the other.

Mack gasped. "Jaxon's here?"

Kate appeared, and Mack's eyes doubled in size. "Kate?" he whispered. His eyes flicked over to me one more time, the question forming. I knew he was dying to ask.

But he didn't; he flew straight for Jaxon and Kalepe's tumbling forms. In all the scuffling, Kory had been dropped and was slinking away. The two fighting monsters were drawing the attention of several other Defenders. Their restlessness was turning into giddy energy, and if we weren't careful, we were about to ignite a nasty spark none of us would live through.

Mack tackled Kory from behind, shoving him to the ground.

"See! This is why Jaxon needed to be the queen," Kate yelled, throwing her hands up. "Sammy, you better do something or we're all dead!"

She's right. What do I do now?

Fly, Sam! I did as I was told, flying above the heated frenzy below.

"Dragon Defenders!" I hollered, with little hope any would

hear me. "Listen to me! You're all in danger!" No one paid me any attention.

The fighting continued below; Jaxon and Kalepe had now drawn at least a half a dozen Defenders into the fight. The stench of blood was already wafting up to me. I searched out Mack, finding him and Kate both trying to hold on to Kory, but Defenders kept throwing them off. I gasped as one smashed Kate to the ground. She didn't jump back up.

Sammy, no one's listening! They don't know I'm their queen! Get Kalepe and Jaxon to show them! she commanded.

I dove down. Not stopping to think or plan, I plowed right into Kalepe. I scrambled to get my body sandwiched between them. The punching and clawing ceased immediately, both monsters freezing to keep from hitting me. I pushed them apart, my hand feeling small on their heaving chests.

"My Queen! Get out of the way!" Jaxon commanded, his eyes still trained on Kalepe.

"This isn't your fight!" Kalepe agreed, glaring at Jaxon.

"Yes, it is. So you're going to have to kill me to get to each other."

Kalepe's gaze finally shifted to me, and then he slowly lowered his arms. "I can't kill you."

Jaxon shook his head, a frown on his lips. "You know I will never hurt you again, Sam."

"Finally, we're on the same team." I exhaled the breath I hadn't realized I'd been holding. "Kalepe, you need to listen. We're not here to fight you; we're here to save you. All of you."

"She's right." Jaxon pointed up to the ceiling, "This place is about to be gassed, and if we don't leave now, we all die, including Sam. I know you've felt the insane desire to protect her, because I feel it too. We need to get this crowd moving, now."

I thought there'd be some long explanation on how I was their queen or an argument of why he should trust Jaxon, but instead, Kalepe's arms wrapped around me. We instantly shot up into the air, Jaxon on our heels.

As soon as we were high enough, they both let out simultaneous roars that echoed across the room, silencing everything and everyone, leaving my ears ringing and my chest pounding.

"Defenders!" Kalepe commanded. "Listen to her!" He held me out to them, keeping his hands on the back of my arms.

"She's your queen." Jaxon's voice carried across the room. "And your rightful leader."

Several Defenders shifted where they stood, but none spoke. All black eyes turned upward. This was it, they were ready, and yet, my eyes sought out Kate in that split second, wanting to make sure she was all right. I found her cradled in Mack's arms as he tried to shield her from further attacks.

"Dragon Defenders, stop fighting!" I shouted down to them. A murmur rippled through the crowd, and the few Defenders near Mack and Kate stopped and turned to face me.

Relieved, I continued, "Up till now, you've followed Kory, but he's never been your true leader." Now the murmuring got louder, mostly around where Kory stood. "Yes, he created you, but he used my DNA to do it. My blood runs through your veins, and I know if you stop long enough, you can feel it."

CHAPTER
Fifty

Kory swore every cuss word I thought I knew, and then some. "Why are you listening to her?" he demanded as a few Defenders stepped away from him. "She's nothing to you! I'm the one who gave you this life, me, not her!"

I shot Kory a withering look. "You may have been the one pressing the needle to their skin, but they are a part of me, not you." My eyes swept the room. "I can show you how magnificent you really are. I'm the only one who can replace the void you have within you."

The hairs on the back of my neck stood on end at my own words. I caught Mack's pale face from below, his eyes wide.

"The Irukas have tricked you into coming here; it's a trap," I continued. "If you want to live, you need to follow me now and leave this place." With that, I shot forward, flying through the air freely until about a hundred monstrous Defenders joined me.

Jaxon and Kalepe flanked my sides, and I could only pray Mack had scooped Kate up and was following us all out. The doors were open, for now. Whatever tactics Blake was using with Tonbo must be working.

No one pushed or shoved. Everyone flew in unity with the strength of an army. The air whipped around us from the force of so many monstrous wings flapping at once. Some deep part of me stirred at the sight of them. They are majestic, I relented. Even if they are bugs.

The Defenders who'd been in the rear were already out the door. I could taste the freedom, the victory. I can't believe this all worked! And with no real bloodshed either! Everyone's in one piece...

I'd thought it too soon—horrible growling sounds made my blood turn cold. Within seconds, a group of Defenders came crashing into Jaxon, Kalepe, and me. They'd been in the corner... waiting for me to come near. Seeing the bloodthirst in their eyes, I had no doubts as to where the twenty unchanged Defenders had gone. The ones that had kept me up all night with their claws trying to reach me through the bars. They'd been here, with the rest, only they hadn't been given my DNA. They had no desire to protect or defend me, so while I gave my speech about being one with them, they must have waited, stalking me from the shadows.

Kalepe and Jaxon reacted immediately, buffering the attacks while shoving me behind their backs. Every other Defender near us jumped into the fight as well. Stunned, I watched in shock and horror as Kalepe didn't hesitate to rip one of his 'friends' in half with his claws.

It scared me how fast the twenty were slaughtered. The metallic stench of blood in the air turned my stomach. No one stopped to think that all they needed was one more injection. They were still human, deep down within, probably some of their closest friends and family. The Defenders had only seen them as an immediate threat to me. End of story.

As much as I'd wanted to scream at them to stop, something prevented me. Was it Sammy? Or was it my own fear of what those bugs would do to me if they weren't destroyed? I shuddered as she seemed to gloat. You never need to be afraid again, Sam.

I never wanted this! To be in charge of these trained killers! Responsible for their actions!

You wanted to save them, didn't you?

Well, yes...

This was the only way. How else did you think this would go down?

We'd passed through the open door, the briny night air a welcome relief to the claustrophobia. My shirt clung to my sweat-covered flesh, my entire body shaking with adrenaline. I searched for Blake. Even if he were holding Tonbo back, surely he'd be here. I couldn't see him, or Tonbo, but I did make out several dragons.

Which, to my horror, the Defenders began fighting off.

"No! Stop!" I screeched, this time making my voice heard. I was desperate to avoid another bloodbath.

The Defenders immediately stopped attacking the dragons, but that didn't stop them from being attacked in turn. Hearing one yelp in agony as a dragon speared it through the chest with a long-handled harpoon, I gasped, grabbing Jaxon's arm.

At the same time, Sammy commanded. Come on, Sam. We've got to get them out of here!

Where do we go? I don't know how to do this! This was never the plan! We were going to just get them out... and Blake and I...

Blake's not here. Sammy's words were sharp. So take charge!

My world was spinning, breathing proved difficult. I knew we had to get out of here, but I didn't want to go alone. I needed Blake.

Jaxon's black eyes peered down to me. "Take them to my caves."

"Okay, let's do it," I breathed out, grateful Jaxon sensed my predicament. I turned to Kalepe. "Tell everyone we've got a long flight ahead. Switch to camo and follow me."

We left the island, only losing one Defender's life. A life that was purely my fault because I had told them not to fight, which meant they didn't defend themselves either. I couldn't think about the twenty who had died within minutes. It made my stomach ill knowing what the Defenders would do if they sensed I was in danger. It seemed either decision I made—to allow them to fight or hinder them—meant death. How could I be the one who decided that?

Trust me; this is a good thing, Sammy reassured.

No. It's not! Where's Blake? I need to find him.

We will find him later once we get them to safety. You think Tonbo's going to give up that easily?

No... but there's something weird about how easy it really

was. I mean, where was Tonbo back there?

I don't know, maybe Blake was retaining him for us. Which is all the more reason for us not to stop, but to finish this.

I wanted to continue arguing with Sammy, but I knew she was right about at least one thing. We did need to get the Defenders far from the island and the surrounding ocean, where the Irukas could be summoned to act again. As soon as we got them some place safe, I would find Blake. In all our haste, I wished I'd brought a cell phone. Some way to reach him quick. Make sure he was okay.

Feeling someone fly up next to me, I fought the urge to drop my camo. My heart surged, hoping it was Blake, even though it wasn't his scent I detected. Blake was warm honey, a sunset in the woods, not a spicy pumpkin pie.

Mack's hand slid up my arm, leaving a trail of goose bumps behind.

"I'd know your scent anywhere," he said, aligning his body with mine. I slowed my pace, allowing us to fly next to each other more comfortably. I could tell by the grumbles from Jaxon and Kalepe that they weren't happy to be moved out of their spots as my personal bodyguards. I sure hope these two don't think they are going to be permanently glued to my sides.

"Funny, I just thought the same thing about you," I answered him, surprised how difficult it was for me to speak at the moment. All of my thoughts were focused on how his hand felt gliding up my arm, toward my shoulder. It more than tickled; it sent tiny thrills through my body.

"Where's Kate?" I asked, clearing my throat. "Is she okay?"

"She's fine. She's with the Defenders holding Kory, toward the back of this mess."

"Oh." I'd forgotten all about Kory. "We'll figure out what to do with him once we land, I guess."

"I have a few ideas," Jaxon growled.

"I bet you do, but we can't kill him right away," I replied, surprising myself.

Why on earth should we let Kory live? I inwardly thought.

Because Jocelyn loves him, Sammy simply replied.

What? Are you serious?

Look, we have several hours until we land. Kory won't dare try to escape now. If he does, it means death. Jaxon will see to that. Let's just worry about Kory later.

I shook my head, trying in vain to figure out Sammy. Just when I think I knew her motivations and feelings, she threw another curve ball at me.

"So we're heading to Jaxon's cavern? You really want to bring this bug army to the mainland?" Mack asked, bringing my attention back to him, and more importantly, to the way his hand felt on my bare shoulder. Did he know how crazy his touch was making me? How fast my heart was beating now?

"I didn't know where else to go," I admitted. "Jaxon offered his place, so..."

Mack chuckled, even if it sounded strained. "This is crazy, you know that, Sam."

"Please don't call me that."

"What? Crazy?" he asked, slowing his pace even more. I matched his speed. Even with the camo making it so we couldn't see each other's faces, I knew what he really wanted to ask. The question hung in the air between us. I was scared I didn't know the answer, and yet, even more terrified the answer was all too apparent. I bit my lip, not wanting to admit to him that Sammy was in my head, telling me what to say and do. It felt like if I were to say it aloud, it'd be permanent.

"No. Don't you call me Sam," I blurted instead as my insides cringed. Sammy, why did you say that? Now he will think...

Mack's hand slipped behind my neck, and before I could counter my statement, his lips crushed against mine. I wanted to pull back, to tell him to stop. My mind screamed that I loved Blake, but my heart ached to have more of Mack. I'd never felt so torn and confused, and yet filled with desire at the same time.

You aren't the only one with a heart in this body, you know.

I deepened the kiss; my hands tangled themselves in his hair, my mouth working with his. Mack groaned softly, pressing me against him, his hands sliding up my back as his lips traveled down my throat.

Sammy, stop it! I pleaded, feeling like a helpless bystander to my own actions. This isn't fair!

To whom? she angrily thought. To you?

To Mack! You're only going to break his heart again because we both know we won't end up with him!

We don't know that, Sammy snapped back.

I hated that she was right.

Mack stopped kissing me and pulled me against his chest, holding me tightly. For half a second, I allowed myself to close my eyes and enjoy the sound of his heartbeat against my ear. His body was warm and I was exhausted, the temptation to drift to sleep was overwhelming me.

He leaned down and said in a low voice, "Sammy, is it really you? Please tell me I'm not making a horrible mistake."

"Honestly, I don't know who I am anymore," I admitted.

"What do you mean?"

"I'm still me but... sometimes, I can hear what she's thinking. All that stuff I said back there was what Sammy wanted me to say."

Mack shifted back, and I felt his eyes. I glanced up, wanting to make eye contact. Stupid camo! Makes every conversation so much harder. But then again, maybe it's a good thing Mack can't see me. I knew I was flushed. It felt like fire was racing through my veins.

"So you're both Sammy and Sam right now?" Mack asked, his arms loosening around my waist.

"I'm afraid so."

CHAPTER
Fifty-One

"Why did you kiss me like that then?" His words were barely audible as he completely let me go.

"Because that was Sammy," I answered, feeling ashamed of myself. Truthfully, deep down, I wondered where the line between Sammy and me ended. When it came to the Defenders, I could see clearly, but when it came to matters of the heart, it got a little messier. The line got fuzzy.

"So you're Sam right now?"

"Honestly, I'm not really sure." Deep within, I was me, but my actions, my words, my feelings, especially around Mack, felt like Sammy.

"Sam, I'm sorry. I wasn't trying to—"

His words faded at my touch. I'd reached out to comfort him before I knew what I was doing. Now my hand caressed his cheek, feeling the scruff he'd neglected.

"Mack, I'm the one who is sorry. I've caused you so much pain. You deserve to be happy, to be loved completely. I don't know if I'll ever be able to give you that. It was selfish of me to think otherwise."

"Sammy? That you talking now?"

"Yes," I said, even though my insides squirmed with resistance. "I need you to know that I never lied about loving you. That kiss was real. I've missed you desperately. More than you'll ever know. Sam feels it, my feelings for you, even though she tries to suppress them."

I laughed; it sounded foreign to my own ears. "Funny, with all my formulas and serums, I still can't figure out a way for us both to be happy. I thought if we were finally one, sharing this

284

body, we'd feel complete. But how can it work when our hearts belong to two different people? Who'd have thought such a small organ could cause such a fuss?"

Mack didn't answer; he only listened. Sammy was speaking freely, without restraint, and I could only listen too. Was this what it was like for her all those years? Was she a helpless bystander as I went about my daily life, only breaking free every once in a while?

Sammy was obviously the smarter of the two of us. She had been the one finding solutions, saving the day. What had I done? Nothing. Maybe it was time I let her lead. Maybe she could keep the army from hurting others and from being killed. Then Mack could be happy...

"Sammy, I need you to know something too." Mack's voice was thick, full of emotions. "I've always loved you. It's like all logic and reason is thrown to the wind the minute I know you're there. I can't help myself. I want more than anything for us to be together, but I care for Sam, too. I can't hurt her, or force myself on her, because you're now in charge. If she's still in there, I have to know."

My heart squeezed painfully, and I wasn't sure who was feeling it. Sammy loved Mack, that much I knew, but hearing Mack stand up for me, not wanting to hurt me, meant a lot to me too.

"She's still here, just as she's always been. Why is it different now? You've always known Samantha was inside of me when I took over." The words just formed themselves.

"Because, if she can hear us, is aware of this now, there's a big difference!"

"You don't think I heard things too?" I snorted, while inside, I cringed. I'm getting how it felt now, Sammy. I was there but only observing, not participating in the conversation my own mouth was having.

"Not all the time, but when her guard was down, like when she slept," I continued to say. "After changing us, though, it's only became stronger. I thought, at first, it meant it had all worked. That we were going to finally be one person, but turns out, I was wrong."

Sammy, can you hear me? I asked within myself. Sammy, please. We need to talk.

If she heard my thoughts, she chose to ignore me. "What do you think it's been like for me, Mack? Sitting back, knowing what needs to be done, but barely having the time to do it! Well, I'm tired of taking a backseat; maybe it's time Samantha takes a turn."

Mack dropped his camo, and I gasped. He grabbed me by the arms and demanded, "I need to see you."

Seeing how hard his jaw was set, Jaxon and Kalepe suddenly appeared as well, growling. All of us had stopped flying, which was bad. We needed to keep moving.

"It's okay," I immediately reassured them, scared what they might do to Mack. "Jaxon, keep leading the Defenders toward your caves."

He frowned, obviously not liking leaving my side. "I'll be fine. Kalepe can stay behind. We won't be but a second behind you, I swear."

Jaxon nodded and took off, the Defenders following after.

Only then did I drop my camo. Mack's eyes widened, his hands still holding my forearms. My body felt smaller, shorter. One of Mack's hands reached up and brushed the brunette hair back off my face. I was the girl I'd changed into when Jaxon had been trying to kill me. The girl Sammy had always wanted to be if she gained control.

Does this mean I'm lost forever? Trapped in a mind where no one can hear me?

Again, she didn't answer my questions. Instead, I met Mack's gaze and spoke with Sammy's voice.

"Mack, I understand if you don't want to stay with me and no one," I shot Kalepe a look, "will hurt you if you leave now, but someone has to help these Defenders, show them how to live peacefully. If you still love me, and can accept me as I am, then come with me. Help me."

Mack's eyes darted between mine; I could tell he had a thousand questions he wanted to ask.

Finally, he sighed heavily. "I may be damning my own soul, heaven help me, but I can't leave you, Sammy. I've never been able to tell you no." He leaned down and kissed my lips softly, and even though the heated passion wasn't there like before, I still loved the way his lips felt on mine.

Sam, Sammy called to me, piercing through my agony—guilt that I enjoyed Mack's kiss and fear that I was forever lost.

Oh, so now you choose to acknowledge me, I thought bitterly.

I was a little busy before, in case you hadn't noticed, Sammy replied.

Actually, I did. What's happening to me? Why can't I do the talking anymore? You're doing everything. I feel like I'm trapped in here!

I'm sorry, Sam. Truly, I am. It seems fate has decided to have us trade places. I'd always hoped there'd be a way for us to... I don't know... maybe meld into one person. But it seems you and I are like oil and water—we just don't mix.

Mack and I had begun flying again, his hand holding mine tightly. Kalepe seemed eager to catch up with the rest by the speed he took off. Since I was lost in my own thoughts, literally, I pushed hard as well. The air slapping against my skin made me feel alive again. Like maybe I wasn't just a shell of a person.

Do I have any choice? I asked. Are you forcing this on me?

What? No! I know what kind of hell this is. I wouldn't wish that on you. Believe it or not, I really love you, Sam. I wanted you to be happy.

So this is just how it is now? You have the reins? I can't control my own body anymore?

Silence greeted me. Honestly, I don't know, Sam, she finally thought. We seem to still have a strong connection. I mean, we can read each other's thoughts. That's got to mean something, right? I swear, Sam, I'm not trying to snuff you out.

But that was exactly how I felt, as if I were slowly being suffocated. My chest felt heavy, like the air was too thick to enter my lungs properly. My vision blackened for half a second, the stars over the ocean disappearing.

Sam? Sammy's voice sounded distant.

I opened my eyes, trying to focus. Sammy, just tell me. Can you do it?

Do what? Sammy asked, an edge of panic in her voice.

Keep the Defenders from taking over the world? You know, ending human life as we know it.

Yes, Sam. We can do it together.

Good, I thought, the darkness pressing down on me was too heavy to fight anymore. I closed my eyes again; it felt heavenly.

Sam? You there still? Sammy sounded so muffled.

I'm fine, I thought, unsure if she could even hear me. I'm just so tired. I think you've got this, Sammy. I just need some rest...

Sam? Sam, you there still?

The darkness won out finally as I drifted into a deep, dreamless sleep.

Epilogue

"**A**re you sure about this, son?" Tonbo asked as the last of the Defenders literally disappeared from view. They'd switched to camo, like they'd assumed they would.

Staring at the fleeing army, Blake knew Tonbo was putting tremendous trust in him, letting them go like this. His heart had been in his throat when he'd seen her, but it hadn't been his Sam. The way she'd just watched as the Defenders slaughtered several of their own kind within minutes in the doorway was proof. He shuddered. She'd come out of that building a different person. He had a hunch who too. As much as he was dying to run to her, he knew if Sammy didn't want him interfering, that would have been the end of him. The Defenders were under her control now. Even his brother.

"It's the only way, Tonbo," Blake answered, the ache in his chest so severe that he was half tempted to rub his ribs to make sure they weren't bruised. Bruises would heal, but not this, not a broken heart. "I won't let her die trying to save them," he muttered. "Tonbo, I wish you would have just been honest with me about all this from the start. Why didn't you tell me you thought Sammy was taking over? That she wanted to steal the army the entire time for herself? I would never have gone along with trying to save them. I could have stopped—"

"Sammy?" Tonbo asked, lifting an eyebrow. "Blake, my boy, I'm afraid she outplayed us all."

"But I would have kept Sam in the cage, like you'd said to do, until after the Defenders were all destroyed. Then we could have—"

"Tried to cure Sammy out of her?" Tonbo asked, finishing his sentence again. He sighed. "I'm afraid nothing is ever quite that simple. I didn't tell you what I saw happening because for one thing, I wasn't certain it was and on the other, I didn't want to cause you more pain if I could help it. You've already had to make enough tough decisions when it comes to your brother."

Guess I know how Sam feels now when I keep things from her, trying to "protect" her, he thought bitterly.

Tonbo's bony shoulders sagged as he scratched his chin. "So now what? We just let them fly away? Enter a world that is not ready for that kind of violence?"

"No. Now, we wait. Let them regroup. If I know my brother, he will take them to his caves. It's a never-ending underground labyrinth. Perfect for hiding and defending themselves. Let's just hope they stay put long enough that I can get to her."

"What makes you think you can get to her?" he softly asked. "Blake, I don't want to be the one to say this... but Sam might be gone for good. Sammy's been growing stronger, taking over more and more of Sam's life, without her even knowing it."

The ache in his chest doubled, and he had to bite the inside of his cheek to keep from wincing. He shook his head. "I won't give up on her, Tonbo. Sam's in there. I know she is."

Tonbo's black eyes saddened as he gazed back at him. Blake read empathy all over them.

"I'm going to do whatever it takes to get Sam back," he said firmly, subduing the gnawing ache with new resolution. "And no one will stand in my way, not this time. Not even my own brother."

The End

Acknowledgements

With every book I write, I have to say a huge thank you to my family. My husband, Josh, and my three beautiful children who not only support my crazy writing habit but also believe in my books and me. Writing takes a lot of time, which in a family is a precious commodity. I'm so grateful to have their support, love, and encouragement. I couldn't do it without you guys. I love you so much!

To all the readers of *Hidden Monster* who have waited patiently for me to finally give them more—your excitement and anticipation has meant the world to me. Don't worry, book three, *Monsters Among Us*, is on its way next. Hopefully, the wait will be well worth it! To my Wattpad readers, I'm forever grateful to you for believing in me before I was ever published.

To all my friends and family who take the time to like, share, comment, and cheer me on through social media sites—you don't know how much it means to me to have your continued support. I wish I could thank each and every one of you personally here.

To my parents, Ralph and Cyndi, and my husband's parents, Eddie and Georgene, thank you for all your love and support. I love how you keep sharing my books with everyone you can. Thank you!

A special thank you to my friend, Roxanna, for your enthusiasm and love of my books. Your support means so much. To Gail, my writing buddy for life, what can I say? I couldn't do this without you. I'm so glad you moved in two doors down from me. Who knows if I'd ever started writing again if you hadn't. To Sheree, thank you for all you do to help me—from the marketing tips to sharing your time with Gail and me. I love how the three of us keep each other going!

A special thank you to all those who created the cover. To Amy Brimhall, with Dramatic Imaging Photography. Not only are you a dear friend to me, but you also take stunning pictures! Thank you for the cover shot and my profile picture. A huge thank you to the gorgeous model featured on the cover, Kailynn Blackwood. I am thrilled you wanted to do this. A tremendous thank you to Marya Heiman, with Clean Teen Publishing, who was the cover artist and mastermind behind this design. I loved that I said, *I want a dragonfly on her face*, and this is what you came up with. It's perfect!

To my publishing team and family, Clean Teen Publishing. I am forever grateful you took a chance on a girl with 'another angel' story a few years ago! I am so blessed that my stories are turned into beautiful books because of you. To Rebecca, Courtney, Marya, Melanie, Cynthia and all those who proofread, market, and share my stuff, thank you. My heart is full with gratitude!

Lastly, and most of all, I want to thank my God, for blessing me with talents I can develop, enjoy, and share with others. For giving me the strength and courage to face each new day. I know every good thing in my life, I owe to Him!

About The Author

B orn in Dekalb, Illinois, Amanda Strong has called Utah, Arizona, Hawaii, Virginia, and now New Mexico home. She has loved to spin tales since childhood. It was not uncommon to find her hiding in some random corner, scribbling away in her spiral-bound notebook, with her bright pink glasses. You could say some things have not changed.

Amanda signed with Clean Teen Publishing in the fall of 2013. She is the author of two paranormal, YA series: The Watchers of Men and Monsters Among Us.

The first novel in The Watchers of Men series, The Awakener, debuted in October of 2013. It has been an Amazon number one best seller in three Young Adult categories. Book two, The Holy and The Fallen, released May 12th of 2015. She is currently working on book three, The Watcher's Mark, releasing spring of

2016.

Hidden Monster released November 4th of 2014, and it finished as a Finalist in the 2014 USA Best Book Award: Young Adult Category. It is book one of a brand-new young adult, sci-fi thriller series called Monsters Among Us.

When Amanda isn't writing, you can find her chasing her three rambunctious children around the house and spending time with her wonderful and supportive husband. On some occasions, you can still find Amanda with her not-so-pink glasses, hiding in a corner reading her favorite young adult fantasy novels or working out only to blow her diet by eating ice cream.

CPSIA information can be obtained at www.ICGtesting.com
Printed in the USA
LVOW07s0200240316

480415LV00005B/6/P